DRIFTING
DREAMING
DYING

GAVIN PIENAAR

First published by Gavin Pienaar, 2023

Copyright © 2023 by Gavin Pienaar

Publishing Consultant: Phillipa Mitchell
(www.phillipamitchell.com)

Editor: Jonathan Amid

Cover Design and Interior Formatting by Gregg Davies Media (Pty) Ltd
(www.greggdavies.com)

ISBN: 978-0-6397-6215-9 (Paperback)
ISBN: 978-0-6397-6216-6 (eBook)

To the most beautiful women in the world,
who have inspired me to complete this novel.

My daughters Bridget Shan and Rachel Catherine
and my Spouse Ivy Noleen.

CONTENTS

PROLOGUE

A ll we wanted to do as children during the summer holidays of
December 1999 was to enjoy our freedom. Much of my original
account of the events of December 1999 was removed by the South
African Government as part of the Official Secrets Act. My hope is that
what remains will provide some perspective on what we endured; how
close our country came to disaster. These words are an account of love,
of family, friends and strangers: how I was held together during the
most traumatic times of my life, intertwined in a dark-hued kaleidoscope where each fragment would reveal itself through the movement
of others bound together forever.

I learned by observing and listening, soaking in sounds and words:
from the long-aged creaking of the evening crickets to my grandmother's stories of the headless horseman. I also loved learning from my
younger brother Morph's outlook on life. I credit much of this story to
him. He remains an inspiration.

Sometimes I would also hear too much. I was the first one to take in
the conversation my grandmother had with the policeman, at our door
to tell her that my parents had died in a car accident. I was the first to
hear my sister's screams, my grandmother's sobs and feel my older
brothers' rage. I could hear Morph's silence, who knew without quite

understanding. Listening drew me closer to the endless expanses of my imagination.

My brothers, sister and I had to move in with our grandmother after the accident. She cared for us, right until the end. I remember all too well what unfolded when Grandma, in the best way she knew how, relayed our parents' fate. Who could explain the state of mind and actions of a taxi driver who tried to overtake along a treacherous bend on the N11 between Ladysmith and Newcastle? Who could predict that we would somehow become involved in a tangled web, in events so strange, convoluted and haunting? Events threatening not only our own lives, but national security. This, then, is the story of those fateful, and strangely coincidental, unforgettable weeks.

CHAPTER 1
TEARS IN THE STORM
(THURSDAY, 09 DECEMBER 1999)

That morning the sun shone warmly, sending rays of light through our bedroom window and onto the foot of my bed, keeping my toes perfectly toasty. I loved these moments, just before my grandma came to wake us. We did not have to go to school today; Grandma agreed that I could stay home, on condition that I did all my chores.

Others attended school every single day. I tried it earlier in my schooling and stopped doing it as soon as Grandma permitted it. For the last semester of every year the Grade Sixers went to school wanting to be elected prefects for the next year. I was not one of them. I lay still in bed, tossing only to reposition the sun on my happy toes, listening to the sounds of people walking by outside – children on their way to school, parents on their way to work. I breathed in smells of chimney smoke mingled with fresh rain on dry ground and limestone from the quarry a little down the way. The quarry boomed those jarring rock-crushing sounds, the noise oddly comforting to me. It reminded me so much of Grandpa who used to hurry off to work there, pausing just to wave us off to school.

Grandpa always brought a couple of toffees or liquorish sticks home in his dusty pocket. He secretly handed these over to my siblings and I at the front door. I still listened out for those heavy footsteps, waiting eagerly for him to march into the yard, his deep voice loudly calling out, "WHERE ARE MY FRENCHIES?!". I missed listening and eavesdropping in on the jovial conversations between him and Grandma. Grandpa was never an intimidating man, but his voice increased substantially in volume when telling a joke or when he laughed.

We were drawn close to the quarry, where our beloved grandfather had worked for two decades before he died three years ago from emphysema complications. He was a tall, proud man with a sharp mind and strong vocabulary. Seeing him waste away traumatized us all.

There was something different about this morning. No matter how hard I tried to shake it, there seemed to be a deeper stillness beyond the immediate sounds of a town wakened to the day. I could not hear the trees rustling or birds singing, leaving me unsettled. These sounds had something uplifting to them; harsh realities turned somehow softer. This stirring apprehension grew steadily. I prayed for the safety of Grandma, my sister and brothers while the sun's rays glimmered and sparkled, offering brief respite to morbid thoughts.

"Shine on, you millions of..." I tried poetry to describe the morning. I closed my eyes tightly, imagining the sun swooping down from the heavens and engulfing me in pure warmth and the brightest light. I scrambled out of bed, hastily slipped on a pair of shorts, my t-shirt, and a pair of slightly worn out takkies and went to Grandma, who was busy preparing breakfast in the kitchen. Without lifting her gaze from the bubbling porridge on the stove she smiled and stretched out an arm to give me a morning hug.

"Morning, Plano."

"Morning, Ouma."

Grandma tapped the ladle on the inside of the pot and moved it off the stove plate.

"Where're we off to without breakfast, mmm?"

"I wanna go write, Ouma," I smiled, trying to look guilt-free and avoiding eye contact.

"Breakfast first. Put the kettle on." Grandma patted me on the shoulder.

We chatted about the summer holidays, Christmas presents and decorations, Grandma's ear keen and attentive. When I was done swallowing the last morsel of porridge Grandma let me go, on condition that I was back in two hours to do my chores.

"There's an early morning storm forecast, Son. Don't wander off."

"Okay, Ouma! Love you, Ouma! Bye!"

Before Grandma could blink, let alone change her mind, I rushed down our cul-de-sac on Rocky Lane, turned left into Alfred Street and bolted down dusty Quarry Road to my favorite old willow tree along the bend of the Bushman River. I enjoyed sitting within the canopy of sweeping branches and fishing in the river below. While waiting for a bite I would use my sling to shoot at various targets. Our older brother William and I used to hunt and kill rabbits, birds and fish, bring these home to clean and cook after teasing our sister May-June and little brother Morph to clean the catch., They would chase us out of the kitchen with broom sticks.

Grandma always made us prepare, cook and eat what we killed. Suffice to say that our actual hunts gradually diminished, but the thrill remained. Now we just caught and released. When with William and our friends we played Cowboys and Indians or cops and robbers in the bushes around the old tree. I often had the best time on my own – playing for hours and writing and reciting poetry. The river, flowing over rocks and down a waterfall, always buoyed me.

Estcourt, our little town, remains a jewel, quaintly beautiful, a place where nature seems to outnumber man-made structures. Graced with the magnificent Drakensberg Mountains on the west, Champagne Castle remains my preferred lookout point. Besides the mountains there are rolling hills spread out for kilometers in every direction, full of green or golden grass, and exquisite Acacia trees that sway with dancing grass and wildflowers in simple splendor.

Ahead of me two dust devils swirled this way and that before racing away through the yielding grass up the bank beyond the river. A year before Grandpa died, he took William and I further along on the road past the Quarry to the Zaailaager Battle site. In 1838, Zulu Amabhuto attacked the Voortrekkers, one of the first bloody battles after Piet Retief and his party were annihilated by Zulu King Dingane kaSenzangakhona and his soldiers at KwaMatiwane. The battle lasted forty-four days; the Voortrekkers eventually managed to repel the Zulus.

The Bushman's River is beautiful, crystal-clear in its meander through town. It forms an idyllic picnic spot at an almost perfect horse-shoe, created by the deposit of millions of grains of sand. Our play-ground was on the opposite bank, where the river flows through Lambert's Park. Most of Estcourt would congregate within the horse-shoe on Saturdays and Sundays. We, however, preferred the wilder outer side. It was far more exciting to conquer the untamed.

Our home was on Rocky Lane. The cul-de-sac is on higher ground than much of its surroundings. It is as though everything else around us had been flattened by some invisible hand, deliberately leaving this one portion of land to stand proudly above the rest. We lived in an old house built at least a century earlier by quarry owners. It looked like many other mine houses across the country. The outside brick walls were plastered and painted light blue. The single garage was free-standing at the back of the property. The roof and garage were red, painted corrugated sheeting, showing signs of wear and tear, while the large verandah – that spanned the width of the house – was the imposing feature at the front.

The front door opened into the lounge with worn but clean and polished furniture. A dark brown display cabinet held a TV set in its center, with various ornaments family photos standing proudly in-between the spaces. The door leading indoors from the lounge opened into a long, wide passage, with doors leading to the dining room and kitchen on the left and three bedrooms and the bathroom on the right.

We always had a clean tablecloth draped over the dining room table. The cupboard held Grandma's crockery and cutlery that she only used for special guests. The first door to the right in the passage lead to Grandma's bedroom, with two single beds, one for Grandma and one for May–June. Large wooden wardrobes stood on either side of the door and a dressing table stood between beds. Grandma's Bible was always next to her on the side table while her rocking chair waited at the foot of her bed with a knitting basket next to it. She loved to knit in the late afternoons with a tot of Old Brown Sherry, her 'medicine' to ward off the pains from aching joints.

The next bedroom belonged to our parents. It was dominated by a brass and ivory queen-sized bed with matching glass topped side tables. on either side of a similar design to the bed, with two matching white wardrobes that stood near the door . The bed was only made up when we received visitors. A picture that Grandpa had painted of the house hung on one wall. Most of the time our parents' bedroom remained locked after their death.

The next bedroom was William's, Morph's and mine. On the left-hand side was a bunk bed that Morph and I slept in and on the right was a single bed for William. Near the foot of William's bed stood a large wooden wardrobe. On the opposite side, at the foot of our bunk bed, stood a chest of drawers with a lamp on it. Our room had posters of Manchester United and our favorite soccer players plastered in almost all the available spaces.

Our favorite room was the kitchen. This room was roughly as large as the lounge, filled with built-in cupboards, Grandpa's hand work – a gift to Grandma he built with money he received from the quarry when ill health stopped him from working there. Grandma said that he was boarded which made no sense to us at the time. A large, old brown table dominated the center of the room. Grandma said that it was the first piece of furniture Grandpa made after they got married. He collected scraps of wood at a building site and put together the table that somehow had stood the test of time.

The electric stove was an old Defy model repaired many times. Next to it was a Kelvinator fridge/freezer that had long ago faded to a light yellow. It hiccupped its way through life but continued without needing many repairs except to service it, change worn parts and to fill it with gas every six years. We believed that when it eventually seized up for good, it would do so with a single, loud bang. Uncle Solly, the handyman keeping the stove and fridge alive, told us this. Half of the chairs around the table were wood, the other half plastic.

Between the stove and the back door stood Grandma's special kitchen chair, another gift from Grandpa. The back door opened out to another verandah narrower than out front. The bathroom had a single toilet, an old ceramic bath and hand basin. Our home was simple, but to us it was special – a place called home.

My dad had French ancestry and my mom had some Italian blood flowing through her veins. They spoke French to us every now and again. My full name is Deplano. Grandma said that it meant that I was 'signed, sealed and delivered.' Morph's name is Adamor. When younger he called himself Adamorf, then settled into Morph. William was blessed with our Dad's name, with May-June named after two great-grandmothers. All of us were caramel-skinned with black curly hair and dark brown eyes. Our surname is Delvaux, 'valley' in French. I was never able to determine for sure whether we were somehow related to the surrealist artist, Paul Delvaux from Belgium. The eldest was fifteen-year-old William, two years older than May-June. She was three years older than me. Morph was the youngest brother, three years younger than I.

My brothers and I sometimes dressed alike, out of necessity more than anything else. Whenever possible, we would dive into shorts and tee shirts and sandals and this was how all our friends dressed to play. Formalwear for us was normally hand-me-down jeans, short-sleeve shirts and pairs of All-star takkies. Although we sort of looked alike, the shape and depth of our saddened eyes told us apart. It stemmed from the day we were told that our dad and mom passed away in what the newspapers dubbed a freak accident, of massive proportions.

Grandma had tried to shield us from the worst descriptions, but we eventually figured out the brutality and senselessness of their tragic passing. Being with my siblings always made me feel brave, like we could overcome anything, but not today. I felt all alone in a troubling world.

We lived quite close to Blurock Quarry. William and I often snuck in and played before he began to trouble himself with the problems of the adult world. Grandpa taught William and I all we needed to know about living and about being kind. He taught us respect and discipline, about being men, about wildlife and hunting and caring for all things bright and beautiful, all creatures great and small. A fond memory was when he chased William and I up the old gum tree near the back boundary fence, hell bent on giving us a hiding. Boy, did he wait! Grandpa always followed through on his promises. He waited almost the entire day for us to climb down. Hunger and the tantalizing smell of Grandma's cooking ushered us indoors after the sun disappeared in a red glow beyond the hills. We received six lusty whacks from Grandpa's old leather belt before we were allowed to wipe our tears and tuck into the meal.

Solitary excursions growing up allowed me special moments to discover the comfort of a willow tree. The covering of willows hung low over the river, sweeping the waters with long, graceful branches. It swayed like a crystal chandelier – glimmering in the water's reflection below.

Occasionally William and I used to climb the tree to swing from its branches into the river. When I was with William, we never rested long in the willow tree. I had tried to take Morph up the tree with me, but his allergies cut this short. His face started to swell up and when he began shaking with sneezes, coughs, runny nose and weepy eyes I loaded him on my back and raced home. We soon learned where Morph could and could not go.

I flopped down under the shade of the willow tree and pinning my back against her trunk and disturbed a pair of Hammerkop birds wading in the shallows at the sharp bend in the river. They flew off, whistling loudly at my unwelcome intrusion. "Sorry, my friends!" I called out. These odd-looking, shiny, reddish-brown creatures with anvil-shaped heads, long beaks and long legs were renowned as mystical creatures that could bring death and destruction to your home if you stole their eggs or killed them. William and I once came across many of them dancing in rings, around and around. I watched this pair fly into their nest high up in the fork of a large Acacia tree. I hadn't meant to disturb them, but said a prayer, nonetheless, to ward off evil, as the feeling of dread grew steadily.

I let my legs dangle down the sides of the riverbank and enjoyed the feel of the cool, clear water washing over my feet. I dipped my fingers into the water and used the moisture to gently rub the tinging scratches on my arms and legs – inevitable badges of an adventurer's journey. I rested for a minute or two, then spent an hour kicking water off the side of the bank, skipping rocks, shooting with my sling, playing and reciting poems to the old willow tree. I eventually climbed up the tree and rested on one of the thick branches.

"Shine on, you millions of..." I wrote, then read the line repeatedly. Nothing came to mind. I closed my eyes, listening to the wind rustling the branches and leaves. The Quarry was quiet, with only the occasional car or truck driving to or fro. Enjoying the warmth of the sun on my legs, the cool breeze swaying gently through the tree branches and the rivers' call, I was lulled into a dreamy state. I thought about our home; about Grandma's old arms and legs and bent back. The deep wrinkles on her face, neck, arms and veins that stuck out on her arms.

Grandma had round, rosy cheeks and deep, brown, beautiful eyes. Charming, happy eyes that spoke of surviving tragedy, eyes that would turn fierce when she was angry or upset. She had two neat, deep dimples on each cheek − hidden slightly amongst the wrinkles − that would appear with her beautiful, welcoming smile. Grandma had hands rough as gravel, hands that would hold you to her bosom to take away all your pains and fears. She always prided herself on neatness and tidiness and having exemplary manners. She never left home unless her shoes, handbag or hat matched her dress. She would always say, "Just because you're not wealthy, don't mean you have to look poor." She was the envy of every woman in our community, hell-bent on making proper gentlemen out of my brothers and I and a lady out of our sister. The rambunctiousness of William and I was curtailed by painful hidings, while May-June and Morph were more naturally timid.

I tucked my notebook and pencil into my pocket, folded my hands behind my head and breathed in deeply. It didn't take long for me to fall into a deep sleep. I was deep in my dreams and did not sense that the weather had changed − from warm and sunny to dark and gloomy. The increased volume of nature's call startled me awake. I had barely a second to register that the winds had picked up speed, throwing the long grass and bush around me violently. The day's shadows were dimmed, and the river was no longer calm and smooth, but choppy.

My willow tree hummed mournfully as her thin branches danced to and fro at the hands of an unseen master. Branches began hitting me on all sides as they flew up and down and side to side in the strong gusts. Before I could secure my grip and foothold for a safe climb down, wind knocked me off my perch. I fell headfirst to the ground − hitting the back of my head against one of the lower branches. My elbow caught a branch on my way down and a good chunk of skin came off. Blood poured from my head and arm, all over my t-shirt and shorts, while the back of my legs scraped against the tree trunk. Pain blew the air from my lungs.

I cried out and must have lain under the tree for ten seconds before lightning and thunder and the increasing darkness of the gathering storm scared me enough to begin the long, painful stagger home. Above the storm's crashing orchestra I could hear insistent banging from Blurock Quarry. The wind blew from town center towards the quarry – I was right in between.

Faintly above the cacophony an animalistic cry curdled my blood. I stopped dead in my tracks. There it was, a fleeting note that whizzed by my ears. Without thinking I veered off the dusty road towards the little Bushman Stream. Pain shot through my body again. I thought I'd have a good view from on top of a large slab of protruding rock that stood lonesome in the veld and slowly I crawled up the flattest side. Between raging winds and stinging whips from the grass, bush and shrubs I struggled on. What I witnessed terrified me. Fear paralyzed me; my body rooted to the rock until those terrible screams stopped at the bank of the stream.

That same morning a young girl, Adelaide Florence, was about to leave home. She lived in one of the boxy houses in Cosmos Township across the Bushman's Stream. Adelaide stood ready at the door of their tiny home in Ash Street. The pretty thirteen-year-old had her textbooks hugged in her arms as she shifted impatiently from one stance to another. Her hair was neatly plaited into two ponytails, her old school shoes shone, and she wore a grey jerscy slightly torn at the sleeves and worn at the cuffs. Her faded blue school uniform was fluff- and crease free. Adelaide waited for her mother, who usually walked her and her friends Delilah and Salome to school, then proceeded to work in town. They did not have to go to school during the last month of the year, except to write exams and to collect reports on the last day.

Living in Cosmos was tough. Many children feared getting caught up in the alcohol- and drug-fueled drudgery that plagued the township.

Adelaide could hear quarrelling from inside the house. She knew that her unemployed, violent father picked fights with her mother.

"Ma!" shouted Adelaide as she peered into the house.

She waited for an "I'm coming, my sweetie!" but heard nothing. The quarrelling grew louder. Adelaide had witnessed fights before – none gave her that morning's sinking feeling.

She walked swiftly but cautiously into the tiny cold, dark house and down the passage and stood at the bedroom door. She heard the whooshing thud of something against flesh and heard her mother scream. Adelaide opened the door. She saw her mother slumped on the floor, hands over her head, clothes torn, her face bruised and swollen. Adelaide's father stood with a thick length of hose pipe dripping with blood, smelling of sour perspiration and alcohol.

Adelaide felt anger and betrayal grip her. She had pleaded so often with her mother to leave her father. He was going to kill her, she knew that. Adelaide's first instinct was to stop this madness. She wanted to charge and begin beating on him repeatedly – until the last morsel of his life left him. She clenched her fists, but her legs stood rooted to the spot. She couldn't move. Fear gripped her as she looked at her mother, desperately hoping for some sign for what to do, but nothing, not even a glance. Adelaide glared at her father. How she hated him.

"Stop it! Stop it! You're hurting Mommy! Stop it!" She screamed.

Her father, panting like a parched animal, turned towards her with mad, coal-black eyes. He lunged, reaching out to grab her with one hand and the raised hosepipe in the other.

"You little bitch!"

Adelaide turned and ran right out the front door, out of the yard, in the opposite direction of her friends Delilah and Salome, who fled when they saw the bloody sight of Mr. Florence chase Adelaide out of the house. She ran down the road towards the quarry where her grandpa worked. She knew he was the only person who could stop his son.

Adelaide was halfway through the veld leading to the quarry when the feeling in her tummy grew worse. Nevertheless, she continued the pathway that meandered along the edge of the Bushman Stream. Coming up the path towards her were three young men laughing and joking as they staggered along. She could tell that they were drunk or high. She wanted to run away, but the thought of watching her mother die before her kept her moving forward. Adelaide had a bad feeling about passing them. She began to walk at a fast, steady pace, picking up speed as she got closer to them. She put her head down and avoided eye contact, her breathing heavier and her heart beating faster. She passed the first man, then the second, but the third put his arm around her and spun her around. She stared into his young, hard face.

"Aweh, dinge!" said one of the men who reeked of stale alcohol, urine and sweat. The other two turned, crowding Adelaide.

"Isn't that Greta's kid?" asked one of the other men.

Adelaide tried to turn and flee, but her arms were caught in a suffocating grip.

"Aren't you supposed to be in fokken school?" asked the first man.

Adelaide nodded. She responded very quietly, "I'm going to my oupa." She kept her head down as her heart pounded relentlessly.

"Aweh! To your fokken oupa? Neh? Do you know what happens to bitches who don't go to school? Neh?" one of them taunted.

"She gets bloody fokken private lessons," another answered.

"Nasty little fokken bitches like you gets fucked!" shouted one of the men, forcing a kiss on her while the other two men laughed.

Adelaide fought hard, biting hard on the one man's arm and spitting in another's face. She pleaded, shouted and cried and fought to get free, but they wouldn't relent. The quarry's bashing and grinding noises seemed to mock the desperate sounds from her mouth. Adelaide tried to scream again. The man clasped his hand tightly over her mouth while she looked around for help, to no avail. She shook her head as violently as she could to get free. For a brief moment his hand slipped from her mouth and she managed to scream before he closed his hand against her mouth, this time digging his nails into the flesh over her jaws, suffocating her.

"You little fokken hoer!" he shouted, unzipping his pants while the other two men forced her down. They tore her school uniform and ripped off her panties. Her worst nightmare was coming true. Grandpa near yet so far. Time stood still. Her screams had no effect. When the three men decided that she could no longer satisfy their desires, the man with the blue pants and black sweater spoke into the wind.

"So ja, you fokken stupid cow!" voiced the man with the coldest eyes.

"I need to take a piss," said the other man who had first held her.

He then relieved himself over Adelaide's broken body. After what seemed like an eternity they staggered away, tipping their hats. "Compliments of Jakes, Raymond and Leon!" They proceeded up the footpath while Adelaide curled up as much as the pain would let her.

I saw everything those vile cowards did but could do nothing to stop them. It was only by some miracle that the three men failed to spot me peering down at them from the top of that rock. Not once did they even look to the top of the rock. Now I would live to tell the tale. My eyes were the only windows to what happened. My stomach had already given up my breakfast all over the rock that I lay on. I could vaguely hear those men in the distance as they danced and sang, carrying on as if nothing had happened, while I lay on the rock, shivering between fits of fear, guilt and rage. My mind replaying the images over and over.

Eventually I climbed down the rock and ran to her. When I reached Adelaide I felt ashamed. I sat beside her, rocking back and forth, caught between wanting to run and needing to stay. Adelaide suddenly opened her eyes. She turned her head slightly in my direction and stared at me, desperately. I knew that she was dying.

She started to cry in a way that seemed to burn into my flesh and memory for many years on end after that day. Before she died, she turned her head towards me, whispered three words, and then fell silent. Something passed between us as she left this world.

I stayed there a few short moments, staring at her dead body frozen in time before me. Rain began to pour, tears running down my face. Why was I being punished like this?!

I wished that lightning would strike me dead. I couldn't live with what I had seen. I had to tell someone! Flashes of lightning ignited within me those brutal faces, beyond the curtain of the storm that surrounded me. The three words that Adelaide whispered rang loudly in my ears. I must have been running aimlessly before I saw my grand-mother in the storm, on the muddy road near the edge of the veld. I ran straight into her arms.

"Ouma!" The only word I managed to shout repeatedly in a frantic chant. I clung to her with all my might, refusing to let go. Grandma just held me close. We stood there in the storm with my head buried in her bosom, sobbing. She walked us home, shielding me in her arms. Grandma opened the door and hurried me inside. I was wet, miserable and sore. I scrambled onto a chair in the kitchen in front of the stove. She kissed me on my head and gently rubbed my cheeks with her hands. I could not stop crying. She left the room and returned with a towel and a scarf, which she draped over her head. It was the one Morph bought for her for her birthday; seeing it covering her damp hair was a small comfort. My crying settled down into painful, throb-bing sobs. I stripped naked in front of the stove and Grandma wrapped me in the towel. She began to dry my body.

"Son, what happened?" Concern etching every wrinkle on her brow.

Looking into her eyes I burst into tears again. Words came tumbling out.

"Ouma, they hurt her! They killed her! She's dead! In the veld! I saw all of it!" I shouted between loud sobs. I wanted to give it all to Grandma – all that I had seen – so that I would not be alone anymore. I wanted her to take it away from me, but I turned my face away. Grandma put her fingers beneath my chin and lifted my face. All I saw was shock and confusion.

"Hurt who?" asked Grandma as she hugged and tried to calm me down.

"Adelaide! I saw it! In the veld, Ouma!" I yelled between sobs.

"Are you sure, Son?"

All I could do was nod. Grandma stroked my back until I finally calmed down. She then walked into the passage. I heard her dial a number on the phone, then speak briefly. The last thing I heard was her giving our home address.

I was roused out of this troubled blackness when Grandma shook me gently.

"Wake up, Plano."

Grandma stood in front of me with the pair of pajamas.

"Come change. You're shivering. You'll catch a cold."

I had forgotten how sore I was until I lifted my arms and the clothing brushed against the cuts on my body. "These look sore," said Grandma, examining my legs, arms and head.

"Don't change yet. Let me fix you up first."

Grandma returned with cotton swabs, Dettol, a tube of ointment, plasters and bandages.

A cup of piping hot black tea was on the table near us.

"Come, drink the tea. I've put plenty sugar into it. Let me see you."

I slowly turned around for her to have a look at me. Grandma began to swab the cuts, scratches and bruises with cotton wool dipped in Dettol. Every inch burned and stung. I wriggled and flinched between tiny sips of tea.

"Some people are coming, Son. I need you to tell them. Can you do that for me?"

I shook my head vigorously as the pain would allow me to. All I wanted was to sleep.

"They can't help her if you don't tell them," soothed Grandma as she helped me change.

I knew that no one could help Adelaide. No one could help me, either.

"You must be brave. You need to talk," continued Grandma.

Grandma was right. I wriggled away from her.

"My head."

"I know," responded Grandma. "We'll see to that; I'll call Dr. John right away."

A loud knock on the front door. Were these the people I had to talk to?

"Plano! Look at me! Son, open your eyes!"

I felt someone shaking me gently. Hands cold and smooth against my cheek.

"Come, Son, open your eyes."

I tried to move, but everything felt so heavy.

"Wake up, Son! Come on, wake up!"

It was a man's voice, speaking with authority.

"Plano, Son, open your eyes."

Dr John! I knew the voice; it had to be him.

"Plano, Son, it's Ouma."

"Ouma," I repeated.

"Open your eyes for me, Son."

I slowly opened my eyes, staring straight into a luminous ceiling with very bright lights.

Grandma grabbed my right hand and squeezed it reassuringly. I turned to look at Grandma, deep concern replaced by a warm smile.

"How're you feeling?" she asked as she rubbed my limp hand. I nodded slowly. "Ouma, where am I?"

"You're in the hospital, Son."

I looked away from Grandma and to the surroundings within this curtained enclave.

"Are you hungry?" asked Grandma as she kissed me on the forehead.

I shook my head. Just looking at Grandma made me feel better, but I felt light-headed.

Dr John kept on with his ministrations to my cuts and bruises.

"Have some water."

Grandma put her arm behind my head, lifted me up and held the cup to my lips.

I took a few small sips, then tilted my head away from the cup.

"You're going to be alright. Your wounds will heal," said Doctor John. "You took a nasty fall, but I've patched you up. Ouma, Plano is to take the tablets that I'll prescribe for the pain." He patted me lightly on my shoulder. "I'll pop in later."

"Ouma, is she okay? Is Adelaide OK?" I asked pleadingly.

"I'm so sorry, Plano."

"[...] Sergeant Van Wyk… on our way, you told him everything. Don't you remember?"

My heart pounded again. How will I ever forget?

"No! No! No! No! No!" A nurse rushed in. They tried to calm me.

Nothing worked. I shouted as loud as I could, wriggling and squirming.
I saw it all over again.

"Plano, calm down, please," pleaded Grandma.

"Plano, Son, it's Dr. John."

It's okay, Son, you can cry. It helps," consoled Dr John.

I closed my eyes. The tears came heaving until my chest hurt.

"It's okay, Plano. You'll feel better in the morning."

I longed for my parents and my grandpa. The ache grew and grew.

CHAPTER 2
BOUND IN SHADOWS
(FRIDAY, 10 DECEMBER 1999)

The five young men sat in a corner of the large verandah of the Estcourt Golf Clubhouse drinking coffee and enjoying freshly baked blueberry muffins after completing a nine-hole round of golf. They glowed from the exertions. There were only three other occupants within the confines of the verandah, but the other two sat as far away from the five as they could. They had paid homage to the gang upon their arrival, who dismissed them with slight shakes of heads. The third occupant was the waiter, who stood at a discreet distance ready to attend to any of their whims. They were dressed casually in jeans and t-shirts, pointy black shoes aiming upward. Each wore a cap plastered on their heads. Their black jackets had "Homeboys" emblazoned across the back. They would terrorize the town gleefully and with impunity.

The 'Homeboys Brotherhood' attended Estcourt High School by day, spoilt brats who enjoyed privileges due to their families' wealth. Their nighttime wanderings were disturbing, to say the least. The boys had adopted the school motto, 'Celer at Audax', but not in the way you would hope. This unholy alliance led by sons of the three most prominent businessmen in town employed such a creed sadistically. Their ethos was simple: 'The Richer, The Stronger!'

With his back to the waiter sat Hermann Combrink. His father, attorney Joe Combrink, served as lawyer to all three members of the

'Three-men-in-a-tub-club'. Hermann was merely added muscle to his friends, not in their class of wealth. A sixteen-year-old, blonde-haired, blue-eyed boerseun with freckles, he had a tough look about him, with a scar above his right eyelid and a crooked nose because of a fight outside the local disco the previous year. He attacked Vusi Duma and stabbed the young man in the shoulder with a pocketknife. Vusi beat him up, to the delight of many. A clear-cut case of self-defense, but if not for local councilors, community leaders, concerned parents and students who toy-toyed regularly outside the court and rallied behind Vusi, chanting, "Racism! Racism!" Vusi would have been in big trouble. Such is the Combrink influence in town. The case was eventually settled out of court.

The three most powerful families, combined with all their wannabe hangers-on, controlled Estcourt. You could hardly work without being employed by one of the three. The most powerful was Ewald Prinsloo, who owned the meat packaging plant, two large farms, two hotels, a wholesale company, three clothing shops and the local weekly newspaper, virtually half of the properties in town and various shares and businesses not made public. Prinsloo was known as The Butcher by the community, though no one ever dared to call him that to his face.

His sons were seated to the right of Hermann. They were also blonde and blue-eyed, taller than Hermann and more muscular, rugged and handsome. The eighteen-year-old twins Ewald Junior and Dewald were mild-mannered and polite around adults from within their circle of friends but were antagonistic towards anyone not white. They fed off each other and would go into a blinding rage if they felt that you offended them in any way. Even looking at them the wrong way could earn you a vicious beating. They allowed others to do their dirty work for them but never shied away from beating people up when the slightest chance arose.

A barman from the Silver Lining Sports Bar and Carwash was beaten to death on a Saturday at about 12h30 in the evening. His body was found a day later by two traffic police from Colenso travelling on the R103 towards the N11 onramp near Frere, where they had intended stopping passing trucks and busses. A flock of Cape vultures drew their attention.

The body was dumped in dense bush about 5km north-west of Chieveley, close to the gravel road that the traffic officers travelled along. They stopped and watched the vultures feed and then dance and hop around with bald necks outstretched, with claws flashing in the air and with their dark brown and white feathered expanse of more than two-meter wingspans fluffing back and forth in mock battles. The cacophony of the feeding was loud; the vultures bobbed, cackled and hissed, blood visible on their long, wrinkled necks, heads and sharp-clawed beaks.

The officers watched this spectacle for at least five minutes. They were not able to make out what the vultures were feeding on due to sheer numbers. The officers were making a U-turn to travel back to the main road when the passenger spotted a patch of bright blue cloth at the feeding. He hastily urged the driver to stop. They fired to scatter the vultures. They had ripped the lifeless shell of flesh and bone into an unrecognizable mess.

There was no substantial evidence at the crime scene or credible witnesses to any crime. An unidentified individual phoned the local police and the Natal Witness and told them that he witnessed the threats made by Ewald and Dewald towards the barman accused of watering down their drinks. The twins left the bar after their friends pried them away from doing bodily harm to the poor barman. The police managed to trace patrons who were at the bar that night, each denying that any wrongdoing had taken place. The twins had good alibis from a police officer, who said that he saw their black Audi S3 Quattro enter the gates at their home at Urban Heights No. 12 at approximately 11h45 that evening. Their parents confirmed to the police that their boys were indoors by 11h40. The case was dropped, the docket destroyed soon after.

Then there was Faizel Ameen, who owned a bakery that supplied the entire Municipal district, two supermarkets, a bus company, a freight service and various properties and shares around South Africa. He was known as The Baker. His son, seventeen-year-old Abubaker, was seated to the left of Hermann. He was the tallest and thinnest of the group, brown-skinned and black-eyed with a hooked nose that gave a sly look. Abu loved flying around town in his metallic gold

BMW 325 with its fancy rims. He regularly aimed his vehicle like a guided missile at slow moving pedestrians – laughing gleefully as they scattered before him. Abu carried an unlicensed gun, unafraid to brandish it around when high on designer drugs. He spent many hours on the internet, telling anyone within earshot of the good extremists were doing by ridding the world of Jews, Infidels, the poor and the weak.

Witnesses at the railway station on the corner of Harding and Lorne Streets saw a motorist in a white Mazda 626 with an NP registration recklessly cutting in front of Abubaker's BMW, right on the ninety-degree bend, on a Friday evening at about 11h00 in September 1998. The vehicle sped off up Lorne Street, heading out of town. Witnesses could not be sure whether Abu and friends followed him or not, although they went in the same direction, but the driver of the Mazda was found the following morning about a kilometer from the N3, severely beaten.

The Estcourt Guardian carried the story the following week and reported that the man's head was swollen to almost twice its size when brought to the Estcourt Provincial Hospital. The man was blind drunk when he decided to leave the Royal Hotel and head home to Pietermaritzburg and had no recollection of what happened to him. Abu and friends were never questioned; no arrests were made. The man eventually recovered enough to head home in his white Mazda and after a week this docket was also destroyed.

The third wealthiest man was Eric Walton. Walton owned three coal mines, a construction company, a cartage company, a large dairy farm, a bed and breakfast lodge and property, shares and other unknown investments. He was known as The Candlestick Maker. His son, seventeen-year-old Robert Walton, was seated on the other side of the table. He was the shortest and stockiest of the lot, with black hair and dark, brooding eyes that matched the sardonic grin that sometimes crooked his stern, full lips. He wore this simmering, violent anger like a cape. Rob was with Ewald and Dewald at the hotel the night the barman was murdered and with Abu the night the Mazda driver was severely beaten. Word on the street was that Rob was the most cold-blooded of the lot; first to attack, cruel and calculated. Some saw a smooth-talking ladies' man, charming and well-intentioned. When the sun set, he hunted ravenously.

"They fucked and killed her!" exclaimed Ewald, all arching eyebrows and wide eyes.

"Yeah! Had my eye on that bitch," retorted Abu with exaggerated sadness.

"They say they bloody kicked her to fucking death," Rob added matter-of-factly. He reached into his jacket pocket and took out a vial containing blue Ecstasy tablets. He passed these around, keeping one for himself. Each quickly swallowed theirs with a bit of water, then consumed the remaining muffins and coffee.

"Pa's hiding those cunts at the stables. He's moving them tonight," Ewald volunteered.

"We'll have to watch that little Bushman shit troublemaker," Hermann contributed.

"Yeah! replied Dewald. "Pa said he'll have to be sorted out."

"Whadda he mean?" Hermann slurred. The other four shrugged their shoulders.

"Maybe we can bloody well do something. Sort this shit out ourselves," offered Rob.

His comrades leaned forward with glazed eyes. Not a sound from the five in the corner by the other three on the verandah above the hum of air-conditioning and East Coast Radio.

The ride home from the hospital at sunrise the next morning was a long one. I tried to busy my mind with trivial questions and simple child-like guessing games, recited poetry and drawing pictures in my mind – doing everything I could to keep the terror at bay. The pajamas I had on smelled of the hospital. Grandma sat in front with the male nurse who graciously gave us a lift home. As we exited the vehicle at our gate we were greeted by the happy faces of William, May-June and Morph. Grandma helped me into a clean pair of pajamas and then fussed me straight into bed as she shooed my sister and brothers out of the room.

I could hear chatter in the kitchen and strained to catch a bit of the conversation but could only pick up on the odd word. All I wanted to do was to sleep and to forget everything.

Dark clouds parted above me I was bound to a fig tree
A clock standing in front of me hands dripping with blood
I saw her standing in front of me a pure white ghost
She had a knife in her right hand and a shiny red feather in her left
She touched my cheek with the feather
Immediately her hand bled her white turned to black
I felt a stream of hot blood covering my eyes
And a rope tightened around my neck
The clock struck twelve the ground fell from beneath me.

Soon I came back from that place of sedation and opened my eyes, sweaty and shivering cold – even though the day was hot and clammy. I glanced around wildly. Grandma was sitting in her rocking chair at the end of my bed, whispering. I knew she was talking to God about me. Grandma put the knitting down, leaned over and touched my forehead. Her cool hands made me flinch. Grandma looked at me with concern.

"You're burning up."

Grandma returned with a damp, cool face cloth that she placed on my forehead and a bucket that she placed at my bedside.

"Nauseous?" I nodded.

Grandma went into the bathroom and came back with a pill which she handed to me with a glass of water. I drank the pill, then lay back down. Staring at the ceiling did nothing to calm me. When Grandma returned, she was bathed and dressed in her Sunday best. She hurried me into the bathroom. Afterwards we sat in the lounge and waited for the taxi. I looked at the old clock hanging on the wall. Seven o clock. My siblings were in the kitchen.

"Do you want to talk about it?" asked Grandma out of the blue.

"I'm fine, Grandma," I responded hastily, avoiding eye contact

Grandma paced the floor, each time feeling my forehead as she passed by.

"You know I hate waiting!" she repeated.

"William, May and Morph aren't coming with us," said Grandma as she peered outside. "Shame, they had a long trip. May said Morph bit the doctor when he tried to put a spatula into Morph's mouth. I'll have to go with next time." She kept pacing anxious.

It was about twenty minutes of waiting before we heard the hooter of the taxi outside. Grandma first called to William and May-June before hurrying me out of the house and into the taxi. Once we were seated in the VW Kombi with torn seats and Grandma explained to the driver where exactly he needed to go, we began our seven-minute drive to the Doctor's surgery. Grandma felt it necessary for us to be driven in a taxi there, because I was unwell.

I loved looking out of the window while being driven in cars. What fascinated me was how fleeting the scenery was as we shot by. Everything so blurred yet somehow stationary. I nuzzled up to the window and pressed my nose up against the glass, resting my chin on my hands and looking out into the near and far distances that slid by in a kaleidoscope of colors and movements. The sun warmed my face. The sound of the spluttering vehicle engine calmed me, much like thunderstorms did on warm summer afternoons. I looked on at a group of children of about my age walking down the road, happily singing and chattering away.

"Why aren't you mourning Adelaide with us!?" I wanted to scream.

The group were adorned in their bright Saturday clothes, colorful dresses, jeans and t-shirts. Blissfully unaware of the evil that lurked all around. How I envied them! I pushed myself away from the window and rested my head on Grandma's lap. It felt like ages to get there.

Town center was mostly old buildings, not many beyond two stories tall. The municipal buildings and town hall were probably the biggest in area, stretching out for an entire block. The Milo factory was the most imposing industrial building, a most wonderful place. My siblings and I loved to sit outside the factory on the days when they sold their products at special prices to shops all over the country. Mrs Jacobsen, one of the factory foremen, would even give us goodies for free! Each one of us would take chocolates and tins of Milo.

That factory was the closest thing to heaven on earth. Some of the other fancier big buildings belonged to the businesspeople who lived to the south side of town, up on the hill. Their grand, double-story houses had long driveways and Olympic swimming pools and houses with enormous TVs, so big that it was like sitting in a cinema. Of course, I had not seen this myself, but heard stories from other school friends who claimed to have been in some of these houses where their mothers worked as domestics.

There are four main roads that lead into and out of Estcourt. Harding, Albert, Lorne and Richmond. The one that we frequented most often was Harding Street, where a lot happened. Near our home at the corner of Harding and Alfred Streets was a little café shop where Grandma often traded Coke bottles for bread. William, May-June and I also regularly helped the owner with stock taking for a few Rands. The shop owner, Mr. Seedat, was kind to us. He would give us extra bread, milk and maas whenever he had some to spare.

Many people in town were very generous to us after our parents died. We were told by Mr. Seedat that this was as a direct result of Grandma's kindness to all people. There was a taxi rank next to the Post Office. This area was continually abuzz with vehicles, commuters and hawkers who spent their days plying their goods to weary travelers on the pavement. Most banks and shops stood as proud sentinels on either side of this long road. The imposing old Estcourt Crown Hotel grandest of them all, testimony to a bygone era.

To the boys of Estcourt the standout place on Harding Street was where it joined Lorne Street. The old railway station was a special place. The deep, rumbling train engines was the stuff of dreams and legend for us all. There was not a single young boy in Estcourt from our generation and circle of friends who did not dream of one day becoming a train driver.

When we had opportunities to see people in their trains passing by, we would wave with gusto until they disappeared. Although modern trains transited through the station, old steam engines also rumbled by in billows of smoke as they dragged their protesting carriages onwards to unknown destinations. It was a sight to behold.

Grandma always respected Doctor John, both as a doctor and as an upstanding man, although she sometimes found his strong opinions about all and sundry a bit sanctimonious. I often enjoyed the playful verbal joust between Grandma and Doctor John. I wondered what they would discuss today. Doctor John also visited Grandma at home on some of his days off work, or after his rounds at the Strelitzia Old Age Home. He would bring sweets, other delicacies and clothes for us. I always found this to be a strange act of kindness, especially from a white man. What was his special bond with Grandma?

I used to wonder whether he was trying to fatten us up like the wicked witch tried to do to Hansel and Gretel. Grandma exuded confidence in him as our family doctor, even though he was barely forty. She praised his 'good heart' and 'pure intentions'. Grandma often told how she had been looking for a good doctor for years before finding Doctor John. His predecessor practiced in an untidy surgery with books and files stacked on desks, chairs and the floor.

"It was as though he was afraid to pack away his stuff and make Estcourt his home," Grandma always reasoned about the previous doctor. Despite my childish concerns regarding Dr. John, I found him to be a gentle, kind man. He always kept up perfect professional appearances when on duty, and always spoke his mind. However, there were whispers about him being a closeted drunk. Grandma said that these were not true, it was just because he was not racist and treated everyone equally in a small town that was still largely segregated. Most people knew each other and generally interacted politely in accordance with their standing.

When the Kombi came to a stop Grandma hurried us out of the creaking sliding side door. She turned to pay the taxi driver his due after I jumped out and turned to watch their interchange. As usual the driver tried to squeeze a few more money out of his passengers. Grandma handed him the exact fee with much haste. After Grandma shut the side door and before she could step away from the taxi, the tough-looking man blurted out,

"HEY WENA, GOGO! Ma! It's ten Rand eighty!" demanded the taxi driver. "You said eight-fifty when I called you!" replied Grandma in exasperation.

The taxi driver eyed Grandma cautiously, but she did not back down.

"Mfana, you're trying to cheat an old lady. Heh!? I only brought 21 rand, which includes the return. Where must I get the extra money from? Mmm!?"

"Ama Boesman!" came the reply before throwing his hand up and driving away.

We walked into the red brick building that stood prettily on the confluence of Wagon, Brewitt and Felgate Streets, across the road from the bigger glass double story and concrete buildings of the Estcourt Victorian Mall. I glanced in the opposite direction to the Estcourt Golf Club. Within my memory of that place was a portrait of glimpses through the dense shrubbery and trees that bordered the entrance way, of silhouettes of shiny cars. William and some other rugby players once caddied there for their schoolteachers and showed me where it was.

William's description of the game was that it was where the rich businessmen of the town gathered on a weekly basis. When we neared the entrance to the building, I instinctively walked faster towards the door to hold it open for Grandma, who patted me on the head. She always said, "Damned be to her if she raised a pack of hooligans like other boys our age!"

I felt worse for wear after walking this short distance. The honey-blonde receptionist with her beehive of teased hair spoke to Grandma about our appointment, while I blankly observed her. She stood up with files and a stack of papers in hand, looked at me reassuringly and smiled before walking into another room. Grandma and I sat in the cold waiting room. The worry on her brow seemed to be etched into place. We were the only ones there that morning. The air conditioning made me shiver. I looked at the light brown walls and white ceiling, then tried to read the medical pamphlets and notices on the wall. Grandma paged through an old magazine. After a while I closed my eyes, hoping to drift into that place of blackness where I would find some peace, but soon we heard Dr. John's voice.

"Good morning, Ma. Morning, Plano. Please come through." He ushered us into his examination room and placed his arm around Grandma's shoulders. After friendly chatter Grandma and I were seated on one side of the wooden desk, while Dr. John sat at his side of it.

"How're you doing, Plano?"

Dr. John scribbled on a page before him as he spoke.

"Doctor, he's burning up. The vomiting hasn't stopped. The other pills are helping to calm him, but he still sleeps restlessly and has nightmares."

The doctor looked over at me. I tried to ignore his probing eyes.

"Let's get him looked at, then."

"Come, Son."

The poking, prodding and probing started. He examined my chest, my back, and then the back of my head. He spent some time on the bump on my head, then removed the plasters off my arms and legs and examined the wounds. I was shivering again.

"Apart from the slight infection on the elbow, he'll be fine." I'll give him some stronger antibiotics that should help clear out the infection. The fever is definitely because of that, but the vomiting probably isn't. Severe trauma can affect one in several ways," continued Dr. John.

When he finished bandaging me up, he lifted me off the bed and gently nudged me in the direction of the chairs. He walked back to his desk, sat down and started scribbling onto that page and then a notepad. I took my seat again next to Grandma, who held my hand.

"I am sending him for therapy," said Dr. John as he finished and signed with a flourish.

"I've recommended a good psychiatrist for Deplano to see early next week." Dr. John put a page from his notepad into an envelope, sealed it and wrote a name. He picked a business card from a little box on one side of the desk and handed it with the envelope to Grandma.

"He needs to talk to someone professionally. It's too much for a young man to bear, we both know that. Don't worry about the cost, I'll settle it with Dr. Carlson."

I didn't know what they were going to do to me. There was a brief pause.

"Thank you so much, Doctor," said Grandma tearfully. "I don't know how I'll ever be able to repay you. Deplano desperately needs help and I've been worrying non-stop."

"Ouma, when I moved to Estcourt, I struggled to build my practice. You were the first patient who believed in me, even though I was young and unknown. You stuck by me when others did not. You befriended me and welcomed me into your home. I am deeply indebted to you. You're very dear to me – like a mother – and I am glad that I can help in some small way." He smiled. Grandma was crying and dried her eyes before blowing her nose.

"Don't worry about Deplano, Ouma. He has suffered a deep trauma. It'll take a while for him to recover, but he will bounce back. I know he will. He just needs time to heal." Grandma could only nod in response. I cannot recall the ride back home.

"Get into bed, I'll bring you something to eat and the tablets you must take. No getting up until you feel better!" instructed Grandma as we walked to the front door.

I just wanted to crawl into bed and sleep past this living nightmare. How would I rest?

My heartbeat faster, my head hurt terribly, and my mind flowed with bloodied images. I yelled out. Grandma rushed into the room and held me tightly.

"Settle down, my child! It's only a nightmare. I'm here." She rocked us back and forth.

"But it's not Okay, Ouma. I saw it!" I yelped. "It's never gonna be okay!"

"It'll take time, but you'll be okay, my child. You'll be alright." Then she sang to me.

"Goosey, goosey gander, where shall I wonder? Upstairs and down-stairs in my lady's chamber. There I met an old man who couldn't say his prayers, took him by the left leg and threw him down the stairs. Stairs went crack! He fell back! All the little ducks went quack!"

I woke up sometime later in darkness with the nursery rhyme on loop in my head. "Quack, quack, quack" I repeated softly. Three quacks, three words that forever bound me to Adelaide.

CHAPTER 3
VOICES FROM THE SHADOWS
(SATURDAY, 11 DECEMBER 1999)

Dark clouds parted above me I was bound to a fig tree
A clock standing in front of me hands dripping with blood
I saw her standing in front of me a pure white ghost
She had a knife in her right hand and a shiny, red feather in her left
She touched my cheek with the feather
Immediately her hand bled her white turned to black
I felt a stream of hot blood covering my eyes
And a rope tightened around my neck
The clock struck twelve the ground fell from beneath me.

I screamed and jolted awake, soaked with perspiration. Grandma hurried into the room.

"It's alright, my child. It's only a nightmare. See! It's morning already."

Grandma dabbed my face and arms with a damp facecloth.

"I'll get you something to eat then you can rest a bit. You had quite a restless night." Grandma cupped my face tenderly and then hugged me tightly. The yelling stopped and the shaking slowly subsided. When I opened my eyes again, two big brown eyes were looking down at me. Still in a dazed place I was startled when Morph spoke cheerfully.

"Hello." His hands pulled my cheeks up then down, then up again.

"Morph, stop it," I scolded softly

"Shush, not so loud. Ouma said you need to rest." Morph put his hand over my mouth.

"Come see, William! May! He's up! He's up! He can talk!" yelled Morph.

"Morph, I told you not to wake him up!" scolded William as he walked into the room.

"But I didn't. He got up on his own. I was just looking at him when he got up."

"Hey, Plano," greeted William, touching me lightly but reassuringly on my arm.

"Hey, bro," greeted May-June and kissed my forehead. "How're you doing?"

"We heard you saw her die! What happened? Was it like a movie?" Morph piped up.

There they were – the never-ending questions I expected Morph to bombard me with for the rest of the day. I turned my head away and stared out the window.

"Come, Morph, let's go help Grandma make pancakes." May-June lifted Morph up off me and hurried away hand in hand with him.

"Hey, Plano, I…" began William. He sat on his bed, leaning forward, arms rested on his legs and fingers anxiously intertwined.

"I'm fine…"

William continued without missing a beat. "I wish with all my heart I was there with you. Know that I'm with you through all this." His eyes fixed onto mine.

With a lump in my throat, I replied softly. "Thank you."

"Ouma told us you must stay in bed today as well. How're you feeling?"

"I'm fine," I replied again.

"Whoah, you got so many bruises and bandages. You can't be alright," William joked.

I felt good with my brother close. I so wished that our lives could be normal again.

"You'll have to do my chores for a while," I joked.

"I know. You'll do mine as soon as you get your butt out of this bed." We continued with lighthearted banter until May-June walked back into the room with a tray of pancakes, syrup and five cups of piping hot tea. She smiled with eyes that could not hide her concern.

"Ouma'll be here soon. She's just with Morph." She placed the tray on William's bed.

It was the beginning of December school holidays. William had collected our report cards this morning. Sudden loud knocking on the front door startled us. William was up in a flash and rushed off to see who it was. I could hear two authoritative voices introduce themselves as Captain Khuzwayo and Sergeant Brits.

"It's the cops," said William. "They want to know if it's okay to talk to you now. Before I left, I heard Ouma say it was not okay, but they wouldn't take no for an answer."

This made me anxious. Morph jumped into bed against the wall next to me. We could hear murmuring voices from the lounge. May-June held my hand while William sat at the ready near the door. It dawned on me then that they had formed a protective ring around me. Eventually we heard the police say their good-byes and the front door close. Only then did we collectively breathe sighs of relief. Grandma came into the room, concern turning to relief.

"Those were the detectives investigating the case. I told them you're not ready to talk and to wait until Dr. John says it's OK." Grandma touched my foot reassuringly. "There'll come a time, Plano, when you'll have to talk. They have a job to do. When you're ready."

The end of year school reports always set the tone for our holidays. If they were good, Grandma would allow us freedom to play much more until the schools re-opened. If there were poor grades the offender would get a dusting from her and then all of us would be woken up early to scrub and polish the entire house and to work the garden until Grandma was satisfied. "All for one and one for all" seemed to be Grandma's motto when it came to punishing us.

In our latter years this bond remained as powerful as ever. Grandma valued education above all else. I soaked up knowledge and enjoyed school more than anything. I supplemented my formal education through voracious reading. I only later realized how much this helped me.

While I hardly spoke in class, I passed all tests and exams with top marks. Grandma knew that I needed to be kept busy learning the ways and workings of the world way beyond the boundaries of Estcourt and she never let my mind grow lazy. When not reading books like *The Fall of the House of Usher* I had to complete difficult crossword puzzles or work through May-June or William's old math or science books.

School was tough for William the past year. He was bullied, but still managed to keep to his high academic standards. It was not uncommon for us to be picked on because we were considered low class kids, who had high standards and didn't act or behave how society dictated poorer people should. Because we stood together as a family, we would end up in quite several playground bust-ups that often lead to the principal's office and punishment. There were also some students from rich families who made life hard for their poorer classmates. They were ruthless in their teasing of our clothes and everything else that did not meet their standards.

Morph had some peculiar mannerisms and was teased relentlessly for being different. From his very early years Morph's uniqueness began to show. When he was learning to walk, he'd only swing his left arm quite aggressively as if he were trying to propel himself into the air. He eventually stopped doing so. Watching Morph interact with the world was like looking at the worst place you could be and seeing it through rose colored glasses, because he had this ability to make everything be filled with hope and goodness. Where the world saw "trash" Morph found treasure. Even a box was a gift, a toilet roll holder was a trumpet. Everything to Morph had meaning and everything was to be protected and made whole.

Naturally we stood up for him. As soon as William tried to explain that Morph was not well since birth, bullies simply elevated their taunts. We never willingly revealed to Grandma all that happened to us at school, but she always knew somehow. Grandma would speak to us about proper behavior and would make it very clear to us that we were under no circumstances to be expelled from school, because we needed an education to survive in the world. In the latter years of our schooling we relied more on our wits to overcome adversity.

We were sufficiently motivated to persevere. It was in our DNA. We had wonderful role models in our parents and grandparents who taught us well. Grandma also often spoke glowingly of President Nelson Mandela and of other stalwarts of the Tripartite Alliance. Grandma and Grandpa were active members of the ANC in their younger days. They shared tales of hardship, oppression, marches and secret meetings and campaigning and going to jail because of their convictions. Taped to the back of our bedroom door was a poster of Nelson Mandela in that iconic moment when he raised an arm and clenched his fist on 11 February 1990 as he walked out of Victor Verster Prison. Emblazoned across the bottom of the poster were the words, "*Never, never and never again shall it be that this beautiful land will again experience the oppression of one by another.*" I glanced at the poster as my brothers and sister chatted while we waited for Grandma to return with those foreboding envelopes.

Grandma walked into the room clutching four brown envelopes with Morph strutting proudly behind, but he dashed for the tray of pancakes as soon as he could. Grandma always made a big fuss of report opening. The buildup to the proud moment was more fun for her than for us. I had faith in my siblings. For the past three years we had wonderful school holidays.

"How do you think you did, May-June? Mmm!?" Grandma sat in her rocking chair that was still in our room and slipped on her reading glasses.

"I'm not sure!" responded May-June, tilting her head slightly and biting her bottom lip.

"You must be sure, mmm!? If you're not sure, then what are you?" countered Grandma sternly as she arranged the envelopes in a neat stack.

"Lost," Morph chipped in.

"And if you're lost, then what are you?" continued Grandma.

A loster!" answered Morph proudly, bouncing up and down on the bed.

Everyone burst out laughing.

Grandma opened the first envelope slowly and cleared her throat theatrically.

"May-June!" enthused Grandma excitedly before she read out the grades on the report card: *"English A; Maths B+; Science B+; Afrikaans C; Biology A; Economics B+. "*

We cheered and clapped. May-June was hugged by each of us, starting with Grandma who enclosed her in a bear hug and rocked her from side to side. Grandma returned May-June's report to the envelope and placed it on the bed next to her before picking up the next one.

As she opened the envelope Grandma said, "How're you doing, Plano?"

"I'm fine, Ouma," I replied on autopilot. Hands under the blankets, squeezed together.

"English A; Math B+; Science C; Afrikaans A; Biology A-; Economics A+. "

The clapping and hugging commenced again.

"Well done, my child!" Grandma hugged me and kissed me on my forehead.

Before Grandma could place my report next to May-June's and pick up the next envelope, Morph knew he was next. He shot up straight from his place next to me and walked in a circle, then sat down, fidgeting and wringing his hands, eyes shifting every which way.

"Morph! Sit still, Son." Grandma opened the envelope. A frown creased Grandma's forehead. *"English B; Afrikaans B; Business Econ D; Economics D; Math C; Art A+. "*

Morph was elated. "I've passed! I've passed!"

Morph and Grandma almost landed on the floor as he flew into her arms. Grandma rocked and congratulated him. Morph strutted back to his seat. Grandma then reached for the last envelope and eyed William. He looked back at Grandma with determination in his eyes and with hands folded calmly in his lap, but his thumbs whirled around and around each other. *"English A; Math C; Science C; Afrikaans B; Biology C; Economics D+. "*

Sighs escaped both William and Grandma, just before the cheering and hugging started.

"No extra chores! Everyone can relax!" Grandma hugged William tightly.

Morph jumped up and down and dashed around the room in excitement.

"Plano, what happened to your head?" Morph queried.

"I fell," I replied between chewing and swallowing my delicious pancake.

"Where?" continued Morph.

"Out of a tree."

"Morph!!" Grandma cautioned.

"Oh! … which tree?" continued Morph.

"Just a tree." William, May-June and Grandma all stared. I refused to relive that day.

"There by the place where the girl pegged?" declared Morph finally.

"ADAMOR!" roared Grandma. "I warned you!"

"No, you didn't," replied Morph with false bravado.

"HAND OR BUM?!?" roared Grandma.

"Hand," whispered Morph sheepishly.

Morph stretched out his hand, but before anything could be done, he bolted like a flash of lightning, somersaulted over the tray, down William's bed and landed on his feet. He ran towards the corner behind the door and turned to face the room with the expression of a frightened animal. Grandma swiftly cornered him as he looked for a way out. He turned sharply to escape between Grandma's legs but poked his bum in the air, leaving it exposed. Grandma seized the opportunity and Morph let out a yelp.

Grandma grabbed Morph's arm and managed to land a few more smacks on his bum.

"Ooohhwww!" cried Morph. He finally managed to dash away from Grandma, crying.

"Don't you dare do that again!"

Morph stood in the doorway, contrite.

"Sorry, Ouma. Sorry, Plano."

"Good, now wash your face and come finish your breakfast." Grandma turned to look at us, all shaking with laughter. The first time that I laughed in what seemed like an eternity.

The rest of the morning was much better than the day before. I remained indoors, meandering and talking to my family, I made sure never to be alone. The medication helped to blunt the pain. I tried with all my might to stay awake but couldn't do so indefinitely.

Adelaide was buried on a somber afternoon. The grey summer sky and afternoon breeze seemed to cry out in despair. I tried to think of other things and to fill my time in conversations with my sister and brothers, but I would unwillingly return to Adelaide and her funeral. I would retreat to the bathroom to cry, silently in anguish. My siblings tried to comfort me, but I could see the frustrations each one battled with in trying to help but failing to get through to me.

Grandma attended the funeral, too. When she returned, she carried with her an air of quiet solemnity. William and May-June quietly reported to Grandma on what had transpired in her absence. I could see Grandma quietly reassure them. Although she said very little about the funeral, I heard William and May-June talking of the simmering anger at the vicious rape and murder. I heard them say that the children from Cosmos were walking around in fear.

This reminded me of a time a year earlier when we were crawling through the long grass below Rocky Lane, playing cowboys and crooks. A friend of William named Victor stopped the game by urgently calling us to the place where he hid. Directly in his pathway was a thick puffadder, curled up but with its head raised as if to strike. It was dead, burnt in the fire that raged through this section of the veld a month earlier. The ants had reduced the puffadder to a skeleton of skin and bones, but the silently menacing sight was still scary. More so that its eye sockets, within a head as large as the open hand of a grown man, were void of any sight. We halted play and sat around talking about how terrifying dead snakes and animals were.

Our imaginations and bravado tended to run wild. It was not long before we were imagining what Victor would have done if that snake was alive. Suffice to say that a lot of mirth was shared regarding the probability of Victor shitting himself from fear. We had a good laugh at Victor's stoic defense of his bravery and how he would have caught the snake with his bare hands, ferociously wrung it to death, bitten off its head and thrown it into the river. We were all aware that Victor would have been killed if that snake were alive.

This thought tempered our games in the veld somewhat from that day onwards. We would always first walk about and make a lot of noise as we beat tins and threw stones into our play area to chase away snakes. The same sense of foreboding prevailed in our home this afternoon. The storm that hit Estcourt felt like a vicious cloudburst lashing out on Adelaide's behalf.

The thunder and lightning were utterly ferocious. The windows in every room rattled and shook, such was the severity of the onslaught. It felt as though the storm had chosen to linger over our home to seek me out in retribution. As hailstones rattled the corrugated roof sheeting so loudly that speech was impossible, so came more rain, so heavy that it sounded as though buckets of water were being poured directly onto our home from above.

The roof leaked from all corners. We hurriedly moved furniture and placed buckets, pots and pans where it dripped, but couldn't manage to keep all the bucketing water out. When I finally managed to fall asleep my dreams echoed the scream of the storm. May-June must have heard me scream. She walked into our bedroom while nightmarish visions dragged me under. I shuddered. May-June crept under the blankets next to me, hugged my shaking frame and spoke soothingly, until my body calmed enough to allow me to breathe normally.

'It's okay, Plano," May-June whispered. Then she sang one of Mom's favorite songs;
"...Hold me close
Let Your love surround me
Bring me near
Draw me to Your side
And as I wait
I'll rise up like the eagle
And I will soar with You
Your Spirit leads me on
In the power of Your love..."

May-June sang beautifully. My heartache – for the loss of my parents and the tenderness shown by my sister – was overwhelming. I hugged

May-June and wept. Grandma appeared in the doorway. May-June gave her a reassuring look and Grandma smiled before shuffling off to bed.

The Butcher, Baker and Candlestick Maker met just before sunset in the Butcher's plush upstairs office on the corner of Albert Street and Shepstone Avenue. It was not unusual for them to meet at these offices, but rather so for them to convene on a weekend. The Butcher and Candlestick Maker were similarly attired in white long-sleeved shirts and black pants, with high-gloss, expensive black shoes completing their outfits. The Baker was dressed in white garments, from the taqiyya on his head, the thobe that covered his body and serval visible from below the hemline of the thobe. Only his sandals were black.

While the setting seemed quite casual their demeanors were anything but. All three men were older versions of their sons. The Butcher, Ewald Prinsloo, was the most imposing and charismatic of the three, the natural leader of this group. His silver-grey hair and coldest of grey-blue eyes were striking. Those icy orbs locked fiercely onto those of Eric Walton.

"What the fuck were you thinking! I told you never to shit where you eat. Your stupid lust for that woman is going to jeopardize our plans!" His hands were on the desk before him, palms down, as if ready to spring up and choke the life out of him.

Eric Walton, The Candlestick Maker, sat impassively on the other side of an imposing mahogany desk, although he clenched his fists below. Ewald could not see this, but Faizel Ameen, The Baker, picked the movement up with shrewd black eyes. Walton also had silver-grey hair, but his was more peppery and untidier. He was short and muscular for his age, looking like an elderly gangster. The skewed nose and scar below his left eye bore testament to his grit. Not a man to be trifled with. His speech was laconic, yet brutal.

"You should be the last one to point fucking fingers," he countered forcefully. Ewald responded before Eric finished speaking.

"That's not the point, Eric! This man is part of our inner circle. A trusted confidant, and you had to choose to screw his wife! Worse! You had to get caught! What the fuck! Our plans are at an advanced stage! He could spill the beans! Did you think of the consequences?!" Ewald's voice rose in volume and intensity after each sentence.

Eric's eyes turned a more opaque, colder cobalt. It looked as though he was about to spring up at any minute, reach across the desk and choke the life out of Ewald.

"I told you I'll fucking handle it! Stop fucking stressing!" His voice matched the coldness of his eyes. Ewald saw the murderous look in Eric's eyes but did not back down.

"Gentlemen, please!" interjected Faizel Ameen. He sat cross-legged while stroking his peppercorn-colored beard. Faizel was wiry and short but lacked nothing in pragmatism.

"What's done is done. Now we simply manage the situation."

Ewald and Eric stopped glaring at each other and sat back in their chairs to focus on Faizel. Tensions between them remained.

"Clearly, if we can't undo this mess, then we'll have to take steps to bury it. We don't know how much of our secrets he has stashed away for a day like this." Faizel made sure that his eyes swiveled equally as he spoke. Ewald and Eric both focused intently at what he said.

"If you were in his shoes, would you not have hidden something incriminating for insurance? Especially after what happened?" Faizel treading on dangerous ground.

"So, we cannot eliminate these problems until we can establish this information. For now, I suggest we buy his silence. If he agrees, then it's going to cost big bucks."

"Who's going to approach him?" asked Ewald, steepled hands under his chin.

"I'll do it on Monday. Eric must stay as far away as is possible from that family."

"How much?" barked Eric, his hands still formed in fists.

"No less than R5 million, but it could go up to ten… I'll negotiate with him."

"You'll have to fork out at least half of that to supplement our operational funds. We must keep the balance healthy for the next phase of our plans," declared Ewald.

"No problem. I'll have the money transferred to the offshore account tonight," Eric added, then took a deep breath.

"Shouldn't we consider wasting that bloody bastard? Would be far cheaper."

"No, under no circumstances whatsoever," responded Faizel. "It'll cause too many complications that would jeopardize our plans."

"R10 million for a fuck. You're a madman, Eric!" Ewald added.

"I said I'll fucking pay the bloody money!" Eric responded heatedly.

"Fine! responded Ewald. "Faizel. I'll start to find out what he's stashed away."

"Eric, have you sorted out the three helicopters for our families?"

"All ready to go in an instant," Eric replied as he relaxed a bit. "Is the Land Surveyor in place? Are we still a go for the 29th?"

"Yes, he is. We're ready," answered Faizel. "His equipment is in place."

"And the rest of the packages?" Eric asked Ewald.

"All in place." "We have two hundred shipping containers packed full and hidden strategically in Gauteng. The other provinces each have one hundred."

"Has Combrink sorted out those dockets of our three shitheads?" asked Faizel.

"I haven't received feedback. Ask when you meet on Monday," Ewald responded.

"We need those bloody fuckers back in town to sort out the shit dump of a mess they've made," Eric said sternly. "They must take care of bloody business before it fucks up beyond our control. Remember, we only got seventeen days to go. We can't have these shitty distractions fucking it up. Bloody hell! I'll phone them tonight to come back on Monday. As for that little cunt who saw them! They'll have to sort out that mess as well."

"Speaking of sorting out… Thank you, my friend. All my systems are set for the millennium change. The guys you used sorted my computers, registers and other stuff out quickly. There'll be no problems with this Y2K bug," Faizel said, looking gratefully at Ewald.

"No problem." This Y2K shit is all a big hype from those who are making big bucks from it. The solutions are out there and have been for quite some time."

"Yeah, thanks, Ewald, we're also sorted," Eric added dryly.

"So, we're all set. The mainframe with all our Vulintaba Manifesto's modelling and strategies is sorted. We had to take it out from the bunker and had to watch those guys like hawks to make sure they didn't get too nosy." Ewald glanced from one partner to the other.

"I have to go, it's time for mosque," Faizel interjected. "We'll talk again tomorrow."

He walked out of the door. As he descended the stairs he whispered "Insha Allah."

Ewald stepped to the window. He stood hands behind his back and watched Faizel get into his white Land Rover Discovery and exit the yard past the manned and electronic controlled security gate. Eric sat quietly and watched Ewald. For a while all that could be heard in the office was the quiet washing sound of the air conditioner. In the distance the rumblings of an approaching storm could be heard. Ewald glanced in the inclement weather's direction.

Without turning around, he asked, "Did you hear what he said, Eric?"

"About stashing info away? Yeah, I heard. I've always said, one can never trust a bloody Coolie. They'll steal bloody milk out of your coffee right if you're not watching them."

Ewald turned from the window and seated himself before talking again.

"We knew from the outset that he was dangerous. No one amasses a fucking fortune the way he did without being shrewd and cold-blooded about it. He controls more KZN municipalities than we do with his bribery and donations. He's untouchable amongst the politicians and officials. But now... I believe our friend Faizel Ameen is running scared. He's letting us know that he also has a fucking insurance policy in place just in case."

"So, how do we handle that raghead?"

"Do nothing for now. TJ said we need him and his contacts in the Middle East. Without them our plan won't work. It's too big to rely only on the Southern African network. We'll also have to watch our backs in case that sneaky little shit has made any plans to take us out. There's a lot at stake and a shitload of money that'll be made from this venture. Much more than any one of us ever dreamed of. A greedy person wouldn't hesitate to eliminate his partners."

Eric steadied his hands on his lap, aware that Ewald could read people well.

"Do you want me to sort the Coolie cunt out?" he asked flatly.

Ewald looked at Eric with a steely glint in his eyes.

"Leave it to me, Eric. If Faizel thinks he can double-cross us he's in for a nasty surprise. Either way, he's still in for a shock."

Later that evening Dan Watts wrapped the coarse, worn sack tighter around his gaunt body as he huddled in the concrete pipe in the dense bush off the R103 to Mooiriver and opposite Fort Dunford. On a good evening Dan would sit on his concrete pipe, roll a smoke of tobacco, light up and contemplate the lights and traffic of Estcourt. At other times he would stare at the grey and light orange building of the fort with its dark, imposing windows and wonder what it was like to live and work in that scary building. But not tonight. He lay in his pipe consumed with fear – not at the ferocious storm, but at its aftermath. The storm had passed, but a cold freshness still lingered. Stars overhead and the quarter moon's glow were displayed in full splendor, with Dan cowered deep within the pipe's shadows.

The ferocious storm filled him with fear, the likes of which he had not felt for a long time past. It awakened within him a sense that he needed to call upon God to save him or die. The pipe he was in was not long enough to prevent the huge, stinging raindrops from pounding him as the wind drove it relentlessly into his meagre shelter. In his drug-fueled haze his soaked legs and feet gave him the impression that he was about to drown. He closed his ears with his hands to try and silence the eerie cacophony of millions of horsemen driving across his pipe to steer him into hell. His efforts were in vain. Soaked in rainwater, fear and perspiration he prayed quietly to God to spare him from his apocalyptic wrath.

"Aweh, ding! We gotta put dat fokken little shit away," muttered

Jakes in the coldest voice that brought an involuntary shiver to Dan's body.

"Ja. We gotta blerry do it," echoed Raymond. Dan could clearly hear him slurp from a bottle. The sound forced Dan's tongue out of his mouth to lick his cracked lips – lips that thirsted for even a drop of the alcohol he knew they were consuming. More slurping followed.

"Jislaaik! Where was the fokker? I looked all around. Didn't see a fokken soul. Where the fok was that stupid son of a cunt bitch?" Leon wheezed.

"Aweh, dinge! It doesn't matter," Jakes replied. "We gorra fokken waste dat blerry cunt. Da boss said we gorra lay low for short shift and we gorra blerry work on da fokken 'plaas' near blerry Wembezi."

More slurping noises. Dan was in agony. "No one will blerry trouble us there," Jake continued. "But his fokken days are fokken numbered. When we come back, we'll blerry waste dat fokken bastard. No blerry witness, no fokken case. Boss said they'll blerry sort out the fokken 'magi.' Plus, the blerry docket will fokken fokoff. He just needs some blerry time to fokken sort it out. While he does, we blerry stay at the fokken plaas."

"Aweh, dinge! There's the blerry bakkie, gents!' interjected Raymond. "Let's fokoff! Shit! I dropped the blerry dop."

"Fokkit!" Leon wheezed. "Der's blerry booze on the fokken plaas, man. Let's go!"

In turn, each jumped onto the pipe in which Dan hid and then scurried off down the embankment to the bakkie. Dan was forced to stick his hand in his mouth so as not to make a sound as they rocked the pipe in their passing. He waited until the bakkie roared off in the distance before he dared to venture out of his tomb in search of his life's sustenance that lay somewhere in the shrubbery near the pipe. He crept about on hands and knees in search of the bottle. To his credit, some survival instinct caused him to tense and try to roll away just as his hand touched the bottle, but it was too late. The piece of concrete block that landed on his exposed head knocked Dan into oblivion. He did not see his assailant who grabbed the almost empty bottle of booze and disappeared into the shrubbery like a whisper in the breeze.

Eventually, ever-so-feebly, Dan stirred into life. He was still bleeding profusely from the head wound as he felt around in tho dark. He touched the suede shoes of a man nearby. With his last strength ebbing Dan whispered hoarsely in a voice not much above a whisper,

"Tell her dey coming for her boy," he begged, holding onto those shoes.

"Please, dey gonna kill the laaitie!"

His last words were barely cold before another concrete block came crashing down onto Dan's already pulverized head, ending his life. The man in the brown suede shoes squatted quietly next to Dan as he listened intently to the night noises.

He was so still that even the male crickets close to him resumed their loud chirping songs. Eventually the man stood up in silent, lithe movement and stealthily glided up the hillside. Not a soul disturbed as he passed by. When he reached the main R103 road he turned and jogged comfortably in the darkness at a rapid pace towards the Estcourt Provincial Hospital, where he turned right near the Department of Transport offices. He continued down New Formosa Road, where his vehicle was concealed. No one saw him drive off or took any notice when he entered Estcourt across the grey steel bridge.

They found Dan Watts covered with early morning dew as they emerged from the bushes and shrubs. Most hurried past his inert body, but a few paused briefly to steal his meagre possessions. Two wizened old ladies took pity on Dan and sent one of the younger men to call the cops. It took an hour for a yellow SAPS van to eventually get there and another half an hour for the Police Mortuary van to come and remove Dan's body. The two policemen had already decided that it was the least tedious to report that Dan had fallen on his head during the storm and died immediately from his injuries. This was despite the two bloodied concrete blocks laying in plain view in front of them. When no one was looking, the two pieces of incriminating evidence were rolled away by the lawmen, out of sight.

"Who cares about these cockroaches?" voiced one of them in Zulu.

The only response was a quick shrug of shoulders. Before another half an hour had passed Dan's body was gone from the hill, never to be seen again.

CHAPTER 4
THE DEEP DIVIDE SUNDAY
(SUNDAY, 12 DECEMBER 1999)

"Come on, guys! Wake up! Wake up! It's my birthday!" Morph flew like a twittering sparrow up and down from our bedroom to Grandma and May-June, tugging at blankets as we moaned and groaned and tried to burrow deeper into slumberland.

"Come on, guys! Wake up! Wake up! It's my birthday! Ouma gorrra bake me scones!" Morph urged us. We eventually tumbled out of sleep and shuffled off, in turn, to the bathroom.

I stood on the back veranda and looked at the gnarled, old, massive gum tree shake its thousands of leaves in the gentle summer breeze. Grandma reminded us of the previous night that the municipality was going to cut it down on Monday. Another part of our lives, gone forever. As I gazed at the old gum tree, I remembered how we decided to climb the old tree during the previous December holidays. Somehow the gentle breezing cooled us down.

Without much persuasion, William and I started our ascent. May-June and Morph went up to the lowest branches of another small tree nearby and there they sat holding on to each other, happily swinging their legs rhythmically over the edge as they urged William and I on to conquer the old giant. We climbed and climbed, rested a while, and climbed and climbed to heights that no other child in our neighborhood ever achieved. William had to stop, eventually, when a breeze came passing through and swayed his perch too much for comfort. I carried on, climbing ever higher. Then the wind picked up and we were swung heavily to and fro.

William shouted at me to come down as he started the long journey back to the ground. I was high above him, where the soft green branches groaned and strained almost to breaking point under my shifting weight. It was one of the simplest yet most exhilarating experiences of my young life: I clung there and felt so free and alive that I cried out as loudly as I could.

I looked to the south-west and saw the dark, ominous summer storm gather for its rapid charge towards us. My euphoria instantly turned into fear. William was about three meters from the ground when he lost his grip and fell, tumbling down, hitting branches with sickening crashes and thuds as he bounced lower and lower to eventually drop like a lump of mud at the feet of May-June and Morph. Both were screaming; I was still stuck high up in the tree.

William lay there, lifeless, as May-June and Morph wept and wailed around him, reaching out, but not touching him. When I eventually got down and knelt beside them, William opened his eyes with a sigh that turned into a long, painful groan. He sat up ever so slowly and we helped him to his feet. Our joy could not be contained as we helped our limping brother hobble home through a stinging wall of rain. We made it indoors just as the deafening thud of lightning lit up everything around us in a blue haze.

That old gum tree lost one of her branches in a loud crash of disdain at our foolish attempts at trying to conquer her. William wore the plaster-of-paris on his left arm and all his cuts and bruises like badges of honor. It was one of the few times in our lives we escaped a well-deserved hiding from Grandma. We were banned from climbing that old gum tree again.

"Come on, Plano! Hurry up! It's time for my birthday scones!" Morph stood at the kitchen door and eagerly called me to join them. Morph turned seven today. Grandma baked fourteen scones for his birthday celebration, two for every year, according to tradition. Morph was seated at the head of the table, bouncing and chattering non-stop.

Grandma and May-June were busy preparing breakfast and William was across from a beaming Morph. I joined them.

"You're fifteen!" demanded Morph. "You're a liar, William! You're fifteen!"

"I'm almost fifteen and three quarters, Morph. That makes me sixteen." William sounded tough like Dad and copied a stiff adult posture. He yawned in feigned nonchalance.

"No! You'll be sixteen in February! You're still fifteen!" cried Morph, throwing a little tantrum as he flip-flopped like a fish out of the water onto the floor, kicking the air as though he were pedaling hard on an upside-down bicycle. William and I barely kept a straight face.

"Morph!" cautioned Grandma walking with the tray of scones to the table.

"Ouma, I also want to be fifteen and three quarters!" cried Morph between tearful sobs.

"Why now, Son?" asked Grandma sitting down on the chair next to his seat.

"Coz' you can eat big people sweets like fireballs and sour worms."

"But you can eat those sweets, Morph."

"But William said I can't!" cried Morph again kicking the air.

"Morph, today's your birthday. Come see the scones I've baked for you."

Morph shot up and into his seat, almost knocking the tray out of May-June's hands.

She placed the seven scones in front of Morph, who looked like he could tip the entire plate into his mouth and down everything in one gulp. Next to him was a butter knife, a tub of margarine and a jar of apricot jam. Morph was salivating. May-June wiped his mouth with a tissue and then lead us in song, "Happy birthday to you! Happy birthday to you! Happy birthday to Mooorph! Happy birthday to you!" We clapped and wished him happy birthday. Grandma and May-June kissed Morph on the head, while William and I slapped him on the back. Morph could hardly contain himself. Grandma added margarine and jam to the first scone and placed it before him. The rest of us watched and teased him as we tucked into our thin porridge.

"Aaah! Lighty! You look like you're gonna faint even before you eat the first one! Come on, Sonny! Eat! Eat! We haven't got all day!" William and I cajoled him.

Morph was utterly unconcerned. His eyes grew bigger and bigger looking at that scone.

"Ahh come now, Morph! Eat it before it grows legs and runs away!" teased May-June. She sounded more like Mom by the day. "Morph! That's yours, enjoy!" William chipped in.

"Oh! My boy, I'm so proud of you! Seven today mmm!" Grandma stroked Morph's head. "Next year you're going to a new class."

It was as though time stalled just for Morph as he slowly lifted the scone to his mouth.

"Well now, you gonna eat it or what?" William chuckled; his eyes crinkled with mirth.

"No." Morph solemnly replied. "I'm not. Not on my own." He handed it to Grandma.

"And now, Morph? Is there something wrong with it?" Morph shook his head.

"I love them, Ouma. Was just thinking… We're a family. Wanna share it. If it's okay?"

"It's your scone, my child. You can do with it as you want." Grandma responded, smiling and giving him a quick hug.

Morph beamed. "Ok. I love all of you very much. I wanna share this one."

"Ok." Grandma conceded. "We'll share the first one with you as a family. Thank you."

The laughter died down for a moment. Grandma sent me to her room to fetch some tissues. When I returned, she took the first bite. Morph beamed as the scone began its journey.

"Love you, Ouma." May-June took a bite. "Love you, May-June." It once again came from Morph. May-June bit her bottom lip to stem tears of joy. William took a quick bite. "Love you, William." A broad smile prevailed. He nodded his head in acknowledgement. I took a bite. "Love you, Plano." I managed to hold myself together, barely.

Morph put the last piece into his mouth and chewed slowly, savoring the moment.

"Love you, Morph," we echoed in unison.

I stepped across the chasm of nothingness, right back into the fold. "You're the bestest family in the whole world!" exclaimed Morph.

Grandma always said that despite Morph's ailments he possessed an uncanny understanding of people, a wisdom far beyond his meagre years. We were again reminded of what it was like to be in a selfless, caring, loving family. Morph could do no wrong this day. He walked around the whole day with a gold star stuck to his forehead. He and I went on our other traditional birthday journey after lunch. Grandma allowed us on these special days to visit the families we knew who lived close by. Grandma had told them in advance that it was our birthday. They would wish us happy birthday and put a coin or two in our hands as a present.

Morph begged Grandma for me to accompany him on his special journey. Grandma hesitated but relented after I assured her that I would be just fine.

"Don't go to Cosmos. Only visit this part of town and come home immediately if there's any problems along the way." William walked with us and proceeded down Rocky Lane to visit friends. Morph and I turned into our nearest neighbor's yard.

I once heard our neighbor on Rocky Lane, Aunty Nishi Ramdan, say in her sing-song voice to Grandma that her dead father-in law was, "A tyrant from Tongaat, I tell you, Auntie. Ooh! His wife and children, and all of us married to that family had some tough times with that man. You know, Auntie? He had a 'short-shit' syndrome." I laughed so hard!

Aunty Nishi was always forthright in her speech. We hardly reached her front door before it burst open. She came flying out in a bright red sari and before Morph could even open his mouth to say something she had him in a bear hug. Her poodle, Snow White, hopped around them, barking in tandem with Auntie Nishi's words.

"Oooohh! My child! Happy birthday, and all!" She kissed Morph on his cheeks. "May God bless you to see many more birthdays. You're such a good child and I'm so proud of you."

Aunt Nishi held a bunched handkerchief. She released Morph to open a bunch of knots.

"Thank you, Aunty Nishi." Morph managed to got in.

"This is for you, my child. I've been saving it this past month, and all." She gave Morph a handful of fifty cents coins and then proceeded to hug him again.

"Thank you, my child, for all you do for me. It's always much appreciated."

"Thank you, Aunty Nishi. Thank you, Aunty Nishi." Morph managed to get in a word or two every now and again between Aunty Nishi's words and Snow White's yapping. Morph was always helpful to the residents around us, doing menial jobs like going to the shops for them and helping with some of the chores at their homes. It took a while before he managed to extricate himself from Aunty Nishi's embrace.

Before we could turn away, Auntie Nishi walked up to me and touched my cheek.

"And how're you holding up, and all, Plano?"

"I'm fine, Aunty Nishi."

"It's not easy to get through what you've seen my child. It'll take time for you to heal, but you will eventually get through the pain." I did not move my face away from her warm touch. Aunty Nishi hugged me tightly.

"We're all here for you, Plano. Remember, we love you lots."

"Thank you so much, Aunty Nishi," I managed. She held me to her as I wept.

"In time, all will be much better. Look after yourself, Plano. You're such a good child. I'm praying for you all." Coins jingled in Morph's pockets at every step as we headed back.

"Aunty Nishi really likes you, Morph. How much did you get?"

Morph took out the coins. We counted R15.50. It was a good start for Morph and a good precursor of the afternoon that lay ahead. I fed on the kindness we encountered from our community like parched earth does receiving rain. I never wanted to let go of that day. Next stop was Ouma Beulah and Oupa Spence Stumbles. This couple was very special to our family, always being there to for us through all the good times and bad. Oupa Spence was Grandpa's best friend. Ouma Beulah and Grandma were just as close, even though none of them were related. Oupa Spence was our de-facto father figure who we turned to for advice from time to time in the absence of Grandpa and Dad. We spent at least half an hour in their wonderful company and Morph was blessed with R 15 birthday gift.

Within a few hours we covered the entire downtown Estcourt, Morph's pockets jingling with coin. He knew that he had more than enough for a family outing to the movies.

"We'll take Ouma along this time. I'm sure they'll like it very much," Morph said enthusiastically, walking backward facing me. I slowed down so that he could keep up.

"Ja, but we'll have to choose a nice movie they'll all like. You know Ouma doesn't like animation and hates action and karate movies."

"We must go early so that we have enough time to check out what is showing."

We reached Ouma Betty's home on the corner of Drummond Road and Alexander Street. Morph opened the gate and lead the way. Ouma Betty was seated on an old wooden bench on her verandah. She was very still as she held tightly onto her gnarled wooden cane. She looked asleep, even though we could see her eyes moving along in our direction as we approached. Her face and hands were wizened with wrinkles and grey blotches and her short, curly hair was snow white.

"Hi, Ouma Betty. How're you today?" Morph greeted.

"Hi, Ouma Betty," I added.

"Hello, boys. I'm fine, and how's everybody at home?"

"They're all fine." Morph responded. "It's my birthday today, Ouma Betty!"

"Happy birthday, Son. May God bless you to see many more birthdays. May you be blessed your whole life." Ouma Betty sounded sad, despite the well wishes.

"Thank you, Ouma Betty."

Ouma Betty sat quietly and stared off into space. We waited quietly with her for a few minutes. Morph eventually shifted and the coins jingled in his pocket.

"I'm so sorry, Morph. I can't even give you five cents this year. I'm totally broke. My grandchildren were here from Joburg for the week end. They cleaned me out. Left this morning when they saw there's nothing left to eat and that my purse was empty." Ouma Betty swallowed a few times and stared off into the distance again.

"I don't know why they bother even coming here. They ignore me the whole time except when they want money or food. All they do is eat, get drunk and party with those Homeboys." Her shoulders shuddered. "I haven't had nothing to eat the whole day and there's nothing for supper. I don't know what to do! I just don't know what to do." Ouma Betty wept.

Morph and I swallowed rapidly a couple of times to keep our emotions at bay. We stood there and shifted and squirmed from one foot to the other, not sure how to respond.

"We'll come back just now, Ouma Betty," I eventually said. We departed hastily.

"We'd better go past the church. Tell them what's happened to Ouma Betty. I'm sure they'll help her. Mrs. Kay must be there, preparing for the Evening Service." I took charge. We walked hastily in that direction.

"Ok, Plano," Morph replied, pensive.

We went down Drummond Street along the grass sidewalk of the road closest to the Bushman's River. Lambert Park was busy. We caught glimpses of the festivities that prevailed between the screen of bushes and trees. I made sure not to look back towards the other side of the river. Just before we turned into Victoria Street, I gently stirred Morph away from the path of two dung beetles. The male was rolling his huge ball of dung with his hind legs while the female hung onto the life-giving projectile as if her life depended on it. A family in unison. Normally I would stop and observe them, but not today.

Along the banks of the Bushman's River a herd of Nguni cattle grazed, while a flock of Cattle Egrets rode on their backs to feast on the parasites that were clinging to their own sustenance. Every now and then these birds hopped off the backs of the cattle to feast on the ground, their heads bobbing above their hunched bodies with every long step they took, as if silently creeping up on their prey. They occasionally clicked their beaks to communicate. The Egrets were sharp-eyed. I hoped that the dung beetles would escape the sharp yellow beaks of the birds. We climbed up the sixty steps on Victoria Road, resting occasionally for Morph to catch his breath. Not once did I look back towards the other side of the river.

We reached St Matthews Church on the corner of Conner and Lorne Streets. The building of grey slabs of sandstone rock and steep roof always stirred mixed emotions in me. We still regularly attended church services on Sunday mornings in the very building where my parents' coffins had lain on the day of their funerals. A place of long goodbyes.

We knocked on the door at the church office and entered when bidden to do so. After perfunctory greetings were made, we told Mrs. Kay about Ouma Betty.

"Pastor and his family are still on leave. We don't have any grocery parcels left. I'll try my best to do something for Ouma tomorrow, but I've nothing left to give tonight. We're also stone broke at home. Can you boys not get some supper from home for Ouma Betty just for tonight?" Mrs. Kay asked us.

"Ok, Mrs. Kay. We'll ask our Grandma for something."

"And how're you doing, Plano?"

"I am fine, Mrs. Kay."

"We're praying for you, Plano. Things will be alright eventually."

"I'm sure they will, Mrs. Kay."

After saying goodbye, we departed for home.

"Why don't we help Ouma Betty, Plano? Isn't it we're supposed to help each other? We can take my money and buy her something to eat for tonight? Even for tomorrow if there's enough left?" Morph asked as we paused on the steps.

I made sure to avert my eyes from the other side of the river during our descent.

"I don't know, Morph. What about the movies?"

We reached the place where we last saw the dung beetles, but they were gone. The cattle and egrets had also wandered further down the river towards the imposing light grey steel bridge on Lorne Street. Even though I loved birds more than any other animals, I hoped those dung beetles were not devoured by the egrets and were safely ensconced within their breeding burrow to live another day. That's what I needed, too – just to live another day.

"We can go another time. Ouma Betty needs food, Plano. I don't think I'll be able to eat my supper while Ouma's so sad in her house." He walked backwards again.

"Please! Please, Plano! Let's help Ouma Betty."

"Ok, Lighty. But remember, it's your money. Don't come crying when you're broke."

"I won't." He skipped towards the supermarket until a coughing fit slowed him down.

Ouma Betty shed tears of gratitude when we walked in with the fish and chips, loaf of bread, carton of milk, small tin of Ricoffy, small packet of sugar, packet of minced meat and two tins of baked beans. She hugged Morph tightly after I told her who bought the groceries.

"Thank you so, so much, Morph. You've a heart of gold. Don't ever change. Thank you. Thank you. God'll truly bless you for your kindness," she repeated as she smothered him in her tight embrace and kisses.

"It's OK, Ouma Betty. No problem." He grinned from ear to ear.

It was starting to get dark by the time we journeyed home.

"Plano?"

"Huh!"

"Were you crying back there at Ouma Betty's?"

"Who me? Tears? must've been you couldn't see properly in the dim light," I responded gruffly. Morph smiled and held my hand as we walked home through the gathering dusk.

The deep ochre red of the fading sun cast long shadows. In the spaces and places where the sun was allowed to still show itself, the settling dust glowed eerily red – a reflection of the day's heat that taunted us into submission. Overhead bats and hawks vied for their insect supper. They clicked and screeched in delight at the abundant gathering of their food in the dimming sky. In the gardens we passed crickets and frogs were heard clearing their vocal cords for the choruses they would orchestrate to the night sky. Today was a good day. I would be seeing a psychiatrist tomorrow and was drinking tablets prescribed to keep me sane.

While Morph was in the bathroom I hurriedly explained to Grandma, William and May-June about Ouma Betty and what Morph did with his birthday money. I thought that at least William was going to squeal about Morph giving his money away, but no one did. Instead, each one of us committed to scrape together whatever cash we had to secretly donate to Morph's meagre stash of remaining coins.

The man with the brown suede shoes staggered out of a shebeen and meandered slowly down the road as if on his way home. Then suddenly he disappeared. The sober man stood still in deep shadows of the early evening on the outskirts of Cosmos Township. No one picked up or sensed him there, not even the roaming dogs going about their scavenging business, scurrying for food from bin bags and rubbish heaps close by. He remained in that place into the evening gloom, while a vehicle carrying three wanted men hurried into the township. It was only after the vehicle with just the driver flew back out of Cosmos that the man stepped deeper into the shadows and removed a cellphone from his jacket pocket.

"As-salamu alaykum." He spoke in the Hassaniya dialect of Morocco.

"Wa'alaykumus-salam." The response tinged with the Levantine dialect of Syria.

"The three infidels have been deposited."

"Were they alone?"

"No. A driver dropped them off at a house known to me and left."

"Do what you must."

"Okay."

'By when?"

"Tomorrow."

"And the boy?"

"Nothing unusual. Any other orders?"

"Not now. Wait for further instructions."

"OK."

The man removed the sim card from the cellphone and snapped it into pieces. He removed the battery and placed it in his jacket pocket. He crushed the phone with his heal and discarded it into a stinking bin bag. He transformed back into a drunk dying for the last dop hurrying to a shebeen close to the house where the men were dropped off.

Faizel Ameen removed the sim card from the cellphone he had used and burnt it. He carefully inserted the cellphone into a box and sealed it with necessary tools at hand. The cellphone would be on sale in a Spaza shop in Phuthaditshaba before the afternoon of the next day. When he was done, he pushed it aside, sat back and gazed at his handiwork.

"Insha Allah!" he said to the long shadows outside the window.

CHAPTER 5
THE DEATH OF GIANTS
(MONDAY, 13 DECEMBER 1999)

At eight fifteen in the morning Grandma and I used Mfana's kombi to my appointment with the psychiatrist, Dr. Carlson. His surgery was almost at the end of Ntabamhlope Road. It was an old double-story house converted and extended to suit his requirements. Throughout the journey Grandma and Mfana exchanged pleasantries. When the taxi came to a stop Grandma paid Mfana the agreed amount and thanked him. He absent-mindedly took the fare while staring at me with his cold black eyes. Just before Grandma and I could turn away, he bellowed.

"Hey! Boy! I see you! You strong! Don't stop fight!"

"Thank you, Sir." I never imagined Mfana being compassionate.

"Hey! Gogo! You phone me ven ready! Heh?"

"Okay, Mfana."

He revved the kombi engine and muttered "Shup-shup!" before driving off with a roar.

"Wow!" exclaimed Grandma. "The Lord works in mysterious ways."

We turned and walked towards our destination.

.   .   .

Dr. Carlson's office was on the first floor. I stood looking at the steel elevator door, squeezing Grandma's hand as tight as I could and stared at my reflection before us. He who stared back looked a lot skinnier – with wider ears and a puffier face. The steel doors yawned open with a loud "pling" and a violent jolt to the sides, shaking me out of my brief reverie. As we rode the elevator, I felt like a fish out of water, even more so when the passage opened before us. On both sides of this imposing corridor were three large brown doors that looked like large chocolate blocks. Reluctantly I followed Grandma, hoping that I would not be subjected to further injections. Thankfully, Dr. Carlson's rooms were the first door on the right.

In the furthest corner from us sat an old man who looked a bit like Crocodile Dundee. He lounged with legs crossed, reading a magazine. I wondered whether he had also witnessed someone die. I stared at the tattoos on his wrinkly arms and legs. He seemed to be well travelled, but unkempt. He wore a t-shirt that read, "I Love Puerto Rico." I smiled because I was the only person in my class who knew where Puerto Rico was.

The old man looked up at me and caught me smiling at him. He flicked one bushy eyebrow up. I looked away casually, but our eyes met once again. I could sense that he was watching me. I was more afraid of meeting Dr. Carlson than this unusual old man. I wondered why he stared so much and paid more attention to Grandma filling in forms. As time on the huge clock ticked closer, I swung my legs back and forth. The weathered old man tucked away the magazine into his brown short pants, sauntered over and took the seat right next to me. He folded one leg over the other one, removed his magazine from his pants, opened it and continued to read silently, with his lips mouthing the words. I pressed closer to Grandma's arm.

"Can I help you?" Grandma demanded politely, wrapping a protective arm around me.

"Agh! I'm sorry Ma'am, my name's Stevie." He presented a hand to Grandma.

"Hmm!" greeted Grandma as she clasped his hand in greeting.

"Whaddya in for, kid?" He had a heavy British accent.

"I don't see how that concerns you?" retorted Grandma feistily.

"Oh, I'm here 'cos of an accident. You know? Check this out, kid." He lifted his shirt to reveal that most of his torso was covered in thick bandages.

"That looks sore," I said softly.

"Yep, took off most of the skin on this side! You know?" he enthused.

"You really don't wanna see what my arse looks like."

Grandma looked up sharply and cleared her throat.

"Like one of those bare-bummed baboons, you know the ones with the pink bums. Had to literally sit on bum cushions at home until it healed up. You know?"

"Shhesh! Ouch!" I remarked in sympathy.

"That's not the worst of it. Old lady didn't make it, you know? Killed in the accident."

I stiffened even more and shifted closer to Grandma who squirmed uncomfortably.

"Yep, a 1980 Harley-Davidson XLS 1000 Roadster. Man, was she beautiful!"

Grandma and I relaxed a bit.

"Was emerald green and silver and shone like a perfect jewel. You know? Was the first bike I ever bought with my own cash ten years ago and then I crashed her in the most epic way. Fitting end to the love of my life. Agh! She was getting old, seen better days. There's a huge gap in my heart and in the garage, I tell you." He crossed his hands over his heart.

"Is that why you're here?"

"No, no!" he chuckled. "I'm here for something else."

"Oh!" I responded automatically.

"What you in for?"

"I…" floundering for words.

"Stress!" Grandma chimed in.

"Oh! At such a young age?! What problems do you have, kid?"

I shrugged. Grandma opened her mouth to respond, but he was faster.

"The world is getting too tense nowadays. Not the same free spirit she was in my youth. Breeding a generation of corporate rats! You know? By 2010 people'll be killing each other purely out of frustration. Mark my words!" He gestured skywards with the last sentence.

"Mrs. Gibbs and Deplano Delvaux, I'm Doctor Carlson. Please come through." His voice was deep and measured but did little to lower my rapid heartbeat.

"Doctor Carlson, just a moment of your time, please. Need my script filled again. You know?" Stevie stood up and rushed closer to Dr. Carlson.

"Steven, we've discussed this yesterday. You need to follow my instructions to receive the help you need right now," responded Dr. Carlson.

"Please, Doctor!"

"Have you booked yourself into Riverside?"

"No!"

"I'm not writing another script until you book yourself in. I need you to do so voluntarily as part of your recovery programme. You *can* do it again."

"Dammit!"

Steve brought his fist down loudly on the desk. Dr Carlson was unfazed by this outburst.

"I'm serious, Steven. If you want my help, then you must do as I say."

"Agh! Doc, the pain is killing me!"

"I'll go with you tomorrow, Steven. Fill this in and meet me here tomorrow at noon."

"This is an admittance form! Dammit!"

"I know. "It's a temporary visit. I won't lie to you, Steven. You know that."

"Okay, then!" responded Stevie in resignation. He grabbed the form and a pen off the desk and scurried off to the corner of the waiting room. I did not want to be like Stevie.

. . .

Dr. Carlson gestured and we walked into his office. The door closed ominously behind him; we couldn't hear anything but the hum of the cool air conditioner.

"Good day, Ma'am. It's a pleasure to make your acquaintance. Doctor John has told me so much about you."

"All good things, I hope," responded Grandma with a nervous giggle.

"Only the best. Pleased to meet you, Deplano."

"Pleased to meet you, Sir."

I had seen 'Frasier' and expected Dr. Carlson to resemble one of those psychiatrists. Dr. Carlson even looked very much like Frasier, just balder. His office had all the furnishings, ferns and ornaments that made you feel at home, but it still intimidated me being there.

Grandma and I sat in these large chairs in front of this massive, polished mahogany desk. Our feet did not touch the ground from these perches. It was as though the furniture was made for giants. Behind us, against the back wall, was an orange lounger with another office chair positioned near the head of the lounger. Along the wall opposite the window were Dr. Carlson's degrees and other important qualifications.

"He must be good," I thought.

"Ok. Mrs. Gibbs, will you please give me a broad outline of what has transpired to date. All the events that have caused Deplano stress."

Throughout her recollections Dr. Carlson focused almost exclusively on Grandma. I knew that his eyes missed nothing: I tried my best to sit as still as possible while the pains were being recalled. I knew also that my face and eyes revealed my inner turmoil as Grandma spoke. "Deplano, can you please take a seat in the waiting room while I talk to Grandma for a bit?"

I nodded gratefully and hastily shot out of my chair. Dr. Carlson glided upright in one easy movement, handed me a lollipop and lead me out and into the reception area. Stevie was gone, but the waiting area still smelt of him. The receptionist looked at me from time to time. When we occasionally made eye contact, she smiled then returned to her computer screen. Every now and then the phones rang; the receptionist spoke in a calm, low voices. The room was warmer and much more calming than Dr. Carlson's sanctum. Grandma and Dr. Carlson were in the room for over half an hour. And just when I started to fidget and fret.

"Deplano?" Grandma stepped out of the room. A catch in her voice and her eyes were red. "Come, Doctor Carlson wants to talk to you." As I entered the room Grandma stepped out smartly. I paused for a moment looking at her with wide eyes.

"It's okay, Son. I'll wait right here.'

Dr. Carlson was seated in the chair near the lounger and gestured, smiling reassuringly.

"Come sit, Deplano."

I walked as confidently as I could to the lounger and sat down. My shaking hands held onto my knees, pinning them together.

"Grandma told me you witnessed a terrible tragedy?" He spoke gently. I nodded.

"Why don't you tell me about it?"

I hesitated, looking steadily at my feet.

"You need to talk about it, Deplano. Healing will come from speaking. Please tell me about it. Remember: what you say in this room stays in this room. It stays just between us."

"I saw Adelaide killed. I saw her die," I finally managed.

Dr. Carlson scribbled some notes on his writing pad balanced on his folded knee.

"Please tell me more, Son. What did you see?"

"The men… they hit her…and did things to her…they kicked her… until she died." I blurted these details out between racking sobs.

"That's really terrible." No emotion registered on Dr. Carlson's face. "And what happened after that? Please tell me. It's okay."

At first, I revealed bit by bit, the words sounding foreign coming out of my mouth. Then the dam burst. Once it started, I could not stop the force of jumbled utterances from tumbling forth. I cried. Dr. Carlson occasionally asked a question, all the while continuing to write on his notepad. Eventually he changed the course of our session.

"Tell me, Deplano, who is your soccer favorite team?"

"Manchester United," I responded automatically.

"Same here!" enthused Dr. Carlson. I was quite surprised – I thought all white South Africans only knew about rugby and cricket.

We went on to discuss the Treble win and the merits of the team and our chances of retaining the Premier League title. The 1998/1999 season was the highlight of Manchester United's achievements. Exciting times. Dr. Carlson moved our conversation along to where we discussed the 1958 Munich plane crash and how Sir Bobby Charlton survived the darkest day of Manchester United. He spoke about the trauma that the survivors had to go through – seeing the bodies of their colleagues and friends all around them.

He told me of the pain and suffering they endured in the hospital where others died and in Manchester where the dead were buried and, in the team, where places were void. He told me about Sir Bobby writing in his memoir many years later that the tragedy had changed him, but that he believed it was for the better. Then he repeated something that Sir Bobby wrote.

"You know, Deplano, he said, 'If you are very lucky, you survive. While you're doing it you fulfill every dream, every ambition, you ever had.' Find your dreams and fly with them, Deplano. You're a survivor. Do so for the memory of Adelaide, not in guilt, or anger, or shame, but to celebrate her life. Live for your sake, for your family's sake and to the memory of Adelaide. The road ahead is not going to be an easy one, but you have within you the capacity to survive and to thrive out of these experiences."

"Let us move back to the desk and I'll call Grandma." He gave me another lollipop.

"Grandma, I am so glad to have met you and Deplano. You have raised a wonderful son and I am convinced that he has the strength and capacity to rise from the terrible events he has had to endure. The medication that I have prescribed is a temporary measure. The prescription is for three months. This will help him get through some of the very rough spots. But heal, he will. I have not found any reason to run any blood tests or have X-rays done." Grandma sighed a deep, audible sigh of relief. Dr. Carlson continued.

"It's important for Deplano to talk more about the events and what he feels physically and emotionally. I'm convinced that he will heal and keep growing into a fine young man."

I stopped concentrating on what Dr. Carlson said from this point.

He and Grandma did not know that guilt and shame were still gnawing at my insides. Despite all that I had exorcised from within me to him in that room, I was not able to tell him about the recurring nightmare and the three words Adelaide whispered to me with her dying breath. I could see the relief on Grandma's face as Dr. Carlson concluded his summation and as we said our goodbyes. Grandma's relief flowed in the taxi ride home. She even joked with Mfana about his love of gambling. For once he laughed at her humor.

"You never know, Gogo. Maybe it's my lucky day." I remained silent throughout the journey. As we jumped out of the taxi Mfana turned to me, "Hamba kahle, Mshana!

"Hamba kahle, Mkhulu."

There we were in our yard on that hot summer's afternoon witnessing the passing of a giant. Municipal workers strained with long ropes attached to the gum tree to keep her in check as the chainsaw did its job. We knew they were never ever going to hold that old tree in place once she came hurtling down. Yet all within the waiting hyperactive group encouraged each other on, closer and closer into the danger zone – generally ignoring Grandma and the municipal foreman's pleas for us to get back. "Grrr! Grrr! Bzzz! Bzzz! Grrr! Bzzz! Bzzz! Bzzz! Craaaaaaaack!' Watch out! She's coming down!" Municipal workers dropped ropes and chainsaws and scattered faster than ants at an anthill exposed to sudden sunlight.

"Run, guys! Morph, run!" William fleeing at breakneck speed.

"Aaaaaahhhhhh! May-June shrieked, bringing more drama to the moment. 'Craaaack! Rrrrrrr! She came down. With a loud thump that shook the ground beneath us, one that blew out a thick cloud of dust everywhere, she was down. She missed our house by at least 10m.

We rushed back to the fallen tree and swarmed all over her. There was also a deep sadness within me at her passing. Grandma stood with a tempting tray of jam and butter sandwiches, Marie Biscuits and Oros, luring us and our hungry friends into the house. William was the last to slide off the tree trunk and onto the sand below. He pressed his back against the gnarled wood and cocked his head to block out the low rays of the disappearing sun.

"It's gonna be weird now that it's gone."

"Yup, how many of us fell out this tree and broke our arms?" I teased.

"Probably like ten people." William scratched the growth of stubble on his chin.

"The funniest was still when Toefy rolled down and left plenty skin on his way down."

"That day was so funny! One minute he was climbing up and the next he was coming down and hit the ground with his boep."

"Hahahahaha!" we laughed.

We followed the group heading indoors.

"Shame, Toefy still had to get up and run like hell. Oupa really chased him that day. Said he had no business playing in trees with young children."

"Where's he now?" I asked.

"Dunno … Toefy… what was the other name we called him?"

"Rapscallion."

"Ouma called him that. Still does."

The noise in the distance seemed to be drawing nearer. I turned to look down the road.

"Speak of the devil! Look, William, isn't that Toefy? Why's he running this way?"

"Hahahaha Toefy doesn't run anymore," declared William.

"Come see. I'm telling you; he's running!" I tapped William urgently on his arm.

We turned and walked to our front gate and watched the scene unfold.

"Sho! He's really trying hard to run! Shame!"

"Run! Toefy, run!" shouted William. We moved closer.

Toefy hobbled along the failing surfacing as fast as he could muster. His arms were swaying and vigorously while his legs shuffled back and forth. Toefy was afraid.

In a flash William opened the gate and ran out to meet the man who was now close to collapsing into the dirt. He grabbed hold of

Toefy and half dragged him onwards. Toefy now put double time into his steps, pumping his free arm faster at his side. His wobbly legs somehow moved in every direction. His old, checkered cap fell off and his shoelaces were loose, but he clung desperately to William. Faintly above the drowning sound I heard Toefy gasp.

"Where's Ouma?" His words came out raspingly as they staggered past me, through the gate towards our door. Instinctively I dashed out of the gate, grabbed Toefy's cap and flew back in, taking a few seconds to shut and padlock the gate.

"What's going on, Toefy?" William shouted with apprehension. The roaring and bellowing cacophony grew louder outside our home.

"Have… speak… Ouma!" Toefy managed to gasp with each shuddering breath. I was close on their heels into the house and shut and bolted the door behind me.

"Ouma!... Ouma!... Ouma!" Toefy managed to blurt out. "What's happening outside, Rapscallion?" enquired Ouma sharply.

"Ouma, dey comin for…" Feebly he raised his shaking hands and pointed a gnarled, quivering finger in my direction.

"FOR WHO? TOEFY! TALK!"

It looked like she was ready to grab him by the throat and shake him vigorously.

May-June handed Toefy a mug of water. He grabbed it and gulped down as much of the liquid as he could muster. Half ran down the sides of his mouth and into his sweaty clothing.

"Rapscallion, what's going on?" Grandma asked calmly.

"Ouma, dey comin for Plano!"

Gasps from the room seemed to echo off the walls of the lounge. All eyes swiveled towards me and then back to Toefy. I was frozen stiff.

"Who's coming for Plano!?" Grandma demanded.

"De people from Cosmos. Dey caught de tree skollies. Dose dat kill'd Adelaide. De people gonna kill dem. Dey wanna Plano to see."

"OVER MY DEAD BODY!" roared Grandma.

She turned sharply on her heels and hurried off to her bedroom. Just as quickly Grandma returned holding one of Grandpa's knobkerries.

"Close the windows! Make sure all the doors are locked behind me!" Grandma strode outside, ready to defend us. Toefy was crumpled in a corner William held a cricket bat in his hands. His friends grasped an assortment of weapons and marched to Grandma.

I stood with May-June and the remaining group near the front door, half-listening to Grandma speak to the boys near her and to my heart-beat thudding in my ears. I could see May-June biting her bottom lip and Morph's eyes wide as saucers. My stomach churned. My head felt light. All I could do was prop myself up against the door as the noise grew louder outside.

I could see Adelaide and the three men. I could smell them, feeling them close to me. I wanted nothing more than for them to die. I wanted them to lay in the dirt, naked, bloodied and bruised, beaten and alone. Morph slipped his hand into mine. Voices approached along the street above the roar of the masses. It was a group of men in hurried discussion, their voices pitched slightly higher and louder than normal, echoing around us like an irregular burst of static. They rushed up to our gate and Grandma called out.

"What are you looking for at my door?"

"Ouma, bring him, bring de boy out!" they shouted back.

"He's not going anywhere with you! What do you want with Plano?"

"We just want him to identify some blerry people!"

"Liar, Jakob! I know what dirt you're doing there near the river! You stay off my property and leave my boy alone!"

"Ouma, he won't blerry see nothing! We just want him to blerry tell us!"

"JAKOB, I SAID NO!

"Ouma, I can fucken bring ten blerry men and fucken take him by blerry force."

"Like hell you will! If any of you set foot in my yard, I won't hesitate to throw you in jail. Plano stays right where he is! If you want to go and kill people in the vlei like dogs, that's your business, but I never want to hear or see you taking any child into the veld to witness it!"

Jakob scoffed at Grandma as he put his hands against the gate. "You won't."

William and his friends moved menacingly closer to them, weapons at the ready.

"MAY!!!" Grandma called out over her shoulder. "PHONE THE COPS!!!"

There was a sudden burst of a large fire beyond where the men stood. The screams near the river grew in violent abandon as the shooting sparks and flames flew high into the night sky. The men before us turned, startled at the brutality of the night. Without a word they sprinted down the road and disappeared into the darkness.

"It's OK, May, you don't have to phone the cops," Grandma called as she ushered us indoors. Faintly we heard the siren of a police vehicle increase in intensity then fade away as it rushed off towards Cosmos. Our phone kept ringing as parents sought to locate their children. The shrill sounds from the river's edge continued to escalate. None of us dared a peek. We could smell the stench of tires burning, mingled with the sickening odor of burning flesh.

The screaming stopped and the mob in the veld scattered into the surrounding darkness. By the time the police vehicle rushed past on the road below our home, the flames had died down. The fear remained. We knew those three men were dead, killed by the mob, but this brought no comfort to us. It all seemed so surreal. More wailing sirens crisscrossed the darkness well into the night. Our friends were hastily collected by their parents who spoke in animated whispers to Grandma before hurriedly ushering their grateful brood into their vehicles. After the last one departed, we sat perched on the edge of our chairs around the kitchen table. It took a while for us to succumb to exhaustion.

Surprisingly, the sound of Toefy snoring in a corner of the lounge brought a bit of comfort. Perhaps it did so because it revived memories of Grandpa snoring. We needed Grandpa. Those men would not have dared approach our home if he were alive. Grandma and William had lowered Toefy to a prone position on the floor where he passed out. She covered him with a blanket. Morph was the first to succumb to fatigue and did so with his head nestled on his folded arms. William carried him to bed. Not long thereafter first May-June then I dragged ourselves to bed. William and Grandma sat talking quietly.

It took a while for me to fall asleep. The living nightmare of the evening kept replaying vividly within my head. Just before I drifted off, I saw William stand at the bedroom doorway to check up on Morph and Ime.

Dark clouds parted above me I was bound to a fig tree
A clock standing in front of me hands dripping with blood
I saw her standing in front of me a pure white ghost
She had a knife in her right hand and a feather in her left
She touched my cheek with the feather
Immediately her hand bled her white turned to black
I felt a stream of hot blood covering my eyes
And a rope tightened around my neck
The clock struck twelve the ground fell from beneath me.

The man with the brown suede shoes stood still under the willow tree near the Bushman's River, deep within the shadows of invisibility, watching as the cops completed their macabre duties in the dark. Earlier he had swirled within the masses of the lynch mob, screaming profanities and waving a steel rod in the murderous air. He was the one who prepared the bottle of Klipdrift Brandy mixed with a large quantity of crushed greenish-grey Rohypnol tablets that the three gangsters consumed in the afternoon. He was the one who prepared the many bottles of Mainstay Cane mixed with crushed yellow Captagon tablets and donated these to the Cosmos community by paying some boys to take a bottle each to specific men that he named, knowing that the recipients loved to share their dop with their friends and would spread the doped alcohol around Cosmos. He was in a different disguise when he dished out the bottles, so those boys never really knew who the donor was. They assumed he was from Cosmos because he gave names of men to receive the gifts. He watched as matters unfolded.

As soon as the three finally consumed the tonic concoction, he arranged for their whereabouts to be revealed to others. There was a moment when nothing seemed to be happening, for the three continued to lounge in drug-filled stupors in Tannie Jane's shebeen. The date rape drug did its job: the men were in a drugged daze, oblivious to their surroundings.

He stealthily sent a message to one of the men who had received a bottle of alcohol that these three men were ripe for the taking. He also personally primed a close relative of Adelaide, reminding him of the brutality of Adelaide's untimely rape and murder. Word spread like wildfire to many homes in Cosmos, then, as if on cue, a group of men burst forth from the home of Boet Sallie and raced off in the direction of Tannie Jane's shebeen.

As they ran many others came bursting out of their own homes and joined them. The man with the brown suede shoes ran with them, concealed in the middle of the mob. The head of his knobkerrie disappeared to reveal a very dangerous sharp point on one end. No one noticed as the dance of death commenced. The man became an invisible force within the crazed mob that overpowered the three incapacitated thugs, viciously assaulted them and dragging them to their execution. He felt ever so satisfied at the outcome. He was still there when the first police vehicle came screeching to a wailing halt near the burning mass of flesh and he remained there until these corpses were loaded into a mortuary vehicle.

He was unafraid of any forensic investigation, because he wore two sets of gloves while at work. The first pair was elbow-length plastic. The second pair was also elbow length, but leather gloves favored by motorbike riders, both pairs pilfered from shops in Durban. He was unafraid that any person from Cosmos would be able to identify him, as a master of disguise: not just hair and face, but also body shape, gait, voice, speech and his accent.

After a while he shifted his hand grip to the center of the knobkerrie staff, held it parallel to the ground, slipped away quietly into the darkness and ran silently to near the Railway Station. He then used his rod to hobble along like a crippled old man to eventually stand amongst the group of people and taxis that waited near the Railway

Station. Just another commuter finding his way home. He stood near enough to them to be part of them, but far enough so that they could not hear what he said into his cellphone.

"As-salamu alaykum," he greeted.
"Wa'alaykumus-salam."
"The infidels have been terminated."
"Any problems?"
"No."
"Will they go to the two agitators?"
"No. They have been adequately rewarded."
"Okay. We will talk again in the morning."
The man removed the sim card from the cellphone and snapped it into pieces. He removed the battery and placed it in his jacket pocket. The phone he crushed with his heal and discarded it into the large blue rubbish skip that stood near the entrance to the station. He waited until a taxi arrived and disgorged its weary occupants, who scurried of in various directions, then joined those getting into the taxi. On a quiet street he got into the old vehicle and drove off through quiet backstreets of Estcourt.

Faizel Ameen removed the sim card from the cellphone and burnt it in an ashtray on his desk. He carefully inserted the cellphone into a box and sealed it. The cellphone would be on sale in a Spaza shop in Madadeni before end of business tomorrow. He rose from his seat and moved to switch off the light in his study at his home and to shut the door. "It's my time now! It's my time now! Insha Allah!"

CHAPTER 6
SUPERFICIAL CONTINUUM
(TUESDAY, 14 DECEMBER 1999)

The call was made at five that morning.

"Shit!" shouted Ewald angrily into the landline. "This is a real fuck-up! What have you learnt so far, Eric?"

"The whole of that shithole township formed into a bloody-thirsty mob that caught the three cunts, busted them up good and fucking necklaced them. So far there's been no arrests. The bloody cops are not gonna arrest an entire township. None of the shits are talking."

"Shit! Shit! Shit!" repeated Ewald. "They were supposed to drive the interlinks. Where're the fuck we're going to find drivers at such short notice?"

"There're some Mozambican cunts I can enlist. They'll abandon the trucks at the bloody rest stop and we'll make them bloody well disappear without a trace," suggested Eric,

"Okay, do that. What else have you heard?"

"They say a group of those bastards tried to take that little shit houtkop to witness the bloody necklacing, but his grannie stopped them. Bloody hell!" Eric replied.

"She's a very tough old bitch with some strong ANC allies in town."

"Bloody hell! I'll arrange for the cops to go and find out more info. Do you think our bastard little Coolie had anything to do with it?"

"He's just as much to lose as we do. Have you arranged for surveillance on Combrink?"

"The guys will be doing their thing from tomorrow. This includes electronic stuff. We'll have to bloody well increase surveillance on that Coolie cunt. I'll arrange for someone to watch his house and businesses. I just don't bloody well trust that fucking crook."

"What about that bloody little shit and his bitch grannie?"

"Leave them be for now. There'll be an inquest and that is where it'll end. What he'll say now doesn't matter anymore."

"Okay. We'll talk later." Eric preferred to close deals quickly. He hated loose ends.

"Okay," Ewald agreed. "I'll phone Faizel to find out what he knows and to fill him in. Those stupid bastards!" he exclaimed before hanging up the phone.

On the other side of the line Eric slowly put the receiver in place.

They met briefly after prayers at the Mosque. They spoke in North Mesopotamian Arabic with the Maslawi dialect of the city of Mosul to minimize chances of being overheard. They paused conversation each time prying eyes or ears came too close.

"Thank you," said Faizel to the man with the brown suede shoes. "I did not trust those three drunken louts to keep our secrets. Not at this late stage in the game. Arrange it so that our own three drivers are ready to take their places. I'll propose the matter to my partners. You must go and check on the Eastern Cape camp near Edwaleni. I've not heard from Bakri since Friday last. See if they're ready to go into action by the 26th. Be back here by the 16th. Be careful in your movements. Knowing my partners, they'll put surveillance on me and my family. I want to keep your movements quiet. I have left ten more cellphones and sim cards for you at the spares shop. This is a list of my temp cellphone numbers for you. The other phones are for Bakri." Faizel handed over the list to the man within a handshake.

The man disappeared into the crowd of men exiting the mosque.

Faizel followed at a more sedate pace, stopping and greeting friends and acquaintances as he made his way to his vehicle. He got into it and sat quietly for a few seconds, taking his cellphone off silent mode. Just as he completed doing so it rang.

"Hello, my friend. I trust you've heard about last night. I found out here at the Mosque."

"Hello, Faizel," Ewald responded. "Yes, that's the reason for my call. We must make other arrangements for drivers. Eric is looking into it."

"My cousin in Nelspruit has more than a hundred drivers. I can ask him to spare three."

"Too many strings. Eric has from Mozambique. We can get rid of them afterwards."

"Okay."

"Faizel, the three of us need to meet tomorrow. You are still to meet with Combrink and make him the offer. Can you do so today? Eric will sort out the drivers and I'll find out what the hell is happening in Cosmos. We should all have answers by tomorrow."

"Okay, where shall we meet and what time?"

"At my office. four thirty. That should fit in with your prayer-time."

"Fine with me. I can phone Eric to tell him if it is okay with you?"

"Fine," responded Ewald before ending the call.

Faizel immediately phoned Eric. "Hello, my friend."

"Hello, Faizel. Has Ewald briefed you?"

"Yes, he has. He asked me to tell you we'll meet at his office tomorrow afternoon at four-thirty. He also told me you're organizing replacement drivers."

"Yes, I am."

"Perhaps I can help, my friend. My cousin in Nelspruit should be able to spare us three drivers." Faizel's voice remained measured.

"Too risky. I've already arranged for the bloody replacement cunts."

"What about back-up drivers, my friend?"

Eric hesitated. "Okay, let's talk about it tomorrow afternoon."

"I'm meeting with Combrink at ten. Perhaps we could meet at nine?"

"Ja. That'll be fine."

25

"Thank you, my friend. See you then."

Eric cut the call before Faizel could finish speaking.

I woke up to the normal sounds of a hot, humid summer's day with doves cooing solemnly and sparrows chattering outside and William and Morph snoring gently to the rhythms of their heaving chests. Feint sun rays peeked from behind the hills. I lifted the curtain to peer outside. The sky was scattered with clouds rapidly covering the morning's red and orange hue. Distant rumblings reminded the tumbling clouds to gather for the afternoon charge.

A knock on the front door caused some consternation. William turned on to his side to face the wall and subsequently drifted off to sleep again. Morph hardly moved. I heard Grandma go and ask who it was before she let the person in. Toefy. I wondered when he left our home, because when I woke up his snoring was gone. The last I saw him was the crumpled heap in the corner of our lounge. The two of them walked into the kitchen where Grandma made coffee and a sandwich for Toefy.

"Ja, Ouma. All tree dead. Deader dan dead I tell you. Dey caught dem at Tannie Jane's Spot. Beat dem up and nek-lis dem. Dere vere Adelaide was killed. T'was dirry buz-nis dat hap-pin las' night. Dirry buz-nis."

"Was anyone caught for these murders, Toefy?"

"No, Ouma. Dey say tings very scared in Cosmos."

"What do you mean by very scared?"

"Ouma, dey not finis. Dey wanna kill all. Even you look at dem. Dey all silen'. An wat-chen ev'body. Silen' en wat chen."

"It's a shame, Toefy, that people had to resort to such violence."

"Ya, Ouma. A shame," Toefy responded mouth chewing and between coffee slurps.

"You be careful, Toefy. You don't have to be caught up in this mess. Stay at home and stay silent. People are going be feeling guilty and they'll do anything to protect themselves."

"Ya, Ouma. I'll will Ouma."

"And thank you, Toefy, for coming to warn us last night. It's much appreciated."

"No problem, Ouma. No problem."

After Toefy finished eating he hastily departed, repeating his goodbyes to Grandma. When we joined her in the kitchen Grandma dished out bowls of steaming hot porridge with a dollop of margarine and a sprinkling of brown sugar. Grandma spoke to us while we ate.

"Those three skollies are dead. A mob of people from Cosmos killed them last night. Things are very tense in the streets…I want all of you to stay in the yard today. If I send you anywhere, you don't go alone."

Morph raised an arm.

"Yes, Morph?"

"Must we go with someone else, even to Aunty Nishi?"

"Yes, Morph. Even to Aunty Nishi."

I chose to spend some of my free time reading. I sat under the peach tree in the back garden and opened 'Sherlock Holmes – The Hound of Baskervilles.' A book recently given to us by Doctor John. He said it was one of his favorite books as a child and he thought we might enjoy it, too. I loved books by Sir Arthur Conan Doyle. I was on page nine when I heard, "Whatcha doing, Plano? Whatcha doing, Plano?" from Morph as he jogged towards me.

"I'm reading, Morph."

"Whatcha doing, Plano? Whatcha doing, Plano?" repeated Morph as he stood before me with hands on hips and a mischievous grin on his face. "There's men in the house with Ouma who want to see you. We must go inside!"

"Sit down, Deplano," ordered Grandma as she took her seat.

May-June and William were already seated, hands folded prim and proper on their laps.

"Children, this is Captain Khuzwayo and this is Sergeant Brits."

"Hello," the two policemen voiced in unison.

"Hello," We replied softly.

"Sirs, this is William, May-June and Deplano." Grandma pointed to each of us.

The policemen sat in their seats, propped up at unusual postures by their holstered 9mm Z88 Beretta pistols and pepper spray canisters. Sergeant Brits was their scribe. He wrote our names and surnames out. Captain Khuzwayo cleared his throat loudly before turning to us and speaking in his authoritative baritone and Zulu accent.

"We were here the other day to talk to you, Deplano." He decided not to attempt our surname and continued, "About the deceased, Adelaide Florence's, alleged murder. Now that case has been changed to an inquest since the three men who've been accused of allegedly raping and murdering her have themselves been murdered last night. I understand you can describe to us what happened the day Adelaide Florence was allegedly raped and murdered?"

I nodded apprehensively.

"You'll have to speak up, Deplano."

"Yes, Sir."

"The statement we're writing down is for an inquest. You won't have to appear in court after you've signed it, unless family of the deceased sues the estates of the deceased, Jakes Gerwel, Raymond Balfour and Leon Hilton?"

"Yes, Sir."

Captain Khuzwayo turned to Grandma. "Gogo, we'll need your and Deplano's ID documents, residential address, home and cell numbers. If you have copies of the ID documents, it'll be okay. If not, we'll record the details. You can bring them to the station."

"I've got copies of the ID documents. May-June will put everything together for you." May-June rushed out, a brief interlude that gave me a chance to compose myself.

"After we've completed the statement, you and Gogo have a chance to read it to check if it's okay. Then Gogo must sign it. Do you understand?"

"Yes, Sir. I understand." Grandma and I replied almost simultaneously.

"Gogo, you may stop us at any time if you feel we're doing something wrong. We've received a report from the dokotela we mustn't push him."

"Thank you. Why have you asked William and May-June to be present?"

"There are questions they may be able to answer."

Morph tiptoed into the room and sat close to Grandma, not wanting to be left out, but Grandma sent him to stay in her bedroom and to close the door there.

"Tell us about the day Adelaide Florence was allegedly assaulted and murdered."

I took a deep breath and relived that fateful day. First through my own words and then through the questions hurled at me by Captain Khuzwayo and Sergeant Brits.

"Thank you, Deplano. That concludes your statement. Please read it. If you and Gogo are happy with it, then Gogo must sign it."

I almost fainted from relief when it was over. William reached out and took the proffered document from Sergeant Brits. "Is it okay if I read it on behalf of Deplano and my ouma? I'll check and sort it out with Sergeant so that my ouma can sign it?"

Captain Khuzwayo nodded in response, took a matchstick from a box and proceeded to clean his teeth. Sergeant Brits carried on scribbling corrections that him and William agreed to. When the document was ready, Grandma first read and then initialed and signed it.

"I'll be given a copy of the document?" Grandma asked Sergeant Brits.

"Ya, Ouma. I'll bring it this afternoon or tomorrow morning."

May-June returned with the ID documents and other information the policemen had requested. Sergeant Brits scrutinized these carefully, even holding the copies of the ID documents close to our faces to confirm the legitimacy. He stuffed these documents into the file. May-June took her seat next to Grandma. Captain Khuzwayo sat impassively throughout. This slumbering posture was misleading. As soon as Sargent Brits completed stowing his paperwork away, Captain

Khuzwayo sprang into life again with the matchstick dangling from one side of his mouth. It bobbed up and down rapidly as he spoke.

"Now, I've another matter to attend to. The murders of the deceased, Jakes Gerwel, Raymond Balfour and Leon Hilton. As you should know, they were beaten and necklaced close to or at the very spot where Adelaide Florence was allegedly assaulted and murdered. Be advised, this is not a formal interrogation. It's an interview because the murders happened not too far from here." He paused a few seconds, then continued.

"Deplano was a witness to the alleged criminal activities of the three deceased. So, he's a person of importance for our investigation. Not a criminal, but a witness. Do you understand?" He said the last bits so loudly that we were startled by their sudden intensity.

"Our discussion is purely informal." This time we were better prepared for his shouting and nodded our heads without much haste.

"You may stop us at any time should you feel uncomfortable, or you can ask us to leave and we'll do so." We nodded.

Captain Khuzwayo rubbed his hands together leaned forward, resting his elbows on his knees. The matchstick poked from side to side like a roving antenna.

"My first question to you is, what do you know what happened last night?" His eyes flicked constantly from one of us to the other as he spoke, as if searching for some weakness. William, May-June and I looked to Grandma for guidance. Grandma was calm and collected as she responded: "I'm afraid, Captain, we cannot be of much help to you. The children and I shuttered ourselves in our home at the first signs of trouble and we remained there until this morning. We didn't see what happened outside in the veld."

Sergeant Brits could not resist. "But we've received reliable information you had other children in your home last night. Some men visited you home. What did they want from you?"

"Yes, there were children in our home. I kept them indoors until their parents collected them. As for men who allegedly came to our home, there were many people running about in the street when we went to lock our gates. In the melee I was unable to recognize anyone, and we didn't speak to anyone. We hurried outside and hurried back in; we were so scared."

Grandma's composure was a sight to behold.

Captain Khuzwyo continued. "What were you afraid of? That you locked your gates? How did the other children get out? If the gate was locked?" Grandma remained unmoved. It was the first time in our lives were heard Grandma blatantly lie, but we didn't dare let on.

She continued unfazed. "We always lock our gates at night. We did so earlier due to the disturbances. We went out each time to open the gate for the children when their parents came and hurried back in. For the rest of the evening the five of us remained locked up, indoors. It was very scary, all the noises and screaming outside."

"Gogo, I think you're not telling the whole truth." Captain Khuzwayo turned sharply to William. With a stern expression he asked, "And where were you when all this happened?"

Captain Khuzwayo asked each of us questions, from eldest to youngest. I thanked God that Morph was not included.

"What Ouma said is true. Each time Ouma went outside I went with," said William.

"Did you see the men who came to your home?"

"As my Ouma said, Sir, no men came to our home. There were a lot of people in the street and I also couldn't recognize one from the other."

Sargent Brits chimed in. "You don't wear glasses and your eyes would be much better than your ouma's. It's impossible for you not to see what was happening."

"I only concentrated on the tasks that we were doing outside, Sir. That was to open and lock the gates. I didn't look in the street." My heartbeat with pride.

"And you, missy? Huh? I suppose you're gonna tell the same story?"

"Not exactly the same, Sir." May-June responded, sitting calmly upright with hands rested on her lap. "I stayed indoors with my two younger brothers and we didn't go outside at all. We could hear the noises, but we didn't go outside at all."

My jaw opened involuntarily and both policemen noticed. "Why's your mouth open?" Captain Khuzwayo's matchstick twirled accuslngly at me.

"He does that sometimes – ever since he witnessed Adelaide's murder," Grandma interjected, before Captain Khuzwayo could continue.

I snapped my mouth shut when the question was asked and slowly re-opened it to emphasize what Grandma said. Sergeant Brits now looked at me as though I was seriously mentally ill. There was little sympathy in Captain Khuzwayo's eyes. Grandma's words knocked them off their stride but soon Captain Khuzwayo was at it again.

"Deplano, what do YOU recollect of the evening past?" he boomed.

"The same as what May-June said, Sir. We could hear the noises outside, but we didn't see anything. We were so scared."

The two policemen glanced at each other in disbelief. Captain Khuzwayo continued. "You're lying to us. We have reliable information. Some men came to your home and made some demands. Isn't that right?"

"At a time like last night, I doubt any person who was so scared could give you very accurate answers, Sirs."

And so the interrogation continued for the next forty-five minutes. The questions were directed mostly at Grandma and William, to obtain names of those who came to our home last night. We stonewalled them, to their visible frustration. They got less than nothing out of us.

"Gogo, we'll be in touch," boomed Captain Khuzwayo as he got up and walked out.

"Ouma, look after yourself," said Sergeant Brits as he gathered their materials and followed Captain Khuzwayo outside. "Goodbye."

"Goodbye, Sir." William, May-June and I responded almost in unison.

"I hope this will all be over soon?" said Grandma as she followed the Sargent outside.

"I hope so too. Let's wait and see."

We walked outdoors and stood behind Grandma as the cops got into their vehicle. Captain Khuzwayo watched us intently as he reversed the van and sped off. What relief!

Grandma put her arm on May-June's shoulder and ushered us indoors. We sat in the lounge, and it was no surprise that none of us bothered to occupy the seats that the two policemen had just vacated. Morph joined us, wide-eyed as ever. Soon my family had a rip-roaring time teasing me and laughing at my open-mouthed antics in such a tense situation. It took a while before we managed to quieten down. Grandma sighed before speaking to us.

"May God forgive me for what I've done to Him and to you, my children. I've never ever asked you to tell lies in any situation and especially on my behalf. We've prided ourselves for being always honest and truthful. But this was a difficult time that could and may still cause lots of trouble for us. The men from Cosmos who came here last night had murderous looks in their eyes. I was not going get us caught up in this terrible stuff. Neither did I want the Cosmos people turning on us for ratting them out." Grandma paused briefly and we nodded.

"I had to tell these lies to keep us out of this mess. Please will you forgive me my children? For dragging you into this horrible mess?"

"It's okay, Ouma. There's nothing to forgive."

"Thank you, my children. Thank you, very much. No one is allowed to stay out late or walk alone. I must know where you are at all times. No more fighting, no more playing outside this yard except with a group of friends – you hear me? And no talking to strangers! Okay?"

"Yes, Ouma."

"I need to find out what happened in Cosmos yesterday and to let them know we didn't rat on them. Those cops deliberately chose today to take the statement from Plano. Doubt is easily formed in the minds of guilty people. The mob from Cosmos will assume we ratted on them if anyone is arrested."

"OK, Ouma."

"Good! Come now, let's watch some TV. May-June, go put the kettle on and make some sweet tea for us, please. Plano, go and help her."

Grandma made a few calls. May-June and I listened to her speak to Auntie Jeannie.

"Hello, Sister Jeannie. How're you doing?"

"Yes, it was terrible last night. In a way I'm relieved that they're dead. You know they wanted to harm Plano for being a witness. I feel sorry for their parents and families, but I won't mourn for them. The cops were here today. No. No. No. We didn't tell them anything. No. No. No, Jeannie. You know me. I wouldn't do that. They came for a statement from Deplano. They said it's for the inquest. There'll be no case seeing that all three of the suspects are dead. No. I read it and had to sign it. They'll drop off a copy of it here by tomorrow. Shame, Sister Jeannie. What happened? Shame, Sister. Yes. They did ask about last night, but we said we saw nothing. Definitely. Yes. The dirty cops are known to spread lies around. Yes, Sister. You and your family be careful, Sister. See you at Church on Sunday. Bye, Sister."

I picked up the tea tray and we walked to the lounge where we waited for Grandma to finish the next two telephone calls. When Grandma returned, she seemed relieved.

"Okay. The matter has been laid to rest for now. There'll be no problems for us from Cosmos. I've spoken to some ladies from there and they said they'll make sure we're left alone. But I still want you to stay close to home. I'm worried. Those men are very aggressive. You never know how they could react. We'll have to wait for them to cool off. The ladies are all saying the men look as though they're high on drugs and they don't know when it'll wear off."

We promised Grandma that we would stay at home and only go out in a group, if we needed to do so. The rest of the day and the evening was beautiful. Spending time with my family after our experience with the cops was rejuvenating. We watched TV together until the sun disappeared behind a mirage of grey and black clouds hanging low. The cool breeze ahead of the storm blew in gentle gusts into our home, cooling the heat of the day and filling us with a sense of peace. I felt relieved that the three thugs were dead and that the police statement was done. I felt relieved that we were alive and well and could face the future together. I could see and sense the relief from my family that we had managed to weather the storm so well.

Morph was the first to go to bed, followed by May-June. William and I did so shortly thereafter. We walked through the house twice to make sure that every window was properly closed and every door locked before retiring to our bedroom. We were laying on our beds, discussing Manchester United's progress when Morph sat straight up in bed and, according to William, with open eyes and a serious expression on his face turned his head towards William and said, "William, where's the North Pole?" William couldn't tell if he was awake or asleep.

"I guess it's in…" William scrambled, trying to figure out which direction to point.

"Oh! Never mind, I found it!" Morph exclaimed gleefully before he flopped back onto his bed and went straight back to sleep.

William and I scrambled out of our beds and raced to Grandma who was in the dining room, patching some of her own and May-June's dresses.

"Ouma! Guess what Morph just did?" William managed between bursts of laughter.

Grandma peered at us above her spectacles. "What did Morph do?"

William continued. "He sat straight up in bed and asked me where the North Pole was. Before I could answer he said that he found it! He was sleeping when he spoke Ouma, coz' he lay back on his bed and went straight back to sleep!"

"Ai! Morph!" exclaimed Grandma. We laughed at his latest antics.

Our laughter woke up May-June up. William had to re-tell Morph's somnambulistic escapades, which led to more uproarious laughter. May-June's laughing – from deep within her belly, making her toes curl with glee – was infectious. We laughed until our sides hurt.

By the time that the storm hit Estcourt, the five young men were still seated at their favorite table in the clubhouse at the Estcourt Golf Course. The staff saw the group take the white capsules and were now witnessing the wild high that they were on, downing beer straight from the bottles. None of the wait staff dared call time on the evening until they departed.

"Shit! Shit! Shit! They killed those bastards! Necklaced them! exclaimed Ewald.

"Who would'a thought those useless scum had it in them to do such a thing. Whenever we went there and took their bitches for a fuck, they did fuck-all and let us do what we wanted declared Dewald, smacking his bottle on the table.

"We'll have to be very careful around them!" continued Ewald before taking a big swig.

"We'll have to make them bloody well fear us again," declared Rob.

"Yeah! They say they tried to take that little shit, Plano, by force to witness the necklacing. His grannie stopped them," added Abu. He was the only one at the table not allowed to drink because of his religion.

"He's the problem. If he was not there to witness what happened to that bitch, Cosmos would still be running scared. It's like they see him as a fucking hero," said Hermann.

"I agree. We have to do something about that bloody shit bastard," added Rob. His bottle was empty and he grabbed another one.

"Wishing for some young pussy. Nothing until we've sorted them out," lamented Abu.

"I organized some prossies from Pietermaritzburg for tonight. I'll be told when they're at the Den," announced Dewald.

"Thanks, Bro." Ewald high-fived his brother.

"Thanks, Dewald. You always get us foxy chicks," added Hermann with a high-five.

"Thanks, Dewald." Rob concluded the high-fives. "Will my whore be into bondage? The last bitch I had nearly shat herself from the bloody beating I gave her," asked Rob.

"Yeah. I know each of you guy's tastes. I've ordered to your needs. You can do whatever you want with them. They've been paid good bucks. In any case, they've been blindfolded at the back of a panel van since they left. By the time they get here, they'll be high and won't remember nothing when they go back."

"What time are you expecting them?" asked Hermann.

"We still have an hour to kill," noted Dewald after glancing at his gold Rolex.

"Do you have some Adam and Eve, Rob?" Abu asked eagerly. "I prefer it to the Ice."

"Yeah. Tell me when you want one," Rob replied.

"Thanks" Abu rubbed his hands together in anticipation.

"Remember the last time we sat here? I told you homies that little shit was gonna make trouble for the boys? Now look" Rob brought the conversation back.

"Guys, it's time for action. We cannot delay any longer. As Rob said, we need to put fear back into Cosmos and I've got a plan," said Ewald. His companions leaned forward, oblivious to the storm outside. The alcohol was briefly forgotten as he whispered to them.

CHAPTER 7
THE SEALING OF AN UNLIKELY FATE
(WEDNESDAY, 15 DECEMBER 1999)

The morning wind blew unexpected, unwelcome visitors to our gate at approximately ten-thirty – the Homeboys. William and I were working in the front garden. Grandma was in the kitchen and May-June and Morph were at the tuck shop down the road to buy some stuff for Grandma. Ewald, Dewald, Rob, Abu and Hermann jumped out of a black double cab Isuzu bakkie. Herman brazenly opened the gate and sauntered in like he owned our home. The others stood leaning against the bakkie vibrating from the loud gangster rap it blasted. The eyes of the Homeboys were glazed and bloodshot. They were ready for a fight.

As for Hermann, we were gunning for him because of his creepy, unwelcome aspirations occasionally directed at our sister. William would have sorted him out already if he was not from the Homeboys. When I saw them, the hair on every part of my body prickled to attention. Adrenalin coursed through my veins. They looked like a ravenous pack of hyenas who had just discovered their prey.

"William!" I called softly.

My brother was also observing them from where he worked. He straightened up and leaned lightly against the flat spade he had at hand.

"Watch yourself, Plano," he whispered quietly when I stood next to him.

Both of us sensed the danger and were ready to fight for our lives, if needed. You have to be crazy, like Vusi, or desperate to fight them. Grandpa said that you may win a battle with one of them, but you always lost the war. There were already many families who were forced to relocate beyond the borders of Estcourt, because job opportunities dried up for them after getting into the smallest of altercations with them. We knew a visit spelled nothing but trouble.

"Seriously, Bushies, it's almost the start of the new millennium. You must stop doing things like this. Heh?" He removed a thin comb from one of his jacket pockets and slicked his hair backwards. I swear Hermann spoke to hear the sound of his own voice.

"What do you want, Hermann?" William's voice hard and flat.

"I want my may-june! my June, my July! my September to December! my winter and my summer. You know?"

"Guys! See! There's the bitch and her fucking crazy brother," Abu pointed excitedly.

They called crassly out to May-June as she walked home, holding Morph's hand and a packet of groceries with the other. She showed no fear as she walked towards the four loiterers outside our yard and straight past them. I could see that Morph was rattled. I was seething.

"Cool it, Plano. They're trying to bait us. They won't touch May," whispered William. He rested the spade against his leg and balled his fists tightly. I did likewise with my knuckles. May-June and Morph hurriedly entered the gate with the gang of four still belittling her and following her into the yard. Morph broke free from May-June and flew past us, indoors. Then Hermann tried to put his arms around May-June.

"Grooming my future wife," he said with a high-pitched giggle.

"Girls with brains like mine don't date boys with brainless faces like yours!" May-June retorted as she jerked away from him.

Hermann grabbed at her again and this time pushed her off balance. May-June went sprawling onto the ground, groceries tumbling out before her. She cried out as her hands and knees scraped the ground. William dropped the spade and rushed to protect May-June. He forced his way between our sister and Hermann and pushed the intruder away.

"FUCK OFF OUT OF OUR YARD! ALL OF YOU!"

Hermann staggered a few paces backwards and ended up close to where I was standing. I grabbed hold of that spade before it hit the ground and held it with both hands, at the ready. Catcalls and jeers increased in intensity and volume. Something snapped. I lunged forward screaming wildly William put out his arm to block me, but I was too swift. I ducked under his outstretched arm, raised the spade and with all my might I swung it at Hermann's legs. He tried to jump back. The front, sharp corner of the spade caught Hermann on one of his shins. He screamed and lurched backwards in agony. All I could see in front of me were those three men from that day, mixed with the smell of blood, urine and death. Horrific screams battered my brain. I raised the spade and brought it down to smash Hermann's head into pulp. William pushed me out of the way. The spade narrowly missed Hermann's head and scraped his arm before smashing into the ground and bouncing upwards.

"PLANO! NO! NO! DON'T!" I could vaguely hear William and May-June's terrified pleading. I watched Hermann writher and scream on the ground. I stood with the spade raised in readiness, watching as Abu and Dewald half dragged and carried Hermann from the danger zone. Rob and Ewald drew their firearms and waved them around, but I felt no fear. We stood still not to antagonize them enough to pull the triggers. I knew that, given the slightest opportunity, I would not hesitate to kill them. The two of them moved ever closer.

"YOU BLOODY RUBBISHES!!!" Grandma rushed out of the front door and onto the verandah. "What the hell do you think you're doing, coming to attack my children in our own yard?! Huh!? What the hell do you think you're doing?! GET OUT BEFORE I CALL THE COPS!!!" Her body quivered as she waved her pointing finger at them.

Ewald and Rob tried to hide their weapons as they retreated towards the gate. Abu and Dewald hastily bundled Hermann onto the goods compartment of the truck.

"I hate you! I hate you! I'll kill you!" Hermann kept yelling between screams of pain.

"I'll get you! You little cunt!" shouted Abu as he closed the bakkie's tailgate and hastily rushed to the driver's seat, where he started the engine and revved it menacingly.

"You" Dewald pointed at William and I. "You're dead shits! Dead! Hear me?!" he screamed before jumping into the back seat of the double-cab.

"I'LL KILL YOU!" I yelled at all of them as I took a few steps towards them. William grabbed a hold of me. I was shaking uncontrollably. Rob walked until he reached the bakkie's front passenger door, climbed in and took his seat. In no time the vehicle sped away from us.

Out of nowhere a group of men came rushing to our gate. They were from Cosmos and had somehow gotten word of our troubles. These were of the wild-eyed men who still had no fear of reprisal from the Butcher, Baker and Candlestick Maker.

"Aweh, dinge! Ouma are you oryt?" screamed one of the men loudly.

"We're fine, thank you."

"Those blerry people must be fokken careful these days," it came from one of the men.

"They can get blerry moered very fokken badly. You know?" Barked from somewhere on the side.

"If they blerry fokken wanna fight us. Neh?" cried another.

"You boys blerry call us next time. Huh?" howled another.

"You blerry watch you fokken backs from now on. You know?" roared another voice from within the swirling mass.

"Ouma, take care. Look after you blerry ganas," screeched the first voice. Without further ado the twirling mass of destructive dust and men disappeared down the pathway next to Aunt Nishi's home in the direction of Cosmos.

Grandma opened her mouth to say something but couldn't. She herded us indoors, shutting and locking the front door before we sat in the lounge. I was still in shock. May-June hastily grabbed Morph before he could open his mouth and hurried into the kitchen with him.

"There comes a time in a man's life when he must fight to defend his family. My boys, I'm so proud of you for defending your sister and each other. Most times you don't have to use violence to win a fight, but not today. You did what you had to do," said Grandma solemnly.

William and I were caught off-guard, expecting to be scolded for fighting and swearing.

"Fine, Ouma," we responded as we tried to absorb the gravity of her words.

"Tell me, why where those hooligans fighting in our yard?"

"They started it. They came to deliberately start a fight," answered William angrily, wiping his face and his palms with his handkerchief.

"What did they do?"

"Hermann picked on May-June and were ready to fight with Plano and I when you shouted. They had guns. Rob had his Glock 31 and Ewald took out his Beretta 8000. I was afraid they were gonna kill us if you didn't come out. They could've cut Plano and I to shreds." William was an avid gun enthusiast.

"I was not sure whether Ewald was gonna use his, but Rob was ready to shoot us if you didn't come out, Ouma," I added my two cents.

"I saw that. I got the fright of my life."

"They're not supposed to be carrying guns! They could be arrested. You know?" William volunteered.

"Which cop is gonna arrest them?"

I had put my whole family in danger by hitting Hermann. I wished we could go back in time and undo it all.

"Everyone is going to die because of me," I thought. I felt short of breath.

"Do you think they'll kill us?" I asked my big brother as he walked into the bathroom, where I was splashing water on my face.

"They can only try, bro. We'll put up one helluva fight, I tell you!"

I nodded my head without any conviction.

"You did well today. Really climbed into old Hermann. Haha! I swear he looked like he wet his pants. Heh!?" William laughed.

I looked glumly into the mirror.

"Lighten up, bro. Those losers won't do anything. They're all talk."

"Okay."

"I'm proud of you, Plano. The way you stood up for May-June and I, considering all you've been through. You'll be just fine. Besides, you can hit like a heavy weight boxer! Woah! Wllllaiii liuud loeliod me under his arm and wrestled me around the bathroom.

"William and Plano, Ouma's calling. She says you'll must come eat," said May-June.

The Combrink family lived near the richest families in Drakensview. They were seated in their lounge. Hermann's leg was raised on an antique footstool. The ticking of a grandfather clock and the faint rustling of their clothes were the only sounds that permeated the hush. Hermann wanted the earth to swallow him whole after what happened.

After what seemed like an eternity, Joe Combrink addressed his son.

"What the fuck made you do such a stupid thing, Hermann?! What were you thinking?"

Herman had similar features, hair and eye color to his father. Joe, however, was more dashing and imposing. He was dressed in a black suit with a waistcoat and a grey tie. He stood near the door that led to their dining-room, feet apart and hands behind his back. He stared intently at his son, drilling him with the intense blue-eyed gaze he used daily in court.

Hermann fluttered under the scrutiny. "In my defense, Sir... I was..." he spluttered.

"Shut up, Son! I'm not here to argue this matter with you." He set about on his measured pacing around their immaculate lounge that smelled of polished leather and furniture polish.

"Hermann, you're accountable for your deplorable deeds. Do you understand?"

"Yuh. Y-y-yes, Sir." Hermann stammered nervously, as he followed his father's pacing with wary eyes, sneaking a few gulps of air whenever not being glaring at.

Susan Combrink could not help herself. "Are you even aware that you could've been killed, my son! What the hell were you thinking anyway, by going to those rubbish people's house? Do you know what that monkey could've done to you? Well, do you?!" The style icon and blonde bombshell wagged her finger at Hermann with such force that it looked as though her appendage was going to launch her entire body off the sofa at any moment. Her voice raised in few decibels and pitch with each sentence. The bun on her head, the strings of earrings and the pearls around her neck bobbed up and down in cadence.

"Susan. Back off, I told you I'll handle this."

"Fine!" "Hermann, what possessed you to do that?! Look at what you've done! What possessed you to enter their yard and attack the stupid girl? Do you realise that if they choose to make a case of this, they stand a very good chance of winning if they find a good lawyer to represent them? You never attack a family in their own home. Do you understand, Hermann?!"

Hermann winced from the onslaught. No sympathy from his father.

"What possesses you to be so nasty to your own child?" Susan demanded. Joe was unfazed. "Your son… Our son confessed that he went too far this time. He confessed that he was going to force sex on an underage girl without consent… Attempted rape, Susan. Have you forgotten what happened to those men who raped and killed the girl from Cosmos, Susan?"

Susan launched her slim frame straight off the sofa and shouted. "Went too far? Sex with a tramp? How dare you even think that my hermann would even look at a Coloured girl like that? They're not his class and nowhere near his type!"

"Please leave us, Hermann. I need to talk to your mother."

"Yes, Sir!" Hermann hobbled out of the lounge and closed the door behind him.

Susan turned a deep shade of scarlet. Faint beads of perspiration escaped on her brow and neck. She knew what was to come. Joe put his hands behind his back, turned away from his wife and stared intently out of the window.

Abu walked next to his father through the cavernous warehouse. Faizel was checking stock and making notations on a clipboard as they marched through the aisles of this colossal building of steel grey shelves packed to the high roof with rows and rows of groceries and merchandise. They spoke in Arabic.

"My son, I trust you were not directly involved in that senseless attack?"

"No, my father. They asked me to drive them there. That's all I did. I was outside when they went into the yard. I only entered to help Hermann after his injury," Abu lied smoothly.

"That's good, my son. They can't really tie you to anything because you were not actively involved in their attack." Faizel stopped at some goods, counted them and made a notation on his clipboard. They continued their journey.

"That boy hit Hermann. Hermann only bumped his sister. It was an unprovoked attack."

Faizel stopped walking and turned to his son. "Abu, think about it. That boy had seen three men rape and murder a young girl. Do you think he was going to stand still while Hermann attacked his sister? Would you stand still if someone attacked one of your sisters?"

"No, my father." Abu bowed his head in supplication.

"Besides," continued Faizel. "They drew firearms and pointed these at the two boys. They could get into serious trouble for that. Their fathers, too, because the guns belong to them." He turned to face Abu squarely. "My son, I trust you did not take yours with you?"

"No, my father," lied Abu, looking his father in the eye. They continued their excursion.

"Abu, there are matters afoot that you do not know of. These will have far-reaching consequences and will bring much wealth and power and prestige to our family."

"What are these events, my father?" Faizel stopped walking and thought pensively.

"At this stage I cannot tell you, except to say that I'm working with the fathers of your friends in this venture."

"Is there anything that I can do to help?"

"Stay away from that family. Do you know your Naana and Ouma Gibbs are best friends for many years? You'll get into deep shit with Naana if she finds out about this."

"Oh! I didn't know."

"And be very careful around your friends. Especially around Rob and Hermann. There is very bad blood between their families. For now,

I think it has been kept from their sons and daughters. But you never know." Faizel shrugged his shoulders.

"Will do so, my father. What bad blood is this?"

"It may come to light in time. Do not ask them anything about it, Abu."

"I will not, my father. Is there anything specific that I am to watch out for?"

"Take note of any changes in their behavior. I want you to report such changes to me, my son. Immediately. No matter how subtle it is."

"Will do so, my father."

"Leave me now so I can finish off here. We'll go to Mosque together this afternoon."

"Yes, father." Abu strode rapidly towards the exit. Staff along his exit route deferred to him out of fear. He needed to soak in the revelations from his father and to plot a plan of action.

Rob sat on the bed in his room and watched as his father's Mercedes Benz drove into their garage. He did not care much about his father' business activities, except to enjoy the benefits that it brought into his existence. There were odd moments, very fleeting, where he might have cared about his parent's lives. These unwelcome intrusions were, however, few and very far-between, lessening with the passing of time.

Normally, it was all about him and how they needed to attend to his needs. He had learnt early in life how to pretend that he cared only to get what he wanted from them. He had also learnt especially how to circumvent his father's temper. The temper that inevitably drove Rob into the inherited hive of heartlessness and cruelty that drove his father. It was said by those who knew the family well that Rob was ten times worse than his father when it came to being cruel, though Rob was still young. These people reckoned that it was not because Rob did not care or could not care much about his family. It was simply not within him to do so.

The front door slammed thunderously.

"Robert!" shouted Eric.

"What?" Rob shouted back when he reached the upstairs railing.

"I bloody heard you going around with that fucking Coolie friend of yours again."

"So?"

"Don't go do all that bloody shit the fucking Coolies been doing all these years. I bloody well don't need you disgracing me in this bloody town. It's bloody bad enough I'm forced to socialize with those bloody shit towelheads that stink of oily curry all the time."

"Aaaggh! Abu's my friend. And he's a bloody good friend. That's all," Rob responded as he descended the staircase.

"I hear the stupid cunt, Hermann, got bloody donnered by a little klonkie. Why the fuck didn't you blerry moer that bloody wanker? I didn't raise you to be a sissy."

"He was saved by his bloody grandmother. His bloody time will come. Believe me."

Eric stared briefly at his son. He walked into his study, pulled a bottle of whiskey and two tumblers out of the cupboard and carried these into the lounge. Without turning around, he said to his son, "Come have a bloody drink with your old man."

"Some other time, have to go somewhere," Rob answered him.

"Have a fucking drink!" Eric turned and, almost as fast as the strike of a puffadder, he caught his son by the shirt sleeve and pulled him into the lounge. Rob was not startled by Eric's actions. He stared at the man's hand on his sleeve until his father let go. Eric poured whiskey into both tumblers and handed one to Rob.

"What the hell do you know about that bastard Bushman family you'll tried to attack today?" Eric asked after taking a sip of whiskey.

Rob took a sip from his tumbler before responding. "They're poor, loser cunts."

"Don't speak of bloody poor people that way. Our family comes from bloody hell worse poverty. And we'd still be deep in that bloody shit if it were not for Grandpa Derrick."

"But they are. And we are certainly not poor cunts now. Are we?"

"That we bloody hell are not. What can you tell me about them?" Eric persisted.

Rob stared at his father before speaking, "Why are you so interested in them?"

"I don't like coincidences. Those three bastard shitheads were killed under unnatural circumstances by bloody bastards that acted bloody unnaturally. I don't like coincidences."

"Well, I don't know anything about them. Why don't you ask Pieter at the workshop about them? He's from Cosmos."

"Because you are in the same regional rugby team with one of them. William, I think."

Rob froze briefly before responding; "I know fuckall about him. Stay away from them. What the fuck will you be able to get from those dickheads about this other shit anyway?"

"Some shit-head bastards on the lot were talking about that bastard William today. They were bloody well saying he's a bloody hard worker."

"Bloody hell!" responded Rob angrily.

"But you're right, my boy. Bastard shits like them bring nothing but bad fortunes."

"Cheers to that!" Rob said as he raised his glass and then took a sip.

"You said you have to go? Where the hell to?"

"Oh, just out."

"Well, don't be an asshole out there. Leave the Glock at home tonight. I don't want an overzealous fucker cop finding it on you."

Rob barely slowed down as he left the glass on a side table and strode out of the lounge.

The twins rode the elevator up to their father's office. His secretary, Mrs. van Niekerk, almost banged her desk with her head as she tried to genuflect in her seat.

"Good afternoon, sirs!" she enthused. "Your father is expecting you."

She quickly picked up the phone and pressed a button.

"Sir, Mr. Ewald and Mr. Dewald are here. Yes, sir!" She put down the phone.

"You may go right in, sirs!" she said excitedly.

The brothers entered the office and shut the door behind them with a thud.

"Hi, Pa," they said before slumping into the two leather seats in front of Ewald Senior's desk in feigned nonchalance.

"Hi, boys! What shit did you get up to today? Huh?" he demanded without preamble.

"Aaaggh! Pa. Just a bit of fun," volunteered Dewald.

"A bit of fun when one of your friends was hit with a spade!"

"Well, Hermann is a bit of a stubborn donkey," responded Ewald Junior.

"Don't give me that shit! What the fuck were you doing pointing the Beretta at them?" Ewald Senior glared at Ewald Junior.

"For protection, Pa. I only took it out to protect us. I didn't use it. Didn't have to." Ewald Junior shrugged his shoulders.

"What you did is still wrong. You don't have a fucking license for it. I let you and you brother have them for protection. Not to point them at innocent people," fumed Ewald Senior.

Ewald Junior shrugged his shoulders and moved his hands outwards with palms upward by explanation. "I swear, Pa. It was only for protection. You should've seen that little fucker with the spade, Pa. If his brother didn't push him out of the way, Hermann would've been in hospital by now. He went totally crazy."

"How did you find out all this?" queried Dewald.

"Don't you get enough pussy from the whores you hire? That township is rife with Aids and yet you still run after bitches from there!" thundered Ewald Senior.

"The apple doesn't fall far from the tree," murmured Dewald under his breath. Ewald Junior heard him and smiled.

"What did you say? What did you say? Huh?" roared Ewald Senior.

"I said it's good business to get pussy for free sometimes, Pa."

"What shit is that? Talk sense, son!" barked Ewald Senior.

"Will there be a case against us?" asked Ewald Junior. "I don't think so. They're probably shit scared to go to the cops. In any event it'll be squashed if they dared. Unless they take the matter to that liberal press in Pietermaritzburg."

"Pa, you know everything. Things are happening, changing here in Estcourt. I feel it and so does Dewald. Look at how the three were killed. Do you know what is happening, Pa?" asked Ewald Junior. Dewald nodded.

"There are forces trying to interfere with my plans. Don't worry. It's all under control."

The twins looked at each other perplexed.

"Boys, I have big plans here in Estcourt. Plans that will have huge benefits for our wealth. What was done today could've jeopardized these plans. Do you understand?"

"No, Pa." "Not really, Pa."

"I can't give you too much detail, except to say I'm working with Eric and Faizel on a huge scheme. It's at a sensitive stage and must be protected at all costs until it's executed. I need you boys and your friends to avoid getting up to any shit for the rest of December, especially here in Estcourt. I'll not be able to concentrate on any distractions during this time. Do you understand, boys?"

"Not really, Pa." "Sort of, Pa."

"I can't give you more details. Be on your best behavior until after the deal is done."

"Is there anything we can do to help you, Pa?" queried Ewald Junior, glancing quickly at his brother. Dewald nodded in agreement.

"Not at this stage, boys, but I'll let you know if something pops up." Ewald Senior sat back and rested his arms across his stomach. The twins copied him.

"What about our friends, Pa? Are we still good with them?" asked Dewald.

"They should be okay for now, boys. But trust no one, not even them."

"Okay, Pa," the twins responded in unison.

"Oh! And stay away from that Bushman family. They could cause serious trouble for us. I don't want that old lady to even get a whiff of our scheme. Did you boys know she was heavy in the ANC in her early days?"

"No, Pa."

"Yes, she was. Quite a firebrand. She probably still has some serious connections within that communist organization. Stay away from them."

"Okay, Pa. We'll keep low profiles for a while like we did the last time."

"You can go with your mother and sisters to Plett. I'll join you after New Year's Eve."

"No, Pa. Let Ma and them go to Plett. We'll stay here to keep you company. Who'll look after you when Ma's not here? The twins finished each other's sentences.

Ewald Senior visibly softened. "Okay. But you'll have to convince Ma. Stay away from those Bushmen, they're not worth the effort." He waved his sons away.

"Yes, Pa."

As soon as they climbed into their vehicle Dewald asked, "What was all that about?" He started the car and put it in reverse.

"Shit! I don't know, bro," responded Ewald, banging a fist into the palm of a hand.

"Whatever it is, we need to be part of it. Huh?" continued Dewald as he changed gear.

"I agree. We have to stay here in Estcourt where it's going down."

"Yea." Dewald gunned the vehicle and headed for the exit.

CHAPTER 8
CATACLYSMIC
CONUNDRUMS
(THURSDAY, 16 DECEMBER 1999)

G randma came at a good clip to my bed, saw that I was awake and hurried me up; "Go top and tail quickly. I want us out of here in fifteen minutes. Almost forgot, you have another appointment with Dr Carlson at eight-thirty. Hurry, son. We don't have much time." I quickly turned to William's bed.

"OK, Ouma!" I flung the covers off and flew past Grandma as she woke William then Morph up. It was a crazy rush to get ready and eat breakfast before we had to leave.

"Dr. John phoned yesterday and wanted to know how you're doing. After I explained to him what happened he made another appointment with Dr Carlson. I'm sorry, Plano. I forgot to tell you last night. I almost forgot about it myself."

Grandma and I ran as fast as her legs could carry her to Mfana's waiting kombi. We passed William at the big gate he was opening for the municipal workers who would be removing the last vestiges of what was once the old behemoth of a gum tree.

"Bye," greeted William as we scooted past him.

"Bye," Grandma and I muttered in haste.

Mfana gunned the engine of his rust bucket of a kombi and we shot down the road. So fast, in fact, that for a minute I thought he was not going to make the turn into Alfred Street. I held on to the handles for dear life as I watched the fence of our school yard rapidly approaching. I thanked God there were no other cars or pedestrians at the intersection as Mfana took the turn on what felt like two wheels. My heart was pumping rapidly in my throat next to my mouth when Grandma added to Mfana's devilish rush down Alfred Street.

"Faster, Mfana! Hurry! We don't have much time!" I couldn't believe my ears! As we turned left into Victoria Street Mfana turned to look at me.

"Howzit!" he shouted above the throbbing music.

"Fine, Sir!" I shouted in alarm as I watched other vehicles take evasive action and pedestrians scatter in fear. Angry hooters blared as we took the bend and roared away.

Mfana said "Shup!" and turned to face the road ahead. He and Grandma carried on with an animated conversation I held on for dear life in this deathtrap of a taxi. "Thank you, Mfana," said Grandma. We reached our destination with half a minute to spare.

"I'll phone you when we're done!" shouted Grandma as we hurried off.

"Shup!" boomed Mfana above the loud music before he revved the engine and shot off.

I ran ahead to open the door for Grandma and then to press the button for the lift. We made it to the door of Dr Carlson's office at precisely one minute late for our appointment. Grandma disliked tardiness. The office of Dr. Carlson was cold and quiet. A welcome relief from our mad dash. The secretary spoke softly to Grandma, while I went straight for the chair I occupied at our first visit. Sadness crept up on me. I wondered whether Stevie was still alive.

"Sit still, Plano." Grandma touched my leg.

The door to Dr. Carlson's office opened. He greeted us cheerfully and ushered Grandma into his consulting room. I leaned forward to listen to their conversation. The secretary laughed merrily and told me the room was soundproof. I would not be able to hear anything, no matter how hard I tried. I sheepishly got up and explored the water cooler and then absent-mindedly brushed the faint dust off the fern leaves. I did not want to talk about those three words Adelaide had whispered. I had once seen a movie where a crook was hypnotized and injected with truth serum to make him talk. I resolved to make sure I do not have to be subjected to such heinous methods of interrogation. I wandered off towards the main door as stealthily as was possible. I was sure I could find something worthwhile to do in the passageway or downstairs.

"Where're you going, Deplano?"

I turned swiftly and looked at Grandma.

"Come Deplano, let's talk." Dr. Carlson held out his hand towards me. I walked past Grandma, who squeezed my shoulder before the Doctor and I entered his soundproof chamber.

There was something else familiar about Dr. Carlson. He reminded me of my grandpa. The more he listened to me and encouraged me, the more I spoke and then listened to what he had to say. Just like Grandpa was when he wasn't working or chasing William and I up a tree, or teasing Morph, or dancing with Grandma, Mom, or May-June. He would always find the time to listen to each one of us and to talk sense to us in a way that made you listen to him. We could talk one-on-one with Grandpa for hours on end He allowed us the time and space to just talk Nothing was trivial. He would listen to my outrageous stories of aliens and heartily join in. My mom used to say that the first time I spoke was to Grandpa. For a long time in my life Grandpa was my confidant. It was his death that silenced me for long periods.

Dr. Carlson was listening to me intently just as Grandpa used to do. The doctor sat with his two forefingers draped over his mouth as I spoke about the nasty happenings affecting us since our last encounter. He listened. After I quietened down, Dr. Carlson got up and sat next to me on the large sofa. He put my head onto his shoulder. I wept for a long time. He said nothing – just let me cry. He then held my one hand and spoke to me.

"Deplano, it's not your fault! It's not your fault, you hear me!"

It was like I was right back in that moment when I was held tightly in Grandpa's tough grip, after I accidentally bumped Morph off the kitchen table and he broke a wrist bone.

"It's not your fault, Son." Grandpa spoke quietly as he soothed me and held me tightly.

I cried again because I missed Grandpa. I missed my dad. I missed my mom. I missed our lives back then above everything else. I didn't like that everything had to change so suddenly and so terribly. I cried because I felt sore – my chest was aching and I couldn't make it stop. Dr. Carlson continued to hold me and to talk soothingly as I wept. Eventually Dr Carlson walked me to the door and into the waiting room. I still refused to share the nightmare and those three words with him, or with anyone else.

"He'll be okay, Ouma. You may phone me on my cell. The number is on my card. Let's make another appointment for the middle of January." He gave me a lollipop.

"Thank you, Doctor, I'll do so right now."

We said our goodbyes. As I reached out to open the entrance door a white couple and their young daughter walked in. I could immediately see the consternation and fear on the parent's faces. The young girl was serene, with her hair plaited and tied with two neat bows. We remained silent as we crossed paths at the sad, sterile doorway.

The ride home contrasted with the earlier death-defying madness. Dr. Carlson had given Grandma more pills to help me sleep and others to improve my appetite. I was to take the one every day, one hour before supper, the other at least two hours thereafter. Pressure to keep the secret was becoming harder by the day. The harder I fought, the more I was torn up inside.

"Boys, please make butter and jam sandwiches and some tea for all of us," said Grandma as we reached the verandah. My siblings were seated in the shade. Morph and I scurried off. I first changed out of the clothes I wore to the doctor before joining Morph in the kitchen, where we began to prepare the tea and sandwiches. I was carefully smoothing the margarine and jam on Grandma's sandwich when my friends knocked on the backdoor.

"Plano! Open for us, and all!" Neville called in desperation.

"No!" I teased.

"Agh. Please, Plano!" shouted Kallie.

I opened the door just enough to peek my head out.

"What's the password?" I asked sternly.

"Please, dude?" pleaded Tsepho.

"Pretty please with sprinkles on the top?" added Kallie.

"Cowboys rule," ventured Neville.

"Indians rule," Kallie tried his luck.

"Plano is the best dude?" was Tsepho's attempt at the password.

"Plano!" they all screamed at once.

"Say Plano is the bestest friend we've ever had," I cajoled them.

"Plano is the bestest friend we've ever had!" they shouted.

"Okay, come in." I smiled, but their faces were all business.

I opened the door, and they made a hasty beeline to the loo, taking caps off their heads as they brushed past me. May-June and William were still in the lounge chatting. Grandma was in her bedroom changing.

"Is Ouma here?" asked Neville, who was the first to complete his ablutions. All three of my friends and I were roughly the same height and build. Neville had an oval face with chubby cheeks and a strong, slightly hooked nose that accentuated these wide, brown, friendly eyes. His thick hair and eyebrows were wavy and shiny black, and they seemed to move on their own volition. He tended to bobble his head this way and that whenever he said something he felt was important. He did so now as he spoke.

"In her room, changing," I responded as Morph and I continued to make the sandwiches and tea. We added more for my friends.

Tsepho and Kallie joined us in the kitchen. It didn't take long before all of us were having a boisterous, and deeply concerning, conversation. Tsepho had high, round cheekbones and a large forehead seeming to bracket these huge pair of black, sharp eyes that missed nothing. His wide mouth continually broke into the widest of smiles bent on crinkling his eyes and revealing perfect white teeth. He loved to stand with his hands on his hips, especially when trying to make a point, looking very much like our school principal surveying children at play. Tsepho was in that stance now walking this way and that, trying to solve a vexing dilemma.

Kallie was wringing his old, weathered khaki cap beyond recognition in agitation as each one of us voiced our concerns at what our world was becoming. He would stop doing so every now and them to wag a finger in emphasis. Kallie had huge ears protruding from a mop of ginger hair, and a freckled, craggy face. In repose, Kallie bore the saddest of eyes and mouth, but when happy his smiling eyes and mouth were infectious. He looked sad today. Kallie's greenish grey eyes can be an intense cobalt blue when under duress

Grandma came into the kitchen to see what all the commotion was about. When she entered my friends immediately shut up and stood in single file, heads hanging, hats in hand.

"Morning, Ouma," they chorused.

Grandma greeted them before joining Morph and I in preparing the tea and sandwiches.

"How come you brave guys had to do a number one indoors today? Heh? I thought you tough guys can stand and do it anywhere?" Grandma teased them.

"It's the girls, Ouma," Tsepho managed to get out.

"What about the girls?"

"They are all over the place watching us, and all," said Neville.

"And they shout and point and laugh at us when we pee outside," added Kallie.

"They're everywhere, watching us, Ouma. Perverts!" Tsepho spat with distaste.

Grandma could not contain herself. At first, her shoulders shook gently as mirth bubbled within. Her laughter could not be corralled, and it burst forth – much to the discomfort of my friends. After a while Grandma was calm enough to say, "Sorry, boys. It is just that it's the story of the ages. You'll learn in due time. For now, enjoy your childhood while it lasts. The girls are beginning to check you out." Grandma burst out laughing. She again had to stop for a while with the sandwich- and tea making, because it was all too much.

"You mean like boyfriend and girlfriend?" Neville was incredulous. "Yes, like that."

The realisation hit the wind out of our sails momentarily. "Don't worry boys. Girls mature quicker than boys. You still have time to play and have fun."

"Then what?" asked Kallie fearfully, scratching his head.

"Then you'll also start noticing them."

We vehemently shouted our response, "Never!" "Will not!" "Ugly pigs!" "Never!" "Ever!" "They stink!" "Girls!" "Yuck!" "Sis!" Even Morph expressed his mortification.

William and May-June joined us in the kitchen. They too were found our discomfort amusing. "Boys! Boys!" Grandma calmed us down. "Don't get your nickers, eerrrr, underpants in a knot. You still have much growing up to do. Tell me, did all of you pass your exams?"

Our agitation was deflected. We stood in the kitchen enjoying the tea and sandwiches and each other's company. My friends had also passed their exams and so the conversation gravitated to going to the next grade in the coming year and what we wanted to be when we grow up. After the meal we got down to business.

"Plano, can you come play with us today?" queried Tsepho.

"Where're you gonna play?" asked Grandma.

"Agh! Just there in Neville and them's garden, there by the tree. We can play cops and robbers," responded Tsepho.

"Stay just there in the yard, boys. I don't want you'll running around anywhere else. Only at Neville's. Do you understand?"

We nodded and beat a hasty retreat out the back door. Grandma's voice chased after us, "Plano, remember we need to go into town at two o clock, so you better be in this house at one, changed and ready to go, you hear me?"

"Yes, Ouma." I called out as we passed the kitchen window.

My friends and I tumbled out of the gate and bolted down Rocky Lane and right onto Alfred Street. Neville's home was four houses down from Rocky Lane. It was a yellow house with a red-tiled roof. At the back of the property stood a huge Syringa Berry tree infused with its yellow berries. Children in the neighborhood were warned not to eat the poisonous berries. We tried it out, but not in large quantities. It was an acquired taste.

Neville's Mom used these berries, the leaves from the tree, and various shrubs of herbs and spices from her garden to make all sorts of potions to ward off every evil and to heal all sorts of ailments. There tended to be a steady stream of customers from all races who called at her door. We reached the shade of the tree and rested on the wooden benches beneath it.

"We were thinking, Plano, we could go play in the veld, and build a fort?" said Kallie.

"A fort? Where?" I queried nonchalantly.

"You know, to play without the lighties troubling us, and all," added Neville.

"Which veld?" I tried to play it cool.

"Here over the fence, dude," pointed Tshepo.

I let out an imperceptible sigh of relief. We had played in the rocky ground behind Neville's home on numerous occasions. It was a good place for such game time.

"My dad gave me some big plastic sheets from his work," noted Kallie.

"And we have boxes there behind the tree," Tsepho enthused.

I watched seven Sparrows and two Indian Mynahs hop about amongst Auntie Priya's plants, picking seeds from the ground. They were so engrossed in their meal they seemed to miss the snow-white cat stalking them. The cat crouched in preparation for her attack. The birds flew off in a whir of flapping wings and chirping into the Syringa Berry tree where they hopped about and continued to chirp, as if mocking the cat. She stalked off to seek more prey.

"Okay, we'll go now, now."

The veld was far from my mind. "Why are the girls so nasty to us? I mean, they used to play so nicely with us. Now they giggle at us for nothing." A berry fell right on the top of my head and bounced off as if to emphasize the point I had just made.

"I dunno, my bras. They could run and play like us and now they dress up and look at us all googley eyes, and all," lamented Neville.

"And start giggling for nothing, dudes," added Tsepho.

"Maybe we should hit them and chase them away. You know?" volunteered Kallie.

And so we delved into a terribly shallow, ill-informed discussion on sex and wet dreams and masturbation that left us more confused than ever.

"Let's make a pact. We'll not fall for the tricks of these nasty girls," I suggested sternly.

"Yeah!" my friends responded. We spat on our hands, formed a circle, and clasped each other's spittle in a silent oath of brotherly camaraderie and resistance.

"Let's go play before I must go to town with Ouma!" I urged. The spell was broken.

We grabbed our boxes and plastics and ran and tumbled over the fence.

"Where're we gonna build the fort?" asked Kallie.

"When we find the perfect spot," Neville led the way.

We ran into the veld nimbly on the spread of rocks before us, singing and joking along those precarious perches. In that moment my life floated back to me: I was overwhelmed with poetry; with words and expressions. The face of Adelaide and the smell of death seemed to be receding. It's not enough to say I felt free in this place and space. It was more than freedom.

It was like I'd died and gone to heaven, dancing on clouds and singing with angels. When we finally agreed on a spot, we collapsed into the grass, surrounded by rocks. We then discussed all the great things we'd accomplish in our fort. After a while it dawned on us that we needed to start with the construction work, and so we did without diminishing our verbal joust. When we finished Kallie raised his hand like a gun and pointed it at Tsepho and I.

"You crooks better run for your lives! We got you now!" he commanded.

The two of us scattered in different directions, hiding, and crouching down low in silence at our chosen places of concealment, listening for the footsteps of the law. I positioned myself low down between a rock and a bush, where the hanging branches offered perfect cover with a panoramic view in front of me. I lay still, with only my eyes moving to scan for any movement. I felt like the Indians in my dad's favorite movie 'The Last of the Mohicans'. I knew it would take ages for my friends to find me.

Suddenly Tsepho appeared and called out, "Plano! Neville! Kallie! Dudes! Come see what I found!" he waved his arms excitedly.

"You're lying, you just want me to move so you can take my spot," I responded.

"No, no really, come see dudes!" he called with real urgency.

"Where?" I asked as I reluctantly revealed myself.

"Over there!" he pointed. "Come see, dudes!"

We followed him as ran off. We were suddenly assailed by the aroma of fish and chips. It was so out of place where we were.

Tsepho stopped suddenly and pointed in front of him; "Look, dudes!" We looked. An emaciated, foreign black woman sat outside a crude structure of cardboard boxes and plastic bags well-hidden from all directions. On her lap she rocked an equally small and frail baby to sleep as she hummed a strange tune.

"Hello," I said as I sat on the rock.

"Hello," the lady responded haltingly.

"Why're you staying here? Where're you from?"

In broken English she explained that they were from Mozambique, travelling from town to town looking for work and begging for food. Her husband eventually found work as a truck driver at Derrick Walton's Cartage this past Monday; they needed to stay there until he earned enough for them to move. She could not yet find work for herself because the baby was too small. A brown locust, with spotted wings, landed on the baby's vest. It swished antennae this way and that as it surveyed its surroundings before whirling off into the long grass.

"Please don't tell we stay here," she begged us tearfully. We promised her we would not snitch. Kallie hurried off and returned with the materials from our fort. These he lay on the ground before her.

"Here's more stuff for you to use, Aunty," he said in offering.

"Thenk you very much," the lady responded in gratitude.

"We gotta go now. We'll try to bring food and stuff for you'll. Ok?" promised Neville. We stood up.

"Thank you very much."

"Bye."

"Bye," she responded, waving her hand. Just then the baby woke up and started to cry.

We bounded over the rocks and fence to our spot beneath the Syringa Berry tree.

"Dudes, we need to help those people," pleaded Tsepho.

"What if they're crooks or terrorists?" asked Kallie. "We can go to jail."

"It's scary! People so close to our home, and all, and we didn't even know it." Neville blurted out. "What if Kallie's right? What if they're planning to rob and kill us in the night?"

"Then where'll they put the baby while they do all that?" I asked.

"They could kill and eat the baby, for strength before they attack us, and all." Neville's imagination was let loose.

"Or they could give the baby away, or sell it, my bras," added Kallie.

"Dudes, we need to help them. I don't think they're crooks," leaded Tsepho.

"I also don't think so. We could ask at Derrick Waltons's Cartage about them," I added.

"What if the manager at Derrick's is also involved? He's a Singh, you know, Hindus always think they're higher up than Tamils, and all." Neville was unconvinced.

We ruminated silently for a few seconds.

"Let's go tell Ouma. She'll know what to do," I suggested.

My friends did not wait for a second invitation to hurry off in the direction of our home.

"Deplano! Do you know what time it is?" scolded Grandma.

"Yes, Ouma. Sorry, Ouma."

My friends fell in line behind me, heads hanging.

When no smile met mine in return, I hung my head and proceeded with caution towards Grandma who stood at the front door. She was dressed in going-out clothes.

"Ouma, we got a big problem," I muttered, trying to smile.

"Are you trying to dodge being late?" Grandma asked with hands on her hips.

"No, Ouma. We got a big problem, and we need your help."

Grandma stared at us quizzically before responding, "Okay. Come into the lounge, boys, let me hear what you have to say. Better make it quick!"

We trooped in and took seats. Uncannily Neville and Kallie, who were the cops in our game, sat in the same two seats the cops had occupied when they interrogated us.

"What's it, boys?"

"Ouma, there's a man, woman and a baby living in the veld behind Auntie Priya and them." I shot out. "Maybe they're crooks, or murderers, and all!" Neville followed. "Or terrorists sent to hunt us down and kill us!" Kallie burst forth. "They're no such things, dudes!" exclaimed Tsepho. He turned to Grandma. "We need to help them, Ouma. Please."

"Can you do something, Ouma?" I begged.

Grandma took a while to absorb our bursts of passion before speaking.

"Tell me, boys, in what condition was the mother and baby?"

"Thin, Ouma. Very thin. Like those Ethiopian people we see on TV."

"And their house?" continued Grandma.

"It's made of cardboard and plastics. It probably falls in the storms," I explained.

"They must try to hide under the rocks when there's a storm," was Kallie's logic.

It made some sort of sense to our young minds knowing that their cardboard abode would be destroyed with each passing storm. They had to ride out the bad weather somehow.

"Maybe they have dug a cave that we didn't see," contributed Neville.

"Did you tell anyone else about them?"

"No, Ouma. We came straight here." My friends swiveled their heads from one side to the other a few times to reinforce my answer.

"But I'll have to tell my parents tonight, and all," added Neville gravely.

"Fair enough," responded Grandma. "Give me until five-thirty this afternoon. I'll make a few phone calls. Someone will go help them."

"Are they going to jail, Ouma?" asked Tshepo timidly.

"No. They'll be taken to a place of safety until they can sort out documentation and accommodation." Grandma always had the right answers. We knew that.

"Ouma, why are they called 'kwere-kwere'?" blurted Kallie.

"Don't call them that, boys. They're good people, just like us. Yes, there are bad people amongst them, just like we have. But they're mostly good people who work hard and want the same things for their families, just like we do. Don't ever call them by that nasty name. Ok?"

"Okay, Ouma," each one of us responded contritely.

"Okay, boys. You better get going. Plano is to get ready to go to town with me." Grandma stood up. We followed suit.

"Okay, Ouma." "Thanks, Ouma." "Bye, Ouma." "Check you, Plano."

"Bye, boys," Grandma responded.

"Spot you later," I replied. My friends departed and I hastened off to get ready.

That afternoon I sat with my friends on our verandah, warily observing some girls playing skipping games in the street. Shadows were lengthening rapidly; much needed shade spread slowly and steadily from everything:

"So whadda you think will happen to those peeps, dudes?" asked Tsepho.

I shrugged my shoulders. "Ouma'll sort it out."

"Maybe aliens will attack them and take them, and all," suggested Neville.

"Could be aliens, my bras, coz aliens take your soul through your stomach. You know? Did you see how big the baby's navel was?" added Kallie.

"So then they were eating fish and chips, they can't be aliens, dudes!" offered Tsepho.

"Can too! They don't just eat people," Neville defended his thoughts.

"Fish and chips have no blood in them. All aliens and vampires need to eat flesh that has blood in it," I added to our conversation.

"Maybe the husband is the alien leader, my bras? And he's captured the woman and the child is his. That's why she's so thin and scared," volunteered Kallie with bravado.

"They have to kill us. We saw too much!" Neville was in his element. We paid no mind.

The discussion on death and a woman and a child started to be quite uncomfortable. I grew steadily quieter as my friends continued. I soon focused on an assortment of birds in a feeding melee near Auntie Nishi's garage. She placed crushed mielies and dried breadcrumbs out for them every afternoon. The birds would come from afar to feast.

"Tell us what you think, and all," I heard Neville say.

"She is dead! Killed! Murdered by those sick bastards! There's no aliens or secret sect! Those rubbishes killed her!" I yelled. I could hear the words come out of my mouth. I was shouting. The girls in the street stopped skipping and stared at us.

I then folded my legs into my chest and buried my head in my knees and sobbed while my friends merely sat there, not knowing what to do.

"Sorry, Plano," they whispered as they shifted awkwardly in their seats.

"I'm sorry," I finally calmed down enough to blurt out.

"It's OK, my Brother," Tsepho responded reassuringly.

We got up and raced each other to the corner shop. When we passed the gang of giggling girls, they stopped playing to chorus, "Hi, Plano!" "Hi, Tsepho!" "Hi, Neville!" "Hi, Kallie!" in between fits of giggling. I felt myself blush.

"Ouma, is that family from Mozambique okay?" I queried as I entered the kitchen door. Grandma was at the stove checking on our supper.

"Yes, my child." Grandma replied. "They're now living in Uncle

Piet's outbuilding. It's a one-bedroom servants' quarters with a shower, but with no hot water. It'll do for now. They don't have to pay rent for the first three months. We've arranged it with Uncle Piet. The Sisters of Charity are going to help with groceries and clothing."

"Thanks, Ouma. I was worried."

Grandma sat at the kitchen table and beckoned me to do the same.

"They're not out of the woods yet. Remember they're illegal immigrants who may, or may not, have bad stuff in their past. They could be deported if the government finds out."

"Oh!" I exclaimed. "Can't they get some papers that'll make them legal?"

"It'll be tricky, but it can be done. I've phoned Thumi at Home Affairs and he'll assist them to get temporary visas. Also, with their applications to get their documents in order. One advantage for them is their child was born in South Africa and it makes him a South African citizen by birth. I don't think the government will deport the parents and keep the child. They'll keep the family if their papers check out."

We stood up to walk to the lounge or verandah where it was much cooler. Grandma switched off the stove. As she turned back to face me, I closed my eyes and hugged her tightly.

"Thanks, Ouma."

"Thanks to you and your friends, Plano, for caring." Grandma hugged me tightly.

The Butcher, Baker and Candlestick Maker met at four-thirty the same afternoon in the Butcher's plush upstairs office on the corner of Albert Street and Shepstone Avenue. All the office staff were already gone home and so they had the place to themselves. Just before they arrived at the office it was swept for any listening devices. None were found. Their diabolical plan was escalating rapidly. It was now necessary for them to meet more often to finalise any details and to institute controlled changes, where required. Tensions were running high.

"These young whelps of ours are really something else," noted Ewald as he sat back in his chair and folded hands on his stomach.

"Yeah! The little fuckers almost caused big shit, agreed Eric. Faizel calmly nodded.

"Talking of shit. What has Joe said about our offer, Faizel?" Ewald asked. Eric scowled, but they ignored him.

"He is naturally bitter and angry. He feels severely betrayed, considering all he does for us" Faizel stated mechanically.

"Will he take the fucking money?" boomed Eric.

"He didn't commit, but he will. He asked for time to consider it," responded Faizel.

"He'd better fucking take it, or else!" threatened Eric.

"He wants out," continued Faizel. Eric's threats did not faze Faizel.

"Can we buy his silence? Is there a price?" asked Ewald of Faizel.

"Yeah! I think so. But it'll cost us big time"

"What if we offer him a minor partnership? He can dump that dame with the money he'll make from us." Eric spoke hastily.

"Do you think he'll take it, Faizel?" queried Ewald.

"He might. What percent are we talking about?"

"The two of you have thirty-three-point-three percent shares. I have the extra point one of a share. If each of us give up one percent plus the fractions of our shares, then he'll get a tidy four percent, max. Start with one percent in your negotiations," commanded Ewald.

"Do you think it'll be enough to buy him off? Can we afford it?" asked Faizel.

"It bloody hell better be! And no! We can't let him go! He's in this organization for life, just as we are! Bloody hell! He even worked on our bloody Manifesto!" Eric responded.

"It doesn't help threatening him, Eric. After all we're trying to fix what your fucking shit dick has caused," Ewald leaned forward and rested his clasped hands on his desk.

"I bloody said I regret my actions!" Eric replied defiantly

"Your fucking shit is gonna cost big boodle. You'll have to fork out whatever extra it may cost." Ewald stared at Eric, who stared straight back.

"Gentlemen, everything is in order. I've even got three extra drivers if anything should happen to the ones Eric has arranged," Faizel interjected.

"I've got surveillance in place on Combrink. I've also appointed an ex-cop who is a top PI to dig deep into his affairs. He's top class and very discreet. I've completed a dummy run for the containers with the men. It went well in all the provinces, except Limpopo. They clocked forty-five minutes later than planned. But we should be able to sort it out before the 29th. The bribe costs to the councilors, officials on both sides and cops and the operation expenses for our men is, however, escalating fast. It's close to R100 thousand per person per month for the big shots and R15 thousand for the small fry. But we're still within our revised budget. The funds from Africa and the Middle East are helping, thanks Faizel," reported Ewald. He leaned back in his chair. Eric unclenched his fists.

"All for a good cause my friend," Faizel responded. "All for a good cause."

Faizel continued, "We've had ten successful transactions in Cape Town since June '98. The vigilante group was willing and eager to test our merchandise and have not squealed about our prices. After all, we gave them free training. I've been informed that their next venture will take place on 24 December 1999 in Cape Town."

"It's keeping the markets quite jittery and that's where we want it to be," Ewald smiled.

"It's a bloody wonder no one has been exposed for their dealings in the bloody Cape. Are we safe from any fucking links to them?" Eric did not look at any of his partners.

"Yes. As you know, we've a host of dummy companies and interme-diaries handling the matter. Each one is unaware of the other." Faizel steepled his fingertips as he spoke.

"The three new stupid cunt drivers are on the farm. I've given them the bloody inter-links to practice with. They should be ready to do a dummy run on Boxing Day. The bloody helicopters are also in place. We'll have to get our families back home by the 28th. It's easier to get to bloody Bazaruto from here. The bloody pilots have tested the route on a few bloody occasions and they're able to get there below the bloody shit radar. The bloody yachts will be anchored and waiting for our arrivals. None of the bloody crew cunts will have any shore leave as of the 26th," Eric reported.

"Joe's sorting out the paperwork for all three drivers," Faizel added. "Ewald, are you sure the Catalyst will be in position at the allotted time?"

"Yes. We've good contacts close to him who'll make it work according to plan. They want it to work just as much as we do."

"Okay. Back to our families. Mine are going to Plett. They'll be back in time. The boys will stay to help out at the offices," Ewald stated.

"Rob is staying. My bitch is going to Ballito with her blood-sucking family. They'll be back on the bloody 27th," Eric spat.

"My family is going to Cape Town. They'll also be back on the 27th. I've asked Abu to stay and help me with the businesses."

"Our most important link is your man, the Land Surveyor. Is he ready and as good as they say he is?" asked Ewald of Faizel.

"Yes, he is. His instruments are ready. He's been officially appointed to survey some land in the Valley of a Thousand Hills, around Greytown and on some plots outside of Estcourt. All three sites have been checked out and the most suitable of each has been established by him. His credentials are legit," confirmed Faizel.

"We've not asked you for more info to protect his identity, but I believe it's an appropriate time to know more about the kingpin. After all, he's the main man who'll drive the success of the plan. What name is he using as the front?" asked Ewald.

Faizel uncrossed his legs and tensed slightly.

"Malik Nader. Our man is also like a chameleon when it comes to blending in."

"Where's his bloody official office? Don't worry, we'll not be checking on him." Eric's words were delivered curtly.

"PE. Staffed and doing legit work. Remember, we've had five years to establish his credentials. When he's done, he'll return to his office," offered Faizel.

"Where the hell is he at this present bloody moment?" Eric was relentless.

"I don't know. He contacts me through an unknown intermediary to protect himself, but he'll be at the right place at the right time where we need him to be. He'll also perform his duties according to plan. He's a proven operator."

"Okay, gents. Any other business we need to discuss?" Ewald asked his partners.

"None comes to mind," responded Faizel. Eric shrugged.

"I have to leave. It's time for Mosque." Faizel was in a rush to get going and said his goodbyes as he arose. Ewald and Eric responded in greeting. Faizel used the lift and as the doors closed, he whispered, "Insha Allah." He wiped sweat from his face. Ewald stepped to the window where watched Faizel get into his white Land Rover Discovery and exit the yard.

As soon as Faizel's vehicle disappeared he turned to Eric and said, "Did you see he was sweating, even with the aircon on?"

"Bloody hell! Could even smell the fucking bastard. He's shitting himself."

"Did you think he gave us accurate info about the Land Surveyor?" Ewald stood with his back to the window.

"I think so. He has all to lose if he's bloody shitting us," Eric said bluntly.

"I'll ask my guy to discreetly check up on one Malik Nader. We need a photo of him."

"I've bloody asked you this before. Tell me when to take him out," he volunteered.

Ewald looked at Eric with that steely glint in his eyes. "Not now, but we'll keep checking on him. Has your surveillance yielded anything?"

"Nothing yet. I If he's bloody hiding something, we'll find it."

CHAPTER 9
MEMORIES IN
FLOWERBEDS
(FRIDAY, 17 DECEMBER 1999)

The two men spoke in North Mesopotamian Arabic with the Maslawi dialect of Mosul.

"Is all well at the camp?" asked Faizel of the man with the brown suede shoes.

"Everything okay. The men are a bit restless. Cabin fever. I gave Bakri his new cellphones and sim cards. He will call you tonight."

"I had to give my partners a bit of your cover story. It's odd they've taken so long to ask. They'll do some checking up on you. Perhaps even try to get a photo of you."

"I am ready. The photos have all been altered with not a hint of any resemblance to me. The real Malik Nader will return from his trip to Pakistan, by way of Okavango, when it is time for him to do so. He has been handsomely rewarded and knows nothing."

"That's fine. I still want to replace their drivers with ours. We'll have to tend to it the night before. Then they'll have no choice but to use mine. You may use Bakri and some of his men to get the job done if you need them."

"Ok. It will be done."

"Be extra careful. They've put surveillance on me and my family."

"They'll not find me."

"Okay. I'll contact you after I've spoken to Bakri."

The man with the brown suede shoes turned the corner at the bottom of the street. He removed the sim card and broke it. These pieces and the phone he placed in a jacket pocket of his jacket, to be disposed of later. Faizel did the same with his sim card and phone. He turned up the volume of the music in his vehicle and patiently waited for Abu to make an appearance.

His son was a popular person in the mosque. The Imam was talking to him. Faizel thought of the entanglement he was dragged into; of the immeasurable rewards he would gather from the success of their plan. He banished all negativity from his mind. He smiled at the wealth and power awaiting him – in South Africa, the rest of the continent and the Middle East.

William and I began with our chores at sunrise to avoid the strength sapping sunlight glaring down on all and sundry until even shadows cowered in small places and spaces. My friends arrived at about ten and they immediately chipped in. I briefed them about the destitute family being relocated and each one was thrilled at the news. Neville had not told his parents about the strange encounter and was now more convinced to keep quite or risk losing our playing field forever. "You know my 'ballie', guys? If I told him, he'll burn the veld down and demand the municipality clean it up, and all. Then where we'll play?"

I wanted to play, but suddenly felt the worst stomach cramps and had to lie down. When I woke up Morph was standing over me.

"Where is everybody?"

"Ouma and May-June went to the shop. William went with his friends. Your chinas went home. I was told to look after you." Morph puffed his chest out.

"Waking me up is not looking after me," I moaned.

"But you can't sleep the whole day! Let's go play! Please!"

"Okay fine, but you're the crook," I succumbed to his urgings. "I need to pee first."

Morph dashed ahead to his bed, put on his hat and jumped into his takkies like a ninja on a mission. Freshly relieved I checked and locked the back door first.

"Let's play on the verandah. You know what Ouma said about dirtying inside."

"Awwh! But inside is so much fun."

"The verandah's part of the house, so we'll be inside and outside. We also can't play in the sun. It's too hot."

"Okay then. But how can we play on there when we can't hide?" asked Morph, surveying our proposed area of battle.

"We can hide behind the verandah walls if we need to, but no further."

"Okay then."

"Hey! Let's divide the verandah and have a shoot out!"

"How?"

"We'll put a row of chairs here in the middle. You'll be that side of the verandah and I'll be this side. First one to get shot ten times loses! You're not allowed to double shoot. Only one shot at a time. Okay?"

"Yippee! Let's fetch the chairs, then." Morph buzzed back into the house.

We set the chairs in place, then hung a blanket over them to afford us some cover.

"Ready, steady, go!" I commanded.

We crept through our lands stealthily.

"Bang! I got you, Plano! I got you!" Morph jumped up and down with glee.

I went down dramatically, holding one hand over my heart and the other over my head as I crumbled to the ground. It was customary at home to always allow the younger brother to win a few games, otherwise the entire contest ends too quickly. The added joy in letting Morph win some was to see the delight on his face. I waited patiently for him to stop giggling.

"Ready! Steady! Go!" We were off again, creeping covertly into position.

"Bang! Got you, Morph!" I yelled.

Morph was scaling the verandah wall when I shot him. Forgetting that he was straddling the low wall, he clutched his heart with both hands and rolled off it. At that precise moment Grandma and May-June entered the yard, each carrying a bucket filled with flowers, just in time to witness this spectacle. Reality dawned on my brother when he was halfway down, and he managed an "Oww!" before the flowerbed knocked the wind out from him in a loud "Whoosh!" The silence was punctured at first by a soft groan, followed by a wailing sound. Grandma and May-June hastened to put their buckets on the verandah while I rushed straight to my brother's aid. I checked Morph's arms and legs. Nothing broken.

I turned him gently over to check his head. No cuts, just bruises and a nice bump on the side of his head where he hit the ground. Grandma knelt next to Morph and cradled him as he cried even louder at the indignation of falling off the verandah wall.

"It's not that bad, Morph. Shush, my child," Grandma consoled him.

"It…it…its brooooooken!" cried Morph.

"Your head can't break, Morph. It's as hard as rocks," I encouraged him.

"It's broooken! I'm broooken!"

"Come on, Morph! You'll be fine! At least you had a soft landing in the flowerbed." May-June tried to comfort him.

"Ooouma!" Morph's siren prevailed. Grandma held Morph and consoled him.

"Feeling better?"

"I'm hurting and I'm sad," moaned Morph, snuggling deeper into Grandma's embrace.

"Come then. Let's go inside. I'll clean you up and see to your war wounds, while May-June and Plano prepare lunch for us." Grandma and Morph stood up and we walked onto the verandah. I took the two buckets of flowers to the kitchen.

"Let's go inside. We need to hurry. May-June and I need to go for more flowers for tomorrow. We're going to help do the arranging for Sunday's Service."

"Even me, Ouma?" exclaimed Morph in excitement, tears and pain seemingly all gone.

"Well, I can't leave the two alone tomorrow. There's no telling what else you may destroy. But you're to stay out of the vestry this time," chided Grandma playfully.

"Why, Ouma?" Morph asked innocently.

"Remember drinking some of the wine the last time, Morph Christian Anderson Delvaux? And you said drinking more of it was supposed to make you more holy."

"It was so yucky. It made me sick and stinky the whole day." Morph pulled a face.

"Now you don't want that again. So don't drink the wine."

"Yes, we mustn't. Okay, Plano?" He looked at me for support. I smiled and nodded. I left them in the passage, cleared the verandah and locked the front door. It had become part of our routine to lock up ever since those men from the mob and the Homeboys came calling.

That afternoon all our friends joined us in our yard for a game of 'Gosha'. It is loosely based on cricket rules, but without bats and a hard ball. The original name of the game was 'Gotcha' and in time it evolved to its present moniker. The major differences were that you had to kick a football-sized ball bowled to you and run like crazy with your surviving team members to amass points. The opposing team tried to bowl you and your team out through a miss-kick or a catch and they tried to hit you with the ball while running between the end zones. A game of Gosha could last an entire day, such was the fun we had. Grandma called time on the game at precisely four, because William had an important appointment to keep.

His friends and I were to tag along with him as his bodyguards and to render much needed moral support. William was spruced up and smelled fresh amongst his rough-hewn friends, Jan, Byron, and Naveen. I followed in their wake. We were on a mission this hot afternoon. Grandma had given her blessings for William to ask Ella's mom and dad for permission to take their daughter to the New Year's Eve Dance to be held at the Forderville Community Hall. My brother's friends teased him mercilessly as we hurried along Harding Street, across the Little Bushmans River Bridge and left into Canna Street.

We knew the family well and the immense struggles they had overcome. Ella's parents were in an unusual marriage in that Uncle UJ was a Tamil and Aunty Rejoice (Thembi) was a Zulu. They previously lived in Inanda until August 1985 when they were forced to flee for their lives. On 09 August 1985 hundreds of young Zulu men went on the rampage through Inanda and Phoenix, beating up Indians, ransacking their homes and businesses and torching their buildings. It was a terrifying night of violence that left at least fifty-five people dead. The mobs eventually reached the Mahatma Gandhi Phoenix Centre, where they rampaged through the settlement that housed a self-help community for both Zulus and Asians. The place was pillaged, books and pictures destroyed, furniture and windows smashed and one of the buildings and a school set alight. Indians had to use live ammunition to defend themselves and to repel the onslaught. More than 1500 Indians were displaced in one night of hatred. It is said that Uncle UJ and Aunty Rejoice were one of the first houses to be attacked. They had no chance to escape from the screaming and chanting mob. Uncle UJ was dragged outside where he was beaten mercilessly and left for dead, while in their shattered home men took turns to violate Aunty Rejoice in her bedroom. The mob soon hurried on to wreak more havoc and left the couple where they lay beaten and immobile.

Fortunately, a young Zulu businessman who knew the couple passed by and saw Uncle UJ laying, bloodied and lifeless in the street. He rushed them to Addington Hospital. That Good Samaritan saved several Indians that night. He risked his own life by going back into Phoenix to help those who needed to escape. Uncle UJ and Aunty Rejoice never returned to Phoenix. Another Good Samaritan helped them relocate to Estcourt, where they were given a house in Forderville. Uncle UJ was employed at the Vehicle Testing Ground and Aunty Rejoice was hired at Forderville Primary School as a cleaner.

Canna Street is a long, busy uphill climb that easily drains energy from those in haste. Our pace naturally slowed down because we knew how to walk this busy road. I also suspected that William was deliberately slowing due to his nerves. You could swear William was being led to the French guillotine. His steady gait with stiff arms looked hysterically funny. Even while being ripped to shreds about his walk, William did not change his resolute tread.

Many of the streets off Canna Street had names of flowers. By some wild twist of fortune, Byron looked at the sign showing Mimosa

Street, "Hey, bro! You haven't got flowers! You gotta have flowers for the stukkie!"

"I agree with boet here. Ladies love flowers. It'll soften them," added Jan ebulliently.

"But I've no money to buy flowers and where'll I get them now?" William's plaintive pleading was met with silence.

"I gotta plan, and all!" declared Naveen, before plucking a bunch of dahlias. These he handed to me to carry.

"Wow, Navs! You're sharp!" marveled Jan at his brazen ingenuity.

"My turn," declared Byron. He bent to tie his shoelaces next to a flowerbed that brightened the pedestrian walkway. When he stood up, he held some white St Joseph lilies, still with their bulbs attached. He placed them in my arms.

"There you go!" he declared as he dusted his hands together.

Jan took out his pocketknife. "You can't take them looking like that, boet. I'll fix them."

And so, as we walked and chatted, our intrepid thieves grew the bunch of assorted flowers and Jan chopped and trimmed and sometimes discarded some of them. By the time we reached the corner of Bougainvillea Street a brightly colored bunch of flowers, with generally leafless stems, was in place. The white baby-breaths added beautiful contrast to the varied colors, but we weren't done yet. "We need some greenery. It must have some greenery," Naveen declared. He dashed off and returned with some ferns.

Byron went on his way and returned with a bunch of stinging nettles. "Oww! Oww! Oww!" he cried wailing towards me to hand over his pain-inducing blossoms.

"No!" I shouted and ran a few steps away from him. "That's stinging nettle! Throw it away!" I urged Byron. He hastily flung the offending flora into the road channel. There already was a nasty red rash on both his forearms and hands.

"Oww!" Byron cried as he hopped from one foot to the other and held out his arms, palms facing downwards. "Yoh! It's stinging! Ow!" he cried in desperation.

William turned to me. "How do you know about the plant, Plano?"

"Neville's mom has it in her garden. She uses it to make her medicines."

"What the fuck must I do to sort it out? It stings like hell!" Byron was traumatized.

"Don't touch it. You'll make it worse. You must get medicine for it," I urged him.

"Let's pour water on it. Maybe it'll wash out some of those thorns," suggested Jan.

"It's itching like hell!" cried Byron, hands red with pimples and whitish blisters.

"I dunno. I once saw Neville use sellotape to remove the tiny thorns," I volunteered.

"Where the fuck must I get sellotape now?!"

"Aunty! Aunty! Uncle! Help! Please!" Naveen called out as he opened the nearest gate and walked brazenly towards the door. Byron followed hastily with arms stretched out like Frankenstein. A wizened, grey-haired old Indian lady came out of the house.

"Please can we use your tap to wash my friend's hands, and all?" Naveen pleaded.

"Whaaaad happened?" the old lady asked.

"He got a funny rash. Maybe he's allergic to something," Naveen lied.

"Shaaaame. Come in and let's see what I can do." Byron and Neville rushed indoors.

Jan turned to us. "You guys better carry on. We'll wait here for you to come back."

"Okay. Shup," William responded.

"Good luck, boet!" Jan called.

We trudged resolutely onwards. It was not long before laughter burst forth at the memory of Byron's antics with the stings from the nettles, but this was short-lived for we spied Ella's home on the corner of Canna and Hibiscus Streets.

"Here we are, Plano." William took a deep breath. This was the first time he had to put himself through serious stress for the sake of a girl and he was freaking out.

"Must I wait outside for you?" I volunteered.

"No, no. Come in. I can't carry the flowers now. I'll drop them." He wiped his brow and pulled and straightened his clothes. He even took out a small comb and proceeded to tidy his hair. Never in my life had I ever seen him preen himself this much. After finally completing this sprucing up to his satisfaction, we walked through the gate, and along the short pathway. William knocked on the door. It did not take long before Uncle UJ opened it. He was barefoot, wearing shorts and a vest. The contrast between his and William's attire was striking.

"William? Plano? What a surprise! Come in! Come in!" he enthused. Uncle UJ was never slow on the uptake. He quickly took in William's dandy garb and the bunch of flowers. His eyes widened, but he kept his cool.

"Rejoice!" he called out over his shoulder. "Come! William and Plano are here!"

"Coming!" Aunty Rejoice responded cheerfully.

Uncle UJ had been clipping his toenails and so he took his seat and picked up a small, red-handled plant pruning shears and lifted his right foot onto the sofa where he was seated. He jabbed the pruning shears in William's direction.

"Why're you all dressed up? And for who you brought flowers?" he barked at William.

"They're for me. Oh! What a beautiful bunch. Thanks, William."

I proffered the flowers to Aunty Rejoice's eagerly advancing hands. She scooped them up and headed straight back in the direction she came from.

"Be with you now, now boys!" Aunty Rejoice called, disappearing into the kitchen.

"Ella! she called. "Come sort out this beautiful bunch of flowers we got from William!"

We could hear mother and daughter whisper and laugh excitedly beyond the closed door. William sat as stiff as a board. I slinked into the furthest chair away from him and sat still and quiet. My seat was closest to the man with the deadly weapon.

Uncle UJ looked at William then proceeded to cut a portion of nail off his big toe. The swishing snip of the shears was followed by the flash of a missile that shot in an arc almost across the room to land near

William's feet. Unperturbed, Uncle UJ glared at William again as if daring him to say something. William gulped a few times and leaned ever so slightly away from the dormant appendage. Aunty Rejoice returned and took her seat next to Uncle UJ.

"How're you boys and how's the family?" she asked cheerfully.

"We're fine. They're fine, thanks," William and I responded. It sounded as though William's voice was going to shatter into a million pieces at any moment. Another piece of nail swished across the lounge. This time it landed on my head.

"So, tell us William. Why the visit?" Another piece of toenail arced through the air to land on the coffee table.

"I... I... came to ask... May I...may I...take Forderville to the Ella Dance on New Year's Eve?" William blurted out.

"WHAT?!" blasted Uncle UJ loudly. That caused William to jump sharply.

"He wants to take Ella to the New Year's Eve Dance," chimed Aunty Rejoice.

William nodded vigorously. He had an ally in Aunty Rejoice.

"OVER MY DEAD BODY!" roared Uncle UJ as he jabbed the shears like a swordsman at William. My brother jumped again halfway out of his seat.

"Sit, William!" urged Aunty Rejoice. She turned to her husband. "Think about it, my love!" In response another shard of toenail flew and landed on Aunty Rejoice's shoulder. She left it in place and calmly continued. "Ella is grown up now and should be allowed to go out with friends. Good friends."

"Ja, but..." Uncle UJ spluttered.

"No buts, Ujjwal. You know William and the family. They're good people. I'll trust our daughter with him. He's far better than the other rubbishes who've been trying their luck with Ella." She tenderly rubbed Uncle UJ's thigh as she spoke.

"Then I'll have to call everybody and tell them about Ella and... HIM!" Uncle UJ sort of spat out the last word in William's direction, as he again jabbed the sharp pointed weapon at my brother. He then proceeded to vigorously assault his toenails: varying shards flew all over the room in assorted trajectories.

William continued to nod his head in agreement with everything Auntie Rejoice said while he ducked left and right. "No need to do that, my husband. He's not asking for marriage proposal. Only to go to the dance."

"And what about Ella? Did anyone ask her? She could say no." Uncle UJ managed to bring forth with a mixture of hope and glee. Snip, whoosh.

"Ella is happy to go with William, but they need your permission." Aunty Rejoice looked at William encouragingly. "You can see what a good boy William is. He came all the way to ask you himself and he even brought flowers."

Uncle UJ completed cutting his toenails. He picked up a piece of fine sandpaper and proceeded to file his knobby appendages that looked like Nik-Naks.

"Then this is only for one dance?!" he asked and demanded simultaneously.

"Just one dance, my dear. Who knows? If they like each other, maybe they'll go out again." Aunty Rejoice was clearing the debris out of Uncle UJ's pathway.

Uncle UJ tried to force words out from his bobbing Adam's apple and opened mouth in an apoplectic outburst, but none would surface coherently.

Aunty Rejoice held his arm tenderly. "It'll be okay, my love. If you say no, then you don't trust your own daughter. She doesn't deserve that. She's always been a blessing to us."

Uncle UJ swallowed hard a few times. Aunty Rejoice must have seen some him relenting. She said, "Are you okay with it?"

Uncle UJ nodded. Aunty Rejoice sighed and beamed in a broad smile.

"It's settled, then. William, we give you permission to take our Ella to the dance."

Uncle UJ burst the bubble soon after. "She's our only child and she's very precious to us!" he shouted at William as he jabbed sandpaper at him. "If you harm her in any way, William! Any way! I'll hunt you down and I'll waste you! … Waste you!" He jabbed the sandpaper at William so vigorously that it flew out of his hand and landed on the coffee table. Aunty Rejoice calmly picked it up and handed it back to her spouse.

I had a brief vision of Uncle UJ sanding all the skin off William. I quickly had to suppress these morbidly funny thoughts.

"I understand, Sir. I'll look after Ella with my life."

It's settled, then. William you may take Ella to the dance."

"You bring her back home BY TWELVE!" commanded Uncle UJ ferociously.

"Let's say one, my love. The main reason for the dance is to welcome in the New Year. That's at twelve. Please give them an hour more?" Aunty Rejoice cajoled Uncle UJ as she continued to rub his thigh.

"Okay, then! But if they are one minute late, he'll deal with me!"

"We'll be back before one Uncle UJ, Aunty Rejoice." William found his voice now that the battle was waning. We hastily stood up to go home, but Aunty Rejoice stopped us.

"Wait, boys! I've got a jar of pickles for Ouma." She stood up and walked towards the kitchen. "I'll also call Ella to make arrangements with you and to say goodnight." We stood and waited. Uncle UJ did not say another word as he sandpapered his toenails into oblivion.

The outside air was a welcome relief from the intensity of that lounge. I waited patiently with the jar of pickles at the gate for William and Ella to say their goodbyes. Once out of the gate, William and I ran down the road as if being chased by a vicious Dobermann. We found William's friends where we had left them. Byron's hands and arms were heavily smeared with Calamine lotion. The quick journey home was filled with light-hearted banter – notwithstanding the fact that we now traversed a relatively steep downhill.

As we turned into Rocky Lane, William and I paused for long while to watch an awe-inspiring spectacle taking place within the valley before us. Swifts, hawks, bats, and other unrecognizable species of birds had put aside their differences to collectively feed from a sumptuous meal of flying ants, mosquitos and other insects. We witnessed a cacophony of clicks and squeaks and squeals and cries within a swirling mass of beating wings and tethered feathers. Because Rocky Lane stood a bit higher than the valley, these creatures swooped low over our heads as they flew and glided to and from the valley.

"Wow!" William whispered in awe. I could not speak, and only kept looking.

The man with the brown suede shoes stood silently in the deep shadows of the school yard. His chosen position was such that there were no distinctive silhouettes or shadows visible from any direction. His breathing was light and measured and his chest barely moved. He had learnt years ago how to allow his stomach muscles to help him breathe quietly. He watched intently as William and Plano walked homeward and paused on Rocky Lane to look at the birds. The man paid these flying creatures no mind.

His employers had asked him to recon the family and their home to find out more about them. Especially the second boy, who unwittingly ventured into the large-scale planning so painstakingly put into place over time. He had to memorize their faces and routines. The man earlier followed Grandma and May-June home and had watched the children at play. He did not follow the boys to Forderville, settling in the school yard knowing that they would return. He averted his eyes when Plano turned to look in the school yard's direction. It did not take long for Plano to turn back to the birds flying above. The moment was lost in the nighttime air.

At the Combrink home, Joe sat alone in his study in the semi-dark nursing a glass of brandy and contemplating his options. He was a bitter man because of his wife's betrayal, screwing around with Eric Walton for God knows how long, and he was a troubled man knowing that any wrong move from him would lead to the demise of his entire family. He had no illusions when he agreed to serve as lawyer to the three men. As their business relationships progressed, his realization that these men were vicious and cold-blooded with no scruples filled him with abject fear, although he did not show this to those around him. Joe knew there was no way out of the sorry mess he had pushed himself into. He tried to protect his family.

What disturbed Joe today was noticing that he was being tailed by a group of men and women. They were good but made the mistake of not changing their clothes over a two-day period. Joe was an excellent lawyer with a photographic memory and this little mistake caused him to pay more attention to them. Even though Estcourt was a medium to large town, people in the smaller communities still generally knew each other. Strangers were often noticed quickly. They were six in total, with two different cars to tail him. At least three of them would be near him when he was not in his office or at home. Joe had long ago suspected that his phones were bugged and used these carefully. It was odd that a stranger, professing to be a cop, contacted him out of the blue to request that they meet urgently to discuss important issues.

Initially, Joe curtly told the man to get lost, but he was persistent. At one point he even shared with Joe some private information about the Butcher, Baker and Candlestick Maker. He had thought of discussing the strange enquiry with his masters, but he knew they would demand facts from him. Information that he was not yet privy to. *Hell!* Joe thought, *"I don't even know the man's name and what he looks like. How do I explain him to the three bosses?"*

Joe deliberated on the possibility that this was a trap set by his bosses. He shuddered at the thought. His thought of his parents and how they adored him. If only they knew the truth. Joe took a sip of brandy and returned to his dilemma. *Don't meet him and I could go to jail as an accomplice or be killed. Go and I could be implicated by my bosses and be killed,* he mused.

The common denominator was being killed. He knew that all three of his bosses would not hesitate to have him murdered if they believed he was jeopardizing their plans in any way. His stomach tightened and his temples throbbed as he ruminated. He took another sip of brandy. The view of his manicured lawn, flowerbeds and trees outside his study always calmed him, but not today. Joe turned off the lights in his study and sat in darkness, drinking brandy. As the level in the bottle decreased, so the optimism drained from him.

· · ·

Ewald and Eric met in the usual place. Ewald went to a cabinet recessed into the wall. He returned with a bottle of Glenfiddich and two glasses. Eric watched as he silently poured the walnut-colored liquid into the glasses. Ewald passed one on to Eric then took his seat. They sat quietly sipping the alcohol. For a while only the steady hum of the air conditioner was heard in the office. The men digested the booze and thought of the way forward.

"Still nothing from those fuckers, Faizel and Joe. They're going about business as usual. I still don't trust that bastard coolie. He's a snake," Eric hissed.

"I've also not found anything. But it's too late to stop the operation. If they're trying something, shit would be flying by now."

"Blood will flow. Blood will flow for them if they try some shit," added Eric.

"We'll have to be careful. If we spook Faizel, there's no telling what that cunt'll do. There's no telling what he's doing to us already. But there's no evidence he's screwing us, so we must tolerate him for now. He's key to our support from Africa and the Middle East."

"Fair enough. We'll dig and see what the fuck comes up," Eric responded.

"Do you think Faizel will be able to deliver Joe to us on a platter?" Ewald asked pensively. He inhaled his whiskey appreciatively and took a sip. The imagery of the head of John the Baptist on another platter was not lost on Eric,

"He'd better, or else we could be fucking screwed big time."

"By paying him out, are we really buying his silence?"

"Yes, that's what we're bloody paying for," insisted Eric.

"Or he wants out?" Ewald took another sip of whiskey.

"Not on his fucking life! He knows too much."

"That man can sell us down the river many times over, either way!" continued Ewald.

"We'll have to bloody well silence him," Eric said with finality.

"You give the bloody order and it'll be done."

"We've made inroads in South Africa and on the continent. Our colleagues, especially the bigshots in the government and in Europe, have lined up some lucrative mining opportunities here and in Africa.

We're talking about Equatorial Guinea, Central African Republic, Ivory Coast and Senegal. There may also be a stake in shipping oil from Nigeria. The deals are all in place if we can pull it off."

"We'll bloody well pull it off, just as long as we're not the fucking schmucks when it goes down," Eric said dryly. He cupped the glass in both hands.

"We're smarter than them."

CHAPTER 10
DANGEROUS DILEMMAS
(SATURDAY, 18 DECEMBER 1999)

After breakfast we congregated on the verandah in happy discussion about buying Christmas presents. Grandma and May-June were seated on the bench, William and Morph reclined on the verandah wall in front of the two ladies and I was on the side wall from which Morph tumbled dramatically into the flowerbed.

"How much do we get this year for presents?" I asked.

"R150 per gift, but we can add from pocket money if short," May-June clarified.

"Remember last month we agreed not to go higher than R200 per person." William added. We nodded in agreement.

"What did you get me? What did you get me?" Morph tried his luck.

"We can't tell, Morph. Then it won't be a surprise," May-June responded firmly.

"Don't go looking. It's locked away. The key stays around my neck," Grandma warned.

May-June smiled in agreement with Grandma and as a co-conspirator with William and me. Grandma was unaware that her gifts were already well hidden in the garage. Unbeknownst to May-June, hers were also safely ensconced in the same cupboard.

"I know a secret!" Morph suddenly sang out, bouncing up and down where he sat.

"If you're a tattle tale, then no New Year's present for you," William warned Morph with a wag of his finger. Morph was the only one who received a 'present' on New Year's Day. It could even be a lollipop or something like it bribe him not to spill the beans before Christmas Day, for he could reveal everything at the tiniest nudge in that direction, especially when promised a reward. The promise of another gift after Christmas always bought his silence.

We discussed William needing new clothes for the New Year's Dance. William turned beet-red at being the sudden center of attention until Grandma gave him her Ackermans' card and a note.

"Thanks, Ouma. I'll go with my friends just now."

"We'll be going to the Church to help with flowers for Sunday," Grandma continued.

"And us too, Ouma!" Morph exclaimed.

"Yes. You two scamps will come with us."

"You sure, Ouma? Them together are worse than the Y2K virus," William warned.

"Is not!" Morph and I responded quickly.

"I've been hearing about that Y2K stuff. Do you think it'll affect us?" asked Grandma.

"No. The government and all other companies have already sorted their systems out for the millennium changes," William responded reassuringly.

"What is a milelinum?" Morph enquired. We burst out laughing.

"Millennium. It's when a thousand years passes. We have lived in the 1000's and we are going to the 2000's." I volunteered.

"Does that make me older than I am?" Consternation spread across Morph's face.

"No. It's just the way a thousand years are counted," May-June reassured Morph.

"So, I don't have to add a thousand years to my age?" Morph had us in stitches.

"No, Morph. Its normal counting. What comes after ninety-nine?" asked Grandma.

"One hundred!"

"The years are the earth's birthday from the time that it was counted after Jesus died. He died 2000 years ago." Grandma concluded.

"Oh! Okay, then." Morph replied.

It was then that I saw the shoeprint. It was in the place where Morph landed yesterday. A left shoe of nondescript pattern, at least a size ten. William picked up my sudden tensing.

"What's it, Plano?" he asked sharply.

"I dunno," I responded. "There's a shoeprint here that was not here yesterday. I know because I raked up where Morph landed." My family walked over to view the shoeprint.

"Remember the yard was full of your friends yesterday. Any one of those big galoots could've done this," Grandma suggested. May-June and Morph nodded in agreement.

"Doesn't look like any of my chommie's shoes," William observed.

"None of mine, also" I added, folding my arms tightly into my chest.

"Whoever it is, we'll catch them. No one broke in; nothing was stolen. Boys, go check the garage and outbuilding." Grandma took charge. William and I did so. Nothing wrong or missing. All we found was a jersey. Probably left there by one of Morph's friends. I took it and the rake to the verandah where William reported our findings to Grandma.

"Okay, let's not read too much into it. Rake it up, William. From now on don't leave anything outside that could be stolen. Always make sure the front and back doors are locked and talk to me if you see anything wrong." Grandma and May-June could not mask the worry. Our happy mood was over. We hurried indoors and William locked the door behind us.

St Matthews Anglican Church on the corner of Connor and Lorne Streets remained an enigma to me in my youth, both a joyous and tragic place. A gathering of fellowship and rejoicing that housed long dead families. We were allowed in the Church and most of the yard but forbidden play in the graveyard. We could laugh and play outside the Church but had to be quiet near the graveyard. Happy memories of baptisms and Sunday school and confirmation conjoined with the coffins of our parents and Grandpa and others dearly departed.

The Church building was small yet imposing, with gothic-styled arches and soaring windows raising steeply up a faded grey slate tiled roof. The walls were light brown cut sandstone blocks all the way up to the roof and bell tower. Some of the windows were decorated with pious and angelic stained glass ghostly artistry. We walked up Connor Street and along the gabion packed fence topped off with black wrought iron palisade fencing enhanced with white crosses. The main entrance was shielded by these imposing dark wood double doors with beautifully crafted stained glass cross insets. Instinctively, we stepped into pious quietness within the cold interior of dark wood pews, railing, organ and most holy altar. I found the sound of the organ was the most enthralling, abiding memory of St Matthews' – it led us through all the trials and tribulations that graced the interior of this ancient Church.

May-June and I lugged the four buckets of flowers to the vestry at the back of the Church. Morph and I hastily retreated from the bustle of ladies who flitted from the vestry into the nave, to avoid being dragged into running errands for them. We peeped into the nave and saw four young white children playing in the aisles while their mothers decorated the sanctuary.

They saw us but paid us no mind. Morph and I decided not to tempt the wrath of Grandma by joining these children at play. Our natural inclination was to play closer to the Church building than to those light grey and gloomy sentinels of headstones flitting in stillness within the light of the sun between the dark shadows of the dark trees. A few birds and butterflies went about their business amongst the tombs.

"Those Boere are naughty," I pronounced with a measure of piety.

"Yeah! Ouma would'a skin us alive if we did that!" Trust Morph to get to the nitty-gritty of it all. I remembered that our choices of play were limited.

"Let's walk around first and see what's up," I said without much enthusiasm.

Our stroll carried us casually past the main entrance and then to the Lorne Street side. We paused awhile to marvel at a long goods train that chugged by across the way and to count cars and trucks whizzing behind it. The furthest end of the yard beyond where the holy altar and holy sanctuary stood was dark, damp and dreary and smelled of rotting vegetation. Our lethargic wanderings perked up sufficiently for us to cross that divide fleet footed. We slowed again to a casual stroll to pass the Vestry entrance.

"Come, Morph, let's play on the kiddies stuff," I suggested. These were designed for children younger than us, but we were bored and there was not much else to do. I played on the jungle gym and practiced hanging head down from the monkey bars while Morph occupied himself with the slide. He got bored quickly and joined me in a new game. We chased each other all over the jungle gym while dangling and swinging from bar to bar. The idea was to catch your opponent within the entanglement of your legs, shake him loose and drop him to the ground. Two of the boys exited the Church to join us. No introductions were made. It was them against us. They were of the same age as Morph and I, so we were evenly matched.

"Stay behind me, Morph!" I cautioned him. "These boeties are both going after you at the same time. I'll take out the big one and you go for the lightie."

"Shup!" Morph responded.

Each team tried to maneuver into an attacking position without engaging in our warfare. Then it just so happened that we congregated on one side of the jungle gym and the rusted moorings below us that anchored it in place all these years gave way. The jungle gym rolled with us on it and came to rest with a tangle of arms and legs protruding in every direction.

"Oh, my arm!" someone shouted.

"Oh, my leg!" someone else shouted.

"I'm stuck!" I shouted.

"Ouma! Ouma!" Morph screamed at the top of his voice.

We moaned and groaned as the aproned horde of bustling ladies descended upside down upon us in a cacophony of shrieks. It took at least ten minutes for them to extricate us one by one from the entanglement of buckled steel tubing.

Nothing broken, just cuts, scrapes and bruises. Aunty Kay used Band Aid to plaster up the more severe wounds with much shushing and clucking. After the last of us was sufficiently patched up she declared ever so diplomatically in her very English accent, "At least it fell with these boys in it. Did you see how rusty those bars and hooks are? What would've happened if there were small babies and kiddies in it? The ladies murmured their agreement and threatened us with death and destruction if we ventured close again.

"I'll put a sign up for no one to play on the jungle gym and will ask the Lay Minister to warn parents that it's broken." Aunty Kay hurried off, while the ladies returned to their chores.

The chastened four of us went to cower within the dark confines of the bell tower where we discussed our intrepid adventure and excitedly compared war wounds. The older boy's name was Timmy and the younger was Sebastien. Our walk home with Grandma and May-June was painful from both the damages we had sustained and from the indignation of being teased. It came to light that our delightful sister had merrily taken photos of us on Grandma's cellphone while we were stuck. They almost forgot to prepare supper; such was all the fun they had at our expense. I needed to remind them to please prepare the meal when the first hunger pangs reminded me that I needed to eat or die. I reminded them of one of Grandpa's sayings. "Shame on them! You don't kick a man when he is down!" It did not stop them teasing us.

The sun was beginning to wane along the hills leading to the Drakensberg, yet the stinging heat relented. The meeting was scheduled to happen casually on a private farm that was soaked in early 1900 with the blood of the fallen who waged war during the Battle of Vaal Kranz. A graveyard of monuments remain to bear testimony to the third failed attempt by the British to liberate Ladysmith from the Boers. The men and their sons who congregated on the farm this day were not there for a history lesson, but rather for bass fishing – one of the most addictive sports in South Africa. They displayed all the appropriate gear with them: fisherman's hat; silicone skirts; fishing rods; reels, assortment of lures; tackle boxes; the works. The cooler bags chilled an assortment of beers, cold-drinks and spring water.

Superintendent Carel van den Beek was Afrikaans, whereas Joe Combrink was English. The meeting seemed to be spontaneous, just members of two families perchance on a guest farm at the same time. When Joe and Hermann approached the silver-grey waters of the pristine dam, Carel and his thirteen-year-old son, Reinhardt, were already waist deep in the water, trying to outthink these m elusive fish. Carel was at least 2 m tall and muscular, while Reinhardt was a smaller and younger version of his father. Joe and Hermann stood at the edge of the rippling water and observed the two in action. They were probably as good as the Combrinks, who had cast many a line in dams and rivers with great success.

"Hi!" Joe called. The two turned from their exertions to glance at the new arrivals.

"Hi!" father and son responded.

"Caught anything?"

"Ja. Five small ones that we released and one five-point-five kg that's in our net. Oberholzer said they'll braai the ones above five kg's," the father said, before turning quickly to concentrate on a feint movement on his line.

"Yeah! We'll go that side and try from there" Joe responded.

"Ja. Ok. See you," Carel answered absent-mindedly.

Joe and Hermann suited up, baited their hooks and got to work. Soon the trials and tribulations of the world were forgotten. Hermann groaned in frustration when he lost a big one.

"Look, Pa!" Reinhardt called and pointed ahead. The four of them paused to witness in awe as a Fish Eagle dived swiftly and steeply to scoop up a huge bass along the other end of the dam and rise majestically into open sky, calling hauntingly in the distinctive sound of Africa to the world around it. There was a sudden flurry of birds as they seemed to realise how close one of them came to being devoured. The sight of the Fish Eagle hunting never failed to amaze.

"Drop it here!" Hermann muttered softly at the rapidly departing bird. Joe smiled at his son. The birds around the dam soon returned to their normal activities. Not even a flock of Lappet Faced Vultures flying high in the sky on their way back to the mountains could deter them from their chirping, feeding and scavenging.

The water's edge furthest away from the fishermen was never quiet with an assortment of birds and small animals venturing to its shore to drink deeply from its clear and cool freshness. At any given time a menagerie of Giant Kingfishers, Black Shouldered Kites, Swallows, and Crowned Guinea Fowl darted to the dam to quench thirsts and just as quickly disappeared into the bushes and shrubbery, calling out in their varied sounds to all and sundry.

The two families even observed a Porcupine and two Spring Hare make brief appearances to quench their thirsts. As the sun grew closer to setting, larger animals started to make an appearance. The first were two Secretary Birds with long black quills dangling from their heads stepped gingerly into the water, carefully scanned their surroundings and then drank their fill. They flew off beyond view. These were followed shortly after by a small herd of Common Duiker and loudly grunting Impala who seemed to voice their objections at the presence of humans within their sacred place.

The loud, aggressive barks of a large troop of Chacma Baboons somewhere in the bush had an immediate reaction on the humans. These primates were on their way back to their sleeping places on the Vaal Kranz and would pause on their journey at one of the dams to drink their fill. They seemed to be warning all and sundry to get out of their way or be ripped to pieces. The men knew that other, bigger game would also shortly appear; they packed away their gear and their catches and took their leave. Formal introductions were made and casual discussions were had as they strolled in the dusk back to their guest cottages at the farmhouse.

In their preoccupation they failed to notice a 2 m long rinkhals pause in fear next to a fully bloomed Pineapple Lilly. Hermann stepped within a half a meter from this venomous serpent and his exposed leg made the snake recoil sharply, ready to strike. The humans moved on and were already a few steps past it when the reptile raised its head and puffed out its hood in a show of bravado before it decided that the threat was past and hastily slithered across the gravel road towards the dam. Such are the fine margins in the African bushveld.

If the snake did strike, the events of the rest of the meeting and the days still to unfold would have taken a different course, but it did not and so the evening unraveled as was roughly planned. The two adults knew that danger lurked constantly in the wild and alertness to potential calamities should be the norm within these wild environments.

Joe and Carel were seated on Oberholzer's deep verandah, ice cold beers at hand. The fish were on the braai being attended to by the farmer's son, Sakkie. Oberholzer and Tannie Rina could be heard chatting away in Afrikaans somewhere indoors. Hermann and Reinhardt were in their respective cottages freshening up. Carel had tufts of blond hair near his temples, otherwise he was bald. The handlebar mustache perfectly framed his slightly pug nose and strong, shaved jawline. Carel's head never stopped moving when he spoke. He always pointed his chin forward as an exclamation mark when making a salient point.

"How long will you be staying?" Carel queried in a deep, guttural voice.

"Until after lunch tomorrow. You?" Joe took a sip from his beer bottle.

"We'll be leaving after breakfast." Carel sipped away while his eyes roved constantly over all before him, registering every detail. He was also keenly observing Joe.

The men paused, listening to the cacophony of frogs and crickets vying to own the sounds of the night. The louder calls of night feeders rose above the somewhat melodious drone within the yard to remind the world they were out there somewhere in the dark night.

"Why all the secrecy? What's this meeting about?" Joe queried.

"We've reason to believe a massive treason, fraud and corruption plot is going down. Your three bosses from Estcourt are involved big time. Masterminds of one of the wings of this organization. I'm heading up the investigation for the Scorpions, Special Ops, to investigate."

Carel turned to face Joe. "What do you know about the Vulintaba Manifesto?"

Joe sat frozen in place and did not respond. He took a while to digest these shocking revelations from this cop and to buy time and swallowed a few long drinks from his bottle. Carel was not fooled. Joe's reaction spoke volumes.

"You can check up on me. But be very careful. I've a team of eleven assisting me. We've gone two years so far without any breakthrough. Nobody's talking about this Manifesto. Only a file we have with too little hard evidence to arrest them." Carel sat back in his chair.

"Unfortunately, we also have evidence about a Mrs. Combrink and a Mr. Eric Walton I can show you." Carel seemed embarrassed. He took a bit of time to clear his throat and then sip from his bottle. Joe waited until Carel was settled before speaking.

"Are you trying to blackmail me?" Joe leaned forward, suddenly much more alert for any signs of danger from this stranger beside him.

"No! It's so that you have a chance to sort out this mess with this evidence. Maybe get revenge. I just think it's somewhat outside the scope of our investigation. But I can help you if you want to get even."

"Thanks," commented Joe dryly, sitting back in his chair.

"You don't seem surprised?"

"Ja-nee! I found out the hard way." Joe's voice and face were unemotional.

"I'm sorry, man. No one should go through such kak." Carel's sympathy fell flat.

They ceased taking as a Spotted Eagle Owl settled in the semi-darkness in one of the Maple trees that lined the driveway. It swiveled its head this way and that way, seeking out prey. The night breeze briefly changed direction. At the first hint of the acrid smell of fire assailing its senses, the owl lifted off and flew into the darkness. Fruit bats hurried to and fro, sharply avoiding the twirling smoke from the sizzling fire.

"And in return?" Joe asked. "What do you want from me?"

"Your co-operation to nail the bastards involved in the Vulintaba Manifesto plot. What do you know about it?"

"At what price? You know they're going to kill me, no matter what!" Joe spoke bitterly into the darkness in front of him.

"Money is no problem."

"I'm not talking money. Death is also a price." Joe's bitterness was palpable.

"Were not gangsters, Sir." For the first time in their conversation Joe turned to look directly at Carel.

"You're a stranger. How can I trust you?"

"You can also sell me out to your bosses. They have big contacts in the police and government." Carel's turn to speak bitterly.

They paused briefly and sat in their chairs when Sakkie passed them carrying a platter of the braaied fish. The aromas were mouthwatering. Questions and answers flowed rapidly.

"I'm being followed in Estcourt by a group of people. Are they yours?" The harshness in Joe's voice surfaced again.

"No, but we'll check them out and let you know. They must be from your bosses."

"We had to lie and duck them to get here."

"Don't worry, man! My team is guarding the route. No one will get here."

"Do you have a wire?" asked Joe suddenly.

"No. I left my phone in the cottage." Carel stood up and patted himself down firmly before sitting again. "No wires. Do you trust the Oberholzers?"

"With my life. I kept Sakkie out of jail when he was accused of raping a fifteen-year-old Zulu girl. We've built a good friendship ever since. They also hate my bosses, who stole a thriving market from them."

"I'm not asking for info about the Manifesto from you now. You have a day or two to think about it. But please hurry. We need something to go on to stop this madness. We've a broad outline about the Manifesto and we know it's an international syndicate at play. We also know it'll go down before the end of this year. But that's all."

"Okay, fair enough. It's a huge deal and prematurely arresting these three will not stop the planned revolution and full-scale massacres throughout South Africa. It starts on 29th December 1999. Something or someone called "The Catalyst" will be used to trigger a civil war. Now where's the file?"

Carel handed over a bright red memory stick.

"On this memory stick. Trust me. It's been bleached off our server. My boss did it himself. That's how desperate we are."

"Okay. I'll think about it. How do I contact you?"

Carel handed over a card.

"You phone that number and ask for Oupa Pless. They'll say it's a wrong number. Don't worry. I'll contact you."

They continued in earnest discussion while waiting for their sons. In the distance to the south-west they could see the intense, multiple flashes of bright lightning and the faint rumbles of thunder heralding the approach of a huge thunderstorm racing along the edge of Ukahlamba Mountains. The Afrikaans name, Drakensberg, refers to 'a place of dragons.' In some of the silent spaces the two men could faintly, but distinctly, hear the deep rumbling of the uThukela River as it barreled resolutely onwards through deep valleys towards the Indian Ocean. The men did not know the Zulu meanings of the two natural wonders of KwaZulu Natal.

By the time the storm burst overhead, the families were safely ensconced within their cottages. Hermann lay on his bed while Joe changed into his pajamas. Their cellphones were off and stored in their vehicle. These were left there deliberately as soon as the Combrinks reached the farm. Joe explained to Hermann that they should not have any distractions during their father-son time together. Hermann reluctantly acceded. Yet it was suggested by Carel before they took the trip. He warned Joe that his clients may have sophisticated surveillance.

"Uncle Carel and Reinhardt are quite cool. They're full of stories and jokes," Hermann commented between loud lightning strikes and deafening rolls of thunder.

"Yeah. They're cool."

"Do you think we can invite them home?" Hermann tucked his hands under his head.

"No. Not at this stage."

"But why not?"

"First of all, we don't know them that well. And we've not asked them."

"We can at least try?"

"Maybe next year. I'll get contact details from Carel."

"Thanks, Dad. Reinhardt said he has a sister my age. Who knows?"

"Ah! So that's why you want them over, you bugger!"

Hermann smiled in response.

"Son, may I ask you to keep them secret for now?"

"Why?"

"I don't want to mess up this friendship. You know how your friends and their families can react if they know we have new friends?"

"Yes, that's true. They can be quite bitchy about it."

"And it'll mess up your chances with the young lady if those guys find out. You know how they throw their money around to get girls."

"I agree, Dad. Let's keep it our secret for now."

"Thanks, Son." Joe sighed deeply.

The storm was unrelenting in its ferocity. It burst some of the trees on the farm that dared to stand in its path, splitting them from top to bottom and shriveling all bark and leaves away forever. In their home, the Oberholzers sat penitently in their lounge and prayed for salvation from this wrath above them. A week earlier they had witnessed the aftermath of a lightning strike that consumed a hut filled with a family of farmworkers. They smelt the charred remains of burnt flesh carried away by the police, burnt beyond recognition.

The strong winds that ushered in the storm caught us by surprise due to the wholesome jollity that had prevailed within our home. Morph was on a strict regime to take his medication and all of us had forgotten to administer the evening dosages. It was not long after the initial sudden burst from an almighty gust that Morph was rendered virtually incapacitated on the lounge floor, battling to breathe. His chest suddenly began to wheeze and whistle at each shuddering upheaval for air. None of us had picked up on any of the known early symptoms that we were trained to look out for, until it was almost too late. Grandma rushed to give him extra dosages of medicine, plus to use lukewarm water to wash out his nasal passages.

The most comfortable places for Morph during these scary moments was either sitting with his head hanging between his legs while sucking life from his metered dose inhaler, or flat on his back on the lounge floor breathing into a paper packet, surfacing to gulp fresh oxygen into his lungs. This was not the only time we had witnessed Morph's entire body convulse.

The first time we experienced this our parents were still alive. Our parents had to bundle him up and rush with him in the rain to the Clinic near the Town Hall for assistance. The nursing staff put him on a drip for least two hours before he could come home. Grandma had a theory that the strong spring and summer winds sometimes carried with them much higher than normal quantities of pollen that blocked Morph's air passages and that this caused this ultra-allergic reaction. His lips and fingers turned a shade of blue. May-June and I sat on either side of Morph, rubbing his cold and discolored fingers and heaving chest as he rattled heavily on. William and Grandma sat on the sofa. William administered the pump every time we raised Morph into a seated position.

We continued to administer to our brother when the storm hit. We soldiered on, despite terrifying lightning strikes and thunderbolts. Morph breathed as deeply as he could, with mouth wide open. Grandma prayed softly throughout as she kept a keen eye on Morph's progress. It was only after the tail end of the storm passed by that some of Morph's color returned and he was able to sit up. Every time this asthma attack pounced on Morph it devolved him for a while into an incapacitated, debilitating and bedraggled existence, barely holding on to life. It was painful for us to see him like this, doing his best to gulp in much needed air into rasping lungs.

"I want my mommy!" Morph cried weakly, his face matted with perspiration and tears.

William hurriedly picked Morph up and put him onto Grandma's lap. Grandma rocked Morph gently and sang to him, trying to calm him down. Morph just kept crying between labored breaths, "I want my mommy! I want my mommy!"

"Morph, calm down, my child. You're with me. You're safe."

The three of us sat around Morph and Grandma. After what seemed like an eternity Morph's condition improved. William carried him to Grandma's bed. I left the three in the lounge and went to Grandma's bedroom. Morph looked sad even in his sleep. He lay on his side, hands tucked under his head and his knees pulled into his faintly rasping chest. He flinched every now and again. I lay next to Morph for a while, keeping a close eye on him. I promptly fell into a troubled sleep of my own. May-June woke me up. Morph was still in a restless sleep.

"You're talking in your sleep, Plano." I carefully extricated myself from Morph's arms and legs and followed May-June out of the bedroom to join the rest of my family in the lounge.

"We'll have to take him to the clinic on the way to church tomorrow. If he's not well enough to go to church, then I'll stay home with him," Grandma said.

"No, Ouma!" William was decisive. "We must stick together. Either all of us go to church, or we all come home."

"What about Dr. John? Can't he make a house call?" May-June queried, close to tears.

"I don't like troubling him on Sundays. He needs a day off."

I failed to understand why a doctor could not be called for an emergency and voiced my opinion. After all, Dr John came to our home when William was unwell last month.

"I hear you, Plano," Grandma responded. "That was an emergency. We had no money for transport to the hospital or to the surgery. Morph is through the worst. The new medication he was given in 'Maritzburg has worked well. He'll be okay. We've seen him in a worse state. I just want to make sure he's okay. Hopefully I didn't overdose him. Aaaiii, Morph."

"Okay. But we'll have to get up a bit earlier, so we can all go," William concluded. May-June and I nodded.

Before we tucked in for the night, William and I patrolled briefly around our home, with torches in one hand and a panga in the other. The night was peaceful and quiet with the occasional sounds of cars and trucks passing by in the distance. Dogs barked their warnings to their masters and their greetings and discussions to each other. Above us the most distinctive sound of the night hunters were the whirring cadence of the Fiery-necked Nightjars.

"Let's go check the gates," William said. We switched off our torches as we approached the front of our home. It was by some uncanny intuition that we had done so. At the bottom of Rocky Lane a black SUV turned into our street, stopped and switched of their lights.

William and I instinctively moved into deeper shadows to try and avoid detection. My heart began hammering my ribs. No one emerged from the ominous SUV. It stood there as a silent nemesis for at least five minutes, before it reversed and turned down Alfred Street towards the darkness of the valley. It did so without switching on any lights.

William and I exhaled audibly.

"That's big trouble coming."

"I think so, too."

"Must we tell Ouma?"

"Not tonight"

"Okay. We'll have to be very, very careful from now on."

"I agree. We'll have to move around with our friends. We'll also have to go with Ouma, May and Morph whenever they leave the house."

"Ok."

"Let's lock up. Not a word to anyone."

CHAPTER 11
STATEMENTS IN BLOOD
(SUNDAY, 19 DECEMBER 1999)

"William, there's a car outside?" I whispered. William arose swiftly and was out of the room with panga in hand before I could take another breath. I grabbed my panga and followed him into the lounge. We stood away from the window, watched and listened. Lights were shining onto the lounge window. It reversed, made a U-turn and drove down Rocky Lane. Only then did we dare peek from the window; all we could see was a dark SUV without number plates.

"What's it, boys?" Grandma whispered behind us. I'm not sure which one of us jumped the highest and yelped the loudest. My panga went clattering to the floor. To his credit, William hung onto his, although he banged it loudly against the wall.

"Shoo! Ouma, you scared us!" William exclaimed.

"Please don't do that again!" I pleaded with my hands over my heart.

"Okay! Sorry, boys! Now let's sit here and tell me what's wrong?"

William and I spilled the beans.

"Ok, then we'll have to move around in bigger groups. I'll call someone to check our locks and burglar bars."

"Can we report it to the cops? Perhaps they'll put more patrols here," I queried, holding with both hands tightly onto my panga.

"Not this lazy, corrupt bunch. They'll just as soon lock you up for disturbing the peace," Grandma responded angrily.

"Who can help us?"

"I'll put the word out to friends and family, and I'll also tell our neighbors on Rocky Lane and Alfred Street to be careful," Grandma answered decisively.

"Otherwise, we're on our own?" William spoke sadly.

"We're on our own."

William set an alarm for every two hours. He and I took turns to prowl indoors, listening for any danger. Grandma sat for a while and shared lighter moments with us.

The five occupants of the black SUV drove off towards their homes in Ezakheni. The plan was to intimidate the family on Rocky Lane and it worked perfectly. By a stroke of luck, the two mfanas walked outside in the yard, so the gang of mobsters could stop and be silent and menacing at the end of the street. They were sure those mfanas were close to pissing themselves from fear. Then came the drive-by outside their home. They almost had to hoot to wake someone up in that house, but three of them were sure they could see the reflections of the two mfanas as they stood in the lounge behind thin curtains. They were seen peeking from the lounge window when the black SUV drove slowly down the street.

Bongani's eyes were failing. He wanted to go and bang on the window to be sure they were awake. Bongani then came up with the idea to liven things up a bit by firing a few shots into the roof of the house, but the rest of the crew shouted him down. He had to reluctantly put away his gun. There was a moment when he perked up again as they entered Drummond Street from the valley. A cop van stopped them. Much to his disappointment, the cops waved them on and beat a hasty retreat in the opposite direction at the mention of the two bosses.

The house music beat blared loudly in the SUV as it flew close to two hundred kilometers an hour in the dark night. The gang smoked weed and drank beer quarts. All eyes were on Skeets in the front passenger seat who was dividing the takings. This horde included an extra night's work that was completed at the train station where some late commuters were robbed of their earnings. They also raided the truck stop where the amahosha ladies of the night attended to the drivers. The men from the SUV had reluctantly given in to Bongani's pleadings to be able to use his gun to rob some people. He was given a stern warning by them not to shoot, or kill anyone, and so he got to work with the help of the two youngest gangsters, Jomo and Papi. These two hardened seventeen-year-olds, still in Matric, took the cash and bling from their terror-stricken prey and stuffed these into various pockets. Three of their victims were even taken to auto banks to draw cash from their accounts. They were released at the edge of the town, unharmed, but with taxi fare to get home. The gang was in a generous mood.

The driver, Mzo, declared that as surely as night becomes day, the two-tweenz would hire them shortly to do bodily harm to some or all that family in Rocky Lane. He spoke of the job they pulled on a farm near Weenen, where they broke both legs of the Mlungu because he owed the two-tweenz big bucks. The driver reminded them that it also started with some intimidation and was soon promoted to bodily harm. This pleased Bongani immensely. More moola was coming and his talents would be needed. It was turning out to be a good Christmas for all of them and for their families. Mzo was supposed to be the only one of them who knew the identities of their benefactors but shared this information with his gang.

Mzo glanced at his comrades. Skeets and Mzo were twenty-three-year-olds. Tough guys who looked dangerous. Jomo and Papi were just as brave and tough. Mzo glanced at Bongani. This mother-fucker old timer was forty, and yet he already looked like a pensioner.

Eish! This democracy in a gang doesn't work! he lamented. But, eintlik! He didn't care. His boys came before his bosses in his world. Otherwise how could they trust him? He glanced at Bongani in the rearview mirror. As for Bongani, this crazy, fucked-up, old motherfucker inkabi was just too quick to shoot targets dead. Mzo cursed himself for listening to his wife's pleadings to give her uncle, Bongani, a chance in life to be a real tsotsi. Chances were they would all die or go to jail because of this crazy fucked up gashu motherfucker shit. Just as well they don't use the igetshas AK 47s In front of him, otherwise he would demand one and then they would all surely die quickly, very quickly.

I may have to shoot Bongani myself and bury him somewhere to save us from his fucked-up shit. His family will cry for a bit until the after-party. Then they'll get very, very drunk and start to forget about this mshiza stupid motherfucker who brings no real value to his family.

The black SUV hurtled ever closer to their turbulent tomorrow. Skeets licked his lips with glee as he neatly stacked the bundles of money for the payout. Mzo turned the SUV slowly and carefully at the right-side junction to Pieter's Station past Colenso. He sped up as soon as they were through the intersection.

We were all up at sparrows and hastened to preen ourselves for the 09h30 Sunday Service. Morph was much recovered, though a bit weak. He nevertheless managed to tend to himself as he chirped continually about Christmas and presents and Christmas lunch. Grandma had to shoo us along to get us moving out of the house.

"Hurry up!" Grandma's outstretched arms herded us to the verandah. "We need to move it if we want to go to the clinic and to church."

After checking every door and window and locking the gate we rushed down Rocky Lane at precisely six-thirty in the morning to be at church at nine-thirty. It was normally a twenty-minute walk to church with Grandma, but we were unsure how long the visit to the clinic would take. William led the way, with Morph on his back, and I patrolled the rear and our flanks. We were wary of everything along our route.

"Not too fast, children, or else we'll be sweating like pigs by the time we get to Church," Grandma cautioned.

"Have you seen a pig sweat, Ouma?" Morph asked.

"Not a live one, Morph, but when you cook it on a spit, then it sweats."

"How do you cook it in spit, Ouma? Won't all the spit dry up if you put it on a fire?"

"It's a machine that allows you to turn the whole pig around and around over the fire to roast it. You don't spit on it. You put sauce on it when it's cooking," Ouma responded patiently between hurried breathing. I empathized with that pig. My life seemed to be spinning faster and faster out of control; from one fire to another.

We reached the clinic precinct in one piece. Grandma held Morph's hand as they hurried into the building. There was a long row of benches outside that William and I flopped onto as though they were inviting beds of repose.

"What happened last night? Why're you guys all so jittery?" May-June stopped us short from entering dreamland.

"What did Ouma say?" she voiced quietly after we told her about the previous night.

"We're to stay together and watch out for each other," I responded, then yawned widely. William yawned as well.

"Sleep, guys, I'll watch over you," our guardian angel volunteered.

We did not need a second invitations.

"Wake up! It's time to go!" we were shaken back to life. Grandma called,

"Come Deplano, we must go." I stood up and followed them. It was only after taking at least five steps that I was fully awake.

"Morph will be fine if he doesn't over-excite himself. Shame, he was on a drip and had oxygen for an hour," Grandma related the news to us.

"Are we still going to church? You boys look very tired." Grandma rubbed tiredness from her eyes as she spoke.

"We'll be fine, Ouma. We'll let 'sisi' sit between us and she can pinch us awake if we start snoring." William laughed and then swung Morph onto his back.

May-June looked at me and smiled. She then stuck her arm around mine and held me close as we trudged onwards. Conversation was minimal. We were just about passing the graveyard when William exclaimed, "There's a Merc SUV, but that one is dark red." The vehicle turned right from Richmond Road onto Lorne Street. Then I quickly spied the metallic gold BMW 325 that followed it and turned left into Lorne Street.

"See! There's Abu's car! But he's alone!"

"He saw us! See, he slowed down!" May-June exhaled and held me tighter.

"He's going now." William noted the moment the vehicle started to accelerate.

"We'll have to be careful when we come out of Church." Grandma was anxious.

"We'll go back down Conner Street and onto Alfred Street after church. It's safer where there's lots of people," William concluded as we entered the church yard.

Sunday School for us young ones was closed for the year. We had to accompany the adults into the main service. Grandma sat on the fifth pew from the back and on the left-hand side. Grandma always took this seat. Morph snuggled up close to Grandma and I sat next to him. May-June took her seat between William and me. All went well until we were about a third of the way through the Service cycles of prayer praising, and reflection. The first sign of impending oddities began with a loud growl from Morph's stomach during silent prayer.

"I'm hungry," he exclaimed to all and sundry. The Deacon who was leading us in prayer and supplication had to pause. All the pious ladies seated around us glanced quickly in Morph's direction with scowls of disdain popping forth from the heavily powdered faces. Grandma gave Morph a stern look that shut him up. A lady in front of Grandma turned and gave Morph a sweet. Grandma hastily took it from Morph and surreptitiously opened it.

Morph tried to concentrate on the service. Unfortunately, the loudest singing closest to us came from a middle-aged lady who sang in this incredibly false vibrato that took her singing close to what a sheep would sound like if it could speak English. Morph tried to copy her. he did so loudly and with much more exaggeration.

The lady was mortified by what she must have thought was a mockery. She turned and would have smacked Morph, but for the warning look that Grandma gave her.

"It's okay, Morph. You don't have to sing like that. Sing normally, but softly," Grandma encouraged a perplexed Morph.

Suffice to say that William and I were pinched several times by May-June for nodding off. Somewhere during the preaching, Pastor Lucas paused for dramatic effect.

"Amen!" William shouted from his somnambulistic haze and the message of the sermon degenerated into loud guffaws of laughter from the congregation. Pastor was an excellent orator and he expounded.

"So be it! That's what amen means and it precisely sums up in one word what Mary said to the Angel when she accepted the calling to be the mother of our Lord and Savior, Jesus Christ. And in our callings, amen should be the firm answer that each one of us gives to our God who is the Great Amen," pointing skywards.

May-June pinched both of us. Order was restored and the service continued to its conclusion without any further mishaps. On our watchful journey home, every sentence that William or Morph uttered was concluded with what sounded like a flock of sheep chorusing "Amens". From that day forth our family always referred to the Sunday that preceded Christmas Day as Amen Sunday.

The Butcher, Baker and Candlestick Maker met at ten am in the Butcher's office on the corner of Albert Street and Shepstone Avenue. They sat in silence as two men with gadgets swept the room for any listening devices.

"This is odd," thought Faizel. "It's been more than five years ago last the office was swept in our presence." Without looking directly at the men, he followed their movements as they systematically scrutinized every nook and cranny.

One of the men gave the all-clear and they quickly gathered up their equipment and left the office. Ewald switched on a small monitor on his desk and followed the men's progress out of the building and out of the yard. No one spoke until Ewald switched off the monitor. The relief of all three partners was palpable.

"The plan's changed a bit. I've received word from Mr. TJ, that our Catalyst will be opening a Clinic in Loskop on the 27th. From there he'll be going to Suncoast Casino. The trips to the Valley and to Greytown have been cancelled. One of his wives is sick. So, there's only one opportunity for him. I don't like doing it so close to our base, but there's nothing we can do about it now. Faizel, you'll have to sort this out with the Land Surveyor. Eric, you'll have to sort it out with the drivers. I'll deal with the teams, handlers and leaders."

Ewald's partners nodded, unperturbed in the least. Their Vulintaba Manifesto was thorough – they were ready for any amendments.

"They hate him in Loskop and don't recognize his authority," Faizel declared.

"All the more reason to affirm his authority in that region," replied Ewald.

"The Colonel hid our first shipment by those fucking people. It's a bloody wonder none of it was found, even after they bloody nailed him for the other stuff," Eric observed.

"Ja, we're still selling to both sides since." Faizel calmly folded his hands on his lap.

"Ja, fok! 1994 to 1996 was good bloody business for us. We literally and figuratively made bloody killings," Eric said, nonchalantly crossing his legs.

"Ja, this time will be even better. We stand to make much, much more." Ewald rested his forearms on his desk and intertwined his fingers.

"We're not the only group trying to effect change," Faizel reminded them.

"Those shysters from the East have wormed their way into the system," Ewald replied.

"They're also trying to buy into TJ's plans, but I hear he's not biting," Faizel said.

"Those fuckers are from the same place as your ancestors. Aren't they your chinas?" Eric spat out as he switched his gaze to Faizel.

"No, they're not,"

These infidel shits are playing me! Faizel thought to himself.

"Do we still have enough chiefs and traditional leaders on our side' considering that at least twenty have already been assassinated?" he asked.

"Ja, still plenty left. A lot of work has gone into this plan by our other partners who've sold it to them. "They're also bloody heavily involved with paramilitary training. So bloody secretive that none of the twenty-eight sites have been discovered, and that number excludes the bloody camps established by the Sheiks. That's a bloody miracle in itself," Eric added.

"But then the other side had at least fifty of their own training bases," noted Faizel.

"Our estimates included the possible discovery of some of our shipments and training camps. It shows what power TJ exerts throughout the country, even though he's not a visible politician and not from here," Ewald responded.

"Everyone trying so hard to fuck the other they can't see past their own dicks," Eric chirped in.

"They don't' see how they're being played by TJ who'll be emperor," added Ewald.

"They're bloody not seeing beyond corruption. Fucking cunts." Eric spoke with distaste. There was no mistaking his dislike of the ANC. "It's a miracle our partners are still able to hide the Vulintaba Manifesto from the authorities," Faizel observed.

"Ja. The Zulus are now in the majority and in the ascendancy within the ANC and all other political parties and they'll not give up this power to anyone. All this posturing by the political foes outside and within the ruling party won't prevent the inevitable," declared Ewald.

"So, as our Manifesto predicted, the Zulus win the prize for now," Faizel said bluntly.

"Ja. Zuma will be the next President after Mbeki and Zulus will rule from then on. They're the future kingmakers. Remember our modelling shows that assassinations will escalate from multiple parties as each opportunist tries to weed out their opponents. Our Province will suffer the most," Ewald expounded.

"But the bloody fucking ruling party is powerless to stop the Zulus from ruling South Africa for as long as they are bloody-well able to. Those fucking commie loving bastards will have to lick fucking arses to stay in bloody power," Eric observed with some satisfaction.

"So it's all about power and money, just as the Vulintaba Manifesto predicted," Faizel said as he watched his two partners keenly.

"Ja, they don't ever want Xhosas, Sotho's, or any other nation on the throne. Even if the others combine to oust the Zulu there'll be struggles for dominance," Ewald responded.

"The Zulus will unify, or should I say have unified secretly across the political spectrum to ensure their rule," Faizel concluded. Ewald and Eric nodded.

"There'll be a massive bloody battle amongst them fuckers to see who the ultimate strongman will be. That is where TJ'll come in. We 'll be ready for that. All future bloody power will rest with the winners," Eric spoke expansively.

"Ja, as the Manifesto spells out, we play both sides until we see clearly who's winning. Then we stay with the winner. They'll need financial muscle to succeed. That's where we'll also come in with TJ and his cronies." Ewald sat back in his chair.

"The Chinese and others are muscling in very fast," Faizel reminded his partners.

"Fuck the Chinese and those fucking coolies. They've no stomach for their own fucking blood being shed in this shithole. If necessary, we go after them as well!" Eric answered.

"That's why we need The Catalyst. Immediately after he's added to the mix, there'll be serious bloodshed in this province and throughout the country. The violence, looting, and anarchy will escalate beyond the control of the government. Remember our modelling has shown that the Chinese will pull out very quickly at the merest hint of a civil war. It's all about their investments and losses. There'll be genocide if the warring nations don't find consensus. Don't forget they're already at war. The others will band together to take on the Zulus. The ANC Alliance are now only the vehicle to power. Whichever ethnic group or faction controls the ANC, controls the government," Ewald offered.

"And that's where the Sheiks come in," added Faizel, compelled to say something.

"How's it going with the Sheiks, Faizel?" Ewald asked.

"All good. Their investment to kickstart the shit is going well.

They're ready to invest big time once the dust has settled. They'll also ship more merchandise over, as the need arises."

"Have you had a response from Combrink?" Ewald continued with his questioning. Eric scowled, but Ewald ignored him.

"Yes. He wants a hundred and fifty million in an offshore account of his choice, but no shares with us," Faizel stated dryly.

"FUCK HIM! FUCKING BASTARD ! FOR THAT FUCKING MONEY I'LL BLOODY-WELL KILL HIM AND HIS WHORE!" screamed Eric.

"Sit down, Eric!" Ewald commanded. He glared at Eric until he reluctantly took his seat. Ewald looked at his partners as he continued speaking.

"I was half expecting such a response from Joe. In any event, this price is a starting point for some quick negotiations with him. Remember gentlemen he stood to make much more over a longer term with the shares we were offering. This gives us a long-term saving." Ewald flicked his eyes from one partner to the next as he allowed them time to digest his words.

"Faizel you will have to conclude the negotiations, but make it absolutely clear to Combrink whatever we settle on buys his total silence. If we go down, he and his entire family will die. We'll kill them first, so he can watch. Eric, arrange for one of his clerks to be eliminated. Make sure it's untraceable. Be as gruesome as you want. He'll get the message."

"How much do we settle on?" queried Faizel coolly.

"Offer him a hundred million, but in phased, equal payments over a period of thirty years and with no interest. We'll take him out before then, just as soon as we find out what he has stashed and can get our hands on the info."

"Has your surveillance yielded anything?" Faizel got their meeting going again. Outwardly he was calm, but inwardly there was deep fear that threatened to overpower him. Of the two men, he feared Ewald more.

"Nothing much. Him and his son went fishing on Saturday at that Oberholzer farm they always go to near Winterton. They returned on Sunday. Same old, same old. We have surveillance on all his phones and computers. Combrink can't take a shit without us knowing about it. We'll find something. My guys are good at what they do."

"Have you checked the timing again?" queried Eric.

"Ja. All ran perfectly this time. I'll let the handlers know about the date shift," answered Ewald. He leaned forward in his chair and looked at Faizel for his report.

"The next venture is set for the 24th in Cape Town. I'll instruct them to escalate matters. With their help we'll have that Province sorted out in no time."

"I've checked on the switching of the dummy companies. All okay," Ewald reported.

"The flow of cash from the offshore accounts is now through Swakopmund. From there it moves to a farm near Doringdam in the Northern Cape where it's sorted. Trompies is handling stuff that end. Then the parcels are distributed by our couriers, starting from their designated collection point near the N10 close to the farm and on to where we need them to go. I'm busy setting up the next route," Ewald spoke confidently. He turned to look at Eric.

"Three new drivers did some dummy runs on the bloody N3 between Maritzburg and Durban and some on the R103 between Drummond and Botha's Hill. All the tests went bloody well. The dumb shits and the trucks are back on the farm where they're practicing. The helicopters are also in place. We'll now have to fly out after New Year's Day to avoid suspicion. So, we'll have to bloody well stick to a good script."

"I agree with you. Let's set it for the 4th January." Ewald did not wait for any consensus as turned to Faizel.

"I trust the Land Surveyor is all good?"

"Yes, indeed. All his instruments are properly calibrated and he's able to use them well. He's ready."

"Okay. Any other business that we need to discuss?" Ewald sat back.

"I'm good," responded Faizel. Eric shook his head.

"Okay. Let's meet daily at five pm from now on. Stay off the phones unless necessary," Ewald commanded. The two men nodded.

"Fuck! I almost forgot!" Eric spoke sharply. "That bloody cunt, Enoch Mathebula, was arrested this morning for fucking fraud and corruption charges. This is bloody odd. The corrupt fucking municipalities close between Christmas and New Year. All the contacts I spoke to were bloody well blindsided by his arrest. They're bloody shitting themselves now the Municipal fucking cunt Manager has been taken in."

"Where is he locked up?" Ewald frowned briefly at Eric.

"The bloody Scorpions took him to Maritzburg." Eric turned to look at Faizel.

"Is he a loose end?" asked Faizel.

"No. We've used intermediaries with him. If he squeals, then we'll eliminate some of those middlemen," Ewald responded.

"I'll keep an eye on this bloody development and report any changes."

"Okay. Then we'll meet tomorrow afternoon." Faizel said stood up. "See you gents."

Ewald and Eric responded in greeting. Faizel left the office. He used the lift. As he entered it, he whispered, "Insha Allah." He then wiped the sweat from his face.

Ewald switched on the monitor before Faizel left the office and followed Faizel's progress out of the office, in the lift and to his vehicle. As soon as Faizel's Land Rover Discovery exited the yard, Ewald switched off the monitor and looked at Eric.

"Anything?"

"Something is bloody well not right with that fucker. I can smell it."

"Well, it's almost too late for him to fuck us around. Why did you bring up the Mathebula matter so late?" Ewald had picked up the flicker in Eric's eyes when they spoke.

"That crooked bastard, Enoch, is one of Faizel's bloody contacts. They were very close in 1996/1997. I wanted to see his reaction, but there was nothing much there." Eric wiped his brow with his hand. Ewald keenly watched this movement.

"Shit!" Eric remonstrated internally. *"I shouldn't have done that!"*

"We'll continue checking up on Faizel, Nader and Joe. We need evidence quickly before shit goes down," Ewald spoke decisively.

He folded his hands in his lap and crossed his legs at the ankles.

"I've asked you this before. Do you bloody well want me to sort them out?"

"Not now, Eric. We'll keep checking up on them. We need to find their caches of info, otherwise we'll be in deep shit if they're buried too soon. You can be sure they've provisos to expose the material if they die suddenly. Nader is another matter. We need to find him and keep tabs on him. We don't want him hunting us. If something blows, then we'll wipe those fuckers off the face of the earth."

"Talking of bloody hunting. I know who to dust. That bloody poofter," Eric spat out.

By eight-o-clock that evening we were deeply engrossed in an enthralling game of Ludo. As usual, May-June was in the lead, mercilessly far ahead of us, roaring with laughter whenever she kicked one of our tokens back to our yards, or reached her home destination with one of her little red monsters. Grandma and Morph shared the yellow. William played for the green and I the blue. The Ludo happiness glint of a winner was in her eyes when the telephone rang and Morph ran to answer it.

He returned and said, "Ouma, it's for you."

"Who's it, my child?" Grandma asked as she rose from her seat.

"Dunno."

We insisted on a quick break. As soon as Grandma entered the lounge, Morph picked up the pair of dice.

"My turn!" he exclaimed, blew on them, shook them and threw them. An eleven.

William, May-June and I instantly saw the ashen expression on Grandma's face. We froze. Morph was in the process of picking up one of their yellow tokens to move along, when he glanced at Grandma and saw her distress. He sat back in his chair.

"Ouma, what's it? What's happened?" William asked alarmingly.

"Oh my God!" was all Grandma could say as she slumped into her chair.

"Hold on, Ouma!" William said. He ran to the kitchen and returned with a glass of sugar water. Grandma drank a few gulps of the sweet liquid, took a deep breath and repeated, "Oh my God! Oh my God!"

"What happened, Ouma?" William urged with real fear in his voice.

"It was Aunty Priya. Her youngest brother was brutally murdered sometime late this afternoon. His body was found behind the Islamic School near the Masonite factory."

"Vinod! The one who lived at the flats in Albert Street?" William was incredulous.

"He wouldn't hurt a fly!" May-June was horrified. Morph and I were too shocked to say anything.

"How did it happen?" William asked.

"They don't know yet. He went for his usual run up Outspan and Industria Streets at about three and didn't return. The family went searching for him in the early evening and found his body about fifteen minutes ago."

"Can we go there to Aunty Priya and them for a short time, Ouma? Neville is my friend?" I asked with a catch in my throat.

"We should. Priya's my friend and she's hurting."

"We'll all have to go. Remember the crooks?"

"Okay, we'll go for an hour, but you'll have to sit with Morph. I don't want you'll to hear what the grownups are saying," Grandma said sternly.

"Okay, Ouma, we'll sit in Neville's room or somewhere outside," May-June offered.

We hurriedly grabbed jerseys, locked up and went to Neville's home. There were already about ten cars and two police vans parked outside. The men milled around angrily in the street and yard while the women wailed loudly. Grandma entered the front door and the despair grew in volume the minute Auntie Priya saw her friend. We walked around to the back. Neville was seated with two of his cousins on the bench under the Syringa Berry tree. We sat near him. Neville's cousins were a girl and a boy, both younger than him. They were sobbing quietly. Neville could only stare blankly off into the distance. William cleared his throat.

"I'm so sorry. Please accept our sympathies." May-June nodded her head, reached out and patted Neville's hand. Morph looked on, wild-eyed.

"Howzit," was all I could blurt out.

"Thanks, guys. I'm fine," Neville responded in tears.

The three cousins held hands as they wept into the night. We fidgeted quietly and uncomfortably in our seats, not knowing what to say and how to comfort them. The cousins were called by their mother and departed. We sat quietly under the tree with my friend, still at a loss for words to try and comfort him. It was hard to keep my composure. The unmistakable smell of burning dagga wafted through the air from the property next door, adding another dimension to the oppressive heat. Two men stood behind the high precast fence and indulged their habit. May-June moved herself and Morph to the furthest seats from the pungent fumes. The men were unaware of us sitting under the shadows of the Syringa Berry tree. I touched the marbles in my pocket and was about to give some to Neville when one of the men spoke.

"Ekse, fucken bad what happened to Vinod, and all?"

"Ya, bro. Dey fucking killed him bad, my bra. Heh?"

"De cop said dey gutted him like a fucken fish, and all. Fuck it!"

These men were bad news. It was best they do not pick up that we were so close to them. May-June gasped quietly and quickly covered Morph's ears with her hands. To his credit Morph did not squirm or squeal. He hopped onto May-June's lap where he snuggled close.

All of us slid deeper into the shadows of the Syringa Berry tree. Neville was absolutely horrified and there's no telling what he would have done if William did not put his arm around his shoulder to placate him. Neville continued to weep and shake silently amidst the gentle rustling of the Syringa Berry tree.

"Eish! Dat's bad, bro. Blood and guts, and all. Very fucking dope my china. Heh?"

"Was a fucking homo. Must be fucking revenge. Heh?"

"Ja, my bra, no one wunds fucken homos eroun. Fuck dem!"

"Whe'rid dey find him, my bra? Heh?"

"At de borom end of de fucken Slamic Skul. But udder side de fucken fence in de fucken Mas'nite fac-tree place. Fucken real dope like. Fuck!"

"Shit, bro! Those fucking Slum-ohs musta wasted him, and all. Heh! Ekse, dey hate fucking homos, big time. Heh?"

"Ja, may-be, and all and all. Fuck, dere's my fucken bitch. Gorra fuck off."

"Ja, bro. Can't fucking win with de fucking bitches and peeps. Check you, my bro."

"Check you in de mornin."

We heard the one man depart. It did not take long before the other man walked off. William continued consoling Neville while all of us tried to make sense of what had happened to Vinod. It was approximately nine-thirty when Grandma came out of the back door and gestured to us. We walked Neville to Grandma who hugged him and kissed him and spoke words of comfort to him. After each one of us also hugged him, Neville went indoors.

We departed. William carried Morph on his back. Much to our surprise, Joe Combrink and some of his staff stood on the verandah near the front door. Grandma said her goodbyes to the group and we moved on. I noticed him intently focused on me, probably because I tried to kill his son. I stared back defiantly. As soon as we were out of earshot, William asked,

"That was Joe Combrink and some of his staff, Ouma? Why're they here?"

"Vinod worked for him. Mr. Combrink was very shocked by what happened and very generous. He's paying for all the funeral expenses. Had only good words to say of Vinod." Grandma drew her jersey tighter around her.

"Do you know what happened to Vinod, Ouma?" William and Grandma continued with their conversation. Morph was already asleep. May-June and I kept quiet.

"Not much. He was murdered and his body was found near the Islamic School."

"We heard some bad things about that, Ouma."

"Tell me about it at home, Son. We'll put Morph to bed first. Don't forget to check the yard and lock the gate."

"Okay, Ouma."

We walked in silence the rest of the way home. William and I went about checking and securing the outside and inside of our home without saying a word to each other, lost in our own thoughts of death and mourning. May-June put Morph to bed and Grandma warmed some milk for us to drink. We joined them in the lounge and William immediately relayed to Grandma what we had overheard. Grandma asked, "What did Neville say?"

"Nothing, Ouma. He was angry, but I held him and spoke to him."

"He'll be hurting a lot, and him and his family'll be teased a lot from now on."

"Can people be so cruel, Ouma? He's dead now, never mind who Vinod was!"

"Unfortunately, fortunes are built on the misfortunes of others. Much of the world still hates people like Vinod." Grandma turned to me.

"Plano, you're his friend. Let him talk if he wants to. I know it's tough for you after all you've been through. I'm not asking you to do much. Just be there for him." Grandma yawned and rubbed her sad, tired eyes.

"Okay, Ouma. I will."

Vinod and Adelaide's senseless deaths merged within a larger cauldron of anger that I did not know how to stop, or even slow down.

"Do you children know what homosexuality means?"

"Gays and lesbians, Ouma," May-June responded, rubbing her own sleepy eyes.

"Don't ever belittle them, my children. They are people who live very tough lives. Vinod's murder was probably a hate crime because he was a gay."

"Okay, Ouma."

"Okay, let's go to bed. I'm sure you boys are very tired"

We said goodnight. William and I switched off all the lights indoors, waited half an hour and went about checking the doors and windows. Soon after we were asleep.

. . .

Vinod didn't stand a chance. He was wearing earphones as he jogged down Outspan Street close to the Little Bushmens River crossing. He paid no mind to the two men walking towards him. This was normal to him; there were always people on this stretch of road when he crossed the river. He did not hear the Toyota Cressida with dark tinted windows approach from the rear. Before Vinod could react, he was bundled onto the floor at the back of the Cressida, handcuffed and a gun was placed in his mouth and the Cressida gathered speed. Not a single witness to his kidnapping.

The Cressida entered a garage that opened and closed electronically. Vinod's hands and feet were bound with cable ties. His mouth was gagged with brown packaging tape. They dragged him into the kitchen and dumped him onto a double layer of thick plastic sheeting. Vinod lay as still as he could, staring wild-eyed at his assailants, terrified of being raped when he saw the men strip themselves naked. These men were seasoned enforcers and had a job to do. Rape had not been included in their instructions.

They changed into surgical clothes, complete with caps, masks and boots. The third man used the packaging tape to close off the joints between the gloves and sleeves and boots and trousers of his accomplices, then did so on his attire. Deep house music played loud enough to drown out the sounds from indoors, but not to agitate any neighbors. All the curtains were drawn and the lights were on. Vinod's heart raced in the darkness of his cocoon at extreme levels from the abject fear that gripped him. He made guttural moaning sounds and tried to roll about, knowing deep within him that they were going to kill him. He knew he was helpless.

The two men each picked up a long, forged steel crowbar with a claw and a point and began their systematic beating of Vinod. The shock and pain of the first strikes jolted Vinod excruciatingly. He tried to scream from the pain that shook his entire being. He tried to swivel into a fetal position, with his hands over his head, but all to no avail.

The beating intensified. They hit Vinod over every single part of his entire body, repeatedly, until bones cracked and his body turned into blood-soaked pulp. Vinod succumbed to a short world of wretched fear, horrific pain and unimaginable trauma. The man who was attacking the lower half of his body then rammed the claw end of the crowbar with all his might up the rectum. Vinod's body tensed with shock, shivered violently, then slumped unconscious.

The man twisted the crowbar in place, and withdrew it, pulling bloodied internal organs out. He dropped the crowbar and accepted the hunting knife that the man with the gun proffered and cut off Vinod's penis and stuffed it into Vinod's mashed, bloodied mouth between smashed lips and broken teeth. When they were done, the men proceeded to wrap Vinod in the plastic sheets, taping him securely closed. Just before they covered his head, the second man slit Vinod's throat. Then they quickly entombed Vinod in the body bag.

"Yebo, Zeph."

"Yebo, my baas."

"Have you finished the job?"

"Ja, my baas. De m'sheen is shup-shup now."

"Have you sent the guys home?"

"Ja, my baas. I also paid dem."

"Good, Zeph. See you tomorrow."

"Shup, my baas."

Eric cut the call and sat quietly for a while.

"The statement has been made! Fuck you, Combrink! And your whore!"

CHAPTER 12
VESTIBULE OF THE DAMNED
(MONDAY, 20 DECEMBER 1999)

They met just after midnight deep in the heart of the scrapyard and were seated in an old Ford Telstar that had long since seen better days. A few minutes earlier Faizel drove into the yard and parked right next to the Telstar. He informed the security guard at the gate and the ones patrolling with Rottweilers crossed with American Pit Bulls to expect a visitor who would identify himself as Mr. Smith and to allow him to meet Faizel at the Telstar. He hinted to them that the man was interested in buying that old car and some others. The guards did not find it unusual because their boss sometimes did business late at night in very strange places. Faizel warned them to stay away from the vicinity of the Telstar. His visitor was afraid of dogs.

The guards and their dogs disappeared into the darkness of the huge lot and Faizel climbed into the driver's seat of the Telstar. He was stunned to find the man with the brown suede shoes already seated in the shadows of the passenger seat. It took Faizel a few seconds to regain his composure.

"What the…? How…?! Never mind!" he exclaimed.

"As-salamu alaykum," the man greeted calmly.

"Wa'alaykumus-salam," Faizel responded He took a deep breath and exhaled audibly.

"How the hell did this 'shaytan' get past the guards and those killer dogs?"

Faizel asked himself even as he voiced the greeting. Faizel took out an envelope from his pocket and used his hanky to wipe his face.

"I have here a list of eleven infidels who must be eliminated within the next twenty-four hours. Even if some are in jail, they must be taken out, no matter what. We're too close to our objective for them to now throw their spanners in the works. The list includes home and work addresses, cellphone numbers and photos of each one."

The man took the envelope and slipped it into an inside pocket of his jacket.

"Do I have any assistance in this short space of time?"

"Use whoever you want from the camps. There's a list of known hitmen in there. Use Doctor Thebe to arrange things." Faizel handed over a briefcase packed with R200 notes.

"Here's some cash. If need be, take out some of those hitmen as well after they've done their jobs. We don't want loose ends."

"It shall be done." The man placed the briefcase on the floor between his legs.

Faizel stared intently through the windscreen in front of him, as if seeking a way through the darkness ahead. On that list was his dear friend Enoch Mathebula. Someone who he knew from Junior Primary School days. The man picked up on the turmoil raging within his client, but he did not respond in any way to this knowledge. He waited for further instruction.

"All well with you?" asked Faizel of the man with the brown suede shoes.

"Everything okay. Your partners have enquired, but not to my face. Questions have been asked of the staff who reported everything to me. The enquirers seem to be satisfied for now, for the questions have stopped since Friday," he responded.

"Good. Don't let your guard down. They may return."

"I will not."

Faizel paused to listen to the dogs bark menacingly in the distance behind them.

"Are you ready for the 27th?" The dogs abruptly stopped barking. "Yes. I've scouted the field, set my calibrations and ran some tests. I'm ready."

"You don't have to do any of the hits on the list," Faizel suggested.

"Okay. The men from the camps must move tomorrow to their assigned cities. I'll let them handle hits that are on their routes. I'll take out those that I consider tough to execute close to Estcourt. The rest will be left to the hitmen. How quick are they to mobilise?"

"They need 24 hours to observe and then execute. If opportunities present themselves during the observation period, take it. They don't have such luxuries this time. Pay them extra if they do the job quickly. Take them out if they fail."

"No problem."

"You must be back by the 26th to take out those Mozambican drivers. I want to replace them with mine. You'll have to attend to it the night before and make it look like an accident. Then they'll have no chance to replace them, but with my own."

"It will be done. Do you want the bodies to be easily recognizable?"

"Yes, but it must look like an accident. I don't want my partners to be suspicious."

"It shall be done."

"Be extra careful of your movements when you leave here. My partners still have surveillance on me. I tried to give them the slip tonight, but I'm not sure if I've succeeded."

"I've seen them. They're not anywhere near here. Do you want me to take them out?"

Faizel was stunned.

"No. Let them have their fun for a while."

"Okay, then. You'll contact me once the list has been attended to."

"Agreed." The man with the brown suede shoes quietly opened the door of the rusty old Telstar. He disappeared just as quietly with the briefcase in his left hand.

It only took Faizel two seconds to scan the yard, but when he turned to where the man was last seen standing, he was gone. Faizel held the steering wheel of the Telstar tightly for a few minutes as his entire being shivered in fear. It took some effort to steady himself.

"Surely he's a 'Shaytan!" Faizel groaned to the creaking edifices surrounding him.

. . .

The telephone's shrill siren jerked us violently awake with an immediate sense of foreboding. William was the first to react and bounded out of bed.

"Hello, Gibbs residence!" he greeted as cheerfully as he could muster so early in the day. He was not a morning person. We could only hear his side of the conversation.

"Hello, Uncle Billy. How're you doing and how's the family?" Neville's dad on the line. I sat up in bed. Grandma came and stood in our bedroom doorway, May-June squeezed past Grandma and sat on William's bed and Morph rushed to the bathroom.

"What time? At your home first? Will there be transport to the crematorium? Okay. Okay. We'll be there shortly." Morph climbed into his bed.

"Okay, Sir. See you just now. Bye." William replaced the receiver. He and Grandma came into our bedroom. Grandma sat on William's bed while he stood near the door.

"That was Uncle Billy. He said they'll be going for the autopsy at eight and it should be done by ten. They'll wash and dress the body there and should be home by eleven. The funeral ceremony will take place at their home, not at the flats. The service at the crematorium in Ladysmith will take place at three. Two kombis have been hired to transport some of the family members without cars to the crematorium. I said we'd be at their home in a bit."

"Thanks, Son." Grandma said. "Remember, they're Tamils. Their services are not the same as ours. You can wear any other color but try not black. The family and other Tamils will wear white for the funeral service. The men close to the deceased shave their heads. I'm not sure whether they do it before or after the funeral. There'll be a lot of burning of incense and using of spices and flowers."

Morph raised a hand.

"Yes, Morph?"

"Must we also shave our heads?"

"No, Son. Only their close family."

"It's gonna be a long day, children. Let's have breakfast and sort ourselves out. We'll try to be there before 10h00. I don't want any one of you viewing the body. You may sit close to Neville when the opportunity presents itself, but don't go viewing the body. And you don't have to take part in any ceremony. The family will not expect it of you. Just being there for them is enough. Ok!" We nodded our heads. Grandma continued.

"I think it'll be better if you keep Morph away from all the burning stuff, the flowers and spices. Sisi and I'll be helping Aunty Priya, mostly in the kitchen. You boys can stand outside near the tent or in the back yard by the tree."

We turned into Alfred Street. There were already at least twenty cars parked along the road. Lots of activity moved between these cars and Neville's home. The ladies generally wore white saris while the men dressed in white cotton shirts and pants. The younger generation were attired in more western style clothing of sober colors. We were not out of place in our casual attire. Neville and two male cousins were standing at the gate to greet visitors and to give directions. Grandma and May-June hugged them, then rushed off to the kitchen. We shook their hands formally, mumbling, "My sympathies" to each one. Although we did not know the cousins, we knew they were closely related. Theirs and Neville's heads were shaven bald. William, Morph and I stood close by within the shadows of the tent in the driveway, watching.

Joe Combrink and his staff arrived and greeted all in their pathway. I quietly crept behind William as they reached the gate, because I did not want to shake his hands. Fortunately, they veered off to the front verandah and thereby avoided us. I watched him carefully as he passed by, waiting for any outburst, but none was forthcoming – even though he glanced in our direction at one stage. I was both angry and glad that Hermann was not with him. I still wanted to hurt him with all my might. The black Merc SUV came to mind, and I kept an eye out for it. These observations receded when William and my friends arrived. The older boys William, Jan, Byron and Naveen liked the vantage point that we were in, for they had front row views of the parade of girls who passed by.

Morph and I were soon joined by Neville, Tsepho and Kallie. Neville was on a short break from his gate duties when he burst out crying seeing Tsepho and Kallie. He sat on a plastic chair next to Morph. We gave him time to calm down.

Kallie asked me, "What happened to Vinod?"

"He was kidnapped yesterday afternoon while out jogging. He was murdered, his body dumped near the Islamic School." I spoke calmly even though I was close to losing it.

"Shit!" Kallie exclaimed in shock.

"Dudes, do they know who did it?" queried Tsepho.

"Nah. Still early days."

"So sorry, Nevs," Tsepho comforted Neville.

"Ja, so sorry, my bro," Kallie said.

Neville shrugged his shoulders and wept quietly; head bowed.

"Hermann's father is here," I told my friends.

"Here, dude! And where's his shit son?" asked Tsepho.

"Not with him."

"Do you think he's involved?" Kallie wondered. "No. Vinod worked for him, and all," Neville perked up and answered.

Three young women came over to pay their respects to Neville. He warmed to the attention and soon went back to his welcoming duties. Tshepo, Kallie and I followed him, leaving Morph in his seat under the tent. Whenever people came to greet Neville and his cousins, we halted our discussion but continued when opportunities prevailed.

"Then why was he killed, dudes? Maybe something to do with that firm," Tsepho asked.

"Maybe they've shady deals and the Mafia was after them." Kallie was on a roll.

The Mafia are Italians and they're in America, not here, you idiot," I reminded them.

"But there're some rich Italians here in Estcourt." Neville's fertile mind was activated.

"Hey Nevs, how come you're suddenly hugging and kissing all these stupid girls so much? Even when they make you cry?" I asked with exasperation.

"I dunno. I kinda like it, and all. They feel nice and they smell nice and it helps me," he responded with a dreamy smile.

Yup. I thought. *Their smells are getting to him.*

"Stay there!" I ordered Morph and went to stand next in line to my friend. Tsepho and Kallie followed suit. For the first time in our lives, we allowed these lovely creatures to hug and kiss us whether they were entering or exiting the yard.

Our deep conversation continued through the breaks from our much-needed duties.

"Ja, but they're not Mafia. We go to the same church as them," noted Kallie.

"No, it's not that," I offered.

"Then what?" both Tsepho and Kallie demanded.

"I'd rather not say," I responded, glancing quickly at Neville.

"Maybe it's aliens."

"No, it can't be."

"Why not? They also abduct people and murder them."

"Aliens don't need to torture people, dude. They can read minds."

"Then why was he tortured?"

"I'll get them! Whoever it is, I'll get the fucking bastards!" Neville erupted.

Just then the hearse with Uncle Billy and Vinod's partner, Ricky, and with Vinod's coffin pulled up, then reversed to the gate where we bravely stood, while every cell in our bodies urged us to run away. We held our positions because Neville had to stand there, and we were with our friend who needed us. All conversation instantly dried up. One was suddenly acutely aware of the agonizing weeping and wailing emanating from the home. This cadence of sorrow grew when it was whispered to the gathered that the coffin had arrived. Except for Neville and his cousins, all young persons near the gate reluctantly relented their positions close to this chariot of death to older men who swamped the back. William was back, holding firmly onto Morph's right hand while I held the other. Our friends remained close by.

I caught glimpses of a light brown coffin as the Tamil Priest sang and chanted incantations to the pantheon of gods and ancestors, while stepping slowly and purposefully towards the home. Neville walked at the back of the coffin next to Ricky. He was a broken young man with a shaven head who looked as though he would collapse and die before they even reached the home. As they approached the verandah, I looked at the people standing there and was shocked to see Joe Combrink wipe his eyes with a handkerchief as he leaned against one of the pillars with sorrow and anger unashamedly etched on his face. Our eyes met before he turned to follow the coffin into Vinod's last farewell in the home of his beloved sister. It took a while before the people were calmed enough for Uncle Billy to make an announcement.

"Thank you for coming ladies and gentlemen... I must announce the coffin will not..." he paused a while. "Will not, be opened for viewing... Only some very close family'll do so..." He paused again and wiped his brow with a handkerchief. "But we'll have to clear the room to do so..." Uncle Billy swallowed very hard and gasped in a few deep breaths for strength. "Vinod's body..." he trailed off for a while again and had to gather himself together one more time before continuing, "Vinod's body and face is very, very badly damaged...And it's not good to view..." Uncle Billy's lips quivered. "I'm so sorry!" He burst into tears and disappeared indoors. Neville and Ricky followed indoors close behind him.

The brutality of death hit me hard in the in the pit of my stomach and I had to quickly sit down and weep as Adelaide and Vinod merged in a mirage of blood and dust and urine and vomit, and from that point on I have vague recollections of the funeral services, intertwined mostly with the saddest of sounds and fragrances of the funeral ceremony that heightened what was already within me such that I could not bear to see more anguish and pain, and was bound in that state until Vinod departed his sister's home forever – in a coffin.

At approximately the same time that the hearse left Alfred Street, the five Homeboys were heartily tucking into their Chicken Licken Family Bucket Fifteen, large Soulfries and ice-cold Liqui-Fruit Mixed Berries juice. They were seated in the lapa near the swimming pool in the Walton's sprawling back yard. It was a large structure with four mahogany patio tables and six matching and cushioned chairs at each table. To one side was a complete bar with the same mahogany counter and liquor cabinets. An 85-inch flat screen TV took center place amongst the closed and locked cabinets. The sound from the TV competed with birds chirping.

"Are you sure it's not one of you crazy brothers from that Mosque who did it?" Ewald waved a partially eaten drumstick at Abu as he spoke with a mouth full of food.

"Ja, they say they're radicalized there." Dewald held his chicken breast with both hands.

Abu was offended but had to swallow his pride and the piece of chicken wing that he was chewing before replying.

"No, I mean, I don't know. We'll have to wait for the cops to find out."

"These cops are too much on the take. They'll find nothing if they're paid well enough not to," Herman added between bites of chips.

"They say it's a bloody hate crime," Rob added his bit, then took a sip from his juice.

"Hate crime, my arse! This is revenge," countered Dewald as he concentrated on another piece of chicken. He settled on a drumstick.

"Speaking of an arse, I've heard they rammed some type of rod up his arse and pulled out his guts. That's bad, man!" Abu tried to steer the conversation away from him.

"They beat him up and slit his throat. That's overkill," said Hermann, shaking his head.

"Or they're sending a message to someone who's fokking gay," Ewald observed.

"Didn't he work for your father?" Rob asked coldly, staring intently at Hermann.

"Ya. My dad is seriously cut up about it. He's even paying for the funeral expenses."

"Maybe your father has a case that's pissing off some big-time fuck-er," Abu offered, glad that the focus was shifted away from him.

"Or he lost one and the crooks after him," suggested Dewald.

"No, I don't think so. It's to do with gay people," Hermann replied automatically.

. . .

A wizened, wrinkled colored male servant approached bearing a tray with five bowls of lemon infused water and serviettes. These he placed on the table nearest to the group, who watched his every move in silence.

"Is there anything else I can get you, my basie?" the servant asked Rob.

"No, Lawrence, that's all. You'll clean up afterwards."

"Thank you, my basie." The group waited until he disappeared indoors before speaking.

"That little fucker needs to be taken fucking out. He's bloody caused us too much fucking grief," Rob spoke angrily as he took out a vial and dished out the capsules, quickly downed with swigs of juice. The others at the table knew exactly who he was referring to.

"Word on the street is he faced us on his own and took Hermann down and we ran away like 'pussies' with our tails between our fokken legs. No mention of his bastard brother and bitch granny. We fokken ran away! Shit!" Ewald's anger was palpable.

"People are laughing at us behind our backs!" Dewald banged a fist on the table. He immediately regretted it when he saw the scowl on Rob's face. He promptly smoothed the portion of tablecloth out with his hands.

"This is fucking humiliation, big time!" Hermann raised his voice in agitation.

"I can put a fokken hit on him," volunteered Ewald.

"No. We'll have to do it our bloody selves," Rob spoke, balling his fists. He glared at each one in turn, daring them to try and weasel out of it. No one flinched.

"When and how?" asked Abu.

"It can't bloody well happen in bloody Estcourt. Too many bloody witnesses. He doesn't move around at night, so we can't nail him in the dark."

"What about kidnapping him?" Ewald frowned as he spoke.

"Too risky. I've seen him around moving with his family and friends. They're too spooked," reported Abu.

"Give them time, they'll slip up soon and we'll fokken nail him," Ewald promised.

"He's an arrogant fucking bastard for such a young cunt," Hermann observed.

"I'll put the word out for reports on that family's movements," suggested Abu.

"Ja, we'll get our break and we'll fokken nail him," promised Ewald.

"I can't wait to bloody well torture that bastard cunt. I want him fucking dead!"

The group finished their meal in silence and proceeded to wash their hands.

We sat in the lounge after supper, each lost in sadness and anger. The only other sounds wafting into the stillness of our company were the night sounds of birds and dogs and cats and crickets and frogs and vehicles.

"Ricky's family were also at the funeral. They're taking him back to Lenasia. They're afraid he'll be next on the list of those who murdered Vinod," Grandma said wearily.

"We saw him walk behind the coffin. Shame, Ouma. It looked like he was finished," William said. He yawned deeply.

The silences were too much for Morph. He slowly but steadily drifted off to sleep with his head on May-June's lap. William scooped him up and took him to bed. We remained with our thoughts until he returned.

"Aunty Priya has asked me to go with her tomorrow to pack up Vinod and Ricky's flat," Grandma cast into the stillness.

"What are they going to do with all their stuff?" asked May-June. She also rubbed her eyes and then yawned with both her hands covering her mouth. Mom used to do that.

"I don't know. Keep some, I suppose. The rest they'll probably sell or give to charity."

"What's happening here in Estcourt, Ouma?" William asked with that frown on his face. "I mean, there's five deaths so far and all were murders?"

"Ja, Ouma. And all in less than a month," added May-June. Grandma thought for a few seconds before answering.

"I don't know, my children. Adelaide's and the three skullies are related – we know that. Uncle Dan lived in a rough place where people are always dying for some reason or another. His doesn't look like it has anything to do with the others. Vinod's death looks like an attack on the gay community," Grandma responded tiredly. She was starting to slur her words a bit. We lapsed into an attentive silence as a vehicle went by below along Alfred Street.

"But what if they're all somehow related?" William asked, looking at each of us in turn. "Is that possible?" We could tell he was serious.

I thought it best to keep quiet. May-June nodded off briefly. Grandma watched her keenly, making sure she did not fall off her seat unobserved. I moved closer to my sister to catch her if she started slipping. I was on the point of waking May-June up when she resurfaced.

"I don't think so." Grandma was reaching a state of total exhaustion.

"Look at what happened since Adelaide's death. What if there's a link?" William said.

"If there is one, then we're not seeing it yet," Grandma said after some thought.

"If there is then something very bad is happening in this town." William looked directly at me. "And we seem to be in the middle of it. Or at least Plano seems to be in the middle of it ever since Adelaide was killed." My heart thudded rapidly.

"Perhaps it'll be wise for us to get out of town for a bit. But we'll have to move quickly and without telling anyone where we're going," Grandma suggested.

"Perhaps forever, Ouma. This place is becoming as bad as the cities," May-June added.

"I'll think about it and make some enquiries. Not a word," Grandma said between yawns.

"Okay, Ouma."

"Okay, let's go to bed. We have a busy day tomorrow. You boys'll have to come with to help carry and load all the stuff. Don't get paranoid about all this. Let's be on our guard but let me try to find out what's happening before we decide on what to do."

"Okay, Ouma. Goodnight, Ouma."

William and I made sure that our home was secured before going to bed.

They were in a Golf III VR6 metallic silver-grey with black mags. It was close to eleven-forty-five pm. Mzo had his eyes on this particular 'Vora-Virus' (VR6) for quite some time. They saw it some months ago when visiting family in Sweetwaters in Pietermaritzburg. On that day the driver was oblivious to them following him to his home in Bombay Heights. They would have taken this beauty that first time while tailing the stupid 'mshana' to his house in Bombay Road, but fortunately for the owner a 'bogata' van with its blue light at rest came cruising by as the Vora-Virus stopped for his driveway gate to open. He was a lucky son-of-a-bitch, but now Mzo was determined to get it.

Mzo and his gang drove especially to Bombay Heights to fetch it. They first had to complete their surveillance of their target area from midday to early evening. They only stopped when hunger pangs elicited nagging moans and groans Mzo took the opportunity to lay out his plan "Haw!" Mzo thought as he viewed the bowed heads of this loudly grunting, munching and slurping 'amajita'. *"Must feed them ven I want sum-ding. Then they shut-up."*

It did not take them long to find the stupid 'mshana' as they cruised the streets of Northdale and Bombay Heights. The owner of the Vora-Virus made it easy for them this time. He came home at about eleven – the car weaving dangerously every now and again. The black Merc SUV followed discreetly behind. The Vora-Virus eventually swung into its driveway in Bombay Road towards a slow-moving gate that it almost smashed into. Then it almost clipped the gate post and the garage door as the drunk driver somehow managed to align himself through these openings. The rest was easy. Skeets was out of the SUV and at the gate as quick as a 'G-String' (BMW), preventing it from closing. The rest of the gang followed behind while the black SUV, driven by Mzo's cousin, carried on cruising Bombay Heights.

That mshana staggered unaware of any danger indoors, making it easy for the gang to gain entry, grab hold of him, knock him out and tie him to his bed. They even switched off all the lights in the house, locked up properly and threw the keys through a slightly open window before driving off with the gleaming Vora-Virus.

"Eintlik, we can't trust what the tsotsis would do if we left the place open. Plus, it gives us time to do the hit shup-shup. This is big bucks moola for the big-time. Fifty thousand Rand is ku million," Mzo reasoned with his gang.

Mzo was pleased at the night's work so far. Even Bongani's insistence that they kill the mshana to buy more time did not irritate him that much. Mzo patiently explained to Bongani about the merits of not wasting this young man who was clearly thriving in life and was not a lova from the loksheen. One day they may return to take bigger things from him. They followed the black SUV to Sobantu Township where it would be parked in a safe place until their return. False number plates were installed on the Golf.

The Vora-Virus breezed into Pietermaritzburg city centre along Ortmann Road. Mzo was sentimental and they made a point of cruising along Chief Albert Luthuli Street until they branched left onto the Old Howick Road. From that point on all sentiment was forgotten as the gang did final checks on the assortment of AK47's and 9mm Taurus pistols and with the magazines of more than 500 rounds of live ammunition. Mzo favored a Heckler & Koch USP Semi-Automatic Pistol. None of the men had any military training and yet the way they handled their weapons seemed to bear testimony to all of them having been trained by a professional.

Unbeknown to the group, one of Mzo's uncles was an askari who was unleashed to wreak havoc on the Soweto youth during the 1976 riots. It was a secret known by only a few family members. Before he died of liver failure due to alcoholism, he spent hours training Mzo on handling all sorts of armaments. Without telling them how he acquired such deadly skills Mzo thereafter embedded this knowledge into his gang through months of intensive training.

At the traffic circle near the Montrose Filling-Station they joined Peter Brown Drive and went over the bridge above the N3 Freeway. Mzo urged his men to be extremely vigilant as they slowed way down to cruise past the staggered intersections of Loveday Drive and Davenport Road. The house they focused mostly on was a nondescript red brick and yellow painted building with a red roof. Like all other houses in the area, it had a 2m high security fence and a heavy motorized security gate. This would be their entry point. They dropped Skeets off at the Loveday intersection. Unbeknown to the locals, the house the gang scouted was a safe house extensively used by the Scorpions.

The caretaker who lived in one half of the building was a ranking police officer at the Montrose Police Station in Henderson Road. It was therefore not unusual to see a regular flow of police vehicles in and around this place. In fact, the residents who lived close to it were chuffed that they had a senior police officer in close attendance. These matters were not in the document Mzo and his gang studied earlier and burnt. Their task was to eliminate Enoch Mathebula. They made a U-turn on Montrose Drive and meandered back along Peter Brown to do another drive-by. As they re-joined Peter Brown Drive the digital clock in the Vora-Virus struck midnight. The area was wreathed in a thick pall of mist. Visibility a mere fifteen meters.

CHAPTER 13
SECRETS IN AN OPAQUE SHROUD

(TUESDAY, 21 DECEMBER 1999)

I t was still their lucky day and night. One of the Scorpions' men left the gate wide open when departing, not bothering to ensure that it had closed properly. He disappeared rapidly in the mist as he headed down Peter Brown Drive towards the city centre. Skeets, who was close to the gate, walked casually to the eye and hung his cap over it, which forced the gate to open again and allowed Mzo to quickly drive the Vora-Virus into the yard. The movement was so unexpected that the other men in the Golf were thrown off balance and the car following them had to brake sharply to avoid a collision. The angry driver of that vehicle hooted angrily, opened his window and raised a middle finger to the occupants of the VR6 before gunning his vehicle and driving off angrily into the thick swirling mist. Mzo and his men casually left the vehicle. Skeets scanned the road outside and gave them the thumbs-up.

To the casual observer nothing seemed amiss, except for the cap over the eye. No passing vehicle paid much attention to them and did not even see the cap, as they concentrated on negotiating their treacherous journeys through very poor visibility along this winding road. Papi waved at Skeets who waved back. The four men walked on, firearms well-hidden behind their clothes. Skeets waited at the gate as if he were a sentry on duty. His AK-47 was slung over his back as he guarded the open gate. They had memorized a map of the place and new which side of the building to go to. Soft music of Brenda Fassie singing 'Soon and Very Soon' was playing from somewhere indoors. The gang paid no attention to the haunting music. They were on a high, riding their streak of good luck.

Mzo grunted an instruction and Jomo melted into the shrubbery close to the back corner on the cop's side of the house. Jomo was also tasked to start the car as soon Mzo signaled him to do so. Skeets would then cover that side of the house as well as the gate. At the other corner of the house, on the Scorpions side, Bongani did likewise. They knew there were three people guarding Enoch Mathebula. One would be indoors with him while the other two patrolled outside. They knew that the cop was on nightshift and was therefore not at home.

The luck of the gang continued, for the two guards were not on patrol. They were taking a smoke break while peeping into the window of the policeman's teenage daughter's bedroom where the curtain always remained partially opened. Tonight they could see the young lady asleep on top of the blankets, almost nude.

Mzo and Papi walked to the front door of the Hawk's side of the house. Mzo tugged at the heavy security gate. It was locked. He tried the door handle. It opened. Enoch was seated in front of a TV set, half asleep, handcuffed to the sofa. The third guard was nowhere to be seen – which meant that he was the one who rushed off a few minutes ago. Mzo raised his Heckler & Koch USP Semi-Automatic Pistol and shot Enoch at point blank range three times.

The first bullet drilled a hole above Enoch's left eye as he turned to see who was at the door. His head snapped back viciously from the force of the bullet. The second and third bullets hit his chest. One of these bursts went through his heart, causing blood to spill onto his chest and stomach. Enoch was dead even before the echoes of the gunfire stopped. Papi waited with pistol at the ready for any other cop indoors, but no one came rushing into the lounge. Mzo pulled the door shut and he and Papi started to make their escape. He called to Bongani who waited at the ready for the appearance of the two cops.

Bongani had stared into light and the flashes from the fired gun. When he turned to the darkness he was blinded for the longest second. His ageing eyes did not adapt fast enough, with the added problem of staring into thick mist blurring his vision even further. He swung his entire body and AK 47 way past the corner of the house, missing the two cops who came running around that corner, guns at the ready. Before Bongani could realign himself, both guards opened fire and four bullets entered Bongani's chest area in a split second. He dropped like a rock into the shrubbery. Bongani did not even get a chance to fire his AK47.

Mzo and Papi turned and quickly shot at both cops before these lawmen had a chance to turn towards the new danger. One of them fell to the ground. To his credit, the other man immediately bent down and managed to drag his colleague out of site behind the corner. The hail of bullets that were meant for his chest whizzed by over his head. Mzo and Papi ran to Bongani where Mzo picked him up and ran for the Golf. Papi picked up the AK47 and followed closely behind, scanning for any further danger from the remaining Scorpions. He fired to discourage any bravado and heard Skeets do the same from the other side of the house.

Mzo dumped Bongani in the back seat and jumped into the front passenger seat while Papi and Skeets took their places in the back seat. Skeets had retrieved his cap. Jomo reversed the 'Vora-Virus' out of the gate just as it started closing. He flew it straight across the road and swung with a handbrake turn down Peter Brown Drive. In a single, fluid movement he sped off towards the N3 Freeway. The hit had taken precisely forty seconds to execute from driving into the yard and exiting. The interior of the Golf reeked of the acrid smell of hot nitroglycerin and the pungent odor of oxidized blood.

The men were high on adrenalin, shock and fear. The adrenalin that coursed through their beings remained at high levels from drugs and violence and the aftermath of what they had just done. The shock trembled through them at the sight of their dead comrade. They knew that the lack of exit wounds were from dum-dum bullets that tore Bongani to pieces inside. This was unexpected. The gang knew and understood the dangers that came with their jobs, but it was always a shock when one of them was killed. The fear stemmed from not properly taking out the two guards who must have already raised the alarm. They feared getting caught.

They needed to get away fast. Their plan was to take a south-bound on-ramp to the N3, but during their recon of the kill zone they failed to take note that there was no south bound on-ramp from Peter Brown Drive towards Durban. They wasted a few seconds trying to switch on the GPS and debating which direction to take. The sounds of approaching police sirens wailing forlornly in the mist reverberated ominously in the interior of the Vora-Virus. The suburb would become a death-trap if they were to retreat.

Without a word to the others, Jomo switched off the car lights and sped the wrong way down the off-ramp that approached from the north. Their luck held, for no vehicles met them down that ramp. Jomo slowed down enough to swing the vehicle in the direction of the traffic flow, without having to touch the brakes. Those red lights from the wrong direction would be a dead give-away. He switched on the dim and fog lights as he cruised briefly in the emergency lane. Within a split second he saw a gap between two trucks and gunned the vehicle into the next lane, heading south towards Durban. The cop vehicles shot by overhead on Peter Brown Drive, paying no attention to the trucks and the Golf VR6.

After breakfast William, Morph and I waited on the verandah for Grandma and May-June to get ready. We were lounging around and goofing off when I espied Kallie awkwardly limping his way up Rocky Lane towards us. We could see he was in some sort of distress. I left William and Morph and ran to assist my friend. The sight was a shock.

His eyes were swollen blue, there was a big black and red blotch on his left check and severe cuts and bruises lacerated his arms and legs. One of his front teeth was badly chipped and his gum around it was blue and swollen. I tried to carefully support him, but he winced and gasped when I touched his back. I quickly removed my arm and held his right arm near the elbow to support him. William followed me out of the gate. He supported Kallie's other arm.

"Kallie, what happened!?" I asked with deep alarm.

"It's my pa again," Kallie responded between labored breaths and gritted teeth.

"What happened at home?" William asked gently.

"My pa beat me up, my bro." Kallie's chest was making a strange whooping sound.

"Why, Kallie? Why!?" I pleaded. I had seen such welts on Kallie on a few occasions before, but those were not as severe as these.

"He was drunk... and hitting my ma. I tried to stop him....to help Ma... So he moered me... very bad." Tears streamed down Kallie's face.

We reached the verandah and gingerly seated him on a bench. Grandma, May-June and Morph came hurrying out the front door.

May-June and Morph gasped involuntarily and with shock at the sight of Kallie.

"My child! What's happened?" Grandma touched Kallie lightly on his arm.

"Hellos," Kallie managed. It took him a few minutes to gather himself and explain to Grandma what he told William and me.

"Have you gone to the cops? He can't do that!" William exploded.

"No, but Ma went to the Welfare office."

"What'd they say?" William continued in the same vein.

"Not much. They said... it's for the cops to sort out. It's not the first time... Pa always hits Ma and us when he's drunk... But it's the first time... Pa beat me up... and sjambokked me so bad," he said with tears streaming from swollen eyes.

"But Kallie, he can't do this. How's your Ma?" Grandma asked with deep concern.

"She's OK, Ouma." Kallie swallowed hard before continuing. "We're leaving today for good." He managed to blurt out as tears continued streaming down his swollen cheeks.

All of us gasped in dismay.

"Where to?" Grandma asked of Kallie's bowed head and shaking shoulders.

"Somewhere in the Free State Ouma... My uncle... Ma's eldest boetie... has a farm there... They've sent two bakkies to fetch us." Kallie said softly.

Grandma, May-June and Morph were sobbing. William and I internalized our shock.

"Oh, Kallie!" was all Grandma could say.

"Why Kallie, why, this is so wrong!" May-June shouted angrily.

"I must go now... I asked Ma if I could say goodbye.... to you.... and she said yes.... but I must go now," Kallie said as he struggled to stand up. William and I rushed to help him.

"Okay, Son. Our regards to your Ma and tell her we'll be praying for you and your family every day. Things'll work out. You must come visit. Our door is always open for you."

"'K, Ouma. Thank you very much, Ouma." Kallie gingerly hugged Grandma. Then he hugged May-June and Morph. William and I held his arms as we helped him home.

"We must be gone before Pa gets back. He went to Newcastle on business," Kallie said urgently. We tried to hurry him along.

"I'll miss you, my bro,'" I managed to blurt out.

"I'll miss you too, my boet... Please tell Tsepho and Neville.... There's no time." Kallie managed to get out. He winced and groaned with each step.

"Okay, I'll do so," I said as bravely as I could.

The two double-cab bakkies each with a trailer, were parked outside Kallie's home. We could count four men who were hurriedly loading goods onto these vehicles and trailers. No one else, no neighbors or friends, were there to help in their time of need.

"Come Plano, we must help them." William left Kallie's arm and rushed forward.

"No! No! Guys! It's ok! Thanks." Kallie stopped us in our tracks. I could see William frown briefly as he watched them loading the vehicles.

"We'll be going to Philippolis in the Free State," Kallie volunteered.

"Will you phone once you're there? You have our number."

"Yes, I will. Please don't tell Pa or anyone."

"We won't," William and I reassured him.

"'K, Kallie. Be seeing you. Don't let this shit get you down. Study hard, 'lightie' and make something of yourself. You can do it." The longest speech I ever heard him make.

"'K, thanks William," Kallie responded with a broken smile They hugged briefly.

"'K, Plano. Check you, my boet." Reality took hold.
"Check you, my brother."
Life was so unfair!

Vinod and Ricky's home was upstairs in a block of flats on Alfred Street, near the Phillips Street intersection. Ricky's family had taken him with them to their home after the funeral and the first cleansing and quenching ceremony was completed at the flat. They packed and removed some of his clothing and personal belongings. Ricky had asked Uncle Billy and Aunty Priya to sort out everything else. He would return for the ten-day ceremony and would take with him anything else they chose to pass on to him. The rest of the items in the flat he left to the discretion of Uncle Billy and Aunty Priya.

We arrived just as Uncle Billy's bakkie went by us in the driveway. Auntie Priya and Neville were with him. Following them was a flatbed truck with a driver and passenger. There was another vehicle already parked in the courtyard. A family of four jumped out. Neville's uncle and aunt and his cousins, Vaughn and Bev, who were with him that night under the Syringa Berry tree. The gathering greeted each other solemnly and in subdued voices.

A poodle barked at us from one of the ground floor flats. Morph grabbed May-June's hand for protection. Before I could reassure him, a lady quickly picked up the poodle and shut the door. We began the laborious trudge towards an unpleasant task that had to be done. Neville and I took up the rear. With each step I filled him in on what had happened to Kallie.

"Why didn't he come tell me also?" Neville wailed forlornly.

"They were in a hurry. There was no time," I tried to speak as comforting as I could muster under the circumstances.

"Oh! Shit! This is too much, and all. First Vinod and now Kallie," Neville wiped his eyes as he spoke. There was a catch in his throat with each word uttered.

"I know. It was hard to say goodbye to him." We walked in silence as we negotiated the landing at the halfway point of the stairwell.

"Will he ever come back?" Neville asked as we started climbing again. He surreptitiously wiped away the tears from his eyes.

"I dunno. I don't think so. You should've seen him, Nevs. He was bust up very badly."

"My 'ballie' dops on weekends and all, but he doesn't go around busting my ma and me up. What's wrong with that ballie?

"I dunno, Nevs. Looks like some can handle dop and others can't." Neville sighed deeply before he spoke. "Well, I'll be a good 'dopper' like my 'ballie', and all, when I grow up." He seemed to perk up a bit at this thought. I kept silent.

"Do you know where they're gone to?" he queried.

"No, I don't."

"Do you have a cell number where we can contact him?" Neville asked.

"No, I don't." I had made a promise to Kallie.

Neville stared at me quizzically as we reached the first-floor walkway. I did not look at him, but instead focused on Uncle Billy opening the door to the flat.

We were energized in a spirit of unity as we worked on sorting and then transferring the contents from within the flat onto the flatbed truck. The ladies did the sorting and packing while the men did the carting.

One of the men assisting with the move was a tall and extremely thin young man called Zane, who was in his early twenties. He moved and spoke in a fidgety, energetic way and seemed to be propelled all over by an invisible wind that tended to blow him off and on course every now and then. He was a great help and did not shirk from the tasks assigned to him.

We were onto the bigger furniture in the flat, struggling in a variety of contortions to negotiate the tough journey down the staircase with heavy cargo in our grasps. Zane was moving backwards downstairs as he held onto a wardrobe. He was almost at the bottom step when that poodle suddenly barked loudly at the man's heels.

It was a shock to Zane's system and so, he stumbled and lost control of his end of the wardrobe. Zane grabbed hold of the railings with both hands to prevent a treacherous fall onto the back of his head. The wardrobe followed his momentum and came crashing onto his exposed spindly right shin. Fortunately for Zane, Neville's uncle, who was carrying the other end, managed to hold on and prevent it from tumbling onto Zane's exposed body and face.

William, Neville, Vaughn and I were returning from the flatbed and we saw the agonizing fall and heard the terrible crack as Zane's shin bone snapped in two. William immediately rushed forward and grabbed hold of the wardrobe that was inexorably heading for the Zane's face. We rushed to assist him and the four of us managed to stabilize the situation as Zane fell slowly back and screamed in pain where he lay at an angle on the stairs. The startled poodle scooted back into his owner's flat.

Uncle Billy and the ladies came rushing out of the flat. With his help on the other side of the wardrobe we managed to carefully remove the furniture and to stand it in the courtyard before we lifted Zane gently off the stairwell and laid him on the ground. Zane was screaming uncontrollably, thrashing about vigorously in distress.

The bottom section of his leg was at an acute angle from where the break occurred. His pantleg around the break was soaked with blood. Zane's screams emptied all the flats as the anxious and the curious came tumbling out to see what had happened. Fortunately for Zane, one of those who rushed outdoors was a qualified nurse who was off duty that day. She immediately took charge of the situation. She needed a big scissors and someone rushed off to get one. She needed her first-aid kit and her child rushed off to get it. She needed a towel and someone rushed off to get one. She needed two makeshift splints and Uncle Billy and Aunty Priya rushed off indoors to get them. She needed strong men to hold Zane still. William, Neville and I joined other men who came forward and held Zane in a vice grip pinned to the floor.

Zane shivered in fear, nodding his head sort of side to side and up and down at the same time. It looked more like he was rolling it about. The nurse methodically examined Zane's body, prodding and pressing him from his head to the bottom of his un-injured leg. She would ask him to lift his hands and move them around, move his wrists and fingers and the ankle and toes on his good leg as she swiftly checked him carefully and slowly.

We breathed a collective sigh of relief when she completed her examination and did not find any other injuries. By then all those who had rushed off to do her bidding returned with the required stuff. The nurse quickly cut open Zane's pants to expose the wound. Some of the surrounding group gasped at the sickening sight of the rapidly swelling break blotched with black, red and blue skin bleeding heavily from that broken gash in his very thin leg. The nurse laid out what she needed on the towel that was brought to her.

"Ready?!" she commanded us and grabbed hold of both sides of the broken leg, tugged the bottom part away from the main body, straightened it and put it back into its proper alignment. Zane fainted at the first excruciating tug and the unimaginable heavy mist of extreme pain that hit him hard when she did so. The sister was expecting this reaction for she didn't bother to resuscitate him after checking his pulse and breathing. She worked swiftly to put the splints in place, and to bandage the leg. With that we carefully raised Zane off the ground and put him into the car. The truck driver jumped in at the back to support Zane. They sped off to the hospital with the nurse in attendance, and with Uncle Billy and Aunty Priya following closely behind in their bakkie.

The somber heaviness returned as we trudged upstairs to continue our work. A few of the men who had rushed outdoors from their homes helped us and we safely carted the remaining heavy furniture from the flat to the truck. The men departed and we continued carrying the packed boxes to the truck. It was back-breaking work for William, Neville, Vaughn and I to haul these full, heavy and sealed boxes down the stairs, especially after witnessing Zane's accident. Voicing our concerns to the hustling and bustling ladies, who were still processing the shock of Zane breaking his leg, was of no help to us for they simply ignored our pleas for the loads to be lightened. They reasoned that if two ladies could lift a packed box in the flat, then surely us four strong young men could carry them down the stairs, or did we want the ladies to do the work for us?

We stopped complaining. We sweated, groaned and grumbled as we carried those heavy boxes down to the truck, but made sure there was no scowl on our faces each time we returned to the flat. Grandma would not hesitate to smack right there for any misbehavior.

Lunchtime came and went with no relief for the sweating and straining and tired bodies and our growling and grumbling and sapping tummies. Tap water had little effect. These acute pangs were aggravated by those lovely aromas of Milo and other nice goodies from the Nestle factory, coupled with the aromas of various foods from nearby homes. These wafted over us as we toiled up and down those stairs. We felt were ready to succumb to the onset of starvation.

"There's my 'ballie'! Hope they brought some chow, and all!" Neville croaked with some semblance of optimism. Vaughn and I licked our lips and William swallowed spit in hope of much needed sustenance arriving.

All thoughts of Adelaide and death and Kallie and Zane receded beyond the veil of primal cravings and salivating for a morsel of food. We huffed and puffed and glared at Uncle Billy and Aunty Priya slowly discharging themselves from the bakkie.

"Woah, boys! You look like you could eat me alive, and all!" Aunty Priya laughed. We shifted uncomfortably and the two adults laughed even more at our discomfort.

"We knew you hungry wolves would be starving to death, so we bought some Kentucky!" Uncle Billy said as he approached from the other side of the bakkie.

"Come help carry boys!" commanded Aunty Priya. The four of us rushed forward to grab the shopping bags and without a word rushed upstairs – leaving the two adults chortling and cackling in our dust. The grown-ups sat on the kitchen chairs and the rest of us flopped on the floor while Grandma and Aunty Priya started dishing up, much too slowly to our liking.

I did not concentrate on their discussion, except to note that Zane was fine and that he would be kept in the hospital overnight. Aunty Priya said he had an open, compound fracture. I resolved to look this up at home. We made light work of the KFC bucket, let me tell you!

. . .

Joe Combrink pushed the grocery trolley rapidly out of the Spar on the corner of Hellet and Wagon Streets. He looked like a man in a hurry to get away as he rushed towards a small flock of doves and pigeons feeding on crumbs ahead of him. Joe was not focused on these birds, for he was seething because of the snide whispered comments and sniggering that assailed him above the piped shop music through the aisles of the shop. He knew that Susan's infidelity was the town's juiciest gossip item. Like the shoppers in the Spar, some of the mildly startled birds in front of him took flight when he approached, circled around Joe and landed behind him on the walkway, cooing their displeasure at his presence. Others merely walked far enough away from him to avoid any unwanted contact. They hastily returned to their feeding spot as soon as he passed by – just like some of the shoppers did.

The swift movement of two pigeons jerked Joe out from that mist of anger and gloom and he braked and jumped back with his trolley as a silver-grey Golf 4 Cabriolet streaked closely by, harshly caught brakes further down the lot and swung with abandon into an open parking space where it came to a sudden stop. It took Joe a few seconds to gather his breath. He recognized the vehicle. He wanted to rush over there and beat the offender into the ground.

The throbbing music from the Golf ceased abruptly as Rob Walton jumped out from his vehicle and jauntily strode with arrogance and abandon towards the entrance of the Spar. He saw Joe Combrink but made no effort to apologise. Instead, he merely glanced at Joe with malevolence, then merely tilted his head and eyebrows slightly upward in greeting as he strode by. An ugly smirk abruptly creased his mouth and rapidly disappeared as he turned his head away from Joe to say something to a parking attendant who rushed forward to fawn upon him.

Without breaking his stride Rob sauntered into the shop. Joe stood where he was for at least a minute, trying with all his might to snap the steel handle of the trolley with his bare hands as throbbing anger coursed throughout his body, screaming for vengeance. When some semblance of sanity returned, he hurried to his car, offloaded the groceries in the boot and sat in the driver's seat, needing to cool down much more before attempting to drive off.

From his peripheral vision Joe could see his minders sitting in a green Toyota Rav4 three parking bays to the left and back of him. He ignored them and put on one of his CD's and turned up the volume a bit higher than usual. Joe then surreptitiously removed the card from his wallet and took out his third cellphone. He dialed the number.

He returned the card to his wallet and the wallet to his pocket while he waited for the connection. An elderly lady with a Western Cape accent answered the call.

"Helloooos!"

"Hello, tannie. May I please speak to Oupa Pless?" Joe spoke clearly.

"You've got a wrong number, Seun. There's no Oupa Pless here."

"Sorry, tannie. Totsiens," Joe responded.

Totsiens, Seun. Hope you find your Oupa Pless." The elderly lady cut the call.

Joe returned the cellphone to one of his jacket inner pockets, started the vehicle and drove sedately out of the parking area. His minders followed closely behind. Joe ignored them. He'd been vexing about the dilemma that burdened him and was on the point of sticking with the three men in a tub, even though he suspected they would kill him one day. Up until that fateful Sunday afternoon of 19 December 1999, he had convinced himself that he needed to stick with them for a while to buy some time. Even the veiled threat Faizel delivered was not enough to convince him that his life and those of his wife and son were in any imminent danger.

He was issued a similar threat in the past when he agreed to be their attorney, but no action was taken against him, even though he had slipped up and in error revealed some important tender prices to one of their competitors. It was the lack of serious consequences then that had lulled him for a while into a misbegotten sense of security. But then they brutally murdered Vinod and he knew without a shadow of doubt it was done as a warning to him. He knew for certain they would not hesitate to do the same to him and to his family if they perceived the slightest inclination that he had somehow betrayed them. Irreversible contact was now made with Superintendent Carel van den Beek.

"Oh God! What have I done! He groaned. He had seen Vinod's

body and now suddenly saw Susan and Hermann gruesomely torn up like Vinod was. He groaned again and then, for the first time since his childhood, Joe prayed that Carel would come through for him and his family and rescue them. The moment he turned into his driveway he felt utterly dejected as the brooding sense of darkness and death washed over him.

The Rav4 cruised slowly by Joe's gateway, made a U-turn further down the road and returned to park outside the Combrink's home. They had seen what Rob did in the parking lot at the Spar. They had witnessed Joe Combrink take, or make, a brief call. But they had no clue what was said. Their listening devices could not separate speech from the loud music and none of them were lip readers. It would take at least three weeks to get call records from the cellphone company and much longer to get a transcript of the conversation. They noted nothing out of the ordinary in their report, unaware that they were also under surveillance.

They paid no mind to the white Nissan Skyline GT-R that passed them by and drove further down the road where it parked out of sight from them. Neither did they pay attention to the lazy group of municipal workers who were supposed to be cleaning the sidewalks and gutters, but instead lounging under the trees. Little did they know that three of those 'good-for-nothing bastards' were Superintendent Carel van den Beek's operatives.

CHAPTER 14
POISONOUS PERSUASIONS
(WEDNESDAY, 22 DECEMBER 1999)

The Butcher, Baker and Candlestick Maker met at six-thirty am in the Butcher's office on the corner of Albert Street and Shepstone Avenue. The meeting was hastily rescheduled by the Butcher at approximately four-thirty that morning. The staff would arrive around seven-thirty and their meeting would be concluded long before then. The tension in the room was palpable.

"Eleven more of our assets dead! And Mathebula! Overnight! How the FUCK did it happen?!" Eric demanded, glaring at his colleagues.

"Does anyone know why they were assassinated?" Faizel chimed in.

Ewald stared back at Eric and Faizel.

"Enoch was assassinated at a Scorpions safe house in Maritzburg. The cops don't know how many assassins did the hit. One of the assassins was shot and one of the cops. But all the assassins got away. They think it was four or five hitmen." Ewald grew up on a farm and spoke fluent Zulu. His pronunciations were perfect. "Three of our other ANC assets – Jackson Nozi Msopi, Weezy Gazide and Ntombifuthi Njilo – were taken out in a hail of bullets on the N2 between Kwambonambi and Mtubatuba. No witnesses. Prelim reports say there were at least six AK47's used. Gift Mvemve, our IFP man in the Dundee region, was assassinated in his house in Sithembile Township in Glencoe. Four men broke in and killed him and his wife but spared their small children." Ewald paused to check notes on a second page before continuing.

"Sesi Mabele was also killed by four such intruders at her home in Alcockspruit near Dannhauser. Her grandchildren who were with her were also not killed. She was another IFP Councillor. Jacob Mgwabi was gunned down by a lone assassin as he walked to a shop in Cleremont. He was DA. Ashok Maharaj was gunned down at his business in Isipingo. Surveillance footage shows it was five masked men who did it. They found Tinus Badenhorst's body in the boot of his car off the N8 near Thaba Nchu. Strangled with fishing line. His hands and feet tied together with cable ties. No witnesses. Both Ashok and Tinus were ANC."

"Speedy Moloi and Bright Chauke were assassinated on the Grayston Drive Bridge coming from Alexandra Township and heading to Sandton. Witnesses said two motorbikes stopped alongside their vehicle and they were shot by the passengers at the back of the bikes. They also said the bikes turned around and went back towards Alexander Township, spraying bullets at motorists as they left. One lady and her three-year-old daughter were killed. Eight other motorists have injuries ranging from critical to mild. Both bikes did not have number plates. Speedy and Bright were ANC." Ewald placed the page down before him, folded his hands together and stared at his allies. The two men shifted uncomfortably in their seats.

"I've already made contact with Enoch's family to express sympathies," Faizel broke the brooding silence. "I'll be visiting them this morning to make funeral arrangements. I'll be paying for the funeral. He was a good friend of mine."

"Do they know any bloody thing? Eric asked bluntly.

"No. They're in deep shock and traumatized. They're blaming the Scorpions for his death. They don't believe the cops version of events." Faizel scratched his beard, dropped his hands to his lap and sighed deeply to recover his composure.

"It could've been them," volunteered Eric.

Faizel swallowed before answering. "It could've, after all, that's what they did during the apartheid era." He knew he was touching a nerve.

"I don't buy it," Ewald retorted. "Not when so many of our assets were taken out overnight and in different places. This is something else."

"TJ's furious and has mobilized his network to search for answers," Ewald continued.

"Was anyone caught?"

"Just a matter of time," snapped Ewald.

Both Eric and Faizel tensed.

"These were mostly your assets. Your contacts through Enoch." Eric's voice was accusatory as he glared at Faizel.

"Mostly, but not all. Four of them were handled by Ewald," Faizel replied calmly.

"TJ's already setting up their replacements. He wants our input before midday today, otherwise he'll make the decisions. "We should try and get some we know. It'll cost us extra seed money, but it's always worth it in the end," Ewald spoke into the brief silence.

"We must promote from inside rather than bring in new ones," responded Faizel.

"Ja. I agree. We don't know what shit fuckers we'll get if we leave it to TJ," Eric added.

"Ok, I'll contact him with our list. Get back to me before eleven-thirty with your lists. I'll make up mine in the meantime." Ewald sat back in his chair.

"TJ warned us. These dead people were in our network," Ewald continued.

"What the fuck do we do now?" queried Eric.

"Keep searching with TJ for answers and hope we get something. Otherwise, nothing else. It's too close to the 27th." Ewald leaned forward and rested his arms on his desk.

"Speaking of the 27th, TJ's confirmed it's all set for the catalyst," he reported, then looked directly at Faizel. "How are things set up with the Land Surveyor?"

"He's done some practice runs and reported to me that he's ready."

"Can that fucker deliver?" Eric boomed.

"Yes. He's had a perfect record over the last fifteen years," Faizel responded dryly.

"And are the Sheiks still a go?" asked Ewald.

"Yes. The money's in place and the ship with more merchandise will dock in Mozambique on the 28th. I've planned for the shipment to be collected and distributed to our storage facilities," Faizel spoke confidently.

"Eric, are the drivers ready?" Ewald asked turning to look directly at Eric.

"Ja. The fucking cunts've done a lot of dummy runs on the N3. They're ready."

"On my side the logistics with the handlers and leaders has been sorted out. They're all ready. I've sorted out more dummy companies and established two more routes for the cash from the offshore accounts into SA. I've checked our investment portfolios, as I'm sure you have done, and everything is perfectly in place. Gentlemen, we stand to make billions."

"Or lose it all, even our lives" Faizel thought as he glanced quickly at Eric and then back at Ewald. Their faces and eyes were inscrutable.

"Faizel have you and Combrink sorted out an offshore account yet?"

Eric's entire frame tensed and he scowled menacingly. Ewald did not flinch.

"Not yet. We need at least four to six more days to have it in place so that we can start the money transfers." Faizel also picked up on Eric's tensing at the mention of Combrink.

"Have you told him what would happen to him and his family if he betrayed us?"

.

"Yes, he knows. Ewald, has your surveillance yielded anything?" Faizel asked.

"Nothing yet. But something will come up. Always does."

"Okay, gentlemen. Any other business to discuss?" Ewald sat back in his seat.

"I'm fine," responded Faizel. Eric merely shook his head. He could not dare speak.

"Okay. Let's meet daily at 6am from now on. Gives us more time to address issues. We can also meet in the afternoons, as the need arises."

Both Faizel and Eric murmured in agreement, rose in unison and departed. Ewald glared at them as they left the building. He picked up an unlisted number and dialed his Security Chief.

"Add Eric Walton to the list for surveillance. Be discreet. I don't want him suspecting anything. Check my office every morning at 05h00 for bugs. You must be done by 05h30. I'll send you an access password every morning and I'll be in the office every time to meet you."

After breakfast Morph and I amused ourselves playing in the yard, while Grandma and May-June sorted through our clothes and toys to give some of these to the local orphanage for Christmas. It was necessary to hide their actions from Morph. To him, giving away something he paid for was no problem, but giving away a gift was sacrilege, a betrayal of the person who bought you the gift by giving it away. No number of persuasive arguments could ever sway him. Losing a gift was painful for him, but it was tolerable. But to give a gift away was criminal.

So, the rest of us had to conspire to have him 'lose' old gifts at least twice a year. Today was one of those days. I could see Grandma and May-June through the window of our bedroom, packing the chosen items for the orphanage into a new big black refuse bag. William was in Grandma's room wrapping up the Christmas presents. The unrelenting summer sun had Morph and I playing only in the rapidly diminishing shadows around our home. I prepared an obstacle course of sand, bricks and tomato box planks for our wire cars. These marvels had these long wire steering columns and steering wheels that allowed the driver to remain upright while driving. It took a bit of talent and precision to construct them using wire hangers and pieces of wire fencing. Old cotton reels, or empty shoe polish tins, served as wheels. I inherited William's pride and joy, while Morph was the proud owner of my previous vehicle.

"Vroom vroom vrooooom," roared Morph as he walked up and down the courseway. "Plano, do you wanna drive now?" he asked handing me the steering wheel of his car.

"Where're you going?" I queried as I applied the finishing touches to our raceway.

"Wanna drink some water." He skipped past me and ran towards the back door. I had to stop him, so I ran after him as fast as I could after him. Morph turned the corner and was instantly surrounded by a kaleidoscope of fluttering Mother-of Pearl butterflies.

"Ooww!" he exclaimed gleefully ran off after them, hopping and skipping this way and that way with joy oozing out from the widest of smiles on his face.

"Come, Plano!" he called.

I followed at a much slower pace since I was past the stage of chasing after butterflies. Then I suddenly remembered why these butterflies graced our yard. Beyond the back boundary of our property was steep, open veld and close to our border was a patch of white, yellow and purple stately wild foxgloves that grew there since I could remember.

Grandpa warned us about the toxic nature of this plant. He even showed William and I how to carefully remove and discard any that grew in our yard. He told us that the entire plant from root to tip was poisonous and we were to avoid going near them. All his pleas to the municipality to have them removed and the area sprayed with a poison to prevent them from growing there failed, and so we resorted to keeping them out of our yard – more so because of Morph's allergic reactions. Because Aunty Priya would occasionally come over to take some away by the roots for her medicines, we grudgingly accepted these plants beyond our yard. I noticed that some were against our fence but forgot to mention this to Grandma and William.

Morph giggled merrily as he veered off down the backyard towards the fence, directly towards the foxgloves where numerous butterflies flitted mesmerizingly between the flowers and leaves. Sudden alarm injected impetus into my legs and before Morph was within half a meter from those pretty bells I rugby tackled him. I scooped my unsuspecting brother around the waist and swung him away from the potential danger. I could not control our momentum and we went crashing into one of Grandma's containers of rose bushes. Fortunately for Morph, we spun halfway around as we went flying. He landed on me as I banged into the container.

"Ooww!" I exhaled in a whoosh as the wind was knocked out of me. I sprang up and attended to Grandma's plant. We recently placed some of these pot plants over the spot where the old gum tree held dominion for many years. A bit of the soil and foliage had fallen out of the container, but it was otherwise fine. I picked it up, returned it to its place and put back the sand before turning to Morph, giggling where he lay.

"You OK?" I asked as I helped him upright.

"We flew faster than the butterflies. We went past them! We were flying!" he chortled.

I laughed, snorting as I recovered from the bruising knock. This made Morph laugh out even louder. He sprang to his feet and dusted his hands on his pants.

"Ooww!" he yelped in pain, holding out his hands. At least two thorns from the roses were pierced into the palms of both his hands.

"Let's go inside and ask Ouma to take them out." I arose painfully.

"Yup!" Morph replied as he started walking off with palms raised in surrender. Near the kitchen door Morph started scratching his arms and legs, avoiding contact with his palms.

"Stop that! We're going inside!" I knew Morph had an allergic reaction to grass where it made contact with his body above his feet. Why he always wore socks with his takkies.

"Can't, it's itchy," he responded sheepishly.

"Let me see, maybe a spider bit you." I reasoned to slow him down a bit. I grabbed his outstretched arms and inspected them closely, then bent to inspect his legs. A faint rash was spreading over his appendages. Morph's eyes began to swell and he struggled to breathe.

I pulled out the inhaler from his pants pocket and put it into his mouth pressing the plunger a few times. Morph sucked deeply of the medicine and sighed just as deeply. Grandma was entering the kitchen when we walked indoors.

"Morph, I heard you breathing heavy, are you okay? What happened to your hands?"

"How did Ouma hear it from so far away on the other side of a closed door? Surely Morph couldn't have breathed that loud?" I asked myself.

"What happened, Morph?" Morph looked at me nervously, then back at Grandma.

"Adamor, what happened?" Grandma asked sternly.

"I got thorns in my hands, Ouma. We rolled on the grass. Ouma, you should've seen it! We flew faster than the butterflies!" Morph enthused as he displayed his war wounds.

"Go fetch the Allergex and Calamine lotion, clean swabs and the tweezer." Grandma inspected Morph's hands, arms and legs.

I sprinted as fast as I could towards Grandma's bedroom, almost knocking May-June and William down in the passage. May-June followed me into their bedroom. I carefully took out a few disinfectant swabs, the tablets and the lotion from the wardrobe and passed these on to my sister who was already halfway out the door. I followed sedately, but did not enter the kitchen, rather silently stood where my family could not see me. Except for Morph who carried on chattering they were also silent in the kitchen as Grandma attended to my brother.

A shiver rushed up and down my spine and it seemed to hold me in that spot in the passageway. I just could not move. Grandma's voice broke into this strange disorientation and dragged me back to the present moment. "Plano, get me a tweezer."

"How did Ouma know I was there?"

Morph did not look like he was in any pain, but had Calamine lotion spread all over his chin, arms and legs. I handed over the tweezer and watched silently as Grandma removed the thorns from his palms. Morph hopped off the chair and eagerly called William and May-June to see the butterflies. Grandma sat on the chair that Morph had vacated and pulled me closer.

"What happened, Son?" I always felt comforted by the touch of her hands and so I stood still as she checked me out.

"He was running after the butterflies and almost ran into the foxgloves by the fence. I had to tackle him. We fell on one of your rose bushes."

"The foxgloves? Are they in the yard again?" Grandma lifted my t-shirt and sighed deeply. She went to the bathroom and returned with the bottle of Savlon. She proceeded to clean my sore places with the strong antiseptic.

"Yes, they're back again." I flinched from the Savlon making the cuts and bruises sting.

"You must dig them out again. Ok?" Grandma said gently.

"OK, Ouma."

"Did one of you touch them?"

"No, but I dropped one of your rose bushes. I picked it up again." The second sentence was said hastily, as Grandma turned me around.

"Give me your hands," said Grandma.

Grandma used the tweezers to remove the thorns from my protesting limbs.

"I'm so sorry, Ouma." Grandma looked at me tenderly.

"It's okay, Son. You aren't the only monkeys to jump onto my rose bushes," she chuckled, cocking her head towards William and May-June.

The truck pulled quickly off to the side of the road near the prick of cut and fill and the driver hastily grabbed a toilet roll, climbed down from the cab and hastened stiff-legged past the front of the truck. He saw a well-defined footpath and followed it, crossed the barbed wire fence with some difficulty and hurried on with this forced gait to a copse of Acacia trees to his left and slightly up the slope of a hill. He was in desperation to relieve himself from a sudden onset of painful diarrhea that was churning his stomach to no end and already rumbling and pressurizing his relief valve to a point of failure. He had driven past the first garage, because traffic cops were stopping trucks on the on ramp and he had no time for such unnecessary delays. He knew that was not going to make it to the next intersection.

Aaaaiii! Must be dat hot bunny chow! Poison! he thought as he moved as quickly as he could into the deep shadows of the trees. There was some evidence of dried out piles of other sojourners who made this same desperate pit stop and the driver grunted and grimaced in mild frustration as he quickly searched for a clear spot to use. He had just enough time to take off his garments from the waist down and to squat before his sphincter muscle released the pent up, broiling mess from within his bowels. The fact that he had the presence of mind to remove his shoes and clothing and to leave them to one side was evidence that he had been in such situations before where splashes from the outpouring of hosed excreta could leave some seriously odious droppings all over such garments. The driver sighed deeply with relief.

As he squatted there, patiently waiting for the second onrush, he took in his surroundings. The light was dim where he was. When he saw it, he thought in wonder, *What a nice branch! I must cut it!* Bursts of moist gasses blew forth towards the pile of excrement beneath him. The driver hurried to get his branch and reached for the toilet roll and began the cleansing process while observing the prized possession about ten meters ahead of him. He looked up to where it seemed to be stuck to a branch that was about three meters off the ground. He was thinking what the best way would be to cut it down without damaging it too much.

Then he looked down and saw it. For a moment he froze in place with one hand holding the toilet roll and another holding a soiled piece of toilet paper.

"Aaaaiiieee!" he screamed loudly as his sphincter tightened. "Mamba!" he shrieked even louder as with one fluid motion he dropped the toilet roll and paper and sprinted with all his might back towards the truck. He had the presence of mind to scoop up his clothing and shoes as he flew in abject fear towards the safety of the cab. His desperation to escape was so strong that he scaled over the top of the 1.5m high barbed wire fence in one giant leap, hardly breaking stride as he landed on the other side. He rounded the truck and used his garments in his hands to try and shield his nakedness from the view of vehicles that rushed by. He needed both his hands to open the door and get into the truck. Angry motorists hooted viciously at him as they espied his nakedness and dangling bits.

The driver was beyond caring as he hastily jumped into the truck, started it, revved it and rushed off as quickly as he could down the road, wildly looking around him and at the truck mirrors as he pushed into the driving lane without a thought in the world for passing traffic. Some vehicles had to brake rapidly or swerve quickly out of his way to avoid collisions. Loud and angry hooters blared all around him until some semblance of equilibrium was restored. It took a while before the driver could calm his heaving breast sufficiently to relate to his assistant how he nearly died under the trees. In the telling of his near-death experience the black mamba grew to at least ten meters in length, with a girth as thick as a man's thigh!

Unbeknownst to them, that 4.5m long black mamba hitched a ride from the Pavilion in Westville and managed to disembark when the truck stopped on the side of the road.

The wizened old herdsman, Babu Fana Ngiba, heard the shrieks and the truck drive off in chaos. He looked in that direction without moving from his vantage point overlooking the busy freeway. He was dressed in faded, dusty khaki short-sleeved shirt and pants that were cut off at the knees. He had on a worn and faded yellowish straw hat and these oversized gumboots that seemed to be too heavy for this frame that carried not one ounce of fat on it. He scratched his crotch lightly while vaguely following the flow of the traffic before him. Then he saw it. A cursed black mamba flying straight at him!

"Haaiibboo! Voetsek! Voetsek!" he shouted, waving his knobkerrie, spear and whip frantically in the air and stamping the ground repeatedly. The black mamba suddenly veered off to the left of him when she was about ten meters away. This was unusual behavior for black mambas. They usually continued with their attack on human or beast who dared to block escape routes. They tended to start their onslaught when they are approximately thirty meters away. They would do so at lightning speed, striking repeatedly to inflict maximum damage.

Babu Fana did not know this as he gave thanks to his ancestors while fearfully watching the mamba disappear into a rocky outcrop at least thirty meters to his left. He waited a few minutes to see whether it would reappear before jumping off his vantage point. He hastily herded the cattle and goats and driving them away from that cursed place with shouts whistles and cracks from his whip. His spindly legs ran frantically this way and that in oversized black gumboots, as he cajoled the herd. "Haaaiii! Jammah!" he shouted at one of the bulls. "Lead us out of here! Away from this evil Satan!"

This Mnguni beast lifted his head and snorted loudly, glaring about with crazy eyes. He began trundling slowly and steadily along homeward bound. His huge horns, strong hump and dewlap swaying magnificently to and fro, tail flicking left and right, as he led the way on the long journey home. He did not look back, with those blurry and slightly mad glares, for it did not need to as one by one the grazing herd followed him. Babu Fana rushed to and fro.

"Velifude! There's no time to lag! This Satan surely will kill you! Buyemendweni, I need you to work with me today. Jamludi! Zondekhaya! No time for that! Go! Go! Hey wena, Bangizonda! Where do you think you're going? Fly Meleko, fly!" he urged them along in a scraggly line, shouting these and other names at cows and goats as they hurried down the gravel road away from this place of certain death.

As the distance from where he had last seen the mamba increased and it did not chase after him, Babu Fana glanced less and less behind him. After they crested the first hill and he realized that the demon had let him live, Babu Fana even slowed the pace enough for the cattle and goats to continue feeding while they meandered homewards.

Babu Fana was still deeply troubled. He continued speaking to the cattle and goats even telling them how he nearly died. A flock of about twelve Crowned Guineafowl suddenly darted across the road just ahead of him, under the fence and across the railway line. Usually, Babu Fana would be alert for such opportunities and would expertly take one down with his spear or knobkerrie, but not today. He hardly glanced in their direction as he tried to make sense of seeing such a large black mamba in a place where he always took the cattle and goats to feed.

In all his fourteen years of doing this job, he had never seen a black mamba as large as this one there. He dragged his gumboots homeward. He vowed to bring someone with him next time he needed to take the heed to that accursed place, in case he died from poison of uSatan!

After lunch Grandma said without any preamble, "Doctor John has invited us to stay on his farm for the holidays. To get away from all our problems for a while."

There was a moment of silence and then we bombarded Grandma with our concerns.

"But is it safe, Ouma? A farm is a very lonely place. There are farm attacks on the news all the time." May-June got the ball rolling.

"I have to be back for the New Year's Dance, Ouma?" William looked sad at the thought of not taking Ella to the New Year's Eve dance. He was not going to give this up.

"What about me? There'll be lots of grass and stinky animals!" Morph added his worth.

"And those guys will know we're there! They'll come and kill us, Ouma!" I shrieked.

"What about Christmas," May-June kept pushing.

"Who'll look after our home?" William asked.

"And who'll keep the yard clean?" I wailed.

"And who'll look after my toys?" Morph lamented.

Grandma raised her hand to stop us and when we complied, she took a deep breath, sighed slowly and smiled at us.

"I hear you and I have some of my own to add to your list." Grandma paused a bit more to gather her thoughts before she spoke again.

"This is merely an offer from Dr John. We need to discuss it. Now, if I remember the order of your questions correctly, I believe we'll be safe at the farmhouse. It has an electric fence and guards patrolling the property day and night. Dangerous situations exist everywhere. We'll need to be sensible about where we go and what we do if we do take up his offer." Grandma paused and we nodded our heads, but Morph raised a hand.

"Yes, Morph?"

"What about my toys, Ouma?"

"I'll get to you now, now, Son." Grandma smiled at Morph and he smiled back.

"William has to be back on the 31st and I believe it is important to attend the Christmas Service. That rules out the 25th and the 31st." William beamed his thanks with the broadest of smiles to Grandma.

"Morph's concerns are very real. If I remember correctly there is not much grass in the farmyard. There's a swimming pool and lots of paving. Morph'll have to stay close to the farm house and away from the sheds. You can take some of your toys with you. The others we'll lock away in your wardrobe." Morph flopped the top half of his body onto Grandma's lap.

"As for Plano's concerns, I have said to Dr. John that if we do take up his offer, we need to keep it quiet. We'll have to spread a rumor we're going to Durban." We nodded again.

"Then, William, you asked about someone looking after our home and you Plano asked about someone having to clean the yard." We nodded.

"I haven't given much thought to these two matters. Give me time and I'll come up with a solution. OK? I think if we clean the yard the day before we go should be enough. We'll only be gone for five days." All four of us nodded.

"It looks to me that, if we do go, it'll have to be from the 26th to the 30th only. But it'll give us a small break from all our troubles."

"OK, Ouma."

"Let's leave it there and think about it. I'll give Dr. John an answer tomorrow."

"OK, Ouma."

"OK. I need to see Doctor Burberry." This was our code for the lady at the orphanage. Morph believed that she was a doctor who dealt strictly with women and their health issues.

We smiled and looked at each other conspiratorially, marveling at the continued success of our con. Grandma displayed a twinkle in her eye as she continued.

"May-June and I'll go see her. William'll be our guard there and back."

"OK, Ouma."

"William and Plano please remove the foxgloves growing close to the fence."

"OK, Ouma." William and I responded in unison.

"Rather wait when it's cooler."

They buried Bongani next to his father's grave, deep in a rural area along the banks of the Swart-Mfolozi River. It was not far north-west from the Hluhluwe-Mfolozi Game Reserve. Probably twenty kilometers as the crow flies, but it could have been a hundred kilometers away, such was the difficulty in getting there. At sunrise they followed a poorly maintained, treacherous gravel road that ran parallel to the wildly twisting and turning route of this great thundering river through deep gorges and valleys. Mzo had to pay a doctor friend ten 'clippers' to organize a death certificate that said, 'natural causes' and not 'lead poisoning'. No relatives beyond Bongani's immediate family knew of his death and not many people therefore attended his funeral. Some who heard of his sudden passing away were not aware of where he was being laid to rest. No one beyond the gang knew how he died – not even his wife and children.

The funeral service was over quickly and interment of the body done rapidly. Graves in these areas were hardly dug beyond one meter deep, because of the hard and unyielding rocks and boulders within very shallow depths in the substrata. It was therefore necessary to stack a high mound of rocks onto the grave to keep it safe from marauding animals and Jack Bemels witch doctors who send izinyoka thieves to steal corpses. Mzo and his gang stayed for the after-party and spent the afternoon in a drunken stupor reminiscing with Bongani's family about him. Mzo passed on five hundred clippers to Bongani's grateful wife who wept even louder after she hid the money in her bag that stayed close to her for the rest of the day.

Before the sun could start drinking water from the earth Mzo and his men departed. They did not want to be stuck in an area where the darkness was so thick at night that people still used rocks to strike together to give them some illumination along the difficult pathways.

"Eintlik, dera maningi Feranjie thugs in deez hills who kill fast if we blom after dark. Dey got good beez-neez selling ganja to Jozi. Dey dink we wanna sum shup-shup." Mzo patiently explained to his gang as their Land Cruiser bounced and grinded its way out of there. Mzo saw his gang draw weapons and sharpen their awareness.

After a while Skeets asked, "Eintlik, who gonna blom with us?" A long pause.

"Eintlik been dinking bout dae-ding." Mzo stuck a matchstick into a corner of his mouth.

"Been dinking 'bout Thulani?" volunteered Papi.

"Fok! He a shyt," grumbled Skeets.

"'Tru dat,'" said Mzo. "He neva eva shup from ubaba we poison." Another pause.

"You see Mduduzi Mgobhozi?" Jomo asked no one in particular. Another pause as the gang waited for Jomo to elaborate. Nothing was forthcoming.

"Dat mshana of Bongani?" asked Mzo.

"'Yebo'," responded Jomo.

"Wharra 'bout him?" Mzo asked patiently as the matchstick moved languidly across his mouth and back again.

"Neva cried for ubaba Bongani." responded Jomo.

"Saw dat. Wharra 'bout him?" Skeets was now interested.

"Maybe he shup-shup," Papi chimed in.

"He no jive-jive, stupid," said Skeets.

"How old is he?" Mzo asked scanning his gang as he spoke. The matchstick continued its journey from one corner of his mouth to the other.

"Thirteen or fourteen," responded Papi.

"We watch him. Give him sum ding to do. Den we see next year," Mzo declared.

"'Ku million,'" responded Jomo. Skeets and Papi nodded.

The gang lapsed into further silence as they approached a deep drift. Each one scanned their surroundings carefully at the place they instantly recognized as a good ambush site. Mzo smiled again with pride at the sharpness of his boys. He opened a bottle of Hennessy-XO Cognac as soon as they passed the danger areas, took a swig and passed it around. Mzo knew with absolute certainty they would gladly drink the same poison for each other that they forced Thulani's father to drink two years ago. Such was the bond between them. It would take a while to train Mfana. He sighed as he contemplated the task.

That evening another thunderstorm marched over Estcourt, daring all and sundry to challenge it, and there was a time when it seemed like we were its target. Our electricity tripped and we dared not touch it or light a lamp. Instead, we cowered around Grandma in the lounge.

The roar of thunder and the loud crack of lightning was terrifying, but more so when the two merged into one overhead and the hot lightning lit up everything in the darkness. We each sat as still as was possible in the darkened Some of the strikes sounded very close to us. Even William kept still as that storm battered and shook our home. Grandma and May-June prayed for our safety between the severe lightning strikes and cried out every time one hit. It took us a long while after the storm had passed before tiredness dragged us to our beds.

CHAPTER 15
DESTINATIONS AND DESTRUCTIONS
(THURSDAY, 23 DECEMBER 1999)

The call was made at four-thirty am. After the customary greeting
were completed, no further pleasantries were exchanged.

"Were all tasks completed well?"

"Yes."

"Were there any problems?"

"No."

"All in place with your plans?"

"Yes."

"When done, we need to settle our business with the two infidels.
Start putting your plans together. It must happen later; the same day
after you've completed your assignment."

"Details?"

"When we meet again tonight. Do you need assistance?"

"No. I've already reviewed options for both men. What about the
attorney?"

"They're settling that matter."

"Okay."

Faizel shuddered involuntarily at the thought that this man has in all
probability checked him out as well for the kill. This lethal being was
only loyal to the Sheiks who use his services extensively. Not to Faizel.

Those Sheiks would have no qualms about having him and his entire family wiped out – especially when the stakes were this high.

"Okay. We'll talk again tonight," he croaked and quickly cut the call. As he had done previously, Faizel destroyed the sim card and re-packaged the cellphone to be sold at another Spaza shop far from Estcourt.

"I'll make other travel arrangements as a safeguard to fool everybody," Faizel muttered.

The man with the brown suede shoes removed the sim card from the cellphone, snapped it into pieces and put it into a small plastic packet and into one of his jacket pockets. He removed the battery and placed it into another pocket. The phone he crushed with his heal, swept up the bits and pieces and spilled these into a second plastic packet. He would empty these at various places on his way to the mosque.

He locked his caravan at the Wagendrift Dam Resort and labored like an old man with a bad limp into his green, old Toyota Hilux 1600. The vehicle started immediately because the engine was in very good condition. Keeping to his alibi, the old man drove sedately towards Estcourt. Even when three official-looking, dark SUVs came barreling past at high speeds, he was not flustered, but merely raised one feeble hand in apology. No one gave him a second glance. This was one of five places in and around Estcourt that he occupied, using different aliases and vehicles at each destination.

Ewald's office was declared clean of listening devices and the security team was packed up and gone before the clock struck 05h28. Ewald put in a good hour of attending to paperwork before his colleagues arrived. As soon as the gate security alerted him of the first arrival, he packed the documents into one of his desk drawers. Their last meeting was an eye-opener. He knew with certainty that both his partners would not hesitate to slit his throat from pure greed. Yet the thought did not cross his mind that he had already put into motion plans to double-cross Faizel and yesterday started on another plan to do the same to Eric. The greetings were stilted. Ewald immediately initiated the order of business.

"It's all a go for the 27th. .TJ has confirmed that the catalyst will be within the kill zone between two and four."

"I'll inform the Land Surveyor," Faizel added.

"I've moved the trucks and the fuckers to Estcourt. My mechanics are busy doing servicing and check-ups. They'll be fueled and ready to go on the 26th" Eric rushed his words.

"I've alerted our commandos to go at dawn on the 28th. First here in KZN, then spreading rapidly to the other provinces. They'll wait for my final order on the 27th."

"The other Western Cape group will stir things up on the 26th," Faizel reminded them.

"We've no control over them. Give them some merchandise and cut ties, Faizel."

"Ok, will do."

"Logistics are in place." Eric's voice drifted. Ewald sat back before speaking again.

"I've some disturbing intel about Combrink. He made a brief call on a different cell on the 21st. We've no info on the details." He did not reveal what Rob had done.

"Can we arrange for a mugging to get the phone?" Eric weighed in.

"Tried it already. He didn't have it with him. His office, house and car were searched, but nothing. This was done by pros and none of the Combrinks suspected anything."

"Can we still trust him, even though he accepted our offer?" asked Faizel.

"No fucking way!" it came from Eric.

"No. He helped draft some parts of the Vulintaba Manifesto, remember? He knows too much," responded Ewald. "We'll have to kidnap Combrink and squeeze the shit out of him for his stash. Use whatever means to get it out of him."

"Eric, you'll handle it. Take him tonight. Arrange a time and I'll have a team ready to assist where you need them. The cops will bugger off from the area for the night. It'll be safe when you're ready to get out of town."

"Yes!" There was no mistaking the sadistic pleasure on his face. "What about his fucking bitch and bastard kid?"

"Them, too. Use them as leverage. None of them come out of this alive."

"Where do we keep them?" Eric rubbed his hands together gleefully.

"Chapman se plaas. You can use the kelners and the slaghuis. They're in the same shed. There're some disposable stuff you'll find in the cupboards. Take whoever you need with you. There's strong chemicals to clean up afterwards. My workers will be bussed to the grain silos near Maritzburg to help there for a few days. There'll be no problems. We've done so before." Ewald looked directly at Faizel when he spoke next.

"Keep up the pretense that you're sorting out the offshore account. Phone him this afternoon with some made up good news. Meet with him to sign some documents if need be. Just make sure he doesn't get suspicious," Ewald commanded.

"Will do," responded Faizel. Ewald glanced at his watch before he continued.

"I'll set it up so his staff believe the Combrinks had to rush off for a family emergency. I'll start putting the plans in place, so it'll be kicking in as soon as you've taken them."

"We're in this together, win or lose. We need to be sharp and zero fuckups for the Manifesto to succeed. No need to remind you what TJ and his cronies will do to us if we fail. But the rewards are endless. Make sure you don't drop the ball on your side."

"No fuckups," murmured Eric.

"Agreed," Faizel responded. *We're fucked!* he thought. "Anything else we need to discuss?" Ewald leaned back in his seat.

"Nothing. I'll let you know about my conversation with Combrink."

"Do you want to know my fucking plans?" asked Eric.

"No. I'll have the keys to the place here this afternoon. Let me know when you've got them on the plaas. I'll come over as soon as I get a chance."

"Okay." Eric smiled.

Faizel and Eric muttered goodbyes and left.

"Insha Allah!" Faizel prayed loudly as he drove away. Doubt and fear churned his guts.

. . .

"Oooww!" Morph's plaintive pleadings woke us up at sunrise. It was a mighty struggle to surface. The previous day's exertions were still taxing us.

"What's it, Morph?" grunted William gruffly.

"Oooww! My ear! It slept on itself!" wailed Morph as he plopped onto my bed and gingerly tried to comfort and console his ear with carefully cupped hands.

"Come here lightie, I'll sort you out," commanded William stretching out his hand.

"No! Last time you pulled my ear out!" protested Morph.

"But it helped, didn't it?" William responded.

"Come closer Morph, I'll massage it better," I interjected before the baiting started.

I gently started massaging his ear as he scrunched his face up with eyes shut tightly.

"Did it grow bigger, Plano? It feels bigger!" Morph asked with concern.

"No, Morph. It's just a bit swollen. It'll come right now-now."

William chuckled at this before commencing with his goading, prepared his hook, line and sinker and waited with a smug grin on his face for Morph to take the bait. Morph did so, tightened his frame like a coiled spring and answered him back angrily. Back and forth they went arguing about who had the biggest ears. Amusement etched across William's face. Morph kept his eyes shut throughout my attending to his tingling and marginally puffed-up ear.

By the time we entered the kitchen I was in good spirits. Grandma and May-June were cheerfully conversing at the table.

"I've spoken to Doctor John and he's okay for us to stay there from the 26th to the 30th."

We had last been on a short holiday when Mom and Dad were still alive. Grandma waited patiently for our questions to dry up before she wiped her brow and sighed gently.

"I hear you and I've some answers for you. Dr. John has a private security company on patrol in the area and at the main gate at night.

He said we'll be safe there. There's also electric fences. Grandma waited for further questions, but we merely nodded in understanding.

"We won't be gone for long, so if we cut grass tomorrow it should be ok until we get back." Grandma paused to give us another chance to absorb what she said. We smiled encouragingly. "Morph, you'll stay mostly with me in the main house. We'll have lots to do together. Like I said, you can take some toys, the others we'll lock up in your wardrobe. Morph smiled broadly and slumped way down on his seat with his back resting on the seating place.

"As for Plano's concerns about those Homeboys, Dr. John agrees we'll all keep it very quiet. I'll spread a rumor we're going to Durban through our Estcourt Gazette." We all chuckled because we knew who Grandma was referring to.

"As for those crooks, I don't think they'll be back and break in here. In any event we don't have much to steal. I'll ask our neighbors to keep an eye."

"OK, Ouma."

"OK, let's carry on then. I'll prepare lunch."

We started to feel excited about our little trip and time away.

Joe and Carel stood just outside the lower Marble Baths Cave overlooking the lush, green Injisuthu Valley formed by steep, craggy slopes. The Marble Baths pools were clearly visible with their lightly greenish tint from the reflection of the surrounding mountains and hills. On either sides and beneath the cool waters the marble rock formation reflected in beautiful splendor off the mid-morning sunlight. The magnificence of their surroundings within the majestic Ukhahlamba Drakensberg Mountains were peripheral to their beings as they discussed a most grave matter. It was a mad dash by Carel and his team to get Joe to this place from the Estcourt Magistrates Court where he was 'in consultation' with a client. To those who passed by the room at the courthouse, Joe was still in there for they could hear him speak and could see his silhouette through the frosted glass in the top half of the locked door. This pretense would be good for about an hour and a half.

The Giants Castle Game Reserve was chosen for the meeting. It was far enough out of Estcourt to have too many day-trippers arriving to mess up the meeting. It could also be surveilled for any potential hindrances and opponents. Carel and his colleagues had used it previously and it served their purposes superbly then. They retained the uniforms and gadgets of the massive sting operation executed to perfection and destroyed a network of international criminals. Mid-morning was already starting to fill with excitedly chattering tourists hopping, skipping and climbing this way and that with cameras and cellphones happily extended to preserve the moments for posterity. The sounds of the living mountain were drowned out.

Their excitement was primarily focused on a herd of Mountain Reedbuck feeding on the lush grass high up on one of the grasslands on the steep slopes across a deep valley. The buck were oblivious to five Bearded Vultures and two Cape Griffon Vultures with their massive wingspans circling high above them in the clear blue sky. Many of those who lingered with cameras at the ready were hopeful for a kill. They moved off one after the other when nothing sensational happened and the graceful loops of these huge Old-world scavengers drifted further and further away. In the caves behind Carel and Joe the voyagers were in reverence of the ancient and sacred rock art of the Khoisan. The area was simply breathtaking.

Carel looked the typical tourist adorned with brightly multi-colored casual wear and veldskoene. He even had a Canon PowerShot Pro70 camera dangling from his neck that he used absent-mindedly every now and then to keep up the pretenses. A red and black baseball cap covered his bald head. Joe was adorned more like an office-johnnie in black pants and shoes and a long-sleeved white shirt were it not for the dark sunglasses and deep seated wide-brimmed khaki hat that disguised him sufficiently. The hat was purchased at the local curio shop. The sunglasses belonged to Carel. To the casual observer Joe resembled a tense businessman entertaining an important client enjoying himself – and in no hurry to move on.

Carel was not too concerned at Joe being identified and their clandestine arrangements being discovered, because his team was all around, most dressed in the uniform of Ezemvelo KZN Wildlife Game Wardens and Guides. Some of his unit were even stationed at the gate and would raise alarms if any locals from the Midlands penned their details in the Mountain Rescue Register at the entrance to the Giants Castle Game Reserve. They could also observe much of the trail to the caves. He had asked Joe to warn him as soon as he recognized anyone approaching. Carel and Joe spoke just loudly enough to hear each other.

"Ja, nee. We need to get you away from Estcourt urgently. We have reason to believe you are in danger." Carel constantly extended his chin towards the open expanse before them as he spoke. His head and swiveling eyes never stopped looking this way and that.

"Oh shit!" Joe suddenly looked worried.

"What have I done!?" Joe cried out.

"You've probably been on their hit-list from the start. We need to get you and all your important stuff away from Estcourt. How long do you need to pack and be ready to go?"

"My family! I have to get back to my family!"

"You can't stay there. You must get away fast. We'll help you escape and hide you."

"What are you saying? We have to run away for good? Into witness protection?"

"Ja-nee. They're going to take you out if you don't get away tonight."

"Not witness protection. They'll find us very quickly. They're part of a massive network in Southern Africa. It's everywhere and in all spheres of governments south of the Equator. You'll be shocked at how big it is."

"What if I help you get out of the country?"

"Depends on where to. Their network extends to some international countries as well. How will you get us proper documents? These things take time." Carel was getting frustrated.

"We need to hide you for a week while we prepare the documents. You'll tell us where to and we'll do the rest."

"Ok. Thank you!"

There was a long pause as they continued to look out into the breath-taking expanse. Then Joe sighed deeply before speaking.

"A copy of the Vulintaba Manifesto and lots of other incriminating documents and memory sticks are stored at the IBV on Rivonia Road in Johannesburg. They have face-, voice- and fingerprint recognition scanners, plus a dual key system to access the vaults. My key is hidden. I'll go with you to collect the stuff once my family is safely out of the country."

"What are we supposed to do with this information?"

"They're going to start a civil war, either here close to Estcourt, or in the Valley of a Thousand Hills. The Catalyst is the key. I wasn't involved with this part of the plan."

"Fok! How?"

"They have commandos in place in all provinces and they're going to ignite civil war."

"Fok! Can you give me more details?"

"Get my family out quickly and I'll help you."

After agreeing to few key details, they began the meandering down the mountain slopes.

Morph and I amused ourselves on the verandah playing snakes and ladders while we waited for Grandma, May-June and William to return from the 'Lady Doctor'. I knew that the game represented lessons on vices and virtues. I worked equally hard to keep these thoughts out of my mind as we blew on the dice, rolled them and made moves amid the tiresome heat.

After supper we sat around the coffee table in the lounge to play Monopoly. This pastime was May-June's forte. She always won, hands down – driving all of us into bankruptcy. Grandma was always given the battleship, William the old boot, May-June the cat and Morph the racecar. I was the banker. My every move was scrutinized. My competitors grumbled out and reaffirmed the game's rules, especially the ones that they believed gave them an edge in the last game we played.

"Ouma, I'm so little. Why must I pay extra money to buy back my properties from the bank? Tell Plano not to do that, Ouma. Tell him!" Morph whined.

"This is only a game, my son, and rules are rules."

Morph always got the game going. He eagerly picked up the dice, rolled them vigorously in both hands and sort of threw them across the board. A nine.

Each one of us has a special quirk when it came to playing the dice. Grandma did a short roll in one hand and a long throw on the board. Grandma threw a two. We sniggered. William was exactly opposite to Grandma in style. His hand preparation was quite long, but at the end of all that he sort of dropped the dice onto the board. He threw an eleven. My hand preparation was somewhere in between I threw a five. It was May-June's turn. She seemed to murmur some words, then blew on the dice in her hands before rolling them out. A four. Those dice moved us onwards in our quest to own the board at the end of the game – no matter what.

I watched May-June as she played. She reminded me of a story Grandpa related to us a few months before he died. Many years ago, three Dutch hunters from Pilgrim's Rest trekked with a tracker and five bearers from Venda to an area north of Skukuza to hunt lion. The locale of the hunt is now within the Kruger National Park. Rugged territory. Rock-strewn hills, deep gorges and dongas, knitted together by dense Marula-knob thorn tree thickets.

A week into the hunt they found the spoors of a pride of at least twelve lions. That night their camp was filled with much excitement and merriment as the exhilaration of the hunt jolted them out of the bone-weary trekking they had been embarking on in the preceding days looking for the spoor of these breathtaking big cats. They heard the mighty roars of the males reverberate through the star-filled night and would pause to listen to that awe-inspiring cadence that stirred their blood with a sense of fear and apprehension.

The Dutch were more determined to possess one of these feared animals. They eventually fell asleep happy in the knowledge that tomorrow they would get their prize. The Venda's tried not to investigate the fire as they stared into the darkness in fear. The tracker told them the pride of lions had not eaten for several days and were hungry for a much-needed kill. This information was not shared with the 'Mlungus' because the Venda's needed the income from the hunt and did not want to jeopardize this. They discussed the matter at length, eventually deciding to take turns guarding the camp, should lions come for them in their sleep.

The group started tracking the family of voracious carnivores in the early hours of a hot summer's day, being very careful to try and stay a safe distance away and downwind of these beasts. They found the place where the lions had tried and failed to take down a Wildebeest and where the hungry pride bedded restlessly down and where they drank deeply from a stream. Then the spoors faded somewhat on the other side of the embankment. It was a tiring ordeal trying to keep up with the pride through the bushveld. They had a lucky break when they paused on a kopje to survey the terrain before them. The tracker spotted the movement of the flicking of rounded ears deep within the shade of a Marula tree.

The rest of the group dropped wearily down to the ground below the gigantic ironstone boulders on the top of the kopje. The Dutch spent a while checking their rifles and whispering a strategy on how best to hunt these impressively powerful animals. The tracker lay still in the midday sun keeping a watchful eye on the pride. The other Venda's sat quietly in the shade, ever watchful. At approximately three-o-clock the lions rose and stretched before gliding off one by one away from where the hunters were perched. When it was safe to do so the tracker gave the signal for them to follow.

The group went as silently as was possible down the rugged slope in pursuit. The men were so intent on their prey none of them noticed a single lioness veer off into the bushes somewhere. The family of lions ahead stopped dead in their tracks and crouched below grass level. Almost instantaneously the formidable predatory force came into being with lionesses beginning their encircling maneuvers while the two males crept steadily forward, stopping every now and then to foil their prey. It dawned on the tracker that a lioness was missing. As he turned his head towards the hunters to tell them he felt, more than saw, the sudden charge.

He had no time to scream before that lioness slammed into him, raking her deadly claws down his back and cracking his neck with her large fangs. The dead tracker crashed into the nearest hunter who was trying desperately to turn towards the danger. A shot rang out as both dead tracker and terrified hunter tumbled to the ground. The bullet went right through the chest of the tracker and grazed the flank of the lioness who took off and was within the deep thicket even before anyone else had time to recover, let alone defend themselves.

The hunters spoke briefly to each other. They and came to the hasty conclusion that they could not leave a wounded lioness in the bush and, after having to threaten the remaining Venda's with imminent death, began to carefully follow the blood spoor of the lioness. They were all vigilant, keeping as much as possible to open spaces while scanning the thickets for any sign of their wounded prey. Suddenly she charged again from out of dense bush.

The five Venda's scattered screaming in morbid fear and panic and fled in the direction they had come from – jerking their heads quickly around every now and then looking for that she-devil who would surely come after them and kill them. They burst through the bush and virtually screeched to a halt almost on top of the rest of the pride of lions that were already tearing their dead brother apart. The acrid smell of lions and death, the cracking sounds of bones breaking and the deeply disturbing growling of the beasts rapidly devouring their kill assailed their senses within a micro-second of them coming to a halt.

The shock stopped four of them dead in their tracks. Before they could turn and flee, the lion pride took them down and started gorging on them even though the morbidly terrified and screaming men were still alive. One managed to escape and ran back towards the hunters who had guns to protect him.

It dawned on hunters that they were in deep trouble when they saw three lionesses circling: one with blood dripping from her left flank. In panicked haste they fired at these beasts and missed. With no time to reload they dropped the useless rifles and took out hunting knives and held these at the ready while trying to retreat, jerking this way and that rapidly every now and then in search of these blood-thirsty carnivores and screaming profanities at the top of their voices at these infernal demons.

Two of them stumbled into the mouths of the huntress lionesses who were waiting for them in the long grass. Their knives went flying out of their hands as the lionesses grabbed them by their throats and shook them around like rag dolls while suffocating their prey. The surviving hunter managed to escape the lions. He met up with the remaining Venda and they veered off away from the kill zone and ran for their lives. When they tried to cross a river, a female hippopotamus reared up from out of the water and wasted no time biting, mauling and drowning them before dragging them out of the water and trampling them into pulp.

May-June did that to us when we played Monopoly. Just when it looked as though she was in a weak place she would find a way to hunt us down one by one. We had no answer.

CHAPTER 16
PERNICIOUS PREPARATIONS
(FRIDAY, 24 DECEMBER 1999)

Superintendent Carel van den Beek stalked through the Combrink's house eerily devoid of life. Carel and some of his team frantically ransacked the rooms for clues to the mysterious disappearance of Joe and his family and in search of any evidence that would help them in their investigation of the Butcher, Baker and Candlestick Maker. His chin was extended further forward than normal as he quickly surveyed Joe's study. His head and eyes swiveled continually this way and that, ever watchful for even the tiniest sign of hope.

Carel and his team had prepared and executed their plan to spirit the Combrink family away perfectly, but when they arrived at precisely two am the back door was unlocked and house empty. The vehicles were still in the garage and there were no signs of a struggle. It appeared the Combrink family had simply vanished into thin air. Carel was one hundred percent sure that no one slipped by his highly trained team of men and women who had embedded themselves in various vantage points in the streets outside and to the sides of the residence. The team now doing the searching was the one tasked, in any event, to investigate the Combrink home as soon as the family were removed by their colleagues.

Carel's deputy, Captain Jabulani Bhengu, led the hunt outside and in the quiet streets of Estcourt. Carel knew their search pattern would widen with every passing minute of not finding the Combrinks. Carel scratched his handlebar mustache as he watched his men tear the place apart. Captain Bhengu appeared at the back door.

"Supe?!" he called quickly and swiftly turned around and strode off into the night. Carel rushed outside and followed the captain.

"What's it, JB?"

"I've found where they were taken out, CJ." Jabulani responded curtly with his deep voice. This tough-as-nails, tall Zulu was a man of few words. CJ and JB came a long way together through extremely dangerous situations wherein their strong bond was forged. Both bore the scars of these armed conflicts, trusting each other implicitly.

"Good man!" Carel responded gruffly.

They hurried in silence and came to a stop at the back right hand corner dividing wall where Jabulani parted the deep foliage that obscured much of the wall within that corner.

"Look!" said Jabulani. Carel walked past him and in the dim night light he could clearly see an old, rusted opened gate and on the ground before it lay a cut open old and rusted chain with an equally old and rusted padlock still attached to it. Carel saw something dark and a bit glossy on the grass near the gate post. He bent down to have a look and immediately discerned it to be a splotch of coagulated blood.

"What's it, CJ?" asked Jabulani as he also bent down to take a closer look.

"Blood!" Carel confirmed. "Not yet dry, so not long ago."

"Ja-nee, JB. You need to get forensics here, ASAP. We need to widen the search. You put out an APB – no details, no press. I'll call the boss."

"Shup!" Jabulani responded.

The two men hurried back towards the house. Before they reached the swimming pool both men were barking instructions on their cellphones.

The faces of the Combrink family remained embedded in Carel's mind as he sent members of his team scurrying off with urgent instructions. He knew that this was a desperate situation. He also knew that without Joe's testimony and the incriminating documents and memory sticks that were in the IBV on Rivonia Road in Johannesburg, there would be no case.

Carel knew that he needed to convince his boss to arrange for the Bank's vault of Joe Combrink to be searched in a national emergency to get their hands on information that may save the lives of the Combrink family and many others in South Africa, who would otherwise die from a looming terrible conflict. The ANC and IFP were already in a de-facto war within Kwazulu-Natal and Gauteng. The simmering hatred between these two political warriors and between blacks and whites was close to exploding. The three businessmen and other as, yet unknown, co-conspirators were untouchable for now; there was no direct evidence linking them and their organization to any crimes.

"It's Christmas eves! It's Christmas eves! I'm so happieeeee!" sang Morph in a merry falsetto chant in the bathroom.

"Aaaiiee! That lightie!" William groaned into wakefulness, then chortled.

"Didn't you also sing something like that not long ago? Much falser, though," I retorted.

"You shut up, Sonny." William chuckled as he removed a pillow and threw it at me before I could begin to imitate his singing. We burst out laughing as I caught the missile.

December 24th was always one of the most exciting days of the year. Not only because it was Christmas Eve, and we all participated in deco-rating our home and wrapping the last of our presents, but also because it was the day that Grandma and May-June, with the rest of us contributing in various measures, baked up a storm for Christmas day! Grandma was in the kitchen making porridge. We needed to eat quickly and work hard. I walked up to Grandma and put my arms around her waist and gave her an extra special hug.

"Morning, Ouma," I chimed cheerfully.

"Morning, Plano, you're in good spirits," Grandma responded as she hugged me back.

Family chatter centered on the plans and preparations for the day. Somewhere within that interaction at that breakfast table I wanted with all my life to hold onto that moment of family togetherness for as long as possible. I scooped the last spoons of meal into my mouth and swallowed it as slowly as possible. After breakfast we got down to making the house ready for Christmas. Morph and I were down to cleaning the bathroom and toilet when loud knocking at the front door echoed through our home. I tensed immediately. We were not expecting visitors. Whoever was at the door had to have climbed over the gate, because it was still locked. I hastily followed William to the source of our sudden alarm. He jerked it open quickly. Tshepo.

"Hi, dudes," greeted Tshepo with a broad smile on his face and in his eyes.

"Tshepo! Why're you trying to break our door down and why did you jump over the gate?" William blasted at him crossly.

The smile never left Tshepo's face even though he took a step back.

"Sorry, dudes. The gate was locked. My mom said it would be rude of us to hoot and shout from the road. So I had to jump over. My mom and dad want to visit Ouma," he blurted out hastily. His parents waved at us merrily near their grass-green old Peugeot 404 Station wagon. William and I waved back sheepishly. My brother grunted something unintelligible, took the front door keys and hastened to open the gate. Tshepo followed. I rushed off indoors to tell Grandma of the visitors and back to the front door in time to welcome them.

"Good day, Mr. and Mrs. Mopantokobogo. Welcome! My grandma will be with you now-now. Please take a seat here in the lounge." I welcomed them in as I am sure William had done at the gate. Their surname meant 'big man' and it suited Tshepo's father perfectly. He was huge, at least two meters tall, with a heavyset body, a colossal belly and large head. Everything about him was massive, including a large bulbous nose, wide grin beneath a large handlebar mustache and a large flat forehead, except his eyes. These were hidden behind bushy eyebrows and thin slits of narrowed eyelids that seemed to be smiling but were forever moving.

"Ha-ha-ha-ha!" Tsepho's dad boomed, his huge belly bouncing up and down with mirth. "You say our surname well! Not many do so!"

"I learnt it from Tshepo, sir. We're in the same class."

"Would sir and ma'am have anything to drink?" William asked.

"Strong coffee for me! I dunno 'bout her!" A tree trunk of an arm swayed in the direction of Tshepo's mom before returned safely to its berth.

"Thank you, *baba*." Tshepo's mom smiled sweetly at her husband before she turned to William, "I'll have a cup of tea with milk and one sugar. uBaba does not take milk but will have five sugars," she said in a cheerful voice.

"Ok!" William hurried off to the kitchen. Tshepo's mom was tiny and slim in comparison with her husband. She was a pretty lady with a beautiful smile. Tshepo looked and was built more like his mom, but he was already almost as tall as her. Both mother and son had rounded, friendly faces and intelligent eyes. Both were soft-spoken but with the toughness of a honey badger about them. Perhaps it was natural for them being encompassed by this behemoth who dominated all and sundry who deigned to be in his presence.

Grandma hurried into the lounge, her apron discarded and the eternal bun on the top of her head neatened. Warm embraces were shared before they took their seats. Tshepo and I sauntered outside and settled on the furthest corner wall of the verandah. All the while the happy chatter of good-natured voices and loud laughter emanated from lounge, constantly drowned out by the reverberating megaphone of Uncle Charles. Even the normally melodious cacophony from the assortment of birds that were ever present in Aunty Nishi's yard were drowned out by the loud merriment that emanated from our lounge.

"Whassup!" was both a greeting and an enquiry.

"Eita, dude! My family are going to Otobotini for Christmas and New Year. There's 'uMsebenzi' festival that must be done for our ancestors. I can't go, dude. Remember last year, dude, I got malaria and almost died. Mom won't take a chance this year. They want to ask Ouma if I can stay with you guys. There's no one else to ask, dude," declared Tshepo.

"Cool! It'll be good to have you here. Hope Ouma says yes."

"Also hope so, my bru."

We changed course and quietly discussed all sorts of mundane concerns about cars and movies while we unashamedly eavesdropped on the conversation from the lounge, waiting to hear whether Grandma would relent to Uncle Charles and Aunty Ntokozo pleading. Not that Uncle Charles did any actual pleading. From him it tended to be like boisterous demands. Grandma must have agreed to keep Tshepo with us, because the next lot of bombastic words from Uncle Charles lifted our levels of excitement.

"How much you want, Gogo? Name it and we'll give you! Neh?! Four thousand?! Five thousand?! Heh?!" he boasted.

"Thank you, 'baba'. Please let us ladies deal with the financial matters. We'll sort it out." Aunty Ntokozo's melodious voice reassured Uncle Charles.

"Ha-ha-ha-ha! Shup-shup den! TSHEPO!" resonated from Uncle Charles, so loudly that the startled birds in Aunty Nishi's yard took off hastily in flight. My friend responded instantaneously and was through the door and into the lounge before I could even stand up. Tshepo stood with head bowed and hands folded contritely in front of him as Uncle Charles told him the good news and threatened to skin him alive and hit him back into yesterday if ever he misbehaved at Gogo's home. All the while Aunty Ntokozo smiled lovingly.

"Yebo, Baba." Tshepo kept repeating as he swayed back and forth from the pulsating forces of these threatening barrage that burst out of Uncle Charles.

"Go fetch your stuff 'uMfana wami'!" commanded Uncle Charles. Tshepo flew to the station wagon and quickly returned with a packed duffel bag, beaming from ear to ear. We sat on the verandah and waited for the visit to run its course in the lounge and for Uncle Charles announced their imminent departure.

"Aaaiieee! Time to go! We still gorra go pass KwaMashu den up N2! Very far!" He must have stood up before speaking because the next minute the giant was in our midst on the verandah. He surveyed us with those dark eyes. Tshepo and I stood hastily to attention. Aunty Ntokozo rushed out in Uncle Charles' wake hugged her son, whispering words of endearment.

"Shup-shup, Gogo! 'Siya vaya' to the township!!" Uncle Charles announced without much fanfare, embraced Grandma in an over-whelming bear hug that lifted her briefly off her feet and strode out of our yard. At the gate he turned towards us, lifted a tree trunk arm and waved his big pointing finger in Tshepo's direction.

"Shup 'umfana wami! Bonana! See you! Watch out'!" The tree trunk arm swayed back to its place of being at Uncle Charles' side.

"OK, Baba. Go well! Tshepo responded and continued to wave goodbye to his dad. I waved briefly. With that Uncle Charles somehow squeezed himself into the driver's seat of that old Peugeot that creaked and groaned in misery from the weight compressing the car's springs to near breaking. Uncle Charles needed to bend his neck awkwardly forward to fit into his seat, pushed as far back as it could go. Aunty Ntokozo ran to the vehicle after also hugging Grandma and I and placing a wad of R100 notes into Grandma's hand.

The three of us went to stand on the pavement and waved to Tshepo's parents as that moaning and squeaking station wagon struggled down the short decline of Rocky Lane. It reached the bottom of our street with a cloud of grey smoke puffing out from the exhaust, before chugging along and disappearing up Alfred Street.

"Aaaii! They'll be using the 4 x 4 to go to Otobotini" offered Tshepo.

"Mmmmm!" Grandma articulated. "Come in, Tshepo. Know that this is your home away from home, Son. You're always welcome here. We still have much preparation to do," Grandma said with her smile crinkling up her face.

"Thanks, Ouma."

The stolen silver-grey Toyota Hilux Double Cab bounced and rattled on the light yellowish brown gravel roads that seem to go on forever. Mzo could swear on the late Bongani's grave they crossed the railway line at least three times without reaching their destination. The brightness of the road shimmered in the noon day sun forced Mzo and his men to don dark sunglasses as they scanned ahead and everything that whizzed by on either side. He was irritated that this spana required them to be amagada security but the moola was hundreds. Also, when mfethu Zeph asks you to do something you do it, no questions asked.

Mzo glanced at his gang. Skeets was in the passenger seat next to him. Papi was directly behind Skeets and Jomo behind Mzo. They looked bored and tired, but Mzo was not fooled. Beneath it all his men were like coiled beasts that could spring into action faster than a Mamba can strike. The fifth person in the 4x4 was Mduduzi, dat mfana of Bongani. He sat wild-eyed at being part of the gang, happy for being invited to this gig and in awe of these men whose reputations were whispered folklore in the township.

Mzo stuck a matchstick into a corner of his mouth and chewed lightly on it as he concentrated on his men and on the road ahead. No one seemed to mind that they were travelling between 100 and 140 km/hour on a treacherous gravel road.

They reached the entrance of the access road to the farmyard. Mzo turned left and was back at 100 km/hour in no time. The huge gum trees that lined both sides of the road towered above them causing deep shade beneath their canopies. Just as Mzo dropped his pair of sunglasses into the compartment between the seats a large and imposing man stepped out from behind a tree about 100m ahead of them. He held along his chest an AK74 clasped in both hands. He stopped in the middle of the road, at the ready.

Around his waist was an ammunition belt with extra pouches, a serrated army knife and a Glock 32 semi-automatic pistol. He looked like a military man.

"Fok!" Mzo swore as he firmly applied brakes. His gang quickly removed their own weapons and were also at the ready even before the 4x4 could come to a standstill. The man ahead of them did not move the AK74. The men in the LDV kept their weapons out of sight.

"Bloma!" commanded Mzo as he stopped the vehicle along the verge at least 10m from the man. He left his weapon with the gang in the car and went up to the soldier with the assault rifle. They briefly clasped each other's right hands and bumped shoulders in greeting. Mzo stepped to one side allowing Zeph to continue having clear field of vision of his surroundings and the Hilux. Mzo glanced admiringly at the AK74 and made a commitment to get one.

"Daai ding?" Zeph gestured with the front of the AK74 to the vehicle. His voice boomed with a deep, commanding timbre to it.

"Hot!" Mzo responded.

"Your men?" he asked gruffly.

"Skeets, Papi, and Jomo. And Mduduzi, mshana of Bongani."

"Your shit!" Zeph said as he withdrew a map from his jacket, moved forward and laid it out on the hot bonnet of the Toyota. Mzo's men got out of their vehicle, firearms concealed.

"Hola, magents!" greeted Zeph.

"Heita!"

Zeph continued speaking brusquely as his eyes drilled into those around him.

"Dis is two-, three-day job; 24/7. You must use amadrugs to stay awake. Don be stupid cunts and get fucked-up. You lose da moola if you fuck up even once. Dis plaas she now Kosovo. Don be cheese-boys. You die!" He glared at each one before him seeking any sign of weakness. The faces staring back at him were inscrutable.

It was clear to Mzo and his men that Zeph had some serious military training and action. He pointed out various positions on the map as he laid out his plans.

"Mzo you hide da bakkie daa and all da shit in da shed daa on da end. Dat your small house. You cook daa and eat daa if you need. Mzo you guada by da slaghuis but also check your men by da hour." He brusquely turned to face the others.

"You must not come by Mzo or you die morsdood. You can ringa him if der smoko shit." The gang nodded curtly.

"Papi you bloma here by da big tree. One or two cars come today or 'morrow. Zeph you ringa me when dey coming. You bloma here when dey come." Zeph warned Papi and Mzo that no one else gets in. Not even the police. If they approach within 100m of Papi's position he is to kill them. "Shoot dem morsdood!" he emphasized clearly. Jomo was to guard the sheds and stables areas. Mduduzi was to climb the koppie at the back of the property and watch from there. He was to be given two fully charged cellphones for each shift. He was the eyes and would see anyone approaching from afar, told to ring when he sees shit coming.

The gang were again warned that no one was go near to the house and the abbatoir no matter what they saw or heard. There were two other amagents with Zeph who would be traversing regularly from one of these places to the other. These men would kill anyone morsdood.

"No matter what, don look and don go daa! Or you die morsdood! Zeph warned them.

One of Zeph's men would relieve Mzo from his guard duty whenever he went to check on his gang or needed to briefly relieve one of his men from their duties or rest a bit. After glaring once more at the men before him, Zeph curtly queried whether they were grand. He removed the layout from the bonnet of the Hilux, folded it and returned it to his jacket pocket.

"Moja shup-shup," Mzo responded. His men nodded in agreement and without another word Zeph walked off behind the gum tree and disappeared into the shrubbery alongside the row of trees. They could see in the distance a double-story white house with grey slate roof tiles, but no sign of Zeph, his men or anyone else. Mzo quickly deployed his men at their designated positions, leaving them with sufficient arms and ammunition and rations for the rest of the day and the night. He realized that they would not be home for Christmas, but then the moola for this gig was exceptional. He banished such thoughts from his mind. Within twenty minutes Mzo had checked and re-checked his men's positions and gone through it with Zeph, who grunted and marched off towards the abattoir with his AK74 slung over his back.

Eric took the call from Zeph in his office at about one pm.

"Yebo, Zeph."

"Yebo, my baas."

"Have the parts been delivered?'

"Ja, my baas."

"And the team for the shutdown, are they in place?"

"Ja, my baas, dey ready."

"Good man, Zeph. Remember this work is very important. I'll come myself tomorrow to see how it's going."

"Shup, my baas."

Eric calmly cut the call, stretched himself out, cracked his knuckles on both hands and smiled at the prospect of getting his hands dirty again.

. . .

The day was long and tiring, but our home was spic and span. Every room was sparkling from top to bottom brightened by the creativity of May-June's beautiful decorations. She used pieces of cardboard, some old clothing cut up, twigs, string, glue, glitter and paint to create an assortment of stars, wreaths, garlands, stockings and various tree ornaments like tiny multi-colored boxes, bells and stars. She collected old pinecones and painted these gloriously like we did up Easter eggs. All the baking was completed, the dishes washed and packed away and we were at rest. Grandma thanked each one of us for the hard effort we had put in and gave us some time to take a breather. Morph, Tshepo and I went out onto the verandah to chill a bit. We had with us a 2l jug of ice-cold Raspberry Kool-Aid and a paper-plate with three scones plastered with yellow margarine and apricot jam toppings. William was helping Grandma and May-June sort out the baked goods he was to take to Auntie Rejoice, Uncle UJ and Ella.

The mid-afternoon sun was relentless. The sting on my skin was almost instantaneous when I inadvertently wandered out of the shade on the verandah. I quickly stepped back from its fiery glare. Even the shimmer from the wilting lawn was blinding. I had to squint my eyes quite tightly to be able to see beyond the brightness of the day. Morph and Tshepo did the same. We chattered excitedly about this and that as Tshepo filled three plastic tumblers with our ice-cold cooldrink. Just as Tshepo returned the jug to its perch on the verandah wall we saw William's friends, Jan, Byron, and Naveen toiling in the heat up Rocky Lane.

Without a word to each other Tshepho, Morph and I each quickly grabbed our scone, stuffed as much as we could into our mouths and with cheeks bulging beyond normality, we gulped these down. Without standing on ceremony Naveen went straight for the jug with juice. He grabbed Tshepo's tumbler and poured a generous helping for himself and gulped it down quickly, then made way for Jan and Byron to follow suit. They were barely perched on the verandah ledge when William walked out. He looked great. First there was a stunned silence, then his friends teased him mercilessly. Naveen even rocked back and forth in a wider pendulum swing, so much that at one point I was almost sure he was going to tip over and fall on his back. Jan and Byron were laughing, rocking and rolling about almost as much as Naveen. It was contagious. Tshepo and I also joined in.

William waited patiently, rocking back and forth from one foot to the other, for his friends to settle down, which they did quickly. William had two packs of goodies and without a word he handed the padkos one to his friends and walked off towards the gate. His friends hastened to catch up and off they went joking and laughing and eating and pushing and bumping each other down the road to Forderville.

Morph called Tshepo and I into the lounge. It was time to decorate the Christmas tree. It was our family tradition that the Nativity scene was always placed under the Christmas tree. The decorated tree represented all heaven and earth celebrating the birth of our Lord Jesus Christ. The scene at the bottom represented His humble birth in a stable. Grandma gathered us around the tree and led by May-June, each one of us had a hand in decorating it. Our chatter was happy. I could see that Tshepo loved doing this for the very first time. It looked beautiful.

We took a moment to stare at our awe-inspiring creativity that flickered on and off, on repeat with some old Christmas lights that Grandpa had purchased. May-June gave Morph the honor of placing the angel right on top of the tree and he could not have been prouder of himself. Afterwards he sat there with the widest of grins on his face staring up at the angel. Then Grandma opened the box of the Nativity scene. We quieted down as she removed the first piece, wiped it gently and placed it in position. Then she started narrating the birth of Christ.

The telling of the story was hauntingly beautiful. Even though it was familiar for me as I watched Grandma tenderly attend to each piece before placing it in place while telling us the story of Jesus' birth. I did not notice when it happened, but I saw tears streaming down Grandma's wrinkled face as she spoke to us. There were tears flowing from May-June's and Morph's eyes as well as they listened to Grandma. Tshepo sat quietly, leaning forward, not wanting to miss a word and following with interest every movement of Grandma's hands. It looked to me as though he was out to capture the moment for eternity.

Grandma ended her moment with words that I have never forgotten. "But we do see Jesus Christ, who was made lower than the angels for a little while, now crowned with glory and honor because He suffered death, so that by the grace of God He might taste death for everyone. Amen" (Hebrews 2: 9 NIV).

I sat up under the tree in the yard and saw Grandma and Tshepo walk towards me. Grandma had on a tan- colored straw hat, using her walking stick to carefully negotiate her way forward. Tshepo carried a wooden bench. He placed the bench firmly in a shade covered spot.

"Thank you, Tshepo." Grandma said sighing as she lowered herself onto the bench.

"'K, Ouma." Tshepo whispered and hurried off into the kitchen.

"Oh my, but it's hot today!" Grandma exclaimed as she used an old piece of cloth to wipe beads of perspiration off her face.

"Mmm." I responded, staring into the light blue distance where I last saw two eagles.

"I miss them, too. .I know we all still do. But we must carry on. To make them proud of what we've become." Grandma said

"OK, Ouma."

"It's okay to cry. I know that. I've done a lot of it. Still do." We again went quiet.

Grandma wiped her face before continuing. This time she first tapped me lightly on my leg with the walking stick to get my attention.

"Looks like we'll get a big storm tonight. We'll have to make sure everything is locked up properly outside. Boetie and Morph will sleep in Mommy's bedroom. That way Morph is closer to me. Tshepo will sleep on William's bed. I've sent William to buy a present for Tshepo. May have to take one of yours to give to him."

"OK, Ouma." Just then May-June, Morph and Tshepo came out of the kitchen door to join us in the shade under the sweet-smelling apricot tree. They settled down around us. Morph carried a rolled-up grass mat, an icansi, that he unfurled. May-June and Morph settled onto it.

It was on all the news bulletins throughout the day and into the evening.

"Seven police officers are injured, two of them critical, by a bomb planted in a refuse bin outside Mano's restaurant in Main Road, Greenpoint in Cape Town. Police are saying that the device was triggered remotely, probably by a cellphone. Police Commissioner announced that no stone will be left unturned in the quest to bring these cowardly killers to book. The country is shocked by these cowardly acts by suspected terrorists. Unconfirmed sources say that this appears to be the work of PAGAD – the vigilante group People Against Gangsterism and Drugs that is itself terrorising the Cape Flats. No comment as yet from PAGAD."

The conference call was made at five to two that afternoon. Ewald got the ball rolling after brief and stilted greetings were quickly exchanged.

"Suppose you got the news?" Eric and Faizel murmured their agreements.

"Are all our links to them cut off completely?"

"Yes. We did sell them some merchandise through four untraceable intermediaries, but no one will find us." Faizel responded.

"Ok. On my side it's still a go for the 27th. The Catalyst will be trussed and gift wrapped within the zone between two and five in the afternoon," Ewald continued.

"The Land Surveyor is ready. It's a go."

"The bloody trucks and the fuckers are ready. It's all a go."

"Remember, I'll give the order on the 27th when the catalyst is on the move. I'll also give the order to our commandos after the deed is done to hit all the provinces at the same time before sunrise on the 28th. I'll personally give you the codes on the 27th when I get them from TJ. Are our escape routes secured?"

"Yes, the helicopters are in place."

"Eric, are the packages ready?" Each man knew who Ewald was referring to.

"Yes! We've got the fucking bastards! Bloody-well trussed and gift-wrapped."

"I'll meet you there in the evening on the 26th. I'll have to be gone by ten on the 27th to sort out the catalyst and the commandos."

"I'll bloody-well be there at seven tomorrow evening. We've got them bloody cunts isolated, blindfolded, naked, on sleep deprivation and starving. They're already fucking shitting themselves and crying like dumb-shit babies. We'll have them fucking sucked dry for what we bloody-well want. They'll be fucking mincemeat long before then."

"Have you got other tools in case we have to break them quickly?" queried Ewald,

"Oh yes, don't you worry."

"Ok, I'll call you if there's anything else from TJ. We won't meet today. We can be in my office early morning on the 28th to get first-hand, live reports as shit goes down."

Ewald cut the call. Eric and Faizel paused for a second to be sure he was gone, then did likewise. They paid no mind to the ominous booming and gusts of wind that rippled through Estcourt ahead of another colossal thunderstorm. Their minds were on much bigger things.

The cloudburst over uMtshezi Municipal District that evening was the worst storm to hit Estcourt in more than twenty years. It was like the earth was warning all of us of terrible events to come. The white lightning strikes were continual, loud, hot and ferocious, seeking out someone to kill and destroy. Claps of rolling thunder sounded as if the heavens were tearing apart as buildings shook and windows rattled in its wake. Then came golf ball sized hailstones that pummeled and pounded everything in its path, shattering windows on buildings and cars and stripping trees and shrubs of much greenery. Close behind the hailstorm barreled the opaque sheets of rain in a hard, heavy wind driven and steady downpour that lasted for hours.

The fearsome beast did not let up, smashing and blasting everything it deemed a challenge. Humans, animals, trees, plants structures – everything struck by one of these bolts suffered either death, in the cases of the living, or very serious damage. Trees were uprooted, houses were damaged and many shacks in informal settlements were destroyed

– the petrified inhabitants having to find cover under anything that they could grab hold of.

An old lady and her two grandchildren were decapitated by flying zinc that flew off one of the shacks roofs. A mother, with her child nursing at her breast, was killed when their shack was struck by a tremendous bolt, and it imploded. The resultant fire took the lives of a neighboring family who could not escape in time and burned alive, screaming in vain for help until they were silenced. The ordeal that the residents of Umtshezi Local Municipality lived through that night would remain forever within hearts that pounded through the darkness in terror. Insufficient disaster management preparations were made by the municipality and the community before it commenced that path of destruction.

An F2 tornado formed just south-east of the Weenen Game Reserve heading in an easterly direction. By some minor miracle no people or their dwellings were trapped in its loudly roaring, erratic pathway, except that it slaughtered twelve cattle of a struggling subsistence farmer before it mercifully petering out less than a kilometer from the Isivivane just off the main road between Weenen and Mount Moriah. Seventeen people lost their lives that night through either lightning strikes, or causes of the wind and hail, or through fast-moving floodwaters that swept away everything in its path.

Such was the volume and ferocity of the flood waters that the R103 outside Colenso had to be shut off. The mighty uThukela River burst its banks and swept a delivery vehicle off the road and into the broiling and murky waters. The driver and his assistant died in the accident. All low-laying houses along the banks of this roaring river were flooded quickly and most inhabitants within these homes had to flee with just the clothes on their back.

Some of these were much, much too close for comfort. So close that we believed with certainty that our home was hit at least once when all the lights went out. The close, purplish-whiteness of the strike made us jump and rattle involuntarily from being at death's door. We took to our beds and cowered in terror as the thunderstorm threatened to destroy us. I jerked awake sweaty when William woke me up for guard duty. Tshepo was back in bed, fast asleep.

That dreaded place of death, darkness and destruction remained within that secret place. When I went back to bed and fell asleep again, I continued hearing Adelaide's screams, seeing her face and hearing those dreadful three words repeatedly like clanging symbols ringing on repeat in my mind. I lay awake for a long time.

CHAPTER 17
THE UNVEILING OF STRATAGEM

(SATURDAY, 25 DECEMBER 1999)

The lightning of that great storm was so severe at the beginning that Mzo had to call his men in to their quarters when the massive hailstones started pounding everything in its path. It was just as well that he gave the command, because the men were hardly indoors when that very tree that Papi was sheltered behind was struck by a powerful bolt of lightning, blowing up in incandescent fireworks display such that not a single sliver of bark and leaves remained. It was split from top to bottom. Even though none of the men complained about the horrendous circumstances that bested them out there the terror on their faces was unmistakable – despite the Red Bull laced with small quantities of crushed caffeine tablets coursing within minds and bodies to keep them alert for long periods.

Mzo knew their abject fear was of Inkanyamba who the Zulus believed rides the storms in anger, so he left his men cowering in the room while he stood outside under cover in a place from where he could watch the access road during incessant flashes of white-hot, hair-raising lightning. He had with him his AK47 and sufficient ammunition to take on any monster that tried to fetch him. He knew that Zeph and his men were in the abattoir. He paid no mind to the occasional disturbing screams emanating from that building above the sounds of the storm. When the vicious Inkanyamba passed by and spared them the men quietly came outdoors and were quickly re-deployed by Mzo to their allotted positions.

At approximately three forty-five am the moon and the stars in the heavenly expanse shone brilliantly on the farm in the early hours of Christmas morning. With eyes adjusted to this light, Mzo and his men could see in the darkness for quite a distance away from where they waited and watched for approaching danger. A few minutes earlier Mduduzi saw the approaching lights of a vehicle long before any sound reached his ears and he reported as such to Mzo. The men, including Zeph and his amajita, were alerted. Zeph took charge. He organised all the men, except Mduduzi, in ambush positions around the farmyard and access road. Zeph and Mzo joined Papi at the most advanced position closest to the district road.

Mduduzi, who was on top of the koppie at the back of the property, kept on giving Mzo feedback on the position of that approaching vehicle. Eventually the men could hear the engine drawing nearer and nearer. Mzo commanded Mduduzi to be silent from the moment he could clearly see the vehicle down the road. The men chambered their rounds and took their firearms off safety, waiting with baited breaths for any sign of trouble. The patrol 4x4 Toyota Hilux LDV in the dark green livery of Sivuma Security Services cruised slowly along the district road outside the farm, East Coast Radio blaring loudly from its cabin.

Two white males could clearly be seen having an animated discussion. The vehicle went past the farm entrance. The waiting men were just on the point of breathing sighs of release when the vehicle came to a sudden halt. East Coast Radio was abruptly switched off.

"Smoko! Shit!" whispered Zeph and he rapidly crept a few paces forward. He re-surfaced deep in camouflage, shielded by the gum trees, on one knee with his AK74 nestled against his shoulder and the barrel pointing down the driveway. The patrol vehicle reversed rapidly and turned onto the access road beneath the canopy of large gum trees, lights switched on to high beam. Their two-way policing radio crackled every now and then into life in communication with other patrol vehicles. The men did not radio in, perhaps because what alerted them to make this detour had to be verified before they could do. Both men kept scanning the sides of the roadway as they slowly progressed.

The passenger held a shotgun, its upright barrel clearly visible through the windscreen of their vehicle. Both protected by bulletproof vests. Other than the sound of the approaching vehicle everything else was quiet, except for the cacophony of crickets chirping and occasional rustling within the shrubbery from a small animal scurrying along in the darkness.

The earthy smell of wet ground mixed with traces of ozone from the storm reminded Mzo of working the fields in the rural area near Blood River and for the smallest split of a second nostalgia popped in and out of him. He could hear Papi shifting position slightly in the bushes not far from him as the sound of the engine slowed abruptly with both its occupants suddenly leaning forward and staring intently ahead at something that disturbed them. The man with the shotgun tilted the barrel to the open window as both stared with absolute focus ahead to try and identify that troubling thing before them. Mzo could see Zeph from where he was positioned, waiting for a queue from him.

Zeph knelt there as still as death ready for the quarry to approach. Mzo was shocked to note that somehow Zeph had installed what looked like a suppressor to the front of the barrel. He did not see him do so. The two men in the patrol vehicle did not see Zeph at all, even when they drew parallel with him. Zeph was a mere 7 m from the passenger side door. Mzo took aim at the man with the shotgun fearing that Zeph would be discovered at any moment. He steadied his hands and body and put slight pressure on the trigger.

Two 5.45x39 mm single-shot bullets from that AK74 whizzed through the open window at 880 m/s, through the cranium of the first security patrolman, through his cerebrum and out his skull on the other side, then through the neurocrania and brainstem of the driver, out of his skull and out the driver side window, pulverizing everything in their paths. The entry wounds were tiny round holes with some surrounding burn marks, but the exit wounds were gruesome with portions of their skulls blown out. Blood, bone fragments and brain matter spurted and pulsed out of these large holes in the right sides of their heads as first one and then the other man slumped lifeless in their seats. They were dead on impact.

Before anyone could move Zeph ran to the vehicle and looked in, his Glock 32 handgun at the ready. He holstered the weapon. Mzo was next to reach the vehicle followed by Papi, Zeph's two men and then Jomo and Skeets. Instructions were rapidly given by Zeph for Skeets to quickly continue with the patrol vehicle along the district road. He was to put on a bulletproof vest of one of the dead patrolmen to try and fool any passersby during the short journey.

Both corpses would be propped up in the seats next to Papi. He was to drive about 15 km to 20 km down the road, look for a secluded place where he could hide the bakkie and burn it. They must remember to put these 'mlungus' back in their seats with their clothes on before they burn it and to bring back the rope. Skeets and Jomo follow in the stolen bakkie.

Under no circumstances were they to call on the radio or on any of the 'mlungu's cellphones that may ring. The vehicle and cellphones have tracking devices. They were to call Mzo if any shit goes down. They must kill anyone who tries to stop them or interfere. Mzo and the amajita helped strip one of the dead men of his bulletproof vest and gave it to Papi.

The mess in the cab and on the driver's side door was no problem to these hardened killers. Neither was Papi squeamish about clothing himself in the bloody garment and sitting in a vehicle that reeked of death. They then maneuvered the two corpses into position and tied them upright into place with nylon rope, trying as best as possible not to leave any unnecessary telltale traces of theirs within that vehicle. Skeets and Jomo ran off to fetch the stolen vehicle and a 5l jerrycan from one of the sheds. They returned just as Papi completed a U-turn.

"Go! You have one hour!" Zeph commanded them before turning to help Mzo and the two amajita get rid of evidence. They hastily broke off some brush from the bushes and proceeded to obliterate much of the blood splatter on the side of the vehicle and on the road and all traces of that vehicle tracks along the access road and of the ambush. The two vehicles sped off, turning onto the district road in the direction the patrol vehicle was initially travelling.

Eric took the call from Zeph in his office at about a quarter to five in the morning.

"Yebo, Zeph."

"Yebo, my baas."

"Any problems?"

"Ja-nee, my baas. De udder mshini."

"We don't need this. Is it sorted?"

"Dey finis, my baas."

"And our work?"

"Ja, my baas, dey ready."

"Good man, Zeph. I'll see you later."

"Shup, my baas."

Eric sat still for a while contemplating this development. He concluded that it was best to leave it all in Zeph's capable hands until he saw him later in the early evening and was briefed in more detail. He walked out of his study, even more anxious to get going.

Morph woke Tshepo and I up at six.

"Wake up! Wake up! It's Christmas Day!" he sang merrily as he went.

Morph was already crouched on his knees in happiness before the Christmas tree, his big eyes sparkling with excitement. Grandma gave him permission to distribute the gifts and he sprung to his task with gusto. I could see that Tshepo looked a bit sheepish, not sure whether he would be part of the celebratory proceedings and I smiled at him reassuringly.

Morph carefully divvied up the boxes according to name tags, shouting out each name like our school principal does when calling students to his office. Morph even cleared his throat before speaking like the principal did. The look on Tshepo's face was a sight to behold when two boxes were placed before him. Grandma smiled conspiratorially at me.

I gathered my presents up and sat them down next to Morph on the floor, but close at hand. The excitement in my heart bubbled as I ran my fingers over my presents, poking and pressing at corners to see if I could make out what lay beyond the bright blue, pink and gold Christmas wrappings. Task completed, Morph sat and gazed lovingly at his two boxes waiting for Grandma to give him the go-ahead. When Grandma allowed him to proceed Morph carefully removed the ribbon and wrapping from the biggest of his gifts.

He revealed a red and yellow plastic tip-truck with black wheels. His second present was a T-Rex that resembled the original Hasbro one from the Jurassic Park movie. Morph was overjoyed. He put the T-Rex in the back of the truck and held his presents close to his chest. He rocked back and forth and beamed from ear to ear with happiness.

"Oooohhh, thank you, guys! Thank you, thank you soooo much," he exclaimed. With that he sprang up and gave each one of us, including Tshepo, a tight hug. He then pushed his truck all over the lounge, growling and roaring truck sounds as he went along.

"Your turn, Tshepo," Grandma announced. He started gingerly on the first box, making sure that the gift wrapping was not damaged.

"HUCKLEBERRY FINN!!!" he exclaimed with joy. Another book from Paruks that I knew was one of Tshepo's favorites.

"A RUBIKS CUBE!!!" His Dad did not see much sense in 'playing with something that teaches you nothing'. It would be interesting to see how Tshepo was going to convince him otherwise. "Thank you, Ouma and dudes!" he purred, twirling the Rubik's Cube.

My first gift opened to a Reader's Digest Book of Facts published in September 1989. I remembered browsing excitedly through it at the second-hand counter at Paruks Stationers not so long ago and I also remembered that William was with me on that day. My second was a pair of sandals. "Thank you very much!" I jabbered. May-June unwrapped a small bottle of perfume, Exclamation by Coty. Her second gift was a Tamagotchi. Many of her friends had one. May-June's smile was a burst of sunshine when she thanked and hugged each one of us.

In all my previous years of knowing William, I had never seen him so excited when he opened his first present. It was a Nokia 8210 – a second-hand phone but still in excellent condition – that grandma and May-June found at one of the Pakistani shops.

"The box also has some airtime in," explained Grandma. William was thrilled.

Grandma opened the small box that was on her lap. It contained a string of plastic pearls.

"Thank you so, so much, my children! I love them and will always treasure them. Today I'll wear them to church!"

"OK, Ouma! No problem, Ouma!" we chorused, hugging Grandma. Then William and May-June almost apologetically removed a large box from behind the door and placed it on the sofa next to Grandma.

"This one's for you, Grandma," whispered May-June, kissing Grandma on the top of her head. We all sat at attention as Grandma carefully unwrapped her gift.

"A SEWING MACHINE!" Grandma exclaimed in wonderment and joy. "How did you lot get the money to buy me one of these?"

"It's not new, Ouma. It's your old one. They found someone to fix it up for you. Now you can sew again," replied Morph from beneath the coffee table.

"It looks brand new."

"We saved up and fixed it for you. We knew how you love sewing. Do you like it?"

"I love it!" Christmas joy filled every nook and cranny of our hearts and home.

Four of the Homeboys were seated around a table in the lapa near the swimming pool at the Walton's home. The pristine garden had taken a beating from the nighttime storm. Portions of the thatching of the lapa and many trees and shrubs were stripped bare and much of this debris was scattered all over the yard and contained within the swimming pool that Lawrence the old servant was cleaning with a net on a pole. It appeared that the subdued chirping of birds were in thanks that they survived and in hope as they searched of others that did not. The meeting was hastily called by Ewald.

"Where the fuck is Hermann? He's not answering his phone," said Rob to no one in particular. They were speaking softly. "Dunno, I also tried the fucker and can't get hold of him," Abu added. He sat cross legged with his coffee mug held steadily on an armrest. It was still too hot for him to drink.

"I heard a rumor his family left yesterday on a family emergency," Dewald offered.

"Fuck!" swore Ewald. "We'll have to carry on without him."

"OK, I'll brief him if we get hold of him later," offered Abu.

"Guys, you remember my old squeeze, Zelda?" asked Ewald.

"Ja, isn't she married now?" Abu asked.

"What about her?" Rob intoned monosyllabically.

"Let's just say that after action we had some pillow talk."

Rob swallowed hard and took a deep breath before he asked the question. "Doesn't she work for that Dr. John?"

"Ja, his receptionist. She told me the fucking shithead and his family'll be going to the Doctor's farm at Old Beacon Hill." Ewald smiled broadly.

"Fuck! We got him!" Dewald almost leaped off his seat with enthusiasm.

"Isn't there a hotel there? We can book in and take him when we want to?" asked Abu glancing at Ewald and Rob. He knew about the shit surrounding that bitch and he's antennae picked up on the grievous vibes that were blowing between these two. He decided it was wise to be cautious around them for now.

"Yes, but we won't be able to cover our tracks there."

"They'll have to move around the farm sometime him and his wanker brother. We can nail them both then."

"I know! My fuck said she's putting together some things for them. I'll get the list from her tonight." This time Ewald avoided looking directly at Rob.

"'n Boer maak a plan!" Dewald puffed out his chest with pride.

"Better still, suggest some activities. Include a fishing trip to Wagendrift Dam. That's far away from the farm. We can get them out there."

"*Crafty old bastard!*" Abu vocalized.

"Abu, can you get us five scramblers with no number plates?" asked Dewald.

"Too noisy. We'll need some old double cab to get us there," Ewald responded quickly.

"My dad fixed a Parks Board Isuzu Crew Cab truck. It seats six. They haven't collected it for the past six months 'cause they can't pay. I'll have it checked and fueled tonight by one of my okes at the workshop."

"I've never seen one" Rob sounded skeptical.

"My dad said it was a gift to the Parks Board from some foreign country. Ten were donated across South Africa." Abu crossed his legs and rested his hands on his lap. He enjoyed being the center of attention.

"How'll you get it?" asked Dewald.

"I'll borrow it. My dad'll never know."

"Fine. Now let's plan what to do and where." Ewald led the discussions.

"We'll wait for them other side of the N3 bridges on New Formosa Road. I know the perfect place to slaughter them. There's a deep cutting that can't be seen from the freeway. It's quiet. Not more than three vehicles a day pass through it. I've used that spot for a fuck now and again. It'll suit us just fine for the kill!"

"Good idea! But what about the trains?" queried Ewald.

"We'll have to time it to get there when there are no trains around."

"They won't be laughing at us no more afterwards," Dewald voiced dispassionately.

"We need guns and ammo that's untraceable," Ewald insisted.

"Eric has lots and I know where he keeps the key. I'll get some," declared Rob. "No matter what we do, I want to open the throat of that cunt Bushman and watch him bloody die."

The Sunday Morning Christmas Service was truly a grand affair. The church was spotless. The brass and wood sparkled as if alive. Warm Christmas greetings were exchanged while others were quite stilted and reserved, but we did not care. We were in a happy space. We joined in loudly with all the beautiful Christmas carols being sung. We were warned by Grandma to be on our best behavior. We assured her that we would comply. Grandma took her usual place and we aligned ourselves alongside, from youngest to oldest. Tshepo took up a place between Morph and I. We behaved perfectly and made Grandma proud.

After the Service the usual teas were not served and everybody abruptly rushed home. We hardly said a word to each other once out of the church gate and as we made our hurried journey home. We breathed sighs of relief and wiped perspiration from our brows as we entered through our gate and then into our home. Without a word to each other we went to change out of our Sunday's best and into our normal attire. May-June and Morph set the table in the dining room while Tshepo and I helped Grandma in the kitchen.

William made a brief call on his cellphone; I surmised to wish Ella and her family. William, Tshepo and I then hurried off to fetch Ouma Beulah and Oupa Spence Stumbles.

It was uncanny how alike Ouma Beulah and Oupa Spence looked. They could easily be mistaken for siblings by persons who did not know them. Both were of average build and height with oval-shaped, cheerful faces. Their high cheekbones and bright eyes were always ready to shine through the wrinkles and blotches of their tanned and wizen faces with the warmest of smiles for everybody. Those intelligent and observant greyish brown eyes peering from behind similar wire-framed spectacles were full of laughter. Our journey home with them was truly an entertaining one graced with good humor. Ouma Beulah stuck my arm around hers and held me there for the duration of the journey home.

At midday Superintendent Carel van den Beek and his team were gathered for an Intel Briefing in one of the prefab buildings they had commandeered at the back end of the Wembezi Police Station in Mashinini Section. A flurry of urgent comms from the Minister of Police to the National Police Commissioner and to his Kwazulu-Natal Commissioner who ordered the Station Commander at Wembezi to urgently co-operate with the team from the Scorpions Special Operations Unit investigating the Butcher, Baker and Candlestick Maker.

He instructed the Lieutenant Colonel that this was a highly secretive, dangerous mission they were on and that his Station Commander job was on the line if even the tiniest of any leaks about the unit emanated from his Police Station. The Station Commander was given a secure number of the Provincial Commissioner to call if there were any unexpected developments.

To his credit the Station Commander knew which of his personnel were on the books of the three millionaires. As luck would have it, two were on annual leave and one was on sick leave. The fourth was on night duty and the Commander hastily arranged for the man to transfer immediately to Durban for a week to assist the police there controlling holidaymakers on the beachfront. The young and unmarried Constable was only eager to comply. He was on his way long before the Scorpions arrived at the Wembezi Police Station.

The Station Commander briefed the remaining force that the team was from the Independent Police Investigation Directorate (IPID) on some matter related to another Police Station within the District. They were not to interfere with the work of the IPID team.

The team spent a moment wishing each other "Happy Christmas" without much cheer before settling down for the briefing. Carel's chin was extended as he briefed his team on the lack of progress so far in their frantic search to find the Combrinks and to nail the three crooks. There was no concealing their desperation. Carel turned to the man seated next to him.

"Over to you, JB."

"Thank you, Supe," responded Captain Jabulani Bhengu. He stood up and consulted pages in his file as he held court. "Looks like finger-prints are from the Combrinks and two others we don't know. Could be from the gardener. We're checking it out. No results yet from all other forensic samples. The latest we'll get anything is two days. The kidnappers were professional. There was six different sets of footprints leading from the Combrinks to the neighbor's yard at the back. Three from the Combrinks. Three from the kidnappers. These disappeared once past the garage. So far, no trace of them from all our searches. Aaiiee, Supe! We must go public quickly." He sat down and gathered his papers into his file.

"Ja-nee, JB." Carel turned to Captain Zodwa Shobe, their Liaison Officer.

"Over to you, Cap."

"Thank you, Supe" she said as she stood up and laid out a map on the table, her file opened in front of her. The team members also stood up and shuffled closer.

"The Combrink neighbors all heard and saw nothing. It's like they were ghosted away. I checked intel bulletins on the wire and there are only three incidents that bear any interest. The first; there was an accident on the R103 just outside Nottingham Road at approximately 01h40 this morning. A pedestrian was killed, but the HiAce with dark tinted windows sped off in the direction of Nottingham Road. Witnesses said there were at least six people in the kombi and it had no number plates. The estimated time of the accident fits with our estimates for their getaway." Zodwa flipped over to the next page in her file before continuing.

"The second, a black SUV also with dark tinted windows, went flying past a Police patrol just outside the Karkloof Nature Reserve at approximately 02h10. They reported that they gave chase but lost them somewhere between the Karkloof Polo Club and iZulu eMhkabeni. The men radioed that there were at least six people in the SUV. I have my doubts they pursued the SUV with six possibly armed individuals at night along those dangerous rural roads. An APB was put out, but the SUV has not been located. The timeline fits our estimates." Zodwa flipped over to the next page. Hope continued to rise within the team. It was plain to see they were eager for some positive news.

"The third: Mooiriver Police believe that a foiled farm attack resulted in the deaths of two security patrolmen near Hidcote. It is believed that they somehow succumbed before their vehicle caught alight and their bodies burnt beyond recognition. Strangely, nothing was stolen, even their severely damaged firearms were found in the vehicle. This could have been a hit, but there were no visible evidence of bullet hole anywhere on the vehicle. There are presently no leads." She left the map in place but gathered up her file.

"Thanks, Cap. You'll stay on the bulletins and the labs. Contact me if you find something. JB, you'll take a team to Howick and work your way to Dalton. We'll meet at the chalets tonight. I'll take a team to Nottingham Road and we'll check out Mooi River. Cap, you'll hold the fort here until 19h00. If nothing new, we'll meet at the chalets. Don't forget to load all our docs when you leave."

JB and Zodwa nodded. Carel then barked orders for the group to split into the three teams and marched quickly out of the office with JB right next to him. The members of their teams followed behind. Zodwa gave instructions to her team then hurried off to the radio room for any further reports that could be valuable in the search for the Combrink family. Carel spun the vehicle onto the Ntabamhlope Road towards Estcourt.

Christmas lunch was lovely. We enjoyed a hearty meal, we laughed and joked and were merry. It felt good to let loose and relax. Goodbyes were long and drawn out, extending to the end of Rocky Lane with Grandma, May-June and Morph confirming promises with Ouma Beulah and Oupa Spence to meet again soon for another meal. Grandma, May-June and Morph reluctantly turned back home, while William, Tshepo and I walked the couple to their home. It was on the verandah that Ouma Beulah and Oupa Spence held me back and asked my brother and my friend to give them a few minutes with me. When I turned to face them their faces and eyes were now tinged with sorrow.

"We know what you're going through," Oupa Spence voiced quietly. Ouma Beulah nodded. The couple drew closer to each other and held hands before Oupa Spence continued speaking, pausing briefly after every sentence.

"We don't say this lightly, but we see your struggle, Deplano. It reminds us of our own. Before we moved to Estcourt we lived in Klip-town in Joburg. We were teachers there. It was a good place for us to be, until our daughter, Leticia who was six at the time died tragically after a hit and run. The person who killed her was never caught. She was right outside our gate, coming in when the driver in a silver-grey VW Golf climbed the pavement and knocked her over." A much longer pause.

"Her body flew into the neighbor's yard and smashed against their front wall. She was dead before we got to her. Both of us saw it happen. Both Ouma Beulah and I literally went off our heads with grief and anger. We spent the better part of six years blaming ourselves and each other for her death. Hunting the driver who killed her. We couldn't live there anymore and so we moved here. It took a long, long time. And much counselling and healing. To let go of our child, but we did. One thing we weren't doing enough of during those years was to talk to each other. It was the hardest thing. But we did it. We could start to live again."

Oupa Spence removed his spectacles and wiped his face and eyes with his free hand. Ouma Beulah did the same before they returned to holding each other's hand. I survived the terrible turmoil within me by rocking mournfully back and forth. Ouma Beulah continued.

"Where we can, we want to help. Anytime you want to, we'll be here for you."

I glanced quickly at William and Tshepo, for it was on the tip of my tongue to cry out to Ouma Beulah and Oupa Spence for help. William flashed me a look that said, "Hurry up!" I could see he was a bit flustered from waiting in the sun.

"Anytime, Son. Whenever you're ready, we'll be here for you."

Ouma Beulah and Oupa Spence took turns to hug me warmly as we said our goodbyes. William, Tshepo and I departed for home.

The call was made at half past two pm. As usual, they exchanged customary greetings.

"My apologies for not meeting up with you last night. I was being tailed."

"You did the right thing."

"Any problems?"

"No."

"It's all a go for the 27th. The asset will be in place any time after one-thirty pm, but is more likely to arrive closer to five pm."

"No problem. I'll wait for him."

"I should get the final confirmation at midday on the 27th. I could phone you then."

"Not necessary. I'll wait for the trucks and then I'll know he's coming. You still have to provide me with that information."

"The trucks will be painted yellow with the full Sunlight Soap logo on both sides. There're two minor differences. The first is that there'll not be a star after the letter 't'. Then the lemons above the words, 'With Pure Lemon' will be a darker green – the color of Paradise."

"I'll familiarize myself with the proper logo today. If no trucks arrive by ten pm, I'll abort the mission if not advised otherwise."

"Please be reminded we need to settle our business with two infidels. The attorney has been cut out of the deal. I don't expect him to return."

"I know where he is. And his wife and son."

The Land Surveyor knew everything. This man reported directly to the Sheiks, who Faizel knew were callous to the extreme. They would slit the throats of their own family if deemed necessary. Faizel wished he had not gotten involved with this everlasting and messy scheme of infidels that was sure to blow up in his face.

"Okay. Don't take out the drivers. They've been trained for the mission. Mine have not." The man with the brown suede shoes did not respond. "Amaan Allah." The Land Surveyor was gone.

Faizel destroyed the sim card and re-packaged the cellphone to be sold at another Spaza shop far from Estcourt.

"Allah help us!" He cried out as he dropped and knelt face down onto the floor. The man with the brown suede shoes removed the sim card from the cellphone and snapped it into several pieces, placing this debris into a small plastic packet and into one of his jacket pockets. He disposed of the cellphone as he had done before, placing the battery and pieces into other separate plastic bags. He stood on the wooden jetty along the trout dam at the Saddle and Trout Resort outside Mooi River and calmly baited his hook before he cast the line.

The rest of the afternoon and evening went by pleasantly. We ate supper, then cleaned up and packed for the holiday. Our chatter was filled with excitement at the forthcoming trip away from home.

Although Grandma called lights out at eight pm, Tsliepu and I spent an hour planning all the fun things we were going to do on the farm.

When the beleaguered Combrinks were brought to their torture chamber in the early hours of the morning, they were stripped naked, blindfolded, gagged and bound to separate metal columns in a building that reeked of disinfectant and death. Their kidnappers left them alone for an hour thereafter to contemplate upon their perils. Not having been subjected to any form of torture before, the initial fears of the Combrinks subsided somewhat during this quiet time. But then, the excruciatingly painful suffering came without warning. They were simultaneously doused with ice-cold water and their gags were removed, but not the blindfolds.

They were beaten with leather straps all over their bodies and heads and on the souls of their feet for half an hour. Each could feel the sickening slaps of leather on their flesh and the terrible pains that shot out from their every pore and there was nowhere to run or to hide. Each screamed, the sound enhanced by the similar torments from their loved ones echoing through this vast and sterile abattoir lined with ice-cold storage freezers that hummed unrelentingly above and below the sounds of torture and the silences. Suddenly it all stopped. The gags were replaced and they were left suspended with a full measure of pain beyond all levels of comprehension coursing through every part of their bodies.

There was no respite. Between the beatings, they were forced to stay awake, suspended upright on painfilled and swollen feet, or else be shocked with a cattle prod whenever they slid into merciful oblivion. It was not because of any sympathy that they were given sips of water every three hours, but no food. It was to keep them barely alive for a while longer.

The petrified family was also forced to defecate where they stood, because there was no other option available to them. Their captors left the Combrinks to stand in the mess of blood and feces and urine and water until they were doused again with ice-cold water to signal the start of another round of severe beatings.

Straps or steel rods were used on them. At other times knuckle dusters were deployed on fists that pounded on already swollen and damaged areas of their anatomies to elicit maximum pain The Combrinks were still alive, but barely hanging on by the merest invisible thread of instinct to live. They were beaten into submission and utterly exhausted, yet there seemed to be no end to the punishment, and neither were any demands made of them.

Their confinement in separate areas of the vast abattoir was particularly cruel. Hearing the terribly painful screaming and moaning and groaning and weeping from their loved ones without being able to see them or run to them made the atrocities they suffered even worse. They knew that their family members were being slowly slaughtered.

CHAPTER 18
INEVITABILITY OF JUXTAPOSITIONS
(SUNDAY, 26 DECEMBER 1999)

T he first thing we encountered when we got out of from the double cab Toyota Hilux bakkie at the crack of dawn was the crowing of roosters waking all and sundry up to a new day. Then came the cacophony of cattle bellowing, sheep bleating, ducks honking and chickens clucking in greeting of the feintest peek of the sunrise as the doors to their sheds were flung open by the farmworkers. The livestock strode out to embark on their day's foraging and feeding.

There was no time for us to linger and behold the beauty of the South African sky. We hurried indoors with our luggage, only to dump them in our allocated rooms, before rushing to the breakfast table. Farm manager Japie told us that Dr John's farm used the entrance next to the Old Beacon Hill Hotel property and therefore it was called the Old Beacon Hill farm. It was ten acres, mostly within the valley of the Roodepoortspruit River. The farmer next door on the western side leased to the doctor about one hundred hectares of land bordered by the N3 on the eastern side.

Japie previously tried to convince Dr. John to use the farm primarily for goat farming, but the doctor would have none of it, due to the rampant theft of goats from within the lowlands. He was nevertheless successful as a part-time farmer. Our hostess Hettie's passion was the poultry farming. She added that the egg market was also very good and that they were even delivering to Ladysmith and Mooiriver. Both Japie and Hettie spoke with much passion about the farm and what was going on here. Japie was a tall, tough as a rhinoceros Afrikaner with blonde hair, smoky grey eyes and burnt and wrinkled pinkish skin severely burnished by the harsh African sunshine. His wife Hettie was a slightly shorter blonde-haired and blue-eyed Afrikaner lady with a kind heart and a warm smile.

Both spoke Afrikaans, English and Zulu fluently and they led by example and loved to communicate with all and sundry and especially with the five Zulu men and seven Zulu women of various ages who lived in the farm cottages. They spoke almost non-stop to the animals they tended. They were well-liked by those who worked the farm with them and there was a genuine camaraderie amongst the entire khaki-clad family. The ladies ruled the roost in the poultry section while the men were responsible for livestock, the planting field and machinery.

The walls of the four-bedroom farmhouse and the four cottages in the backyard were constructed of sturdy yellow sandstone blocks with imposing bay windows that glowed brightly in the early morning sun. Each of these buildings were separately enclosed beneath their own dull grey corrugated roofs. They looked stunning against the backdrop of green vegetation and blue sky. Added to this beauty were the two bright reddish brown gravel roads that went parallel past all the buildings and joined everything together.

The main entrance road ran along the river and continued through the farmyard area, past all the buildings at the back and onto the grazing fields. There was a place further on where it dipped down to the river and up the other embankment to disappear in the direction of grazing land beyond. The internal gravel road ran from the back section of main farmhouse and dissected the sheds and cottages to the end of the last shed where it turned and linked to the main access road close to the river crossing. On the left-hand side of the internal road, at least 100m from the farmhouse, stood a perfectly aligned row of five huge steel framed sheds with red corrugated sheeting coverings, large barn doors and rows of fine mesh covered windows.

These fenced off buildings had separate accesses to the two gravel roads on either side. The cottages of the farmworkers were in another neat row on the right-hand side of the internal road, at least 100m from the row of sheds. The symmetry and beauty of natural and man-made, color contrasts and light and shadows were simply perfect. A sudden unexplained joy filled me. I felt like I was finally at home and did not ever have to or want to leave this place.

The first of these colossal buildings housed all the farm equipment and vehicles. The second was the barn that stored feed and produce. The third held all the poultry with separate compartments therein for nesting, breeding, egg-laying and incubating and other poultry farming necessities. Geese and fowls were partitioned therein but were let loose to range free within the ten-acre yard during the day. The fourth shed held the cattle and sheep safe at night. The last shed was the manure processing plant. Overhead pipes from the poultry and livestock sheds ran to this building where manure was processed and sold as compost. We were warned by Japie not to venture into this building

Ten extractor fans that lined each side of it were there for good reason. In the poultry shed and where the cattle and sheep were housed there were one-and-a-half-meter high wood framed and paneled partitions within the approximate center of each unit. A standard door gave entry from one side to the other for the humans. The cattle entered from the main access roadside and the sheep from the internal roadside.

When all the animals were in full voice, the contrasting assailment of the varying cries of birds and beasts, each trying to outdo the other, was simply spectacular, bringing much happiness to my heart. Hettie declared that the animals were putting on a show for us, because they were normally not so noisy all at once. The cows and sheep tended to be much quieter and the chickens generally made most of their noise at feeding time. The geese were the loudmouths. Nothing moved within the farmyard without them raucously complaining.

The last structure on the side of the cottages was a newly refurbished windmill gently moving according to the whim of the morning breeze. It fed water from a deep borehole to three five-thousand-liter dark green Jo-Jo tanks. Water was also reticulated to the tanks from a concrete lined sump along the Roodepoortspruit River near the farmhouse. This sump was at least fifty meters above stream from a big concrete lined duck pond conveniently constructed alongside the river.

Japie explained that they could also pump water from the tanks to the pond during the drier winter months. He briefly pointed out how the borehole purification system contraption with cylinders and copper pipes worked and we were taken aback by this simple, highly effective water supply system.

An anomaly in this symmetrical wonderland was a clear blue Olympic-sized swimming pool on the other side of the main farmhouse, enclosed with a high chicken wire fence. Japie clarified that it was to keep poultry out of the swimming pool, although they had used it once in the past when the pump failed. They could not reticulate water to the dried-out duck pond.

It was an exciting morning to explore the farm and to get involved with whatever chores were allocated to us. We were all kitted out in oversized black gum boots, blue overalls, protective gloves and floppy hats that were thoughtfully provided by Dr. John. He was only told two days ago that Tshepo was coming along, so William had to don Japie's stuff, while I took his and Tshepo was attired in mine. Grandma and Morph were assigned to the main house and to the cooking, while Hettie linked arms with May-June and they marched off happily to the poultry shed. William, Tshepo and I followed Japie to the cattle shed. There were five bulls, forty-three cows and sixteen calves of the Mnguni breed.

The bulls resided in the pens outside. They always looked mad at each other and at the world around them, ready to fight at any given time, more so when they snorted out steam and bellowed menacingly. Even their trudging around the enclosure warned of danger in their massive sizes, bulging muscles and sharp horns. We gave them a wide berth as they were herded out by the farmworkers with their cows and calves to the grazing fields.

The biggest and scariest of these behemoths bellowed loudly and led his troops out. The sights and sounds of these animals moving off with the two cowboys pushing them onwards gloriously stirred our imaginations and our hearts and we inevitably crept closer to the fence – to be close to the action. But the infernal beast closest to us cunningly decided to test our resolve and he sort of casually sauntered over and bumped against the fence that suddenly seemed to be very flimsy and paper-thin. All three of us almost jumped out of our gumboots in fright as that fence shook and rattled before us. I could swear that bull curled his lips in disdain as he went by. The men on horseback behind the cattle smiled sympathetically at us as they whistled and cracked their whips to move the cattle along.

Next it was the turn of the herd of Zulu sheep to be guided to pasture. William, Tshepo and I were tasked with getting them out of their enclosure onto the farm road and across the Roodepoortspruit River where two farmworkers would drive them further on. As soon as the gate to their yard opened and we entered all the sheep rushed to the furthest corner and mingled there at the ready. Japie closed the gate behind us and instructed us to take over.

There were seven rams, twenty-nine ewes and twenty-two lambs. The mature sheep were multi-colored shades of brown with darker reddish-brown heads and small ears with fat and flat tails. Lambs were mostly black fading to the dark brown in age. *Easy-peasy!* we thought after witnessing the cows and calves follow the bulls out to pasture. We thought it wise to try and herd the rams out front close to the gate to lead the rest of their families out.

We rushed in to get to work shouting and whistling and chasing them. The sheep tended to stand and stare quizzically at us as if waiting for some verbal instruction whenever we stood and watched them, or when we approached slowly and carefully, but were able to shoot off rapidly in different directions when we came too rushed or too close to them. Some bleated loudly and mournfully as if we were about to kill them whenever we got within touching distance. Japie and the two farmworkers stood languidly near the closed yard gate and had a rip-roaring laugh at these mshizas running this way and that way, slip-ping, sloshing and splashing throughout the yard in pursuit of elusive, bleating, wailing and running sheep in mortal fear of their pursuers preventing them from going out to eat and rest.

It was only when Hettie came out of the poultry shed and shouted at them did Japie and the men open the gate and make whistling calls to the sheep who calmly whizzed out of the yard and slowed to a steady walk as they headed towards the river, in complete contrast to the fren-zied chase around the enclosure. Japie and the two men herded them unhurriedly with the sheep obeyed their every command – unlike with our comical attempts. We huffed and puffed, dragging the heels of our heavily muddied gumboots along the rough ground as we followed.

In no time the sheep were at the river where they stopped to have a drink before crossing over and up the opposite bank, followed by the Zulu men. Some of those sheep turned their heads to stare at us, as if relieved that we were not going along with them any further. I had this sudden urge to lay on my belly and to also drink deeply from the cold waters of the river but was too tired to flop down there. Instead, the three of us wearily followed Japie, tiredly dragged ourselves back towards the farmhouse in his wake. There was no time to rest, because the moment we shut the sheep gate Hettie called us to the poultry shed. "Eina!" Japie teased with a rueful smile before disappearing into the processing plant, leaving us to face a small army of honking African geese blocking our paths.

As the big red African sun peeked above the horizon in a spectacular display of light and color Zeph reminded Mzo and his men to be vigilant, because some 'mlungus' bosses will come today or tomorrow. Mzo, Papi and Skeets were deployed to guard at the entrance road. Mzo must let him know when the bosses come. Zeph marched off to the abattoirs while Mzo and his men hurried to their assigned posts. Hardly five minutes after they were settled a fast-moving police van appeared on the district road and Mduduzi radioed in. Zeph and his men quickly stuck package tape over the mouths of the Combrinks and sneaked out back.

There was no time to set themselves in a better place of ambush, because the police vehicle was already swinging sharply into the access road. Zeph quickly whispered something to one of his men who laid down his arms and ammunition and brazenly walked towards the sheds. He picked up a rusted steel pole that lay on the ground before him and rested it on his shoulder as he hurried to the edge of the farmhouse. As soon as he stepped into clear view of the entrance road, he whistled a quick note of warning. – loud enough for everyone in the yard to hear. Then he transformed into a limping man who came to a gradual stop when he saw the hated and feared bright yellow and blue van approaching fast.

The two young Zulu policemen would never know how close they came to dying at the hands of Mzo and Papi. The inkabi were slowly exhaling and steadily pulling their triggers when the first notes of the whistle pierced the morning air. It was to the good fortune of the policemen that both Mzo and Papi recognized the call immediately and were able to stay the executions. The cops saw the farmworker and drove straight for him. Mzo and his men stared incredulously at the spectacle before them as the tough hitman now transformed into a scared, worn-out farmworker. The contrast was unbelievable.

The dreaded van screeched to a halt close to him, the cops yelling for him to come over. The crackling communications over their police radio added even more fear and apprehension to the moment. The hitman truly played the part of a frightened farmworker perfectly as he carefully laid the pole on the ground and reluctantly and cautiously approached the driver's side of the vehicle. He even stopped at least six meters from the van and waited expectantly, looking terrified of the lawmen, not making any eye contact.

Rapid-fire questions were blasted at him. With head tilted downwards and eyes steadily on the ground he responded hesitantly at first, but a bit more assured when he realized that they were not about to load him into the back of the vehicle. The policemen were unaware of five assault rifles pointed extremely steadily at their heads and hearts throughout the exchange.

Clearly not wanting to waste their important time on this idiot, the driver started the police vehicle and roared it into life. Without any further acknowledgement of the presence of this useless farmworker, the van made a sharp U-turn and sped off back up the access road and onto the district road, disappearing into a cloud of dust.

The inkabi was back to his normal self when he explained to Zeph that the cops wanted to talk to the 'mlungu' farm owners or manager. He explained to them that the manager and most of the farmworkers were gone to the other farm near umGungundlovu Pietermaritzburg to help and didn't know when they were coming back. As far as the owner was concerned, he didn't really know. Their Afrikaans surname was too difficult to remember.

The maid was in the house cleaning and two other men were gone to check on the cattle in the fields. Perhaps he'll have to go get the maid if they wanted more answers. She was old, senile and a bit deaf and that's why she doesn't work outside anymore. The cops left without another word spoken to this hapless and scared farmworker. This encounter thrilled Mzo and his men. Never in their wildest imaginations did they see in this dangerous murderer an accomplished thespian. The visit of the cops troubled Zeph and he decided to speak to his boss about it when he arrived.

The gaggle of African geese blocked our pathways to the poultry shed and, for that matter, to the sanctuary of the beckoning farmhouse. They seemed to be strategizing on how best to sort us out as we steadily, tiredly and innocently approached them. There seemed to be at least five ganders, thirty female geese and two dozen gosling in the melee before us. The female geese were dirty, fawny brown with irregular patterns – some fawny light brown below the wings. The males were bigger and whiter with grey wings.

All the grown-up geese had a dark stripe down the back of their very long necks and these soft dewlaps hanging from their beaks. What made them look sophisticated and somewhat mysteriously and dangerously imposing was their faces that were sort of cut in half near their ever watchful black and beady eyes. The foremost parts of their faces was black and this included their beaks and knobs. Just into the black portion two white stripes looked like the stitching that separated the black and white sections of their heads. The gander's honks sounded like tugboats coming into harbor. The female's voices were flatter and abrasive.

Through some premonition I suddenly stood still. Tshepo did the same. William gave us this look of disdain as he carried on dragging his heavy gumboots onwards towards the shed – his pace and posture showing more aggression towards these cumbersome birds before him. The gaggle of geese honked ferociously as if gravely aggrieved then en-masse turned away from William and hastily waddled off in front of him with many necks turning every now and then this way and that way to watch his every move.

William relaxed his stance and turned his head again towards us with this, 'I-told-you-so' look, and perhaps this was the sign the geese were waiting for – I am not sure. Perhaps they just needed a bit more space to viciously launch their attack. Suddenly that fleeing mass made these abrupt U-turns, gurgling out strange guttural hissing sounds from wide open beaks and rushed very fast straight at us with necks extended like crude jousting lances pumping up and down. Wings flapped and webbed feet pounded the earth in a maddeningly scary din aimed straight at our hearts. Some even lifted off at least a meter above ground and flew awkwardly in their murderous quest to get at us.

These fat, waddling birds were now quickly transformed into high-speed hissing and honking projectiles, ready to destroy all who dared to challenge them. We needed no invitation to stand there and deliberate on the concepts of fight versus flight as we instinctively chose the latter. Tshepo and I had a lead on William as the three of us ran very fast away for our lives towards the swimming pool, screaming and crying out for salvation above the loudly approaching crescendo drawing ominously closer behind us. The farmhouse doors remained shut and so we motored on to the back of the swimming pool, leaving our gumboots behind or else we die. Fortunately for us the geese saw our offending rubber footwear quivering on the ground. They descended on these, pecking and pulling and scratching the defenseless boots until their primal bloodlust was sated.

We stood behind the fence of the swimming pool, blood pounding in our ears and lungs rasping for air, peering at the crazy geese and shuddering at what they could have done to one of us if we fell to the ground in our haste to get away. Suddenly it was all over. The geese calmly waddled off in the direction of the river, happily feeding as they plodded along as if nothing unusual had just happened. None of them bothered to turn their heads in our direction.

I was determined to get to know these lovely birds better and for them to get to know me. We hesitantly emerged from our place of concealment when Grandma and Morph appeared from the farmhouse and May-June and Hettie did likewise from the poultry shed. We retrieved our gumboots and went to the verandah to recover our tattered self-esteem.

"My children, what happened?!" Fortunately, the gumboots were fine. We donned them after dusting off our socks. May-June and Hettie hurriedly joined us.

"My, oh, my! I thought you guys were dying the way you were screaming! Then I saw the little geese chewing up your gumboots and you big guys running to hide by the swimming pool!" May-June had this naughty twinkle in her eye. We scowled at her but did not respond.

"Why'd you guys scream and run away like that? You don't have to do that!" Hettie admonished us with hands on her hips and a frown on her face.

"But you should've seen them! There was murder in their eyes," William pleaded. Tshepo and I pumped our heads up and down like the geese did with their attack weapons.

"Nonsense! They're just defending their territory. When they start to be aggressive again, just give them space and back off – but don't turn your back on them, don't scream and don't run. You upset them if you do." Hettie was having none of it. She made her points by wagging one of her pointy fingers up and down like the geese did their long necks and heads.

"But there were too many and they all ganged up on us!" William pleaded.

"Normally one or two will show aggression if you come too close and they don't know you. They calm down if you quietly back away and give them their spaces."

"But they pretended to walk off when I approached them!" Those sneaky little…!" William stopped his sentence short when he espied Grandma's stern look.

"Maybe you were too close or rushing them!" added May-June.

"Okay. We'll stay far from them!"

"Let them get used to you first. Don't fall and don't be aggressive. They'll attack you if you do. Were any of you hurt?" asked Ouma.

"Ja, Ouma, I took a few hits on my back and head. Those things have sharp beaks or claws or whatever!" responded William.

"Let's see, Son." There were at least three nasty looking and blood red scratches and two bruises on his back and three such bruises on his head.

"Aaaiee! Ouch! Eina! Yoh!" exclaimed Morph, Tshepo, May-June and I.

"It's OK, Ouma, I'm a nurse. I'll attend to him," offered Hettie before walking indoors.

"Yoh, but you big guys can run fast when chased by little geese!" May-June's teased. We hung our heads contritely, but she was in no mood to let up. "And scream like little girlies on top of it!" she continued laughingly. Morph joined in with the mirth. Grandma tried hard not to, but her face scrunched up and her shoulders shook as she swayed left and right.

"How'd you get out of the gumboots when you were running?" Grandma asked after some semblance of order was restored.

"Dunno." William and I answered

"Aaiiee, dudes. I think I sort of jumped outta them like the Road Runner!" Tshepo explained and this broke the dam wall of our family's constrained laughter.

Hettie's return with the first-aid kit quieted our standing comedians down. She got to work briskly and in no time cleaned William's wounds, put ointment on them and plasters on the worst ones. William remained stoic throughout, even when she gave him a tetanus shot.

"Ok, that's that!" declared Hettie. "You guys're coming to help in the chicken shed, but make sure you're always near the ladies to learn what they're doing. Watch out for the geese!"

With that we left the sanctuary of the verandah. Grandma and Morph returned indoors and the rest of us traipsed off to the poultry shed. Some of the geese were back and they made some squawking, gurgling code noises when they espied their newly acquired prey, but made no attempt to take matters any further as we calmly walked close to Hettie and May-June. It surprised us to see that the geese already accepted May-June into their family when she calmly walked amongst and spoke to some without any concerns from her and the geese.

· · ·

Ewald made the conference call to Rob and Abu. They still could not get hold of Hermann and he did not need to phone Dewald who was with him in their bedroom. As soon as the connections were made, he got down to business. "My fuck's sorted the funksies and I got the list," he pronounced.

"Yesss! You the man, boet!" Dewald shouted.

"Ok, and?"

"They go fishing tomorrow afternoon at the Wagendrift Dam."

"We've got the fucking bastards!" Abu pronounced.

"Ya, we do!" Dewald added.

"What time'll those cunts be there?" asked Rob.

"From two to five," Ewald answered.

"I'll check train timetables. If I remember right, there shouldn't be trains between quarter to and half past two. We'll have less than twenty minutes to wipe those sons of bitches out," said Rob.

"More than enough time. Abu, do you have the bakkie?" inquired Ewald.

"Yes, all arranged."

"Shup! And you, Rob?"

"All sorted my side. Where do we meet?"

"Abu, can you start picking us up from twelve?"

"No problem. What about Hermann?"

"Leave him out. I don't think he's around," Rob spoke roughly.

"Ok, I'll start with you, Rob."

"This is it! We know what we gonna do. If anyone wants to chicken out, say so now."

"We're in. We've done this before." Ewald responded.

"Me too," It came from Abu.

"Ok, see you guys tomorrow, then," declared Dewald.

"Let's get all our final prep work done today. No fuck-ups!" said Rob.

"Oki-doki." Ewald cut the call.

Hettie explained to us that these were Boschveld Synthetic Indigenous Chickens bred in 1998 on Mantsole Farm by the Bosch brothers. All I saw was light reddish-brown feathers with white ones in-between and many heads that looked very much alike. The ladies pointed out to us that the cocks were bigger and lighter with crowns on their heads and tended to strut around the place like young men did. One of the Zulu women even showed us how men tend to walk when they want to show they are bigshots, and it was funny.

Although the shed was airy, with extractor fans on the roof, the smell of chickens and the manure on the floor and on conveyor belts and the many thousands buzzing flies were overpowering. It looked as though the ladies were unhurried and not working hard as they went about their business checking the birds, collecting eggs, counting them and cleaning out the place. They even put some drops of clear liquid into the mouths of each hen they picked up. How they managed not to put drops in the same bird many times I do not know.

We were the fetchers and carriers. On many an occasion the ladies would stop us from picking up a specific hen and direct us to another. We found out fast that this was hard work, especially the constant bending to pick up the agile and squawking birds and to put them down again. In no time we were part of the stink, and it was part of us. Every now and then the ladies saw our unhealthy countenances and discomfort and they all clucked sympathetically. None of them however showed any real concern that we were close to collapsing onto the manure-stained floor. All they did was to give us more work whenever we completed a task, or even dared to slow down to a virtual standstill.

Eventually I could not make out the difference between their clucking and that of the hens, such was the loudness of my tired heart pumping through my heated ears. We plodded on to finish our toil, even when this meant passing those geese that still eyed us as their prey. Those geese ambled out of our way without taking their eyes off us. I felt right at home.

Carel looked in turn at his anxious team of dedicated police serious crimes special investigators as he briefed them about there being no trace of the kombi that killed a pedestrian just outside Nottingham Road. The black SUV spotted near Karkloof Nature Reserve was traced to a hippie-like commune outside Stanger. It was suspected that they had either bought or sold drugs somewhere and were using back roads to get home.

The Stanger police would be raiding the commune tonight. The third case of the murder of the two security patrolmen near Hidcote troubled Carel, because he did not buy the talk of the Mooiriver police that the dead security men foiled a possible farm attack. He had gone to the mortuary and examined their remains. A melted plastic-like substance was evident on the wrists of both victims, which meant that their hands were tied when the van was set ablaze. The bullets entry and exit wounds were still visible and the signs were they were shot from close range with a high caliber rifle. Carel was sure that someone made it look like a foiled farm attack. Those murderers had something to hide.

"Over to you, JB."

"Thank you, Supe." Captain Jabulani Bhengu shuffled the pages before him and placed some in a row from right to left. He picked up the first one. "Eric Walton has suddenly gone off the radar. We don't know where he is. His vehicle left the factory at about 10h00 and went straight home but didn't come out again. What's strange is he was not driving it. This is not his normal travelling time. But we're still there by his factories and his house, watching? Then we see him, then we don't, but all is shadows – can't say it's him."

He dropped the first sheet of paper and picked up the next one.

"A delivery van from one of the factories, a closed panel van at about 10h15, but nothing else. Except his son who goes out and in, out an in, now and again. The delivery van went out of town on the normal run to Durban. All his usual transport's still around, but we don't know for sure if he's still at home. Maybe he ducked in that van, or fooled us at the factory, maybe not. It's worrying not knowing where he is right now."

JB discarded the page in his hand and picked up the next one and scanned it quickly.

"Any other leads yet?" Carel wiped his face with his two large hands and then rubbing the perspiration off on his pants.

"Still no other positive IDs. No fingerprints."

"Anything from the neighbors?"

"All of them heard nothing and saw nothing. Had some small leads, but nothing in Estcourt and from my intel sources. We're walking around like kittens on eggs, Supe." Jabulani gathered his papers together, raised them vertical and stamped the pile a few times hard in frustration on the desk. He closed the file and placed it on top of the chaotic scramble of other documents on the table. He then folded his arms tightly close to his chest.

"And you're still following up on the Mooiriver / Hidcote farms angle?"

"Yes, Supe! Almost done. Cap'll give report on intel there," JB grumbled.

It was then that Carel flipped in the blink of an eye from that place of meditation into sudden energized life and sat bolt upright – startling everyone around the table but JB.

"Thanks, JB. The Boss said we can go public with the Combrink disappearance, but not yet about the three masterminds. Cap'll handle the press angle. JB, you and I'll start busting rocks and shaking trees. We'll begin with all their known sources in the force, then go after the politicians and officials. Time to push!"

"My bones are saying the Combrinks are still here, somewhere close. Just out of reach."

Carel nodded and turned to Captian Zodwa Shobe.

"Over to you, Cap."

"Thank you, Supe," she responded. She stood up and consulted her files that were laid out very neatly on the table before her. "The Mooiriver/Hidcote investigation up to yesterday afternoon has cleared all but ten farms. Some are outlying places that have not yet been assessed. The teams are travelling to those today. Four of the ten are smallholdings near Mooiriver and the rest are large farms. Three of these only had skeleton crew working on them. It's apparently a common occurrence for farmworkers to be transported to other farms to help harvesting or pest control."

"We'll have to go today or tomorrow morning to the other farms that don't check out properly. We can take one of our colleagues from

Mooiriver for each of our three groups. With the twelve from the Boss, we'll have enough firepower to counter anything."

"JB, you commission whatever more arms and ammo we'll need from here. When we start operations, we'll invite those sell-out fokkers to briefings, then nail them. No need to remind you all this is top secret."

"Shup, Supe!"

"Back to you, Cap."

"Thank you, Supe. The gang of Homeboys are planning to take down a young boy who witnessed a murder in town a couple of days ago. There's some bad blood there. The sons of the 'Three Men in a Tub' Should be considered armed and dangerous. What we don't know is the where and when."

"The little fokkers may lead us to their fathers. Put one vehicle with two to tail the Walton fokker only for today and tomorrow. See if there's a trusted local who can go with one of ours. If nothing comes up, pull back the tail by tomorrow 13h00."

"OK, Supe, will do. Another bit of intel that came up while checking out the farms is there's a Land Surveyor, Mr. Malik Nader, who apparently did some survey work in the Valley of a Thousand Hills and is now surveying some farms near Wagendrift Dam. We've tried to find him but were unsuccessful. The construction industry shuts down for builder's holidays, so this is very suspicious. He was not hired locally and not even the government and farm owners' association know what he's doing and why. He's apparently somewhere from the Eastern Cape. All calls to his office end up at an answering machine, and he has no local address, and we get very mixed descriptions of him from the very few who've seen him or spoken to him. No one knows where he's staying. The more I dig, the more troubling this elusive man is. He's like a ghost."

Carel slapped his thighs so hard with the palms of his hands that the sound ricocheted around the room and startled everyone.

"Combrink said a civil war is coming and they'll start it here close to Estcourt, or in the Valley of a Thousand Hills. You said he's done the Valley and is now here. Combrink said the Catalyst is the key." Carel's normally ruddy complexion flicked ashen. Something scared him mightily. Zodwa handed over the file and sat down primly. Carel ran as fast as he could out of the meeting room. Before he exited the door JB and Zodwa barked orders to the team.

The Combrinks were left alone in the cold, cavernous abattoir for the rest of the morning. When their captors left the building, the Combrinks tried to call out to each other, but it was all in vain. When the door suddenly banged open and their torturers strode rapidly towards them, the Combrinks jerked violently and whimpered again in apprehension. Then Susan Combrink smelled it; Giorgio Armani's Aqua di Gio Homme Eau de Toilette! For a split-second she froze, rigid with shock.

She managed a muffled scream before her mouth was smashed with a knuckleduster wrapped around a powerful fist that bust her lips open wherever the metal made contact. The hammer blow broke off her two front teeth below the gum line. Her head snapped back and she was knocked unconscious.

Wide strips of packaging tape covered by a wide rubber band was again roughly placed over her torn lips and over Hermann's and Joe's mouths in quick succession. Joe's heart was ripped further asunder, because he thought Susan's screamed was accusingly directed at him before they silenced her. Those disturbing contrasts from loud sounds and sudden silences played heavily on each one's mind. It did so to Joe as he strained hard to hear what happened to Susan and what was coming next.

He did not see Susan's lover leave her slumped naked and unconscious in her place of confinement and move silently to stand before Hermann. Neither did he see that Eric held a special tool in his hand; a Picana. It was like the cattle prods his men were using, but much more powerful and effective, delivering high voltage and low currents that jolted the recipient with maximum pain every time it touched and burnt skin. This contraption was connected by electrical wires to a control box with a rheostat where the voltage could be raised or reduced. Already set to maximum. The unit was attached to a mini transformer that led to a wall socket.

Eric waited patiently while his men strung each of the Combrinks up at least half a meter off the ground. The blindfolds were to ensure that the captive could never anticipate which part of the body was to be attacked next. For the briefest of moments there was absolute silence in the abattoir, then water was thrown over Hermann's naked body to reduce electrical resistance of the skin and to increase the effects of the shocks. He shivered involuntarily a few times from the ice-cold water hitting his naked body and before he stopped moving the tape over his mouth was crudely ripped off.

Then Eric commenced delivering 50 000 volts with every touch to Hermann's head, mouth, genitals, stomach, nipples and other sensitive parts of his anatomy, pausing fleetingly after each application for utmost effect and to shift his position. Hermann jerked violently like a puppet on strings and screamed from in pain and terror each time the shock was applied.

The unbearable shocks were so severe that Hermann lost all control over his bowel movements, and he splashed urine and feces all over the floor beneath him. Each time he was allowed to recover for a tiny bit he begged and pleaded and wept, but to no avail. From his place of suspension Joe's distress reached unimaginable levels where it threatened to burst his viciously throbbing heart open. He tried hard to scream but little was heard beyond the tape over his mouth and above Hermann's piercing screams.

Joe thought he was all cried out from that which they had endured before this round of torture, but volumes of hot tears filled his eye sockets behind the blindfold and some of it found miniscule places from which to streak in tiny threads from his eyes down his cheeks. Somehow Joe sensed there was another tormentor in the huge building and that they upped their cruelty, starting with his son. They were doing so to get at him, but there was nothing he could do.

All hope of their survival was dashed into dust at the first blood curdling scream of intense pain from his son. They left Joe alone to suffer as they slowly and methodically worked on hurting Hermann, then Susan, then Hermann, then Susan, again – driving Joe to surrender.

Suddenly it all stopped. Unbeknown to Joe both Hermann and

Susan lapsed mercifully close to states of being in comas, so the torturers lowered them onto their blood, urine and feces, with their hands still tied to their captive poles. They ripped off the tape from their mouths and left the building. For almost an hour Joe called out his wife and son's names, searching for them He wished then and there to die with his family.

The man with the brown suede shoes was already safely embedded within the kill zone. He checked and re-checked his data book on what to expect from the tools of his trade and then re-set the lenses and confirmed both vertical and horizontal alignments before dialing in the ranges. He knew the vertical distance was 1600m that translated to 1603 at vertical drop of 150m and angle of 3,579 degrees. Finally he walked the route surreptitiously gathering the last bit of data on the different wind speeds. When he was satisfied that all was in order, he carefully set up his dirty-looking equipment, fixing each in place on a mild steel frame that was securely anchored into the ground on both sides of the anthill.

Pride of place on the top was a McMillan TAC-50 anti-material, anti-personnel sniper rifle he had removed from the corpse of a dead American soldier in Bosnia those many years ago. He made sure his line of sight was clear by cutting off with a sharp field knife any branches and leaves that were intruding and then retreated far enough away from there to eat his last meal for now until the job was done. He then went further on where he dug a hole and relieved himself in it. All his left-over rations were also chucked in the hole before it was closed and lightly compacted. He even expertly scattered dust and dry foliage over this spot to hide it from animals and humans. The man then carefully covered his embedded equipment on the anthill with a dark green canvas sheet that had tufts of grass like the surrounding area sown to it and a Mylar foil layer underneath it.

From close up the fairly dense foliage growing over most of what was clearly an anthill was not convincing, but he was not worried about this. He secured the outer edges of the covering with pegs and rocks to keep it from being disturbed by night animals and any strong gusts of wind. The man settled for the night within a clump of trees close to his equipment.

The site for the operation was chosen for two main reasons. The first was the sounds from the roaring water and traffic within this valley. It would muffle that single shot. Secondly it fitted perfectly with his three planned escape routes. There was no easy way for anyone to get to where he was, unless already in the valley and off the freeway, and this afforded him more than enough time to disappear.

The only problem with this kill zone was the traffic speeds. He needed the Catalyst to be slowed down enough for his purposes. Normally he worked alone, but in this case, it was necessary to use the inter-links. If they failed to do their job, he would have to adapt accordingly. He knew that it was not impossible to do what he needed to while tracking a fast-moving object. A spotter at hand to perform this function made it easier, but he was alone and would have to make it work if needed.

He was confident he could do it again as he had many years ago in Sarajevo. It would mean more than three shots and his employers had insisted on a single shot kill to make a big political statement. The man strung a hammock in between two trees, climbed into it and was soon fast asleep. The moonlight across his body expertly cast these camouflage contrasting patterns of l He did not snore, breathe deeply, or make any sound as he slumbered, waking every hour on the hour to check on his surroundings.

CHAPTER 19
IN SHADOWS OF VALLEY BEAUTIFUL
(MONDAY, 27 DECEMBER 1999)

PART 1

The man with the brown suede shoes was up at the crack of dawn. After morning ablutions were done and buried the man went about building himself a small mound of clean sand under the trees where he slept. He was careful to select sand without any visible contaminations for this purpose. When he was satisfied that it was sufficient, he prayed over it then stripped completely naked and performed Tayammum, rubbing the sand over his hands, arms, head, feet and finally over his entire body as he quietly murmured 'As-Salat.'

There were not many people remaining in the world who knew that the man with the brown suede shoes was a whizz at pure mathematics at a university in his home country before having to drop out and join the resistance in a civil war that exploded into being in his beloved homeland. It was there that he honed his skills through applied mathematics as an exceptional shot with one of the highest kill rates in the entire world. What kept him largely out of the radar was that most of these kills were attributed to a host of other snipers and no one in the spy agencies and militaries of the West knew him by any name or moniker. He was anonymous – a well-kept secret amongst a select few of the Sheiks in the Middle East who used his services extensively. They provided him with whatever latest technology he requested, who shipped his hardware through diplomatic channels to and from the kill zones and who sowed disinformation about this jinn who served them well over the years.

After getting dressed again in the summer uniform of an Ezemvelo Ranger except for his shoes, he took a handful of the sand to his equipment at the anthill, removed the covering and performed 'Tayammum' over each item, being very careful not to get sand and dust into places that will hinder him taking that shot. He then re-checked his calculations for range, first with a laser rangefinder and then with the mil dot scope. Next, he removed from his button-down top pocket his small notebook of many charts and annotations and painstakingly went through the chart for bullet drop compensation. He had another look at the angle cosine indicator and referred to another small chart to confirm his findings for a moving target estimated to be travelling at 60km/hour at the point of impact. He adjusted the swivel on the tripod to suite the expected trajectory.

A few years earlier the man had modified the tripod mechanism to allow him to set the rifle to shoot at pre-determined angles and directions for moving targets. It was made perfect when used in accordance with his spotter markers in the kill zone. This tripod was so well developed that once set to whatever regular terrain in front of him the man did not need a spotter to tell him what adjustments he needed to make.

Using the sustained-lead method, he picked the target up at a pre-determined position along his spotter markers, held his estimated lead in front of it while moving in tandem with the quarry. For the briefest moment he maintained the same lead distance. When he was ready, he breathed out slowly to steady himself further, then gently pulled the trigger.

There was always the element of instinct involved where he would make minute adjustments to compensate for what he believed was the best point to shoot at. This instinct never failed him in all kills that he executed thus far. The first time the man used this tripod adaptation was in July 1996 just outside Passu Village in Hunza (Heavan on Earth) Valley in Pakistan. He assassinated a high-ranking Chinese Army

General from Xinjiang Province selling arms and ammunition to both sides in a local conflict.

The Chinese intelligence operative was killed while driving an open-topped jeep on a badly corrugated gravel road, from 1 km away at an elevation distance of 120 m from a very rugged stretch of the mountain. The man with the brown suede shoes re-calculated the Gyroscopic (Spin) Drift and Coriolis Effect on the bullet trajectory. Only when he was content that his calculations were correct did he re-set the focus of the reticule on the range of irregular looking spotter markers he had set low down on the opposite embankment and along the asphalt surface shoulder lane of the freeway – just before where the Bushman's River flows under the highway into New Formosa (Beautiful Valley).

From his scope the swivel of his rifle was in a perfect alignment with the downhill slope of the roadway and at the continual perfect height that he needed. The man with the brown suede shoes carefully laid out five 12.7 x 99 mm Barnes 50 caliber cartridges of 700 grain 45g, bullets next to the rifle and covered these with a soft cloth. He knew the missile would be travelling a distance closer to 1610 m at a speed of Mach 1.0 to the target before drilling through the window of the vehicle and through the head of the subject.

Satisfied that all was in order, he packed up his duffel bag with everything he did not need and placed it out of the way from where he would lay to take that exceptional shot. He was approximately 1350 m above sea level, and he silently climbed a further 50 m to a well-hidden vantage point deep in shadows amongst rocks and thorn trees where he could scan around him for three hundred and sixty degrees. He had with him a bottle of water and a packet of lightly salted biltong to quell any thirst or hunger pangs during the long wait.

On his left-hand side was the last cellphone to receive the final instructions. As was pre-determined, he switched it on after every forty minutes and left it on for one minute before switching it off again. The cellphone was connected to a portable battery charger pack. From his vantage point he could see quite a distance up the freeway and would be in place and ready the minute he spotted the three trucks. In his hands was a pair of military binoculars.

· · ·

I was the first one up, dressed and standing on the back verandah long before the house stirred to life. I had a good night's sleep and was feeling grateful, hopeful and refreshed. Japie quietly joined me on the verandah. After a short while he took out his pipe and tobacco, prepared the smoke, lit up and puffed away. Every now and then he sort of chewed something from the pipe and spat it out beyond the verandah. Japie killed off the last embers of his pipe with his thumb before knocking the pipe clean against the closest bin. He packed everything away in his pockets and came back to stand in his original position and folded his arms.

"Jakkals trou met wolf se vrou," he said.

"Pardon?"

"You know?" Japie tried to explain. "It rains and the sun is shining. It makes a rainbow."

"Oh! The monkeys are getting married!" I exclaimed.

"Hmmm." His turn to look bamboozled.

"Same thing." It was my turn to shrug my shoulders.

"Oh, ja. Monkeys getting married!" We burst out laughing.

The geese had enough of our nonsense and started their own loud cackling, honking and hooting racket that woke everyone and everything up in the yard and in very short shrift my entire being was fully stirred into life at the loud crescendo of varying sounds bouncing of the verandah walls all around me. Japie was still cackling when he walked off towards the sheds. I was beaming as I sniffed the air to catch the hint of impending rain that Japie picked up on. When I could not do likewise I reluctantly walked into the kitchen.

The rest of us were gathered around the kitchen table while Grandma and Hester sorted out the bowls of porridge and coffee. The conversations were flowing along happily.

"Jakkals trou met wolf se vrou vanoggend," I declared and sat down at my place like a seasoned farmer, looking at no one in particular.

Grandma, William, May-June, Tshepo and Morph all swiveled to stare at me.

Hettie explained.

"Oh!" they exclaimed.

"Why didn't you just say, the monkeys are getting married?!"

"I didn't know you Could speak Afrikaans?" Hettie exclaimed, smiling at me.

"'n Bietjie. Japie het my geleer."

"Jy praat heel mooi. From now on you and I'll speak in Afrikaans!" Hettie declared as she placed a bowl of porridge and a steaming cup of coffee before me.

I was so happy I did not care that muscles on my body ached I never knew existed. We were again called upon to help getting the sheep out. We managed it with aplomb, such that both Japie and Fana the foreman gave us a thumbs up. Then it was onto the poultry shed.

The rain shower came while we were cleaning out the poultry shed. There was no thunder and lightning, just a quick hard downpour that lasted about thirty minutes. Just as Japie had predicted, the sun shone all the time. The coolness it brought was a welcome relief from the oppressive heat of the morning. There is no better natural aroma in all the world than that brought forth from the soil of Africa after good rains on a hot summer's day. There is hardly a more unpleasant smell than a whole lot of wet cattle, sheep, geese and chicken ammonia dung vying to occupy the last vestiges of breathable air. I saw William and Tshepo turn ashen.

Fortunately for us Hettie spotted our dire misfortunes and she shepherded us to the storage shed to collect some tools and materials to clean out the geese pond. With our wheelbarrows loaded, Hettie led us to the pond along the banks of the Roodepoortspruit River.

"First, we wait for ten minutes for the water from the rain to pass by. You don't want to be in there when it comes," she advised.

"But it wasn't a big thunderstorm, Hettie?" asked Tshepo with genuine puzzlement.

"It rained in the catchment. It'll come down for sure. Just wait ten minutes, OK?"

The view from there had this miniature valley feel because larger vegetation was kept out of the vicinity of the pond to prevent their roots from damaged the concrete structure. When the pond was brimming over, as it did then, that place looked like a beautiful natural pool along a gently flowing river in a small valley overflowing with all sorts of wonderful flora and fauna. I marveled at the ingenuity of the person who designed it, more so because this creation brought a thriving eco-system to this charming miniature valley when it fully served its purpose.

Within a few minutes there was this feint rustling sound upstream of us and then in almost a blink of an eye the water level rose a few centimeters above the pond and quickly took with it most of the floating debris that was visible a moment ago. Then the flood waters tumbled by, and the water level gently subsided to about a centimeter above the level of the pond.

"It'll go down now-now," remarked Hettie as she walked down the slippery slope. We grabbed all the stuff we brought with us and followed her.

"When the water level drops below the level of the pond, use that pipe here to drain it. You must catch all the fishes, frogs and crabs in there, and whatever else. Don't worry about those that hop into the river. They'll come back later." Hettie showed us what to do.

"River Frogs! 'Letlametlu'! Dudes, I'm scared. They're deadly. If you kill one, you'll shrivel up and die, dudes!" exclaimed Tshepo loudly, grabbing and holding tightly onto my upper arm with both hands.

"They're not dangerous, just don't kill any," I suggested as I tried to loosen his grip.

"You guys'll have to catch them! I'm not going in there 'till they're out!" Tshepo eventually let go of my arm.

"It's good to have frogs and fishes and crabs. They help keep the pond clean." Hettie admonished him. Tshepo did not respond but looked at her as though she was crazy.

"Also watch for two Brown Water Snakes. They come around every now and then to eat frogs and fishes. Don't kill them," said Hettie sternly.

"Ivuzamanzi elimdubu! Like hell am I getting into that pond!"

"Dudes those snakes are very, very dangerous. They cause water spouts! If one of them bites you, the only way you live is if you drink water from the river before it does!"

"Nonsense! These snakes are the most harmless in South Africa. There are some more dangerous ones that live on the farm and visit the pond," answered Hettie firmly.

"That's settled, then. If it bites you then just quickly drop face down into the pond and suck up the gooey stuff at the bottom before it does. You'll be fine," countered William dryly.

I tried hard not to laugh out loud. Hettie could not help grinning.

"Yuck! I'm not drinking that!"

This time none of us responded and Tshepo looked really troubled.

Hettie showed us how to remove the barley straw filter. Next, she picked up a small fishing net and expertly cast it into the pond. When she drew it a bit out of the water, there was quite a bit of wriggling and squirming therein, mostly small fishes and frogs and other stuff entrapped. She beckoned Tshepo over to hold it in place. This he hastily did, with eyes forever watching everything that moved and every shadow that stirred around him and in the water. She then explained about catching and storing of the fishes, crabs and frogs in the containers we brought and half-filled with river water. We then started emptying the net off the catch, grabbing hold of these slippery, wriggling creatures and dropping them into the respective jars.

Hettie watched us for a few minutes to ensure that we were doing all things right. This was much fun for my brother and me as we happily moved between net and jars with each catch of assorted squirming and wriggling amphibians, laughing merrily all the way. Our actions brought out smiles and some outbursts of laughter from Hetttie and Tshepo as they watched two crazy kids enjoy themselves.

"Also, clean the White Water Lillies with a few sprays of water. This will chase out any goggas hiding by them. Don't stick your hands there. Use these toilet brushes and spades to clean out algae. I'll come add some hydrogen peroxide when you're done," said Hettie before turning and striding quickly towards the poultry sheds.

"Yes." "Okay!" William and I responded.

"Who's with Shorty checking the little fokkers?" Carel asked without turning to look at Zodwa. He shaded his eyes with one hand as he gazed northwards. They stood close to the landing strip at the Estcourt

Aerodrome that was approximately 2km south of the town along the R103 and less than 1km from the New Formosa Nature Reserve.

"Warrant Officer Meisie Mtambo, Supe," Zodwa responded.

"Is she OK?"

"She's shup, Supe."

Not far from them a SAPS Pilatus PC6/B2-H4 STOL fixed-wing aircraft was being refueled while the pilot and his crew of two did their flight checks. They normally waited until fueling was done before they proceeded, but time was of the essence. The airmen were already briefed by Carel and knew precisely what they needed to do. This plane was sent to assist Carel and his team because it was mounted with a Terrain Awareness and Warning System (TAWS) and a Forward-Looking Infrared System (FLIS) that used thermal imagery. The plan was for them to fly the designated route several times and to report any extraordinary events to Carel and to the helicopter crew that was en-route to the aerodrome.

"Have you got everything?"

"I'm okay, Supe," she responded tapping the rifle case slung across her back. Therein was a fully loaded bolt action Sharpshooter SSG 69 P1 Sniper Rifle. She held over the other shoulder a rucksack containing five rotary magazines each with 5-rounds of 7.62 x 51 mm Nato cartridges. There was also a specially adapted ACOG Scope that fitted perfectly on the rifle. It was inscribed by the manufacturers alongside the model number with the Bible verse JN8:12, "I am the Light of the World." Zodwa's handgun and a pair of SAPS issued binoculars were also strapped in. Zodwa ranked amongst the top four snipers within the Police Force, known to be unerringly accurate to 800 metres, although she once took down a drug lord over 1 km away.

The approaching helicopter had a faint initial buzz, but it quickly grew in volume as it drew nearer. Carel was pleased that the Boss acted very fast after the briefing phone call. There was another airplane and helicopter assigned to the Valley of a Thousand Hills. They were under the direction of another colleague who was based in Durban. Both that team and the one in Estcourt were mandated to follow and protect prominent VVIP individuals who would be in or close to the designated areas over the next two days, while searching for an assassin.

The boss managed to obtain the itineraries of all such VVIP persons who have plans to visit these areas and the teams were acting upon this information. Some of the subjects listened to reason from the Minister of Police and the Police Commissioner who made personal calls to them, and they changed their plans, but there were some who refused to do so, believing that this was nefarious disinformation from the ANC. The most prominent was already en route to Loskop to open a newly constructed Clinic there.

Carel desperately needed the plane in the air to help keep 'Amandla Entabeni' and a host of other ANC and IFP leaders alive and safe. Ironically, some of the Councillors initially heeded the calls to change their plans to go to Loskop, but when told that 'Amandla Entabeni' was on his way, they went to the gathering. The Boss, Carel, JB and Zodwa were convinced that 'Amandla Entabeni' was the target – The Catalyst – as Combrink said not long ago.

The President was informed by the Boss and the Minister of State Security of these developments at a hastily convened Cabinet Meeting at Mahlamba Ndlopfu, the official residence in Pretoria of the President of the Republic of South Africa. Both the Ministers of Defence and Police loudly and forcefully advocated sending in the Army and Police troops to KwaZulu-Natal to quell any hint of an uprising, but sensible voices prevailed.

All leave within these two forces was summarily cancelled and members were instructed to report to their offices and bases within three hours to receive further instruction. Increased Police presence was hastily assigned to where major political figures were scheduled to attend. More Army units were assigned to protect airports, harbors, borders and all national and legislative buildings and the homes of senior national and provincial leaders. Ministers of State Security, Justice and International Relations were urged to make every effort to get to the bottom of the intended sabotage and treason.

There was very real concern amongst the leaders regarding the perceived interference from international countries who were thought to be friends of South Africa and had already invested heavily into the local economy. To accuse them of sedition would require absolute proof. The word was put out that this was a training exercise to test the readiness of the Army and Police. Code named Operation Sputla, ministers were instructed by the President that they would be remaining at Mahlamba Ndlopfu until further notice. They hastily ordered their assistants to get whatever was needed for what could be a prolonged stay.

The SAPS Eurocopter AS350 with FLIR landed and the pilot and his crew of two hastily disembarked and ran over to where Carel and Zodwa stood. The pilot and crew from the SAPS Pilatus PC6/B2-H4 STOL also ran over to join them. Quick introductions were made and Carel hastily briefed them. The Pilatus crew ran to their aircraft and were airborne within a few minutes while the Eurocopter, with Zodwa now part of that crew taxied to the fuel bowsers to be filled up. Carel ran to his vehicle that held the men who were assigned to him. He sped off in a cloud of dust out of the aerodrome and onto the R103 heading towards the N3.

"Guys, we need to be careful when emptying the nets," I interjected urgently. "Let's just say anything that's brightly colored, especially red, we don't touch. Let it go on its own. Remember what Grandpa taught us, William?"

"Why? What did you see?" William asked.

"There was a Spotted Shovel-nosed Frog and a Banded Rubber Frog with those Platanna and River Frogs with the first catch."

"Saw them. I let them hop outta there," William intoned dryly.

"I saw that. Let's watch out for any surprises."

"Ok!" William and Tshepo responded.

"Dude, why those frogs?"

"The Banded Rubber Frog is definitely poisonous. Don't remember whether the Spotted Shovel-nosed is the same. Best to avoid them because of their reddish color."

"Dudes, there's snakes that disguise themselves as pretty mermaids or something like that and can attract left-handed people into the river, hypnotise them and suck out their brains through the nostrils." Tshepo looked pointedly at William.

"Well, they can't do that here," responded William. "This pond is not deep and has a concrete floor. How are they gonna do that?" He deliberately stepped into the pond, where the water did not even reach halfway up to the top of his gumboots and helped drag the net out of the pond. We worked on sorting out the next catch.

I was attuned to my surroundings and to the various sights and sounds emanating from all around us. To distract Tshepo I commented on all that was visible in the net and within eyesight and earshot. It did not take long for him to let go of his inhibitions and to work alongside us clearing the nets, although he wore long rubber gloves.

He also shied away from anything slimy and suspect. He even climbed into the pond with us to catch whatever was left and when we worked on removing the pockets of algae with the toilet brushes, flat spades and splashes of hydrogen peroxide for the difficult spots, Tshepo was so engrossed in learning about many of the creatures he could see or hear, he bombarded us with all sorts of questions, while we answered as best as we could.

My brother and I were well taught by Grandpa about nature and history, especially when he took us hunting or fishing. It was natural for us to pour over books related to South African flora and fauna so that we could impress Grandpa with our knowledge. After his death we honored him by continuing to learn about our natural environment.

We moved from identifying frogs, fishes and other crustaceans from the nets to focus on whatever emanated from the grasses, flowers, shrubbery, bushes and trees. We started on the numerous flies that buzzed all over. Other than the normal range there were also some Mayflies with long tails and wings that do not fold flat, Cainflies that swim erratically in short bursts as though they were undecided where to go next. We showed Tshepo the Caddisflies that look like tiny floating sticks. He marveled at the Blue Emperor Damselflies and Dragonflies and the Red-veined Dropwings flitting this way and that way beyond our reach.

We witnessed the fast swimming and diving of Diving Beetles, the Rhino Beetle with its pronounced horn and the bold tapping Beetle that walked with no care in the world and stopped every now and again to rhythmically tap the ground with its overweight behind. It did not surprise us that Tshepo laughed joyfully as he tried to mimic this behavior by tapping his behind on the edge of the pond We joined him and had a good time.

We followed the flights of a host of African Monarch Butterflies going about their business in the golden sunshine on the other side of the river. Above them, on a Sweet Thorn tree, a pair of loud 'zaaak' squawking Lilac-breasted Roller birds sat and quizzically watched the dancing butterflies go by. They were expert hunters of larger prey and showed no interest in going after the butterflies. William explained that these birds got their name from death-defying courtship, tumbling and rolling towards the ground only to rectify falls last minute.

Not too far from them on another torn tree many bright metallic green males and olive-grey females Malachite Sunbirds flitted here and there within a crescendo of loud calls to each other. I explained to Tshepo that their long beaks were used to suck up nectar and insects and that their long tails helped them to perform difficult maneuvers in flight and when they hovered like hummingbirds to suck up nectar.

On our side of the river a pair of Purple-crested Turaco shifted their Mohawk heads with what looked like some concern this way and that from where they perched deep in the shadows of another tree. One called loudly before stopping to hop about a bit and to preen itself. The other one responded with the same call, stretched its wings and preen William told Tshepo that these were the national bird of the Kingdom of eSwatini and that their crimson flight feathers were used in the ceremonial regalia of the Swazi Royal Family. Tshepo was quite taken by this because his ancestors on his mom's side were from the eSwatini Kingdom.

Near to the barns were numerous Crowned Lapwings scratching the ground and flitting about. It looked as though all of them were wearing black beanies with white stripes. Those on the ground ran about in short bursts and jabbed quite hard onto the ground to grab their food. I Despite all that haste, not one of them went after the same morsel. I told Tshepo that these birds were known to dive-bomb, with accompanying loud screeches, towards any intruder that dared to go too close to the nest.

It was one of those unspoken moments when a group of young men have a sudden urge to pee at the same time and so we lined up next to each other downstream of the pond and urinated into the flowing river. Before anyone was declared the winner, there was a sudden loud splash about ten meters further downstream and we swiveled our heads to look.

A leguaan, at least a meter long, laboriously dragged itself out of the fast-flowing water and stretched out on a rock to warm itself. It lifted its head off the rock and looked menacingly at us with its tongue flicking, but then ignored us from that frozen posture as it warmed up. We hastily tucked away our suddenly vulnerable dangling appendages and quickly retreated to the relative safety of the empty pond. At first sighting the Leguaan looked scarily like a miniature crocodile. William and I knew enough about them to leave this one alone, but not Tshepo; he watched it like a crazy hawk.

"What's wrong?"

"Dudes, do you know tokoloshi lives with uXamu? William and I shook our heads.

"Dudes, its true! If that thing stamps its feet, it's dancing with tokoloshi. We'll have to run away from here fast before tokoloshi comes!"

This Nile Monitor Lizard however remained immobile for quite a while before it eventually slipped silently back into the water with hardly a ripple. Tshepo eventually breathed a sigh of relief when it did not resurface.

We then saw what could have disturbed the sunbathing leguaan – a massive, shiny Brown Forest Cobra, that was close to two meters long, stood at the ready on a rock above where the Monitor Lizard had rested. This magnificent snake's huge, longish hood was fully extended, and the front portion of its body raised up high from the ground, exposing two broad dark brown bands on its yellow, blotched black stomach. It waited in this pose swaying from side to side to be sure that the lizard was gone before it lowered hood and head and slithered down the rocks towards the water's edge to drink from there. The snake was yellowish brown near the head, darkening gradually to pitch black near the tail. Close to its big eyes were dark brown streaks that looked like war paint.

"Haibo!" Tshepo exclaimed in wonderment that this large, shiny

Cobra could so easily chase away the mighty feared uXamu. If there was a snake that could do so simply by its large, menacing presence, this one fitted the bill. It was highly unusual to see this species around Estcourt, because it was not their normal habitat and these snakes were shy, hunting mostly in the early morning and evening.

Suddenly those highly aggressive screeching and screaming Lilac-breasted Roller Birds dive-bombed that snake, pecking it from all angles as it writhed and rolled and desperately tried to strike back at these very quick antagonists who were rapidly tearing it to shreds.

"Haibo!" Tshepo exclaimed again at this unusual spectacle happening right before our unbelieving eyes. Perhaps it was because the snake dared to enter their territory during daylight hours, or maybe they just happened to be quite temperamental, or had some long memory of a previous snake attack, or they were thinking of lunch, whatever the reason, they were merciless in their destruction of this now bloodied reptile that had absolutely no chance against them.

Grandpa taught us to leave all Cobras alone, unless it was necessary to remove or kill them, because they hung on after striking to chew the victim and needed to be removed forcibly. It would be a very painful experience for one of those birds to be struck by this two-meter-long monster, and yet miraculously none of them were. We stopped working and watched in awe as they hit the snake with deadly accuracy from all angles until it ceased moving and played dead, although its body still jerked with every devastating strike from these unrelenting vicious avian species. The creatures would have none of that play-acting and went in for the kill. In a last burst of energy, the snake rolled into the river, but before another second flew by a Leguaan shot upright, grabbed the snake by its head and disappeared with a splash underwater.

"No ways!" Tshepo exclaimed in awe. "This is bad for someone!"

Those Rollers were not done and patrolled the river for a brief while before they flew back to their tree and continued with their loud chattering and preening.

"Wow!" was all that the three of us could immediately exclaim at what had just taken place right before our disbelieving eyes.

"What's up, guys?" Hettie spoke in the silence behind us, and we jumped and spun quickly around like spinning tops in flight.

"Did you see that?" William shouted in excitement, pointing at the rocks where all the action took place.

"See what?"

Then it was like a dam of words burst as we simultaneously tried to shout louder than the other in explanation.

"Woah, guys! One by one!" Hettie laughingly raised her hands in surrender.

Tshepo and I deferred to William to be our spokesperson. He dutifully obliged.

"A Brown Forest Cobra chased away a leguaan and those Roller Birds went after the snake and were killing it alive, blood and guts spilling everywhere, before it fell into the river and was eaten by the leguaan!" Tshepo and I nodded our heads vigorously in agreement with happy grins plastered on our faces.

"Ja, those Rollers can be very aggressive. They even attack each other during mating season. You mustn't go near their nests; they'll attack you too." Hettie responded.

"Dudes! Didn't know uXamu eat snakes!" Tshepo's eyes were as large as saucers.

"Those little shits eat anything alive or dead, even our geese and chickens. We'll have to catch it – to relocate it. We must also catch other Forest Cobras. They also eat our stock" Hettie answered him. We shook our heads, and this made Hettie laugh merrily.

"Come on! Let's finish here! It's lunchtime" still chuckling she helped us get everything done. We joined in, still chattering about our experience of the rough and tough and so unexpected violence in nature. It was hard to believe what we just witnessed in this miniature beautiful valley that initially looked so calm and restive. At lunch the three of us held court as we explained with happy grins the gory details of the death of the magnificent Brown Forest Cobra. Grandma eventually had to tell us to not talk while chewing.

· · ·

Abu collected Rob, who carried two bulging rucksacks, Rob went to commandeer and sprawl across the back seats of the Parks Board Isuzu Crew Cab truck. It did not take long before Ewald and Dewald were also on board. They sat in the middle, but on opposite sides. There was this strong buzz and bounce of heightened excitement charged up within the confines of the Cab. They were all dressed alike in black Chinos and black golf tee shirts; black caps and unzipped and sleeveless Homeboy jackets.

Trust these guys to think of padkos! Abu mulled to himself as he watched Dewald carry on board a big cooler bag. Instead, Abu patiently waited for instructions from Ewald.

"We brought drinks and things in case we have to wait," Dewald offered by way of explanation. No one bothered to respond.

"Do you have everything?" asked Ewald, glancing at each one, but more pointedly at Rob who was tasked to bring the most important stuff.

"Yes." "Mmm."

"Locked and loaded. I've also got the boosters and the downers. We'll take them there."

"OK, we'll dish out guns and ammo at the same time," Ewald said.

"Right."

"Been thinking. On the left side of the first cutting after the bridges there's a nice spot under some thick bushes where we can hide the bus. Been there few times with that bitch. No one caught us. It's like a completely carport closed on all sides. I'll show Abu how to reverse in. We can wait there, but we must be quiet. Those cunts'll be dropped off at the same cutting, almost right below us. We'll take them as soon as their transport disappears," said Rob calmly.

"Sounds good to me. Have you checked train timetables?" Ewald was all business.

"None from half past one to half past two."

"Right. I've made sure they'll be dropped off between ten to and two."

"Last chance, guys! If anyone wants to chicken out, say so now and you can fuck off!"

"We're in!" Ewald and Dewald responded without hesitation.

"Me too," said Abu.

Let's fuck off! It's already quarter past one," declared Ewald.

Abu started the truck and drove off. No further words were spoken on their journey through Estcourt, along the R103, then onto New Formosa Road from where they joined it opposite the Estcourt Provincial Hospital. Abu did not pay much mind to the battered, faded yellow and rusty, Toyota Hilux that managed to overtake them along this windy gravel road and speed off somewhere in the dust cloud ahead of them. To Abu it looked like two poor Zulus heading home with some junk in the back bin of the LDV. What he did not know was that the scruffy looking driver, Lieutenant Shorty Setene, and the equally disheveled woman next to him, Warrant Officer Meisie Mtambo, were tailing them. This was one of Shorty's signature strategies to avoid being detected by going on ahead for a brief while and then allowing them to pass him a short time later, before repeating the process, if necessary.

Shorty started this maneuver on a relatively straight section of road just past the first smallholding. There was always the risk that a suspect could branch off somewhere behind him and so Shorty did not go too far ahead of them. He hastily pulled off into a side road bell mouth near the Roodepoortspruit River crossing and quickly opened the bonnet and made like he was fixing something. Meisie stood watching him while fanning herself with a pamphlet and talking on her cellphone, reporting to Carel about these developments. Abu and his friends paid them no mind as they shot by into the long right-hand loop across the river and quickly disappeared, but for the dust cloud trailing their murderous journey.

Shorty gave them a short lead before Meisie and he continued with their pursuit. This time they followed much more sedately behind the truck's dust cloud, at most times totally unseen by those ahead of them. Just as they approached the freeway overpasses Shorty quickly slowed the vehicle down to a crawl and peered carefully ahead. All his internal antenna were jolted suddenly into very high alert, screaming, "Ingozi! Ingozi! Danger! Danger!"

"Passop!" He hissed.

Both quickly removed their firearms, released safety catches and kept them below window height as Shorty allowed the old van to travel sedately onwards, their highly focused and alert eyes scanning everything in all directions around them. Both saw the fresh truck tracks where the Isuzu Crew Cab diverted off the road up the side of the cutting. Shorty stuck his head out of the window to smell for traces of dust in the air ahead of them. There was none.

He increased speed and drove for approximately one hundred and fifty meters onwards to a place where they could safely pull off the road. Shortly quickly jumped out the vehicle and removed his shirt and jeans while giving urgent instructions to Meisie. Without waiting for a response, he grabbed the recently issued Heckler & Koch USP 9 mm x 19 caliber semi-automatic pistol loaded with fifteen rounds of Parabellum bullets and ran back towards the embankment where the truck went off the road.

Keeping as much as was possible to the vegetation cover on the side of the road he sprinted silently and quickly towards the cutting and slowed down to a fast and stealthy glide through the thick undergrowth when he neared the destination. He stopped about twenty meters from the vehicle, deep in the shadows where he was confident no one would see him in his dark and dusty skin, navy blue t-shirt, boxer shorts and black canvas shoes. The occupants were not speaking and except for the ticking and creaking of the vehicle he could hear and see them checking and loading handguns, then drink from plastic water bottles. Shorty slid up a thick low-hanging branch to get a better look into the side of the vehicle. He lay flat on his front and settled carefully in place – and then he saw him!

There was another man hidden in the shadows behind the vehicle. Shorty immediately shut his eyes, waited about five seconds then opened them to slits, making sure not to look directly at the man. The man must have sensed something, because he peered intently in the direction where Shorty lay hidden, trying to seek him out. Suddenly he disappeared. Shorty steadied the pistol in front of him, heart now heavily pounding adrenaline through his electrified body, in anticipation of a deadly firefight.

PART 2

The silent watcher, who looked more-or-less like a tanned White man with a long, hooked nose suspiciously dressed in the uniform of Ezemvelo, reappeared at the front of the truck where he carefully peered around this side of the vehicle before slowly swiveling to check out the bushes and trees in Shorty's direction, looking for a quarry he sensed was there. Even though the man did not draw out the handgun that was clearly visible, Shorty could sense the very real danger permeating across that deadly supercharged space between them. The man waited, slightly crouched, in place for about two seconds before dropping onto the ground to peer under the truck and then the undergrowth all around him. Shorty thanked his ancestors for their foresight in urging him up to that vantage point. If he had remained at that spot on the ground near the base of the tree, the man would most certainly have spotted Shorty.

The man was up and back behind the vehicle in a few silent strides and the next time Shorty saw him, that man was going up the hill like the big cats of Africa. Shorty breathed a slow and very steady, quiet sigh of relief, then waited precisely ten seconds before carefully and silently retreating. This time he sprinted zigzag from one clump of thorn tree bush to the next, pausing each time to check around him for any lurking or tailing antagonist.

Just as Shorty settled on that branch a few minutes earlier, the man with the brown suede shoes peered into the truck and saw these young men sitting there checking their firearms and taking drugs. He was on the verge of eliminating them for being within his kill zone were it not for the presence of Abu amongst them. The man also picked up on the scent of another quarry in deep shadows to his left. He narrowed this person's position down to within a few meters after surveying the surrounding thick thorn tree bushes on that side of the truck.

He had deliberately exposed himself at the front of the Crew Cab and as he went up the hill away from his sniper rifle position. He did so hoping to draw this person out from hiding. He stopped at a good vantage point in the shadows of some massive rocks halfway up the hill, took out his handgun and waited for this 'infidel' to follow him; but no one did.

The man with the brown suede shoes soon caught a glimpse of a black man in a dark top and shorts at least one hundred meters off running away from where the truck was embedded. The assassin was quickly on the move again, hurrying to his sniper rifle position. He knew he had twenty-six minutes remaining to take that shot. He also knew that the plane and helicopter that flew off in a north-westerly direction were spotter aircraft mounted with thermal imagery equipment. He had seen this as they flew by close to his position.

He needed to be ready for them when they surely would return, searching along the freeway. First the plane would come, flying low along one side then circling back on the other before moving on to the next stretch of the highway. The helicopter would follow the same pattern, except at a much slower pace, pausing to investigate any areas that were deemed suspicious. The sniper was unconcerned that his equipment on the old anthill would be discovered by the spotter aircraft, because it was covered in the deep shadows with the dark green canvas sheet with a Mylar foil layer underneath.

When the time was right, he would also be safely enclosed under this protection. It would be very hot there, but he had been in worse hellholes and survived. The sniper reached the anthill and carefully removed the rocks and pegs from the edges of the covering. He then grasped the canvas sheet with his hands spread as far apart as was practically possible and in one fluid motion quickly flipped it off the tools of his trade.

As he did so that massive Black Mamba shot out faster than the blink of an eye from a hole in the anthill and struck the man quicker than he could react, first on the knuckles of his left hand, then on his left side and finally on his left thigh. A pair of fangs that were at least 8m long injected large amounts of deadly neurotoxic and cardiotoxic venom into him with each penetration. At the first hit the man quickly dropped the blanket and tried to reach for his sidearm. The second got to him long before his hand touched the weapon. The man staggered backwards from the third strike, and this gave the mamba enough space to flee.

By the time the assassin drew the firearm out, he barely caught a fleeting glimpse of the snake that looked like tyre treads slithering at high speed past the trees where he had slept, and it disappeared. A terrible burning sensation assailed him from the puncture wounds. The man immediately holstered the handgun and removed his razor-sharp field knife. Without any hesitation he sliced open the skin and flesh on his knuckles across the puncture holes. Blood came pouring out. He quickly pulled off his pants and lifted his shirt and did likewise to the snake bites on his side and thigh.

The pain from what he did to himself was excruciating, but the man neither cried out, nor did he flinch. He knew that unless he received an anti-venom injection for a Black Mamba bite within the next twenty minutes, or so, he was going to die. He doubted whether anyone in Estcourt would have these supplies; the nearest cities were too far away. He quickly pulled up his pants, tightened the belt and got down to business making final preparations for the shot.

He used rocks and stones to plug as many of the larger holes in the anthill. He then did his final checks and calculations before laying flat across the anthill in the sniper's position and tested his tracking of vehicles along the south-bound lane. None of the drivers and passengers he sighted on were aware of a red dot that stayed unerringly fixed on the side of their heads for five to eight seconds as their vehicles roared by.

The final practice run was sighted on a bawling toddler strapped into his baby car seat behind a clearly agitated father who was shouting some unintelligible words into the hearts and minds of the mother and child who had no options but to suffer from the abusive tirade within the confines of the high speed, whistling BMW 325i. "Bang!" the assassin said softly, without any hint of emotion, at the precise moment he would have taken the shot and killed the crying child. He then checked his cellphone and the time.

The Catalyst was between twenty and twenty-three minutes away. He had between fifteen to twenty minutes of life on earth remaining in which to make the kill. He could taste this metallic sensation in his mouth that made him nauseous. His fingers and toes were tingling and the hair all over him stood somewhat painfully erect. His blood felt like it was slowly but steadily heating up towards boiling point. Paralysing pain radiated from the bite wounds. He could feel strength draining from him with every passing second. The killer prayed for enough life to take the final shot. He quickly disassembled the rifle barrel and just as rapidly cleaned it, repeating the procedure ten times. He also cleaned the recoil lug recess and the action area. Within two minutes the rifle was re-assembled to perfect position on the specialized frame.

He wiped each of the five 12.7 x 99 mm Barnes 50 caliber bullets clean with the soft cloth, then loaded them into the detachable box magazine. This he loaded and locked into place on the McMillan TAC-50 anti-material and anti-personnel sniper rifle. He pulled the bolt action all the way back, chambered one round and re-set the bolt over the first cartridge in the magazine. The man carefully disengaged the safety lever and re-focused on his markers, trying to negate the deadly neurotoxic and cardiotoxic venom coursing through his body as he did so.

The assassin was satisfied that he was ready for the kill, but he was not sure whether there will remain sufficient life within him to do so. As he covered himself and his equipment with the canvas sheet, he prayed for the energy reserves to enable him to complete the kill shot.

Japie guided the double cab in a scary blur along the noisy graveled Nine Hills Railway Road towards Wagendrift Dam. I was eternally grateful that Japie had the foresight to securely pack the fishing gear, including (and most especially for the three adventurous huntsmen) the small picnic basket that Grandma prepared for our survival.

And so, at least for me, that picnic basket was more important than the fishing rods and other stuff. My levels of consternation remained very high, because Japie seemed so relaxed, even taking his eyes off the road every now and then to look at us when speaking while we flew along that narrow and unstable road, through some dangerously sharp bends that were not meant for vehicles hurtling around them close to 140km/hr. He laughed merrily every now and then at our discomfort of potentially being confronted by Rangers with big guns.

"I'll fetch you after two hours, OK? I've got stuff to fetch in Ladysmith. The gate key is in the cubbie. And stick to the marked path to the dam wall."

This side of the dam was forbidden to the public because of the many petrified trees, but also because of the soft and treacherous ground where one wrong step could result in death by drowning. With the flick of my internal switch my mind drifted happily away from the conversation as I espied the shimmering waters of Wagendrift Dam sparkling invitingly.

My eyes were suddenly drawn to and followed an airplane flying low and relatively slow above the waters towards us. In less than five seconds a SAPS Pilatus PC6/B2-H4 STOL whizzed by overhead and disappeared beyond the hill on the other side of us. Then I caught a fleeting glimpse of a battered old Toyota Hilux van parked on the side of the road and a seemingly agitated Zulu couple on their cellphones marching hurriedly up and down close to it. The two of them looked up, saw the occupants within our vehicle and froze in shock, before the dust cloud from our wheels swallowed them up. I hardly had time to catch my breath or try to make sense of it all, because we suddenly screeched to a halt in a cloud of powdered sand tumbling over everything and were out in a jiffy to off-load our fishing gear.

"You've got the key?" Japie asked William while lighting up his pipe.

"Ja" William responded.

"OK! There's the gate," Japie pointed with his pipe.

"Ok! Thanks!" William, Tshepo and I responded.

"See you later!" He concluded as he hurried to the driver's seat and roared off down the road with a new dust cloud tailing the van. My first port of call was to grab the picnic basket and to peep inside to make sure everything was still fine. It was. I closed and latched it while keeping a firm grip on the life support container. We distributed the contents between us.

We were just about to move off when Tshepo piped up, "Dudes, there's that mkhulu whose bakkie was broken down the road!"

"I saw them. Wonder what he wants," William questioned.

I did not say what I saw when we passed them by, but rather moved to stand closer to my brother, and furtively unlatched the picnic basket, placing my hand on the 30 cm stainless steel carving knife that Grandma had packed next to slice a mouthwatering slab of biltong.

"Dudes, what's wrong with that ballie? Why's he running in and out of the bushes?" Tshepo queried while moving closer to my right-hand side.

"Why's he bent over like that?" William reflected our concerns.

The running man suddenly melted into the shadows of the bushes on the side of the road and did not reappear. We waited, unsure of what to do.

"GOT YOU, YOU FUCKING SONS OF BITCHES!" Ewald screamed behind us.

We spun around stunned by this frightening menace suddenly surfaced from a nightmare. Ewald, Rob, Dewald and Abu strode towards us. They each had on their signature Homeboys black caps and black jackets, but what was most frightening were the guns in their hands and the assortment of weapons in their belts and around their shoulders. They stopped a very uncomfortably short distance before us and pointed those very big handguns unerringly at our rapidly beating and terrified hearts. Without warning, Dewald shot William, who went tumbling backwards into a heap onto the gravel road of New Formosa Valley.

I spun around towards my brother who was groaning deeply. I took two quick steps towards him, screaming my distress, and then I saw the stranger crouched in the shadows, partly obscured by a tree trunk, pointing a firearm towards us.

Rob grabbed my left arm and roughly jerked me towards him. Without thinking, I dropped the picnic basket, but held onto that knife, spun around and in that micro-second place and space of time undying, I plunged the knife high and deep into his chest and left it shuddering there. He tried to cry out, but horrible gurgling sounds escaped instead. He tried to stagger away, but fell backwards onto the gravel and sand, his weapons falling away. He feebly tried to move, but life quickly drained from him in tandem with his jerking movements and the lessening blood pumping out of his chest next to the accusing knife.

Dewald took two bullets to his chest and was thrown backwards onto the ground next to Rob. He made no sound where he lay spread-eagled with blood and foam spurting out from his shattered lungs. The third bullet shredded Abu's left ear causing him to scream with terror, drop his firearm and run away down the road clutching the side of his head, crying at the top of his voice for help. I do not know where the fourth one hit. Ewald spun around in bewilderment.

"BOETIE! NEE... NEE... NEE... BOETIE!" Ewald was mortified as he ran to his twin. He was on the verge of placing his firearm on the roadway to kneel and cradle Dewald when some primal instinct kicked in and he instead crouched, searching wildly behind us for the shooter. He must have seen the culprit, for he stiffened into a shooter's stance, screamed all sorts of obscenities and swung his handgun towards the stranger.

The dying man with the brown suede shoes saw the three trucks with the missing stars and lemons the color of Paradise coming down the freeway towards him. They were already in formation, with one in the slow lane and two in the fast lane lined up to overtake the slower one. Behind the trucks a metallic black Mercedes Benz 300E Automatic, with blue lights flashing their impatience and authority, rode on top of the right-hand white line, continually flashing their indignation to these imbeciles before them. Behind them the Police car blared its siren in short bursts to get the trucks out of the way. Unbeknownst to the driver of the Merc and the two bodyguards, a single red dot appeared on the right side of the head of Catalyst and remained steady in place on the target who was occupied with his cellphone.

Tshepo suddenly flew by me in a blur, virtually airborne.

"SIYADOOMA!" He shouted in a battle-cry. He hit Ewald hard on his right upper arm with the undersides of both his takkies, causing Ewald to tumble violently sideways then backwards as his firearm went off. The bullet pierced Ewald's stomach and a sharp rock protruding from the edge of the gravel road cracked the back of his skull open. By the time he came to rest blood poured from his wounds staining the ground where he lay. Tshepho staggered upright with some bloody scrapes and bruises on the palms of his hands.

The three Homeboys lay there lifeless. It triggered within me those nightmares from my deep, dark shadows, I kept hearing Adelaide's screams, seeing her face and hearing those dreadful three words repeatedly like clanging symbols ringing on repeat in my mind.

The assassin carefully aimed the McMillan TAC-50 anti-material and anti-personnel sniper rifle to that place ahead of this convoy where he needed to, sighed a slow and steady expulsion of breath and pulled the trigger at the precise moment his whole self was within that zone of perfect balance, releasing the 12.7 x 99 mm Barnes 50 caliber bullet to kill a man and destroy a country. "Insha Allah" he whispered as the rifle kicked hard against him.

At the precise second the assassin lined up for the kill, 'Amandla Entabeni' looked up and took in what was happening with the trucks. "'Go 'round!'" he commanded sharply. As the killer reached the point of steadiness, the Merc swerved sharply to the left.

"WILLIAM!" I screamed as I ran towards my brother, stopping again in my tracks. The man was using his torn t-shirt to try and stem the flow of blood from William's side. A Heckler & Koch USP 9mm x 19 caliber semi-automatic pistol was on the ground next to him.

"It's OK! I'm a cop!" he said firmly as he kept right on attending to my brother who continued to writhe, moan and groan from the shock and pain. Tshepo and I rushed forward to crouch next to William, unsure how to help him. That old, yellow Toyota Hilux came flying around the corner, gravel and dust scattering from its churning wheels. The driver saw us, braked harshly to avoid running us over and skillfully stopped no more than two meters away.

"She's also a cop. I'm Lieutenant Shorty Setene. She's Warrant Officer Meisie Mtambo," our savior announced gruffly. He picked up his firearm and gave up his space to Officer Mtambo.

"Let me see to him," she said when kneeling on the gravel next to William with a small first-aid kit at hand. Then all hell broke loose.

A loud gunshot went off close by, followed by a loud bang, then screeching of tyres and more loud bangs from the direction of the N3 highway.

"Get down! Get down!" Officer Mtambo urged Tshepo and I as she hunkered protectively over William and carried right on working on his wound.

Lieutenant Setene ran to the van, grabbed a R5 Assault Rifle and two Army issue radios. The one radio he tossed to me and was off, running at top speed into the bush and up the hill. I caught the radio and placed it on the ground next to Officer Mtambo. It crackled to life.

In the instant the man with the brown suede shoes pulled the trigger and released the bullet, the Merc was already entering the emergency lane, overtaking the slow-moving truck with the SAPS escort car following close behind. The bullet shattered the hip and groin of the policeman in the SAPS car, who lost control of the vehicle and bashed into the side of the truck, causing the Police car to spin out of control and smash into the bridge over the Bushman's River. The truck knocked heavily into the one next to it and these caused a chain reaction of accidents and near misses behind them. The Merc was untouched and within a second it roared past the foremost truck and was cruising at 200km/hour in the fast lane.

The driver of the Merc was radioed to carry on and he obeyed without needing a second invitation. The assassin did not see or hear any of this, because the deadly neurotoxic and cardiotoxic venom was rapidly rendering him paralysed and mere seconds away from cardiac arrest, hypoxic brain injury, severe anaphylactic reaction and death. He heard the helicopter behind him and somehow managed to roll onto his back and withdraw his handgun.

"This is 9845. Code 999 on Code 3 to 104 Hotel Oscar Tango. On the move. Going up," Lieutenant Setene reported.

Although Officer Mtambo tried not to show it, her tension was palpable.

"Alpha Sierra 202, 10-4. On approach, two clicks north by northeast," the pilot responded.

"Roger. Is there 10-25 on me?" queried Lieutenant Setene.

"10-4. Coming in now."

"Roger. Subject Lima Sierra is 10-32. Must be Army Sierra Foxtrot (Special Forces). Be careful." Lieutenant Setene reminded them.

"10-4. Go to 10-23."

Whooshing helicopter blades screeched dangerously low over our heads as the SAPS Eurocopter AS350 swooped by in a frightening scream to hover about three hundred meters above the tree-tops close to the crown of the hill.

"Alpha Sierra 202 on 501. Subject Lima Sierra is active," the pilot reported.

Three thunderous booms burst forth from up there before the helicopter spun screeching away from the hover position and flew rapidly downhill towards Old Beacon Hill. There was a short pause on the radio as the it circled on the other side of the hill.

"9845 is there 10-25?"

"10-3." Lieutenant Setene responded. Another pause.

"9845 on 10-97. Go to 10-23."

"Subject Lima Sierra neutralised. Three stars." Officer Motambo breathed a deep sigh of relief. This did nothing to stem the fear and tension roiling from within my heart and stomach.

"Roger 9845, incoming." The helicopter flew to a position on the hill and hovered out of our sight. High above it circled the SAPS Pilatus PC6/B2-H4 STOL airplane.

"Alpha Sierra 201 follow Alpha Echo." A distinct Afrikaner accent commanded.

"10-4, Sir." The pilot responded as the plane banked and flew southwards.

"This is Code 13 and 999. 201A on N3 south-bound lane. Activate immediately!"

"10-4, Sir! Roger, Sir!" several responses echoed over the radio.

"Send two other vehicles from Mooiriver to 10-14 Alpha Echo all the way home."

"10-4, Supe."

"This is 111334! CODE 998, 999 CODE 998, 999." Popping sounds could be heard in the background.

"10-4! 111334 give us your 10-20?"

"KWA-CHUPPIES SHESHA". The radio on that side went dead.

"111334 give us your GPS location." There was no response.

"111334! Come in, 111334!" Three times with no response.

"Sir, 111334 is with Cap Juliett Bravo."

"Where are they?"

"Checking out farms near Mooiriver, Supe. Don't know where precisely."

"I can show you," I said out loud. Officer Mtambo looked quizzically at me, made a snap decision and picked up the radio.

"This is 101037. Sir, I've a civilian who knows. Says he can direct you there."

"OK, 101037! Alpha Sierra 202. Execute 10-42 on N3."

"10-4, Sir." The helicopter dived towards the freeway.

"This is 101037, Sir. Also need Code 902M here for another civilian. Code 914CSF and 914C needed. Subject Lima Sierra and three other subjects."

"10-4! 101037. 84582 is on it! Code 507 to Maritzburg State Facility for all subjects."

The helicopter rose with a high-pitched scream up from in front of the dam wall and came to a low hover in a clearing near the fence and on the fishing spot pathway.

"Go and show them!" Officer Mtambo said urgently, shooing us on with her hands.

I hesitated, looking with deep concern at my brother.

"Don't worry. He's fine. We'll take him to hospital and fetch Gogo." Officer Mtambo spoke compassionately, but still with that urgency in her voice. It did not click in my head how she knew our grandma and how they happened to rescue us. I glanced at the helicopter. Lieutenant Shorty stood near the door and beckoned us over. I turned to face William.

"Go!" William commanded between gritted teeth, and without a word Tshepo and I spun around and ran half bent over, like we'd seen in the movies, to the helicopter. Lieutenant Setene dragged us in and strapped us to seats. I was closest to the open space where a door should have been closed. A giant Afrikaner cop stuck his face close to mine.

"Which way?" The giant barked loudly with spittle flying all over my face.

I was too scared to wipe it off and rather shot my arm out and pointed without hesitation.

"How far!" He barked even louder, emitting a larger avalanche of angry body liquids out of his mouth. I again let the flow be.

"About fifteen kilometers, Sir!" I screamed above the roar of the blades.

The giant glared at me for a second, made a mental decision, put on his headphones and spoke. The helicopter obeyed his command and shot dizzyingly vertical and off in the direction I pointed – so fast, that my stomach struggled to catch up.

Tshepo and I gripped each other's hand during those death-defying moments, only finding some semblance of balance when our stomachs returned to us. There were two pilots in the cockpit and one air crewman where we were. Lieutenant Setene sat on the other side of Tshepo. Then we noticed a female cop next to the air crewman. Across her lap lay a bolt action Steyer SSG 69 P1 Sniper Rifle with a rotary magazine. I guessed that it was probably loaded with five rounds of 7.62x51 mm Nato cartridges. An ACOG Scope completed the rifle. I saw inscribed on the side of the rifle the Bible verse JN8:12, "I am the Light of the World." The giant said something. The air crewman handed earphones to Tshepo and I.

"Hi, I'm Captain Zodwa Shobe. How're you guys?"

"Fine!" Tshepo and I responded in tandem and quite loudly.

"No need to shout. What's your names?"

"Sorry, Ma'am!" We responded automatically, then said our names. The coded chatter could be heard in the background.

"Plano tell me about KwaChuppies? How did it get that name?"

"It's 'Chapman se Plaas', Ma'am. It is known in Zulu as KwaChuppies."

"How do you get to know the farm?"

"We used to hunt there with Grandpa, Ma'am. He taught us about its history, Ma'am."

"What did he say about it?"

"The Boers and the British fought the Battle of Willow Grange there on 23 November 1899 Ma'am. The Boers were on Brynbella Hill and the British on Beacon Hill. They fought mostly along a stone wall that runs on a ridge between the two hills. The wall is still there."

"Can you tell me about the farmyard?"

"Yes, Ma'am." Through her gentle promptings I quickly told her about the long driveway with its massive gum trees, the location of the farmhouse and buildings, including the abattoir, sheds and servant's quarters.

"Did the owner ever know you guys were hunting there?"

"No, Ma'am. Mr. Ewald Prinsloo would've killed us if he found us there."

"You mean The Butcher?" The giant cut in. This took me by surprise.

"Yes, Sir." My response triggered a flurry of activity and further sense of impending danger within that helicopter.

"We've got it, Sir. The wall and everything the boy said. And Cap Juliett Bravo's vehicle." The pilot reported.

"Is that it?" the man demanded. I took a quick look out of the scary, whooshing open door. Someone was high-tailing it down the hill along that stone wall amongst fleeing sheep and goats.

"Yes, Sir!" I gulped and in no time leaned back into the relative safety of my seat.

"ALL STATIONS!" he barked.

Captain Zodwa quickly lay on the floor near the door and the air crewman strapped her in place. It was a further shock to Tshepo and I that she was the shooter. We ignorantly assumed this petite lady was holding that big gun for the giant. Him and Lieutenant Setene checked their R5 Assault Rifles and handguns and strapped these to their bodies. Next to each other their differences in height and size were drastically magnified.

"You keep those headphones on. Keep your eyes closed."

Tshepo and I nodded our heads vigorously, and with that they shut off our headphones. We initially blocked our eyes with our hands, but boys being boys, we were soon peering around us through gaps that magically appeared between aiding and abetting fingers. No one paid us any mind, even though they must have seen us do so.

The giant and Lieutenant Setene were crouched at the door opening. They had bulging rucksacks strapped to their backs. The air crewman held another open for Captain Zodwa.

The helicopter suddenly pulled up to a hover that must have been at least one kilometer away from and above the farm buildings. There was no time to think as I struggled to pull myself back from sliding out of my seat onto the unsteady floor. I do not know how and why it happened, but Tshepo and my headphones were suddenly back on.

Captain Zodwa let fly those 7.62 x 51 mm Nato rounds from her Steyr (Sharpshooter) SSG 69 P1 Sniper Rifle. She handled it superbly and quickly removed the spent magazine and passed it to the air crewman who, in turn, handed over a loaded one.

"Circle!" She said sweetly, it sounded like she was going to add 'please' to her request.

"10-4, Cap." The pilot responded.

"Stop!" the helicopter shuddered. "BOOM! BOOM!"

"Circle to discharge behind the servant's quarters."

"10-4, Cap." We circled once more.

"Supe, two armed subjects retreated to the main house and two others to the abattoir. Cap Juliett Bravo and one colleague are approaching on foot. They'll come around the side of the quarters in forty-five seconds."

"Roger, Cap. How many other 10-32's?"

"Two neutralized near the driveway. Unknown how many others in farm buildings."

"Roger, Cap. We'll go through each one!"

"10-4, Supe."

Our screeching and screaming protective shield suddenly banked sharply and shot groundward to hover hardly a meter above the fever-ishly waving grass. Supe, the giant, and Lieutenant Setene jumped out of there in a flash, and we were back up in the sky with our stomachs somewhere on the ground below.

I caught a glimpse of Supe and Lieutenant Shorty handing out some stuff from their rucksacks to the two colleagues before they ran in skirmish maneuvers towards the back door of the servant's quarters. One man followed the giant while Lieutenant Shorty and the other man each went around opposite sides of the building.

"Servant building cleared. No 10-32's," a new voice reported.

"Roger Cap Juliett Bravo. No movement outside," Captain Zodwa responded.

The next time I caught a glimpse of them they were running zigzag to the sheds.

"Sheds cleared. No 10-32's." Captain JB reported.

"Roger Cap Juliett Bravo. None outside."

"Stables cleared. No 10-32's."

"Roger Cap Juliett Bravo. Still no movement."

Around and around we went, Captain Zodwa and the pilots carefully searching for foe.

"Code 998 (gun battle) at farmhouse. Go to 10-23."

"Roger Cap."

"Two 10-32's sorted. No other in farmhouse."

"Roger, Cap."

"Cap, secure delivery doors at the back and windows on the other side of abattoir. Twenty seconds from now give covering fire for five seconds. We'll have to go in."

"Roger, Supe."

The helicopter went to guard that side of the slaughterhouse. When the time was right Captain Zodwa drilled holes through the door and spectacularly shattered all the large windows, spacing the shots about a second apart.

"Code 998 at farmhouse. Go to 10-23."

For about fifteen more minutes there was radio silence as we waited for information. Nothing could be heard outside above the roar of the helicopter.

"Five 10-32's sorted, including two 'Nkunsi' (big shots). Found two 920A (missing adults) and one 920Y (missing youth). Need Code 902M (medical assistance), Code 914CSF (crime scene forensics) and 914C (coroner)."

"Roger, Cap," Captain Zodwa replied.

The helicopter landed between the farmhouse and the abattoir and switched off, but the chatter from the radio persevered, with the pilot making all the arrangements. We heard him say that fuel would have to be brought in because they did not have enough to fly out. Captain Zodwa was freed from her harness. She dismantled and packed away her sniper rifle before handing the case to the air crewman for safekeeping. She turned to Tshepo and I and smiled brightly, even though she carried a measure of solemnity and deep sorrow.

"You may get out but stay close to the helicopter. The farm is now a crime scene." We nodded. The air crewman unclipped us and we gingerly wobbled on unsteady legs to sit on an old bench under a large oak tree.

All sorts of extreme emotions battled for supremacy within me, beginning with strong revulsion for what I did to Rob and for seeing and being part of all the death and dying we survived through in less than half an hour. Deep concern vied for space, wanting desperately to know how William was doing. High levels of excitement still persevered from the violently undulating, bobbing and weaving helicopter ride and being in the middle of a hectic and scary gun battle. Boiling anger was there for what those Homeboys did to us and made us become. Gratefulness was soothing for the timely interventions of Lieutenant Setene and Officer Mtambo who saved our lives. The most overpowering was fear, starting when Ewald screamed, which drove me to kill Rob. It now enveloped me to face an unknown future as a murderer.

There were many other emotions seeking their own dominance in those shadows, but I tried hard not to find them and feel them. I also scanned my surroundings and listened out for my feathered friends that are many times in my life sources of comfort during the most trying and turbulent distresses. They were there all around us but keeping a safe distance from the noise and death in the yard. The sparrows were the bravest and closest. A pair of Jackal Buzzards flew high above on their way back to the Drakensberg Mountains. Grandpa said all hawks are symbols of courage, so my spirits lifted when I saw them. Grandpa said that to many people they were symbols of death. I made sure not to draw Tshepo's attention to their passing.

Two tough-looking Zulu men came out of the abattoir carrying a bloodied, beaten, disheveled and crudely bandaged Hermann Combrink on a makeshift stretcher. Anger again forced its way ahead of the other emotions. The men laid the hated stretcher on the floor of the helicopter and one of the men returned to the abattoir.

"Thank you, Cap. Good shooting. Shorty said you also took out LS. Well done."

"No problem." The two of them stood and conversed briefly, then they called us over.

"Hi, I'm Captain Jabulani Bengu." A voice like rubbing hard, coarse gravel together.

We feebly mumbled automated greetings and gave him our names.

"Lieutenant Setene said the two of you saved his life on New Formosa Road. Superintendent Carel van den Beek said you directed them here. You saved us. Thank you."

"No problem, Sir. He saved us" Tshepo and I responded, at a loss for words.

"Can you do me a favor? Can you keep an eye on him until the paramedics come? He's not right." Captain JB rolled his forefinger around close to his temple indicating madness. Hermann did look badly damaged, wriggling and flinching on the hard planks.

Tshepo and I nodded our heads automatically and yet reluctantly. After all, Hermann was one of the Homeboys and went to stand in the long shadows near the door of the helicopter. Captain JB and Captain Zodwa brusquely walked back to the abattoir.

EPILOGUE

Ouma, Aunty Ntokozo, Uncle Charlie, May-June, William, Tshepo and I were bound by the State in terms of the Protection of Information Act 84 of 1982. We swore not to disclose certain sensitive information related to the activities of the Government pertaining to the Vulintaba Manifesto and to that which transpired in our presence on 27 December 1999. Some of this information was bound then to a twenty-year non-disclosure period. More will be released by the State after fifty years, but other matters will remain official secrets for hundreds more. This story had to be proofed by the State and was only approved for release after certain portions were changed and others removed. It is important to note that names of certain individuals have been changed to protect their identities.

Susan Combrink was subjected to a most sadistic cruelty that even sickened hardened police officers. She died before she could be rescued. Joe Combrink's bullet-riddled body was found tied to a pole close to his wife's. Police concluded that he was forced to watch the torture of his wife and killed by Eric Walton, during the Scorpion's insurgency and rescue operation.

Hermann Combrink was found lying on a stainless-steel table that was used to skin and cut up livestock carcasses. He ended up in a psychiatric hospital in Pietermaritzburg. His family and the State requested that the name of the facility remain undisclosed.

The Butcher, Ewald Prinsloo, and the Candlestick Maker, Eric Walton, chose not to surrender. Their clothing were found to be drenched in the blood of the Combrink couple when the SAPS examined these in the forensic lab. They were killed by the Scorpions during the gun battle in the abattoir.

The Baker, Faizel Ameen and his family attempted to escape South Africa in a hurry but died at sea when the helicopter they were in crashed. The bodies of Faizel, his wife, their daughters and the helicopter crew were recovered, but not that of Abu. Rumor persists to this day in Estcourt that Abu Ameen was alive and living quite the life of luxury in Dubai. His living relatives have long since given up try to quell this talk, but their inaction, coupled with annual trips to Dubai continues to feed this conspiracy theory.

Business interests of the Butcher, Baker and Candlestick Maker were eventually carved up amongst their wives and children, sanctioned by the State after a five-year investigation.

The real Malik Nader was arrested at his offices in Port Elizabeth and incarcerated at a secret location for fourteen days, without trial or access to his attorney. He was questioned by experts until they were satisfied that he was a victim of identity theft, with no links to any persons with criminal interests.

The man with the brown suede shoes was buried with his shoes on in a nondescript grave at Mountain Rise Cemetery in Pietermaritzburg after succumbing to the poison from a Black Mamba. Zeph, his two hitmen, Mzo, Papi, Skeets and Jomo were all killed in the exchange of gunfire on the farm. All their weapons were eventually linked to the assassinations of a number of councillors and rival businessman, including that killing of Enoch Mathebula. Traces of blood found on Zeph's knife linked him to the murder of Vinod Thulsiram.

The Butcher, Baker and Candlestick Maker and their sons were tried and convicted in absentia. It was proven in the High Court in Pietermaritzburg that the sons were tasked to guard the assassin and were taken out by a member of the Scorpions "with some assistance from unnamed civilians" who were not named when they resisted arrest. According to the Court's final verdict, we happened to be at the wrong place at the wrong time. We were never called to testify, even though we provided statements to the Scorpions.

One SAPS Officer was killed by the Land Surveyor on the N3 freeway. Another died along the farm access road. Both were buried with honors. On Thursday 13 January 2000 they posthumously received the Gold Cross Medal for Bravery bestowed upon them by the President. Codename Amandla Entabeni was the honorable guest at the event. He thanked the families of the deceased and those who received medals for bravery in service to South Africa.

Superintendent (Lieutenant-Colonel) Carel van den Beek, Captain Jabulani Bhengu, Captain Zodwa Shobe, Lieutenant Shorty Setene, Warrant Officer Meisie Mtambo, the assault team and the helicopter pilots and crew were each awarded the Gold Cross for Bravery. Other team members involved were also awarded medals ranging from the Gold Cross to the Silver Medal for Outstanding Services.

Superintendent (Lieutenant-Colonel) Carel van den Beek was promoted to the rank of Colonel. Both Captain Jabulani Bhengu and Captian Zodwa Shobe were promoted to Major and given their own task force teams to lead. Colonel van den Beek retired in 2018. Both Jabulani Bhengu and Zodwa Shobe are now Lieutenant-Colonels with the Hawks.

Of the one thousand two hundred shipping containers, one thousand and sixty-one were discovered and raided by the Scorpions. Thirty-nine were found to be empty. It still vexes the SAPS that one hundred and thirty-nine of these deadly containers remain unaccounted for.

As the Vulintaba Manifesto predicted, Mr. Jacob Gedleyihlekisa Zuma did become the fourth President of the Republic of South Africa on 9 May 2009. He resigned on 14 February 2018due to intense pressure from the ruling party and South African citizens, because of his alleged involvement in the State Capture criminal activities, was recently under the investigation of the Zondo Commission. The amaHlubi and other smaller kingdoms are still being stymied in both the political sphere and in the courts in their attempts to be formally recognized as separate kingdoms. Disgruntled leaders regularly make unproven assertions of a conspiracy between the ANC, the IFP and the Zulu Monarchy that they believe was forged in January 2000. These two political rivals and the Zulu Monarchy refer anyone who asks to approach the courts that are there to handle such cases.

Although the Scorpions found evidence of the involvement of some of the Sheiks in the conspiracy to commit treason, no official link to any specific individual or country was ever determined from any coded communications that were unraveled. Official approaches were made to all the Emirates, but without any tangible evidence to bait their hooks these fishing expeditions were dead in the water. The Scorpions did find that a Mr. TJ was the mastermind, but they were never able to uncover his identity. All leads ran cold.

It was almost inevitable that attempts would still be made by individuals and entities to exploit a young and vulnerable democracy. Where the conspirators of the Vulintaba Manifesto tried violence to get what they wanted, other ruthless opportunists have used their wealth and subterfuge to open the rich coffers of South Africa to themselves. The Zondo Commission is investigating extensive corruption and what has come to be known as State capture.

After extensive surgery to successfully remove the bullet in William's chest, my brother survived and went on to become the boy hero of Estcourt. We were just happy to have him back alive and home. For his bravery the SAPS offered William a bursary to study BTech in Criminal Justice. True to his nature, William would go on to become one of the most successful and decorated detectives with SAPS Bloemfontein. He couldn't take Ella to the New Year's Eve Dance in Forderville on 31 December 1999, but the pair were officially an item soon after William's surgery. They married in 2007 and live in Bloemfontein with their children; Adam, John and Isabella..

After receiving a bursary from the University of Cape Town, Dr. May-June Delvaux MBChB studied and fell in love with the city and its people. She now permanently resides in Stellenbosch with her husband, Nicholas Matherson who is the managing director of Campbell and Murphy International Consulting Engineers. , and their two beautiful and smart children; Blake and Kelly. When I tell you that May-June's graduation was the happiest and most celebrated moment of our family, this would be a great understatement. I still remember that after graduation party lasting well into the early hours of the next morning!

May–June, protective as she is, sought to keep Morph close to her. He lives in an apartment in Stellenbosch, barely a 10-minute walk away from her home. Morph is a photographer who offers his best self to the world and touches the lives of everyone he meets. He is in a long-term relationship with an artist, Taylor Beauford, just as incredible as he is.

Burying Ouma in 2012 after she passed away from a stroke was one of the saddest days in our lives. It felt like a final chapter in our book. Each of us owed our lives, everything that we have become and achieved and everything that we are yet to strive towards, to our beloved Ouma. Since her passing we make an annual visit to the graves of our parents and grandparents.

I went on to study Family Law after a few years of getting into trouble with the law. It was only fitting that my defense attorney became my mentor and managed to guide me back on the right path.

I always refer to my university days as the turning point, even though it did not go well initially. Meeting and establishing a bond with my wife Seme; Susanna Elizette Magdalena Prinsloo, will always be the pinnacle of my healing process.

Back in 2005 I stumbled out of a local bar at 2 am in the morning. I spotted the most beautiful girl in the world who had just exited the bar herself. Boldy, I offered to escort her back to her residence where Seme and I sat on the steps at her residence and chatted until the sun came up.

Seme is the youngest daughter of Ewald Prinsloo. By some strange coincidence we never met in Estcourt, or even knew about each other those years. Seme was shipped off to St. Dominics Academy Boarding School in Newcastle for most of her school years. During school holidays she lived a very sheltered life in Estcourt and remained totally out of all spotlights shone on their family due to all the nefarious activities of her father and brothers.

We very quickly found out about our past lives in Estcourt and broke up in spectacularly unpleasant fashion. We hurled abuse, horrible words soaked in years of anger and resentment, bordering on hatred.

A week after our break-up, Seme pulled my miserable self out of a pub where I was determined to drown my sorrows after another particularly difficult day. We took a bus ride to the Union Building gardens where we spoke, yelled, cried, laughed and spoke of all things past and present until we got to a place of complete understanding. We vowed to stick together and support each other no matter what. Throughout those days at university the most vicious attacks came from her family and friends who refused to accept our union. But we found our own flow as a couple and persevered. I love this wonderful person who chose me above all else.

It was about nine months after our small private wedding that one of her family members happened to mention that Seme lied to her family about being pregnant when stiff resistance from them tried to put an end to our wedding plans. She always denies it with a laugh and twinkle in her eyes. Seme is a charted accountant with her own accounting firm.

Our home in Brooklyn, Pretoria is her inheritance from her father's estate and we have lived in it since our wedding day. During renovations Seme and I found the Vulintaba Manifesto in a secret basement in our home almost ten years to the day after 27th December 1999. It was my spouse who discovered the hidden door hatch on the floor, deep in a corner of one of floor to ceiling cupboards in the garage that we were clearing out. We had to hire a company to open the door to the secret room and to open the safe therein. It was scary finding this hidden basement that we were unaware existed, but a thousand times more frightening to read about the destructive and evil road greedy men were prepared to walk so that they could make a financial 'killing'. We read the manifesto before handing it to Colonel Shobe, elated to finally pick up the cold trail of the case.

Seme was the one who helped me piece together much of the story concerning the Butcher, the Baker and the Candlestick Maker and their sons from her own recollections and through information she gathered from Estcourt for me.

I told Seme one day that the name I call her means "covered with small bearings of indefinite number of stars arranged all over the field" and that it aptly describes who she is. It was Seme who encouraged and supported me all the way to tell my story.

For the first time in my life I told Seme the three words that haunted me for such a long time – the words Adelaide whispered when she died. *"Did you see?"* How I didn't want to see. Didn't want to hear. Didn't want to remember. How I felt so ashamed for seeing and hated myself so for not doing anything to save her. It has taken Seme's unconditional love, years of counselling and the births of our four children, beautiful triplet girls, Juliet, Marelise and Zoe and a laatlammetjie boy Francois to guide me into a place of normality.

There are times, although fleeting, when I find myself within that deep, dark place. Where I still see Rob dying, hear him gurgle with the shuddering knife in his chest, hear Adelaide's screams, see her face and hear those dreadful words, "Did you see?" All I want to do is to keep Seme and our children safe. It is in those moments I know with absolutely certainty that I will defend them at all costs, no matter what – even if I have to kill again.

Made in United States
Troutdale, OR
06/10/2023

10523018R20213